PRAI
LISA L. HANNETT

"*Lament for the Afterlife* is a war novel unlike any you have read before. Visceral, surreal and unsettlingly beautiful, it combines an unflinching portrait of the way war deranges both individuals and societies with an achingly tender portrait of the capacity of individuals to endure the unthinkable."

—**James Bradley**, author of *Clade*

"Mirror shards and broken shadows make up this stunning dark mosaic of a novel. Lisa Hannett's debut is a haunting mirage of war and love, and the cost of both. Unmissable."

—**Lavie Tidhar**, author of *The Violent Century* and *The Bookman*

"Dark and mesmeric, Lisa Hannett pushes at the boundaries of fantasy writing to dizzying effect."

—**Robert Shearman**, author of *They Do The Same Things Different There*

"A stunning page-turner of a first novel, with a bracing freshness and authority to the prose. Entertaining and startling, gritty but also darkly beautiful, *Lament for the Afterlife* is the real deal and marks the arrival of a major new talent."

—**Jeff VanderMeer**, author of the Southern Reach trilogy

"*Lament for the Afterlife* offers a gritty commentary on the nature of language itself and its potential for violence. Here words can wound, and the damage they inflict is terrible indeed. Be warned: This book does not reveal its secrets easily. It flickers like zoetrope through images of heartbreak and loss. Like the best fantasists of our time, Hannett brings an awareness of the human cost of war that will resonate with contemporary audiences."

—**Helen Marshall**, award-winning author of *Gifts for the One Who Comes After*

"Australian author Hannett's first collection shows off her fondness for lush imagery, unsettling concepts, indirect prose, and multilayered plots. The stories push boundaries and experiment with style, form, and meaning, rarely straightforward and often hovering between fantasy and horror . . . this is a collection for fans of weirdness, wonder, and oft-disturbing twists."

—*Publishers Weekly*

"The apparent timelessness of Hannett's stories, that eternal fantastic present, is persistently if quietly undermined, disorienting the reader time and again."

—**Maureen Kincaid Speller**, *Weird Fiction Review*

". . . fantasy fiction down under is in good hands."

—**Peter Tennant**, *Interzone*

"Such assuredness in the storytelling is what helps makes the world of *Bluegrass Symphony* so palpable. Words are Hannett's friends here, too. She knows when the story allows her to show her mettle with poetic description and when such language would be obtrusive. Restraint is not always the virtue of the debut writer, but Hannett understands its power, both in plot and prose."

—**Jason Nahrung**, *Australian Speculative Fiction in Focus*

"Lisa L. Hannett's collection plays like a country music album composed in the darker places of imagination, the little corners that you don't want to look in as you tap-tap your foot to the catchy beat. Coolly beautiful, then coldly brutal, this is one of the most unnerving debuts in years."

—**Robert Shearman**

"Hannett is able to turn the brutally ugly into something darkly compelling."

—*SQ Mag*

"Hannett is one of those rare writers who can write using a variety of voices—and does so wonderfully. It's not simply having an ear for dialog, but possessing the ability to translate what's spoken into the written word and using it to convey to readers the mindset, upbringing, and culture of her characters."

—**Charles Tan**, *Bibliophile Stalker*

LAMENT FOR THE AFTERLIFE

LISA L. HANNETT

ChiZine Publications

FIRST EDITION
Lament for the Afterlife © 2015 by Lisa L. Hannett
Cover artwork © 2015 by Erik Mohr
Interior design by © 2015 by Jared Shapiro

All Rights Reserved.

This book is a work of fiction. Names, characters, places, and incidents are either a product of the author's imagination or are used fictitiously. Any resemblance to actual events, locales, or persons, living or dead, is entirely coincidental.

Distributed in Canada by
Publishers Group Canada
76 Stafford Street, Unit 300
Toronto, Ontario
M6J 2S1 Canada
Toll Free: 800-747-8147
e-mail: info@pgcbooks.ca

Distributed in the U.S. by
Diamond Comic Distributors, Inc.
10150 York Road, Suite 300
Hunt Valley, MD 21030
Phone: (443) 318-8500
e-mail: books@diamondbookdistributors.com

Library and Archives Canada Cataloguing in Publication

Hannet, Lisa L., 1977-, author
Lament for the afterlife / Lisa L. Hannet.

Issued in print and electronic formats.
ISBN 978-1-77148-347-6 (pbk.).--ISBN 978-1-77148-348-3 (pdf)

I. Title.

PS8615.A556L34 2015 C813'.6 C2015-903027-7
C2015-902028-5

Edited by Samantha Beiko
Proofread & Copyedited by Michael Matheson

A free eBook edition is available
with the purchase of this print book.

CLEARLY PRINT YOUR NAME ABOVE IN UPPER CASE
Instructions to claim your free eBook edition:
1. Download the BitLit app for Android or iOS
2. Write your name in **UPPER CASE** on the line
3. Use the BitLit app to submit a photo
4. Download your eBook to any device

CHIZINE PUBLICATIONS
Toronto, Canada
www.chizinepub.com
info@chizinepub.com

Canada Council for the Arts Conseil des Arts du Canada

We acknowledge the support of the Canada Council for the Arts which last year invested $20.1 million in writing and publishing throughout Canada.

ONTARIO ARTS COUNCIL
CONSEIL DES ARTS DE L'ONTARIO
an Ontario government agency
un organisme du gouvernement de l'Ontario

Published with the generous assistance of the Ontario Arts Council.

Printed in Canada

Helen and Laura Marshall,
thanks for the nudge.

LAMENT FOR THE AFTERLIFE

They'll eat your dog and skin your wife,
And suck your soul from the afterlife!
Here or there,
There or here;
How many fée folk will appear?
10, 20, 30, 40, 50 . . .

Abulayfee Abulafiah,
Queen of the fée;
Stole your eyes and turned the world grey!
Single jump,
Double jump,
Balance on a rope;
How many days 'til we give up hope?
1, 2, 3, 4, 5 . . .

Daddy's gone a-soldiering,
Mamma's at the 'port;
Baby's found a tunnel to the faery court!
He slid down sideways,
Flat on his back;
How long 'til he becomes their snack?
(Tick tock, ask the clock!)
1:00, 2:00, 3:00, 4:00, 5:00 . . .

Big ones, little ones, duck out of sight,
Big ones, little ones, turn and fight;
Big ones, little ones, go underground,
Big ones, little ones, get out of town;
Big ones, little ones, please come back,
Wrap a paper parcel for the Pigeon's pack!
Send it to the officers,
Send it to their wives,
Send it to the vultures and save their lives!
Tell us, Mr. Pigeon,
Have you seen the greys?
And this is what he had to say:
Yes, No, Maybe so,
Yes, No, Maybe so . . .

Children's skipping tunes
Bibliotheca 34°24'N, 132°30'E
'Wind-pressed ink, Stamp Nos. 00212—01999, c. Evac.St.2 ±80 years.

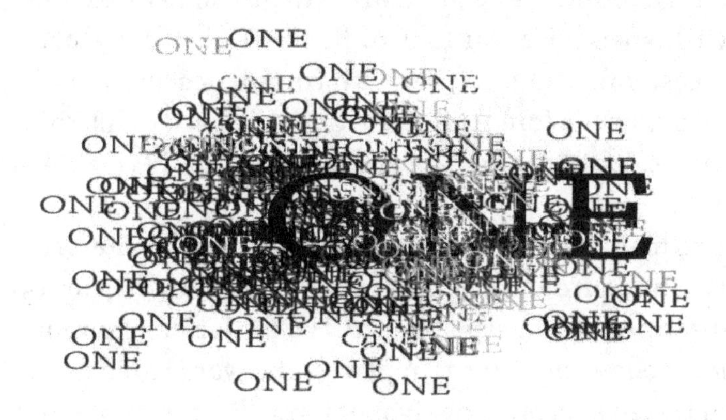

Before leaving, Peytr is given two farewell gifts: a clutch of hollow grenades from Ma and a set of camp cutlery from Borys. He barely gets a feel for either before Jean takes them back again. With a wink, she says, "I got it, Peytie," then begins unloading and repacking his rucksack. Tossing Borys's gift aside, she buries the mute shells under vest and goggles, spare hood and multicams. She folds and refolds sheaves of white muslin, the ones she'd ironed crisp as envelopes the night before. Her hands brisk, but stiff; the scars on her palms tugging fingers into claws.

Peyt avoids looking too close. Focuses on the streaks of silver glinting in her hair instead. Eddying in the air, Jean's wordwind colours with pride. *That's my boy*, it says. *My one and only* . . . Stray 'o's loop Peyt's eyes like specs. 'M's and 'n's peck his cheeks. 'Y's hook his collar, urging him across the house's narrow hall, toward Daken Miller and the front door.

"Ma," Peyt snaps, swatting the letters away, squirming at their intimate touch. For Daken's sake, Peytr sighs. Rolls his eyes. Puffs his chest and peppers his wordwind with curses. *You're fuckin' killing me here, Ma. . . . Let's go, let's go, let's fuckin' go. . . .* The words lilt up to the bare bulb dangling overhead, ugly petals on an unfelt breeze. They circle once or twice, then gasp and deflate, sinking within seconds. Peyt glowers. He wants the cyclone of sentences to rage round his head, to drip sweat and testosterone, to beef up with speed. He wants it to be like Daken's; a cluster of contempt easily floating, corded with confidence and muscle. Daken's 'wind skims his forehead and gropes the back of his thick neck like a mullet. It's slick and dark and anxiety-free. It's eighteen and macho.

Peytr tries to match him. Always has. But his thoughts are weak. Florid. Frilly. They pirouette on his shoulders. They hiccup on *cocksucker*, intentionally misspell *faggit*. His air-letters shimmer, now pink, now yellow, now puce. In places, the words aren't even legible. When Daken snorts at the sight of them, Peytr's paragraphs crumble.

"Stop crying, Ma," Daken says, patting Mrs. Miller's arm as he passes, hitting the head one last time before they go. *Hitting the head. . . . Soiling the shitter. . . . Tanking a turd. . . . Fuckin' a. . . . Fuckin' a . . .* Jaw clenched, Peyt smacks his pathetic alliterations as soon as the bathroom door clicks shut. *Ah, fuck.* He exhales and drops the act. For months he's been trying to roughen his poetic mind; he practises swearing daily. Soon he'll swear like a soldier. Every second word will be *fuckin' this* or *cunt that* or whatever slang the grunts use on the field. Being a poet won't help him kill any better. Curses are stronger weapons than rhymes.

For now, obscenities slur down his fresh-shorn scalp, trickling behind his ears, tumbling the length of his scrawny biceps. Broken words crash in the crook of his arm, snagging in the rolls of his pushed-up sleeve. One by one, he squashes them into the mottled skin on his forearms. The words wriggle under his thumbs. Meanings lost for a few seconds until, reabsorbed, they're remembered.

"It's all right, Mrs. M," Peyt says, flinching. His voice is still too high. He clears his throat, tries again, tilting his chin down this time. "We'll be all right." Deeper. Better.

Daken's mother sniffles and fishes a hankie out of her sleeve. She scrubs her nose, tamps the wet from her eyes. Her 'wind open, raw, vulnerable. Peytr drops his gaze. *Put it away*, he thinks, embarrassed by her outburst. Her emotion. What's she crying for? If any of them survive, he thinks, it'll be Dake.

Mrs. Miller crosses her arms and slouches against the hall closet. Her housecoat sags open above the waist-ties. Underneath she's wearing an old cotton nightie. White with purple flowers. V-neck. Cut so low, Peyt can clearly see the ribs stretching between her small breasts. For a second, he wonders what it would sound like, running a finger over those bony ridges. *Corduroy friction? A stick striking fence slats? Thumbnails zipping along a comb's plastic teeth?*

Squinting to read, Mrs. Miller follows the trajectory of Peyt's thoughts. "You're not a kid anymore, Peytie." She straightens, expression and robe pulled tight. "Grow up. And no more of this 'Mrs. M' shit. It's Ann. Just, Ann."

"Okay, Mrs. M."

Huffing, Jean hefts Peytr's bag and sits it upright in the middle of the hall. She scowls as it teeters, top-heavy. "Peytr will speak as befits his station." She crouches, knees cracking. Unbuckles the flaps she's just buckled. Hunkers for a third go at arranging his kit. "You'll be polite, soldier. Respectful. 'Mrs. Miller' will do fine. 'Ma'am' if you want variety. Got it?"

Peyt's dad coughs. Out of habit, Borys hitches his belt while clunk-thunking closer. The harness jangles, the hold it's got on his right leg secure. "Boy's got to get a move on, Jean."

"I'm more than aware of that, Borys."

Dark 'winds coalesce above Jean's spine, dagger-shaped and stabbing. *Traitor. . . . Deserter. . . . Home-wrecker. . . .* The word-blades are clichéd but acerbic. *Action instead of reaction. . . . All's fair. . . .* They move with such energy, slicing back and forth so quickly, it's hard to tell which feelings are Borys's, which Jean's.

"Got it," Peyt says, reining in his 'wind. Concentrating on keeping it beige, noncommittal. He lifts his hood and shepherds his thoughts under its quiet cover.

While he waits, Peytr shifts from foot to foot, *left, right, left, right*, and listens to the final chorus of his departure. Floorboards creaking underfoot. A clock in the living room, ticking, chiming the quarter hour. Jean snapping leather straps in place, calling Euri and

Zaya up from the basement. His sisters' little boots clomping on the stairs. Mrs. Miller—*Ann*—blowing her nose. Daken whistling in the private john. The toilet flushing. Such familiar, mundane noises. So *regular*. Part of him wants to shout: that's it? That's all? The rest memorises every sound.

"Don't forget these," Borys says and instantly his hand's a blur. Too late, Peyt snaps to attention, fumbling the catch. He traps the cutlery with all the grace of a newborn. Wrists thwacking, fingers splayed, arms jumbled against his belly.

"Thanks, Da."

They've got a good heft to them, a jangle like well-earned coins. Stainless steel, nicely polished. Solid knife, three-tined fork. Spoon gently pointed, a mini spade. The lot strung onto a thin metal ring from holes in their handles. Bones, Borys calls them. Rattlin' bones.

Peyt shakes his head and clips the set into his jacket pocket. What sorry goodbyes, he thinks. Bombs and bones. He musters something like gratitude, pins it to his face. Says he's as glad to have one as the other. They'll both come in handy. Really.

Borys grunts, eloquent as ever. In that one syllable, Peyt hears a lifetime of his dad's rants. How *the gov't hasn't got a fuckin' clue, boy. Grant a soldier the basic necessities, my arse. Nycene's cabinet supplies tents for the grunts and the mess slops up three squares daily, sometimes hot. The forces'll shower you with all the shells we can produce, the ships we can rally—and they'll chuck in a fuckload of acronyms for free. DLBs and E&E—invented for the greys, that one—MIAs and KIAs. So many fuckin'* As, *Peyt, it's hard to keep track. AAs and AAAs, AAWs and AWOLS—then there's shit like Comms and Landops and Sigs and Intel. Yeah, they'll fuckin' glut you with intel about the greys—where they've been, what they've hit, what they've stolen—anything except where they are, of course, or where they're going. Finding that out's all up to you, son.*

At the end of the day, Borys always said—Peytr hates the expression—*at the end of the day, a soldier's got to be vigilant. He's got to watch his own back—and equip it to boot!—if he wants to fight the fuckin' greys.*

Peyt doesn't want to fight, but he's going, anyway. Lugging his top-heavy pack, his parents' hand-me-down patriotism. Borys's posture, Jean's pride. His new empty shells and his bones.

Outside, the local boys are gathering. Nate and Cheff and Grig and all them, a dozen or so guys from the block, called up in the last draft. Just like Dake, who inspires a cheer when he poses in the doorway, stepping out before Peyt. Pants tucked in his tall boots, fists on hips, Dake whistles in his stained field-mask. A snug, goggle-eyed skullcap that snaps onto his jacket's high collar at the back, it's got two lamps inset as nostrils in a long leather beak that curves to a point below his cleft chin. Designed, apparently, to siphon wordwinds, keep them close to the face, safe from theft and contamination.

Following Dake's lead, Peyt slips on the vulture helmet Borys once wore. The pigskin smells of old polish and new glue; it's stiff with disuse and rubs uncomfortably against his Adam's apple. The small sockets give him tunnel vision and he has to breathe carefully to avoid choking on his 'wind. But he likes how the thing hides the white blotches on his light brown cheeks, mouth, and chin. The white lace of skin that gleams whenever Peyt blushes. The white that raggedly, doggedly, beards further and further down his neck.

Beside him, Daken's whistling is leather-muffled. Still the finest whistling Peyt's ever heard. Man, the trills that guy can manage! Man, what a warble. Peyt swears it's sweeter than birdsong. Less sombre, less harsh. Less likely to be some fuckin' unnatural code.

To hear better, Peytr listens to Dake's song with his eyes closed. His goggles reflect sights he's seen all his life—sights he doesn't need or want to see now. A long street of identical duplexes, two-storeys turned bungalow after one blitz or another. Cream brickwork pocked and grimed with mortar. Burnt struts and roof beams exposed, jagging to the sky. The destruction left standing, reclaimed as camouflage for ceiling cannons and snipers. The whole suburb a mishmash of repairs: in time, in progress, impossible. Above and below, green brightnesses bloom in the grey. Illumination flares bursting in the smoke-heavy sky. Carrots and onions and cabbages flowering in window boxes and raised beds. Peytr can picture it all without even trying.

He blinks and blinks and blinks, defying the heat welling under his lids.

Dake's final note swells into a whoop. He claps Peytr on the shoulder and gallops down the front steps. Here we go, Peyt thinks, hesitating on the porch. We're going. Dependents of the state. No—*defenders*. He meant defenders. Out on our own. Pursuing invisible footsteps down well-trodden paths. A minute passes before he follows.

Around them, unboarded windows and doors gape, most filled with wishers-well. Peyt focuses on the gutters, kicks at piles of ash and dead 'winds. He doesn't need to look up to know that everyone's there. Borys and Ma. Euri with little Zaya perched on her hip. Mrs. Miller. *Ann*. The Gorevs and Baltharssons next door. The street-broomers and cannon-men. Old ladies peering through sheer curtains, peering through time, seeing ghosts. A flock of photographers swooping, clicking.

Fuckin' crows, Borys calls them. Snapping at meat, living or dead.

"Give us a smile, son."

Peytr doesn't. What's the point? They can't see his face anyway. The flash pops and he's blinded. He tastes magnesium through the mask.

"Once more," says the crow. "For luck."

Why not.

He looks up. Scowls. His parents wave.

He falls in line as the boys start to march. He loses sight of Borys in the hustle, the attempted order. He loses sight of Jean.

I shouldn't be here, he thinks. I should turn back.

But he goes.

He knows they're watching.

Peytr's only sixteen, so they put him on stretcher duty to save him from the horrors of war. They pair him with Angus, a kid from farther South, who's been hauling bodies for almost a month—the division's best triage man. First flares of the morning have crested the grey when Peyt peels off his helmet, hiding nothing, and shakes the wiry boy's hand. *Don't get attached* floats round Angus's shaved head, but Peytr's not sure if it's a suggestion or a reminder.

Angus takes the lead, which is A-OK with Peyt. He likes how Angus gives clear orders. How he tells him to warm up before they set off, getting him to do a few laps with the mules around the mess tent. How he shows him to breathe through his mouth without eating 'wind. How he runs fast but not too fast. How he jogs diagonally across roads, sprinting at intersections, keeping low between houses. How he seems to have one eye on the sky at all times and one on the ground. How he doesn't turn around to see if Peyt's keeping up. How he brooks no complaints about side-stitches or blisters or fear.

Staying a block or so behind the fighting, they treat what they can on the field. Just pull out of the firing line and start working, Angus shouts. What line? Peyt shouts back. Where? Columns of smoke rise from grey-fires, marking enemy territory. There are so many, so near . . . what makes this patch of concrete more protected than that one? Peyt thinks they're sitting ducks, about to get shelled right there on the sidewalk, elbow-deep in some guy's belly. You got a better idea, Angus yells, twisting a tourniquet above a shredded forearm, leaving the near-dead behind. Mouth shut, Peytr helps lift a wailing kid onto their stretcher, and then they're off again. They never stop for long.

Most of the time, a pearl-eyed Whitey keeps pace by their side, transmitting messages in myriad voices, telling them where to find the latest fallen. The girl's words are garbled, a muddy stream of moans and cries and *mamamamamamamas*—but Angus directs her as they run, leaning close every time the mentalegrapher starts babbling. Listening hard, he nods or shakes his head. Too far gone, he says after one shrieking transmission—"They got me! They fuckin' got me!"—blowing a shrill whistle to summon the skybunker corps instead. Moving on, Whitey's throat gurgles as, far away, a soldier chokes on his own blood. Not worth it, Angus says, perking up when another voice screams and screams and screams through Whitey's lips.

"Which way?" Peytr says. "Where is he? Where is he?"

Angus slows down when the screaming stops.

"Save your energy, Borysson," he says. "Some of them's just meat what hasn't accepted it's dead yet."

The division's best triage man.

Peyt's grateful Angus doesn't laugh when they reach their next call, when the soldier's scooped-out sockets and pulped legs leave him puking his borscht on the sidewalk. He even loves Angus a bit, just a bit, when he says "Happens to the best of us," and passes his canteen. By their fifth shouter, Peyt's chucking bile. By the twelfth he's got the dry heaves. He keeps taking Angus's water until it's empty.

"Thanks," he says, again and again.

He likes how Angus mostly keeps his thoughts to himself.

Next morning, Peyt's paired with a grunt called Willard.

"Where's Angus?"

Willard shrugs, buckles straps and helmet, turns vulture. He kicks the stretcher laid on the ground between them. "Which end you want?"

"Gotta warm up," Peyt says, then runs round and round the mess tent until the weak has left his legs. The following day, he's teamed with Barnard. Then Singh. Newcombe. Haas. Tierney. After that, he stops asking their names. Calls them Head or Foot, depending on which end they take. Within a fortnight, he just calls them Foot.

By then, Peytr's Head by default.

The division's best triage man.

In theory, the grunts' mission is simple: clear the staging area for phase one, Operation VERNA.

Take point through grey territory, lure the fuckers out of hiding; play sparrow to the infantry's hawk. It's a three mile hike from base camp to the CBD through five suburbs, down a long stretch of highway and across a belt of parklands that was shot to shit long before the greys ever got a hold of it. Cross the gravel-lands and onto the asphalt. Conserve ammo, if possible—let the hoofmen blow their loads on the cocksuckers. Set up a perimeter, four blocks squared, starting on the city's western border, two clicks away from the football stadium. That's it. Air force will patrol from above while special ops recaptures the complex. Hoofers will bring up the rear, taking RPGs in shifts, squad after squad enlisted to help hold the grunts' defensive line. Two hours from initiation to extraction. Simple enough, in theory.

Five hours later, they've covered lots of ground, but won next to none of it.

How can they hold a line when not a fuckin' thing is straight between here and there? The front is one fuckin' joke of a term, Peyt thinks, stepping over a heap of minced civvies. On three, he and Foot heft a wailer from a pile of clipped vultures. Shrapnel-grated and crusted red, the grunt's eyes and limbs are intact. His 'wind's gone haywire, though. Ranting and raving about underground labyrinths, warrens, rabbits disappearing in fuckin' hats. Peyt hups the litter, palms slippery. He ignores the squirm and creep of someone else's 'wind touching his body.

"Sorry," he mutters over his shoulder, the guy's bloody skull bouncing on the stiff tarp with each step. "Sorry."

"Why you apologising, kid? You gone grey? Then shut the fuck up."

"Sorry."

The front isn't a fuckin' line, Peyt thinks. It's a round-robin of grey artillery ravaging human flesh. It's a fuckin' red splatter with a thousand fuckin' edges splashed every which way and back. And the enemy has a lock on each angle—N, S, NNW, SSE, wherever—they come from all sides, unseen, unsmelled, unfuckin'detected until they're right there, *right fuckin' there*, stabbing, digging, goring and gouging. Blinding. Vanishing. Though tunnellers have burrowed for decades and skybunker girls have given troops the bird's eye for twice that long, scoping for weak points, entry points, *any* points, they still haven't got the skinny on the whereabouts of those fuckin' grey bastards' lairs. . . . The fuckin' grey bitches? Fuckin' grey . . . *whats*?

Whats . . .? Whats . . .? And for what?

They've covered lots of ground.

Won next to none.

There's an eruption two streets east of the plaza where Peyt's crouched, scrubbing bloody gauze in a still fountain's scum. Scrubbing old blood from his hands. Scooping water into the wailer's mouth. Sand rains down as ships cut too close to high-rises and bunkers, the air under their wings thick with grit and silt. Peyt looks to Whitey, waits for more calls to come in. Tilts his head the way Angus used to, but only receives a clusterfuck of nonsense. He's heard the word mayhem before, but never really *heard* it until now. Mayhem is so fuckin' loud, all noise blends to white. Mayhem is supersonic. Peytr watches Whitey's mouth move as if in slow motion. Through her, some guy's shouting "On me! On me!" Peyt can't tell if the kid's calling for support or saying there's a grey . . . *what?* . . . right there, right fuckin' there, right then.

A numbered civvie streaks past, waving the seven digits carved into his palms. "Get down," Peyt yells as the man dashes into a known grey corner, looking around for photographers to catch the moment his body explodes.

Ears ringing, Peyt sits up. Watches the dust settle. Breathes through his mouth until his pulse slows. Clenches and unclenches hands gone numb from the stagnant water, numb from clutching the stretcher's cold metal grips. Echoes compound the noise in the square, doppelgangers of sound shouting from building to building, shouting from Whitey's lips, pinpointing every soldier's location, and none. Across the way, using dumpsters for cover, men bound over trenches, jumping for years before touching down. Sounds throb in Peyt's chest, making his helmet vibrate, shaking all sense from his 'wind. The in and out of his breath is loud, so very loud in his ears.

"Which way?" he asks, leaning close. Whitey could bite his ear off if she wanted.

Which way?

Which way?

Whitey jibbers, deafening.

Peyt grabs the stretcher, grunts at Foot. They take to the alleys, moving closer to the blast point. Not too close. As they pass, shopkeepers bolt their doors. Security blinds roll shut. From upper storeys and balconies, people watch the action. People living their lives. People going about civvie business.

"Get the fuck out of here," he shouts. The curse sounds almost natural now, almost convincing.

They stay.
Tomorrow he'll be back to collect what's left of them.

"Move," Peyt yells at Foot, trying to sound like an officer, not just an angry stretcher-bird. The pretence makes him angrier. There are no real ranks here, no staff sergeants, no orderlies. They're a *division* only so far as provisions go; their names inked on one camp's bunk and footlocker, one mess tent's rations list. Loyalty exchanged for a full belly and a place to take cover—mobile loyalty, sure, but deadly sincere while it lasts. It goes with their nameplates, carried if they're too wounded to move camp on their own steam, staying put when they're dead.

There's no secret to promotion, Peyt's Captain tells them, over and over again. "Just stay alive and open wide."

The men laugh as if the gag is a new one. "Good one, Borys," they say, or "Fuck right off, B." Peyt joins in, but calls the joker Cap—out of respect, mostly, and because he can't call him Borys. He can't. This Borys is nothing like his father. This Borys is tall and fit, blond as pine. This Borys makes eye contact when he speaks, squints when he laughs. Yeah, this Borys laughs.

"I'm being serious." Cap searches for a horizon through the smog, pupils dilating, soaking in colour the rest of them can't see. "What ye gotta do is listen—got it? *Listen.* What's this remind ye of?' He barks up a phlegm of 'wind. Raises his eyebrows, waiting for an answer, when it squelches words into the dirt.

After a minute, someone calls, "Landmine."

"Good," Cap says, then proceeds with his version of training. "Ye got yer Screamin Mee-Mees—sounds like a pig-squealing bitch. *Help meeee, help meeee, help meeeeee!* Let's hope we don't hear none of y'all in them Mee-Mees any time soon." Nervous laughter. "Then y'also got yer Oh-Twos, yer Dee-Fours, yer Rababou. . . . Keep an ear cocked for those fuckers, I tell ya. They sound innocent enough, like a trumpet blaring. A sharp brass note, held louder and longer the closer it gets. Fuckin' killer if ye're there when it hits."

Cap's litany of weapons goes on and on. Scattershot bottled from lunatic nightmares. Firebombs of distilled hatred. Teargas wrung from desperation, tapped and capped on the field. And who the fuck knows what we're hitting with any of it, Peytr thinks. Almost a month as Head and he hasn't scooped a single grey on his rounds. Not a one. Maybe their bodies dissolve, he thinks. Maybe the survivors gather their fallen when the grunts aren't looking. Maybe they come and snack on their dead. Gnashing and gnawing on grey meat down back alleys, leaving nothing but fuckin' grey crumbs.

Grey whats?

Peyt's got proof enough the fuckers exist. One blood-soaked stretcher, two well-worn steel handles, palm-loads of calluses. On the ground, a generation of corpses. Ahead of him and for miles around, a sorry collection of men, of boys, aiming at something. Returning fire.

Most of Peyt's long days have two nights. Some even have three. He sleeps when it's quiet, regardless of what the sun's doing. He tracks peace from bunk to bunk.

The cot they've supplied isn't much. Khaki sacking stretched over a metal rack that's two inches too short for his frame. One steel bar will dig into his ankles if he doesn't want the other cutting into his head. The canvas is almost new—he'll give them that much—and it's taut under his back; the same gauge and hue as the mildewed tent he can't see, but can sense, peaking a few metres above the platoon in the dark. It reminds him of the one he slept on back home. The yellow tarp smell of it. The fabric squeaking as it gives, millimetre by millimetre, beneath his weight.

As a kid, he'd drum his heels when he couldn't sleep. *Left right left right left*. Lulled by spiral echoes of his pounding, the sproinging rhythm, erratic but persistent, he'd start to relax. He'd tire his buzzing brain by working his muscles. Small, repetitive contractions. *Left right left right left. . . . Flex flex flex flex flex flex . . .*

Sleeping—trying to—on the floor next to him, Euri would whine at him to stop his twitching. But he couldn't. *Left right left right. . . .* He'd kick and kick until his calves chafed. *Flex flex flex flex flex. . . .*

After a minute or two, Dake would pipe up. Annoyed less at Peyt's wriggling than he was that he had a real bed. Ever since the Millers had moved in, Daken had been stuck with a whisker-thin slab of foam on the tiles.

Better than the folded towel Euri called a mattress, Peyt thinks, before realising she's probably taken the cot for herself now.

In the barracks, Peyt keeps his heels low so the other guys won't hear, tries to shake out his jitters.

What do the greys look like, he wonders. *Flex flex flex . . .*

What do they look like? *Left right left right left right left . . .*

"What do they look like," he'd asked, when Jean came to tuck him in. "Have you seen one?' Her silhouette detached from the doorway, crept on silent feet across the bedroom. A hand stretched out. Fingers warm and firm and reassuring, splaying across his shins, pressing him calm. His skin cooled the instant her touch withdrew. "Well? Have you?"

Feigning sleep, the other kids rolled closer. Wordwinds shaped listening-horns around their ears.

"If only we could talk to them," he'd begun, as Jean took a round clunking off the dressing table. She palmed it before scooching Peytr's legs to one side, sitting in the crook of his knees. Questions rained on his pillow—*Where are they hiding?*—tripped down his chest—*Why? Why? Why?*—and over Ma's knuckles, slinking a chain of need-to-knows around her forearm. *Can't we just talk?*

"Filthy thoughts," she'd whispered, flicking word-flies, pinching any she could catch. "Filthy." Running her fingers through Peytr's thick hair, she sifted, nails snipping and popping two kinds of lice, those with wings and those with serifs.

Tension eased in his limbs with each thought shorn. One by one, Jean crammed them into the metal shell cupped in her hand. "You know what to do," she'd said. In the half-light fogging down the hall from the living room, her face was inconstant. Shadows clung to her wordwind, sluggish darkness that shifted her features into something monstrous, something resolute.

"Yes," he'd said, though it made his stomach churn—until Ma plucked unanswered questions, rotting above his belly, and packed them into the grenade. Just to be sure, she screwed the lid on, mimed shaking the capsule. A couple good hard jolts to really stir up the contents. "Anyone tries to come through . . ." she'd said in lullaby tones, nodding at the boarded-up window. Cocking her arm, she exaggerated a fake throw, as she did every night, trying to make him giggle.

"Everyone has ammo, son. But not everyone has the good sense to use it."

Peytr's laugh was hollow. "I know." He submitted a cheek to her kiss, returned the gesture. "I'll use it. Promise."

"Cross your heart and hope to die," she'd said.

"Hope to die."

When she left, he was never totally drained. He simmered as Dake and the girls drifted off, their 'winds pristine and intact. New filthy thoughts fidgeted at the edge of his mind, danced on the tip of his tongue.

Flex flex flex flex flex.

The loaded grenade rattled on the table next to his head. Alive with his worries. They'd be back, he knew. Full-blown again come morning. Set to keep him awake.

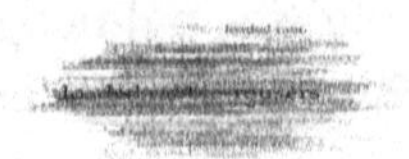

Before lights out, when the other grunts let their guards down and their 'winds loose, Peytr reads what they think about him.

The kid's wrung.

He's fucked.

Is he okay?

Hasn't blinked in hours.

Is he okay?

Fuckin' wrung.

Ask him. Somebody ask him.

Later.

"There's no later in war." Cap is cleaning his pistol, hood laced tight to prevent accidents. When Cap shoots, it's intentional. No exceptions. His 'wind is controlled, neither touching nor being touched. "There's only, forever, now."

Cap's fuckin' wrung.

Kid's wrung.

Is he okay?

Ask him.

But they never do. And that's fine, Peytr thinks. He's fine. Though his eyes are red, strained, bugged out from staring. He's fine. His senses are honed at night. Heightened. He's on the lookout. He's vigilant. He's deciphering shadows.

Daybreak and the highway is empty except for the vultures. Helmets on, masks and hoods up. Weapons locked, loaded. Six riflemen, six grenadiers, four medics, including Peyt, hanging back. Cap and Daken, with maps and a Whitey, leading the platoon on the first sweep of the day.

Until yesterday, Peyt hadn't seen Daken for—what? Three weeks? Five? Since they arrived at HQ. Selectors took one look at young Miller, with his robust wordwind and broad torso, and stamped his papers with a black triple-helix. Peyt's forms got a little red star in the top right-hand corner, some kind of kindergarten endorsement. Different age groups, he told himself, different missions. But still it rankled.

Now Daken has shrapnel scars on his left forearm.

He's lost the mullet; now a steel-mesh bandanna plasters his 'wind in place.

He's got a comfortable grip on his crossbow, and a swagger that shows he's used it.

The trill in his whistle is sharper than ever, Peyt thinks.

When Dake and the other helixes came into the mess last night, he pretended not to know who Peyt was. His glance oiled right over him. But after dinner, back in the tents, he kicked Jepp Rhysson out of his rack, the lowest bunk in the joint. The one right next to Peyt's.

At each street corner, Cap signals for a halt. Peyt stops immediately; if nothing else, he's well-trained in holding back. Waiting for hours, if need be. Being quiet. A quick nod and smoke bombs are tossed onto roofless condos, through glassless windows, into brick husks with tin steeples. More smash through a closed dance club's beaded doors. Another skitters across a paved schoolyard. Golden clouds gout from the cannisters, mixed with a smog of deception that stings the sinuses like fuck. The bright dye is supposed to be cheery, Carclew says, coughing, muffled behind his beak. Like a sunrise, someone else replies, Hackett maybe, and they all laugh. A golden dawn without any hint of the greys.

They musta *caught 'wind* of us coming, Rhysson says, and everyone gives him shit for the pun.

Yellow groundcover billows, swells, obscures half a city block. In taupe and beige, with hints of green leather peeking through the talc on their boots, the vultures blend into the fog. Streetlight bulbs are muted or broken, but their stalwart posts make good landmarks in the haze. There's still enough shadow to camouflage ten thousand greys, Peyt thinks, and Cap seems to agree. Before advancing, he lobs an orange streaker, then a crimson, and another yellow for good measure.

Peyt and Foot wait down the street in front of a convenience store. A faded *closed* sign hangs crooked on the door. Inside, a pale blue glow emanates from upright coolers. Peyt sure could use a drink. A fuckin' two litre spring water. A gallon of Pepto. His morning borscht isn't sitting well. His shoulders are caning. The stretcher's getting heavier by the second. Empty or not, the thing weighs a fuckin' tonne. But still, he can't put it down.

"Ready, Foot?"

"Ready."

Waiting for the go-ahead, they jog on the spot. Short hup-twos. *Left right left right lefts*. Within seconds, Peyt's breathing hard. Sweat soaks into his skullcap, burns his eyes. His stomach somersaults and his guts rumble. Fuckin' borscht, he thinks, clenching his asshole tight.

"Ready, Foot?"

Foot sighs. "Borysson."

Peytr curves in on himself, crimps his groaning belly. He inches closer to the corner where Cap and Daken are scoping the deadzone, performing smooth, even scans with their binoculars. The two of them poised, in synch. Cap lowers his specs for a second, three, five.

Watches Daken watching for the scurry of rats. *Go*, Cap signals after a minute, and Dake's across the road. Just like that. Always first, always Alpha, always brave and bold. Leader of the pack.

The rest of the guys crouch or lean against the building behind them. They pick at their nails. Whisper mods onto their bullets. Lift their helmets, scratch their melons. Dead words slough into the gutters. *Disco, centrefold, sassafras.* Useless conglomerations of letters. *Penny farthing, Cyclops, rhubarb.* In a minute, street cleaners will scuttle out of their foxholes, brooming stray thoughts, lifeless chuckles. Collecting them for incineration. Ensuring no secrets are spilled on the sidewalks. Hackett peers into a rainspout as if that's where the brooms are hiding. Others gaze up, staring at nothing. Yawning so wide their chins triple below their helms.

The stretcher is going to break Peyt's fuckin' arms. Dust clogs his mask, so thick he's going to fuckin' suffocate. Grime itches under his collar, his cuffs, in his fuckin' fly. Every step he takes grinds more sand into his creases and fuckin' ass crack. Peyt's so filthy he's chafing. He's raw.

Daken whistles the all clear.

Man, what a warble.

Cap turns and points. You and you and you. There and there and there.

One after another, soldiers dissolve in the yellow gloom.

Peytr would fuckin' kill for a bath.

"You ready, Foot?"

"Yes, Peyt. I'm fuckin' ready."

That night, Jepp Rhysson reclaims his old bunk. He rips Daken's nameplate off the footlocker, tosses it on the packed dirt floor, then flops down next to Peytr, snatching the blanket and bunched jacket Daken used as a pillow. Before stretching out, Jepp reaches over and quickly ruffles Peyt's hair, fingering his 'wind in the process.

Blushing, Peytr glares iron, his balls shrivelling at Jepp's shameless touch. *Fuckin' carrion bird. . . . Fuckin' vulture. . . .* The words rev with fury and now Peyt's up and towering, quivering, quaking. He throws curses like darts, aiming for the head.

"Fuckin' right," Rhysson says, easily backhanding Peyt's attack. Hand lingering until the letters disperse. "Finders keepers."

Just as quick as it swelled, Peytr's rage deflates. Adrenalin drains through his heels and he finds himself sitting, balanced on the edge of his cot. Doesn't remember bending his knees or propping his elbows on them. With bare feet, he stamps what's left of his fallen 'wind. Wishes the words would burn his soles like embers.

Earlier, Cap dug a couple jars of grog from his stash, generously passed them around. Peyt took one long haul after another, but didn't taste a drop. Sweat broke out across his brow and trickled down his neck. He knuckled the water leaking from his eyes, smeared the snot dripping from his nose. Carclew came up and nicked the bottle, chuckling at the sight of him. "You're fuckin' wrung, Borysson."

"Fuckin' fumes," Peyt managed and Carclew hooted, pulled down his pants, and blasted some fumes of his own.

The guys were rowdy, revelling in booze and life, their laughter extra loud, drowning out voices of the recently lost. Lamps swung from the tent's crossbeam and flickered in corners. Shadows danced wildly on the canvas walls, aping the boys' movements, crowding them into the narrow aisle between beds. Soldiers and spectres stripped to their undershirts, socks off, cargos rolled to the shin. It's fuckin' hot in the hootch, even with the flaps roped open, even with four bunks out of sixteen now empty. Hackett was swept first today. Two newbies soon after him. And Dakes . . .

"Just fuckin' up and vanished." Merv's been explaining what happened all evening. He whistles through his teeth, focuses on the candle in his big hand, melting wax to plug holes in his boots. He spits on the rubber, shakes his head. "I was right there, Cap. Right fuckin' there, practically clipping his heels." Next to Daken, Merv's the fastest runner in their crew. Played quarterback for the Blues, once upon a time—scored two touchdowns in the very stadium they're supposed to defend—but even he couldn't catch the bastards that sacked Dakes. "He rounded the corner right infuckin'front of me. Three steps ahead, max. I took that corner three steps behind him, I was clipping his fuckin' heels, and he was whistling like a champ, whistling into the schoolyard—and gone." Merv's wordwind spun in confusion, dogs chasing tails. "Just fuckin' up and vanished."

Peyt refused to believe it.

Cap refused to meet his eye.

"Poor fuck," Rhysson says, his voice all heartbreak and wistful. "Wouldn't even've got a grope on one of them Skybunker girls before his 'wind gave out. Hackett got hisself a good feel, I can promise you that. Chick swooped down on that glider of hers, swinging her big tits right in Lars' gob. . . . She was into it, leaning close so's he could make her wriggle while she took extra-long scooping up his 'wind . . ."

"You're full of shit," Foot says. "Hackett's fuckin' arms were blown clear off when me'n Peyt saw him."

Peyt nods to himself.

"Never said he was using his hands, corpse-mule," says Jepp, snaking out his tongue, quick-licking an imaginary nipple.

The guys howl and Cap passes him the jar. Young Foot hurdles one cot then another, rams into Jepp, sends the grog flying. Glass smashes and the drink is wasted, the night's long buzz reduced to a small wet patch on the floor. Peyt shudders as Foot's 'wind tangles with Jepp's then, both guys huffing, limbs locked and writhing. Shards bite their arms, shoulders, cheeks; blood speckles their sweaty beige skivvies. Jepp dominates, then Foot—they roll twice before jamming to a stop against Cap's trunk. With nowhere else to go, Jepp frees a hand, pounds the ground in surrender. Soon as Foot relents, Jepp goes in hard, ploughs his elbow into the younger boy's guts, gets a stranglehold on his 'wind. Foot flops around like a herring until Merv jumps in, tackling Jepp from behind.

Peyt watches from his cot, doesn't join in. He's slender, muscles lean but too small for grappling. Most of the guys have shaved heads, nothing to snag the points of their 'winds, thoughts flinging free as their punches. Peyt's got a thatch of straw that spirals from his crown and spikes at the forehead. It's thick and babyish, but makes a good buffer under his helmet.

The other guys drink and wrestle to avoid thinking. Of today. Tomorrow. After. What they'll do if, when the war ends. Useless speculation, Peyt knows, but they wrestle and drink and merge 'winds like they're strong and tough and in the now. *Only, forever, now. . . .* Merv and Jepp are grunting and rearing like stallions, bucking each other off. Their knees grate red on the broken glass. Almost as red as their faces. Maybe I'll tend mules, Peyt thinks. Nothing fancy. Instead of being one. Maybe I'll get a stable of cart-pullers. He likes the army's workhorses well enough. Likes the steam rising off their flanks in the morning, the velvet on their muzzles, the way their lips probe his fingers, toothless maws seeking something soft to gum.

Be my stallion, Peytie, Euri used to beg, when school was off, the neighbourhood gone grey, and they had nothing to do but wait for the haze to lift. They'd tell stories to kill time, make up fake accents for all the different characters, while Daken whistled a soundtrack. They'd play-act the parts, Daken always the sheriff and Peyt the deputy or, if Euri got her way, the horse. A palomino, she claimed, on account of his dappled skin. A Dalmatian, Daken always corrected and they laughed hard at that. *A Dalmatian*. Peyt wheezes, wipes his eyes. You make up the dumbest stuff, Dakes.

Peytr lies down, zips the black-out netting around the head of his cot to keep his dreams private. His blanket scratches like fibreglass. Brown, regulation fabric, a flimsy shield against fire and penetrating 'winds. There is no real conversation here. There are jokes, sure. Jibes, insults, machismo. There are instructions. Debates. Orders. But no one tells stories. No one really talks.

He rolls over, tries to block out the sound of skin slapping against skin, boots skidding, thundering, grunts and snarls. Tries to ignore the cheering when skulls crack against dirt. He flexes his legs, *left right left right left right*, working his muscles, pretending he'll be able to rest. Pretending Dake's not gone, not a traitor. Pretending he's not so alone.

Without sleep, there's no dreaming. Only sketches of memory, flickering reels of scenes from the past. Peyt kicks his heels, watches phantasms play across the tent wall. It's late, or early. He blinks. Can't pinpoint the time. It's late.

He blinks.

Down the hall, the front door creaked open, creaked shut. Footsteps feathered past the kids' room, but the floorboards tattled, giving her away. A slow clunk-thunking emerged from the living room. Clunk. Thunk. Clunk . . . thunk.

"Where have you been?"

"Sorry. I didn't want to wake you." Pause. "I waited as long as I could."

"No, Jean. Jeanie. What have you done?"

Who's that? Peyt wondered, rushing to the bedroom door. Ma always left it open a crack—for Euri and little Zaya, she said. Knowing full well it was Peyt who needed that line of light in the dark.

"What have you done, Jeanie?"

It didn't sound like Borys. The timbre was wrong. Nasal and wild, like a horse with a grey-snapped leg. Must be someone else. A crook. A dream-thief. But it's so late, Peyt thought. Even robbers and greys have to sleep . . .

"Clean yourself up. Now." The words more whinny than command. "No. Leave that on. We'll take you to the doc, get you stitched up."

Peytr inched closer. Put his eye to the gap and breathed silently, through his mouth.

"Won't make a difference," Ma said, smearing red on her coat and hood as she hooked them up next to Peyt's schoolbag. A row of numbers was scored into her palms, seeping. "My part is red-written now." Borys grabbed her hands, blotted them with his shirt, pressed hard.

Be careful, Da, Peytr thought. Don't hurt her.

"Scrub and stitch all you like, love," Ma said, suffering his ministrations. "I've made an oath."

"But, *Jean*."

Peytr stopped breathing. Borys's wordwind was thick, flaking on his shoulders like fallout. It sputtered about shackles, constraints, handcuffs. Flaccid penises. Balls being twisted, severed. The 'wind throbbed, clench-pulsing, and blanched to the colour of aching.

"When will you go?"

Peytr blushed when Jean took Borys's face in her bloody hands, kissed his tears. When she stroked his frantic 'wind, when she touched it. Fondled it. Brushed it with salt and iron. "When I'm needed."

"You're needed here," Borys said, a crack undermining the force in his tone. "The girls. . . . And Peytr . . ."

"I'm not going anywhere now." She laughed, her 'wind drooping. Condescending. Jean kissed Borys again, long and hard. She smiled. "But when I have to, I will go."

Sirens blare like the world's fuckin' ending.

"Get yer gladrags on, kid." The netting flings back and a lamp's in Peyt's face. Around the tent others flare and bob around, lightning bugs against the dark seeping in from outside. Peytr stretches for the grenade Ma left on the dresser. Arm flailing, whacking a strong pair of thighs. He sits up, blinking stupidly, 'wind lethargic. *Don't hurt her. . . . Don't hurt her. . . . Daken. . . .* Jepp reaches over, traps hovering 'D's and ellipses between his fingers, and gives them a liberal squeeze. Peyt gasps, pain shooting right down to his calves. He kicks out, screaming awake.

"Get the fuck off!"

Jepp loosens his grip, brushes off clingers. He's full-dressed and sober. The sour stink of grog oozes from his pores. "Haul ass to transport. Cap's got us a wagon. Leaves in ten."

Peyt's head is pounding. His hands operate on their own, grabbing pants, fumbling them around his feet. "What's going on?" He stands, pulls. Does up his belt, then his vest and jacket are on. Never mind the mask and helm; can't see a fuckin' thing with it on, can't distinguish fuckin' wordwinds from the black. He grabs his ruck, already packed. Cinches the straps. "What is it?"

The greys are here the greys are here the greys . . .

Sirens keen his legs into motion. He's running, he's out in the cold. Sky-fallen clouds are puffing from soldiers' mouths. For once, there's a moon. So bright Peyt staggers. Frost on the concrete, sparkling dust, gets trampled dull under stampeding feet. On the strip, propellers whir to life, catching the moonlight. Chips of ice spin off blades, glistening Catherine Wheels.

"One fuckin' job," Jepp says, slinging a rifle across his back.

"Dumb cunts in Nestor's crew got fuckin' overrun tonight. See that?" He gestures at the pickup hitched to a team of roans; the black carcass of a Chevy with dubious tires. Cap stands in its gutted cab, reins in hand. Jepp dekes right, heads for the parking lot. Pushes Peyt toward the med-tent. "Get yer meat tray, mule, and meet us there fuckin' yesterday. We got ourselves a breach."

Peyt wishes they could've run the three miles instead. The wagon gets them there too quick; before he knows it, they're unloading at the convenience store, all in a clump. No hanging back this time, no smog-yellow cover. Peyt's out in the open, deep in the thick. Can't feel his fingers his hands are clenched so tight. He runs through the smoke, the bombing, the fray—the fuckin' grey. Can't see a fuckin' thing beyond the length of his stride, but he keeps running, keeps running, no Whitey to guide him, just the bone-shaking eruptions, the trail of broken words, the screams. He follows the same route they took that morning, past condos, churches, into the schoolyard. Loses count of how many trips he makes back to the wagon, delivering load after load of the near-dead. Has no idea whose men they are, just that they're men, real men, spilling red, spilling syllables. He's got good instincts, he finds them by gut and groan, the division's best triage man. "Sorry," he says, over and over, jostling, bumping, tripping over curbs. "Sorry." Ears bleeding from all the screaming Mee-Mees, the Rababou, he keeps running, a mule hauling meat, kicking corpses face-down so Foot will stop trying to help them, stop bending to pick them up. Then it's Foot on the stretcher, wordless and chalky, and Peyt wraps the stump of the boy's arm in the last of Ma's gauzes, knows it's too late, the kid's fucked, but drags him back anyway, he was a good Foot, and he probably deserved a name.

"Sorry," Peytr says. "Sorry."

Dawn brings more warmth than light, but even so Peyt's got gooseflesh and his teeth won't stop chattering. He trails the litter behind him, no replacement for Foot, not enough able men left to waste on retrieving the wounded. Plodding now, no gumption even for walking. Words bullet past his ears, explode in trenches, shoot blaspheming gouts to steeple-height—and he goes as far as the school and back, again and again, camouflaged in a silt of grey, wearing gloves made of other men's blood. Deaf to whimpers and last words, he hears the sputter of curses, bullets, grenades, and quiet whistling, hears the stretcher's steel handles scraping on concrete, thudding across fabric, whistling across skin, hears his pulse throbbing out of sheer fuckin' luck, breath ragged in his ears, sobs stuck in his throat, and whistling he hears grey whispering, grey snickering, grey snares and trapdoors, grey skittering, grey roars, grey whistling, he hears the clunk-thunking of Borys's metal leg, the clunking of Ma's grenade, the jangle of bones clipped in his jacket, horse-knees thudding on bedroom floorboards, cot springs squeaking, glass shattering, grog seeping in the dirt. He hears, clear now, whistling.

He stops at the end of the alleyway.

Whistling in the schoolyard.

Man, what a warble.

I got him, Mrs. M.

Peytr edges around the corner, afraid to take a wrong step now, afraid to be mistaken.

I got him, Ann.

"Good work, Borysson," says Cap, clapping Peyt on the back. Big meaty whacks of the hand. Dake's alive and *he* saved him, he dug him out of the playground rubble, he dragged him back to the truck. Fuckin' right he deserves Cap's praise—he deserves a fuckin' medal. But what he gets is shoved into an alley, no wider than two men standing side by side, and Cap yanking Daken in behind them.

Soon as Cap saw him on Peytr's stretcher, he hauled Dake up by the collar, angled his face to catch the light.

"This him?" he asked Nestor's boys, who nodded without hesitation.

"That's the turncoat," says one.

"Close enough for gov't work," say another.

Before Peyt can stop him, Cap strips Dake to his filthy jocks, tears the bandanna from his head and binds his wrists with it. The other soldiers block the way out as Cap hooks Dake's legs out from under him, though he can't hardly walk; the brick and mortar all but crushed the pep from his calves. Nestor's guys are tense. Angry. Embarrassed at failing, Peyt thinks. At being ambushed. The men thrash their wordwinds, wield them like cat-o-nine-tails. Take their frustrations out 'til Dake's cheeks lips are swollen, his eyelids purple-blued, his cheeks plumped with red. Daken closes his eyes, suffers it silently. His 'wind close-cropped and blurry.

"Enough," Cap says and Peyt starts breathing again. He tries to turn, but Cap holds him firm by the shoulders. Thumping with gusto. Thump, thump thump. "Enough. This one's all yers, Borysson."

"But it's Miller, Cap. It's Daken."

Thump, thump, thump.

"He's one of ours." Peyt's voice breaks and his guts turn to vinegar. "He's like—" A *what*? A brother? A roommate? A lifelong friend? "I saved him from the greys—"

"Did you? Or did they send him back for more intel? Ask him that, soldier. Ask him where he up and vanished to this morning. Where he's been burrowing all day. Ask him why he fucked us over."

Peyt's legs twitch, *left right left right*, and he's got a desperate urge to piss. He's seen the kind of questioning Cap's talking about. Back at camp, with some twelve-year-old runner they accused of squealing. Peyt carried the kid's body away on his stretcher. "I'm no Whitey. I can't read this fuckin' guy's mind. Never could."

Dake? Dake? Dake? Dake? Dake? Dake?

"You damaged, Borysson?" Cap sighs and Peytr lowers his gaze, ribs contracting, burning around his lungs. "Don't use yer fuckin' egg. Use yer fuckin' gob. Use *this*, fer fuck's sake." Cap yanks the cutlery still dangling against Peyt's chest, hands him the sharp spoon. "Dig in."

"Why me?" Peyt whispers. His hands shake so badly, he drops the utensil without even feeling it. Cap picks it back up, closes Peyt's fingers around the shaft.

"Might be we got ourselves two traitors here," he says. "How am I to know? You and Miller go way back, right? And I seen you snuggling bunks, whispering late at night. . . . What's to say you ha'nt been planning this all along?"

"Planning *what*?"

"Don't play dumb, Borysson. You can't tell me you ain't heard Miller communicating with the greys today, warning them whenever we was coming. Man's got a whistle on him all right—now we got to find out what secrets he's gone and trilled."

"But—" Peyt wishes he'd brought his mask tonight. Wishes he could block out Cap's accusations, his glare. "What am I supposed—"

"You know what to do."

Blocking off the end of the alley, Nestor's brutes cross their arms, 'winds glowing encouragement. Rough bricks scrape Peyt's back as Cap pushes him down. After a few seconds, his legs give out, too tired to maintain a crouch.

"Did you do it?" Peytr asks. "Did you?"

Do it do it do it do it do it do it do it . . .

Daken's glance oils over him. As if they've never met.

"Get on with it, soldier," Cap says. "Or else I will."

"No," says Peytr. "I'll do it."

Do it do it do it do it do it do it do it . . .

The spoon rasps against Daken's stubble as Peyt scrapes into his wordwind. A whisker of thought curls beneath the bowl, mismatched letters and codes that smell salty, musky-sweet in the gaps. *Greys. . . . Doorway. . . . Conc—* Daken bucks so Peyt throws his weight into it, pins him against the brick, bony shoulder against naked chest. He jams the spoon into Dake's scalp, seeking purchase, seeking a crack. But Daken's thoughts are steel-girded, giving up little but meaningless filings and tiny hickory-scented details.

Cap snatches the bones, gives Peyt a shove. "Try harder, Borysson," *pussy pussy pussy* "Unless this is you volunteering for interrogation?"

"No," Peytr says again, forgetting the cutlery, favouring the tools he was born with. Leaning closer and closer, he scrabbles with his nails, then sticks out his tongue and *licks*. Spit dribbles down Daken's temple. Shatters his calm. For a split-second his concentration wavers, and Peyt bites. He tongues the sections around Dake's ears, gnaws chunks of his fear, his tension. Vague emotions distil into coherent thoughts, memories of today, this afternoon, this morning. Peyt breathes the other boy's breath, inhaling him, nibbling him, sucking to catch any wriggling lies.

Daken thrashes beneath him, pummels with joined hands and knees and hips.

"Well?"

"It's grey—"

Cap cuts him off, pushes Peyt's mouth back down. "That's a start, soldier. Not an answer."

There's blood on Peyt's tongue as it darts and scoops, jaws aching, lips and chin chafed raw on Dake's bristled head. He starts gagging, retching up bits of iron-tinged 'wind. Placing a boot on Peyt's heaving back, Cap says, "Keep it down, soldier." And it's enough to make Peyt swallow, swallow, swallow, swallow, a lifetime of stolen words shredding the full stop lodged in his gullet.

Jamming fingers into his mouth, Peyt tries to puke up all he's ingested. He tastes Ann Miller's face powder on his lips, knows what it's like to kiss her goodnight. He remembers a father he's never had, a man who could lift Daken overhead with one muscled arm. He feels what it means to be strong and hard and cool. He knows what it's like to fuck without regret. He sees himself through Dake's eyes, the little Dalmatian, and chokes on a bellyful of shame, neglect, love.

Knuckles scrape bloody on Peytr's teeth. Bile juice-burns his throat.

Beside him, Daken is babbling, his limbs lax. Listless. His tongue, suddenly too big to be stowed in his mouth, bulges obscenely from his frothing lips. Aphasic gibberish spills from his forehead. Primal verbs: eating, shitting, fuckin'g, fuckin'g, fuckin'g . . .

"Sorry," Peytr whispers, then vomits long and hard, spattering truths all over Cap's boots. Etched in acid and bile, stark against dull green leather, they reveal everything Peyt has discovered. Everything he'll never forget.

His wordwind screams humiliation.

"Well," Cap says, reading the sludge. A few chunks about a grey IED.

Merv hightailing at the first click of trouble. A squelch of falling breeze blocks, then hours of digging, digging, digging . . . "Tell Nestor to cordon off the schoolyard, pronto. And Borysson—"

Peyt's vision is clogged with words. Tremors rack his guts, his legs, his arms. He tries to shake it off, left right left right, but has no control. He cannot stop, cannot be still.

"Get yer meat tray, kid," Cap says, nodding Nestor's men out of the alley. He strides to the truck, grabs the nearest Whitey. "We got a man down. I repeat: we got a man down. Medics, run your asses over here to the All Night and parlez with Borysson."

"Ten-four, Cap."

"Good work," Cap says again, coming back to the alley to help Peytr up. Thump thump, thump. He hands Peyt a rag from his pocket. "All good, soldier?"

Cap watches Peyt spew for another minute or two, then leaves him to clean up the mess.

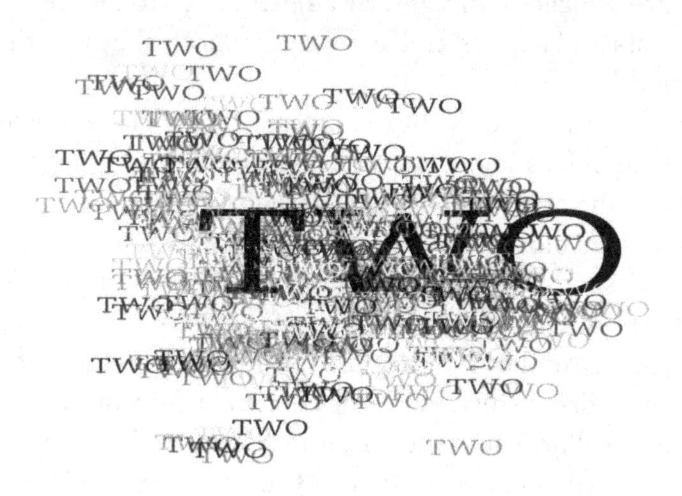

For almost two years, the same routine.

Borys wakes between noon and two. Swings his good leg over the edge of his single bed. Places his good foot on the floor. Keeps the sweat-dinged sheet draped over his lap, his thighs, his knee. In case Euri or the little one barrel into his room. In case Jean forgets to keep the growing girls out. In case Jean forgets herself. Borys bunches the sheet around him. Bolsters himself with threadbare cotton. Creates an impression of presence, of bulk. He leans over and his undershirt gapes. Musk and milk, dried stenches of night, waft from the scooped neckline. Out of habit, he clutches the fabric. Grabs at dog tags that aren't swinging there, aren't clinking together, aren't giving away his position. Deep breath in. He presses the silent shirt to his chest. Exhale. Tomorrow, he thinks, I'll do a load of washing. Tomorrow.

He reaches down, through his absent shin, and pulls a box from under the bed. Takes the shoes out, left first, then right. Fine black leather. Lace-up. Toes tapering to a blunt point. He polishes them with a brush and shammy. With spit and elbow grease. Left, then right. Left, then right again. Once they're gleaming, he takes the balled cotton out from beneath their stiff tongues. Two black socks and one yellow-white. He slips the black pair on two feet—one flesh and, collected from the floor, one cast steel—then stretches the white over the scarred stub of his thigh. Quickly corsets the stump in the metal leg's brace. Cinches it in tight. He adjusts straps to relieve the pinching. Adjusts and adjusts and adjusts. Puts both shoes on the floor. And stands.

Clunk-thunk, clunk-thunk, Borys crosses to the closet. Hips swivelling his kneeless leg onward, leaden heel propelling the nimble. He takes the only pair of slacks off their hanger. Navy twill, no belt. With fingers more than eyes, he inspects pleats and creases for crispness. Satisfied, he balances against the closet's sliding doors. Get the pants around his ankles. Hops them up, hop-hops, pulling both legs at once, careful not to snag the fine material on his brace. Next he puts on a dress shirt. Pale blue cotton, button-up, with a stiff semi-spread collar. Tucks the tails it into his waistband. Jams them flat against his boxers. From the breast pocket, he takes the cufflinks Jean gave him, oh, ages ago. Before. When they first met. Stupid in love, he'd thought them precious. Their shape so intriguing, so abstract, so avant-garde. A curving swirl, fat at one end, narrowed at the other. A teardrop? A whooshing zeppelin. A yin, maybe, or a yang. For years they'd been bright, burnished gold. Now the finish is wearing off. The brass beneath rubbed visible, dulling the gilt veneer.

He fastens one at each wrist.

Reaching for his tie, crimson faded to rust, Borys hears the back door creak open. Seconds later, it gently clicks shut. A pause as Jean heel-toes her shoes off. Bare feet pad across the kitchen. Rattan scratches on melamine as she slides a basket onto the counter. Window-box vegetables for her supper, his breakfast. Turnips, baby carrots, beets. A cupboard door opens, closes. The cutting board is placed, quiet as a piece of blank paper, close to the basket. A knife slinks from the block and slowly, carefully, begins to chop.

That's my Jean, Borys thinks, noosing the silk tie around his neck. Deep breath in. Yep, that's my girl. Treading softly while the rest of us sleep. Always thinking of others. Always putting their wellbeing before her own. He snugs the knot up to his throat. Exhales. Smooths down the flaps of his collar. Discreet, industrious Jeanie. Always busy. Always planting and planning and preparing, hardly making a peep in the meantime.

I didn't want to wake you, Borys.

I waited as long as I could.

Well aren't you just a lamb, dear Jeanie. Aren't you just so fuckin' considerate.

Borys gobs into his palms. Attempts to smear his hair flat. Fails. The thick brown mass is reinforced with grey. Little spirals of age that tease the strands up and out, even when wet. Lack of colour that leaches his wordwind, slows it down, encourages repetition. *I didn't want to wake you, Borys.* He crams a wedge cap onto his head and feet into shoes. *I waited.* Unhooks his cane from the doorknob, hoping the oak's sturdiness will offset his wobbles. *I waited.* Clunks out of his room. Into and down the hall. *I waited.* Passes the living room and there's Ann Miller, staring out the window in nightgown and robe, tearing tissues into snowflakes that collect in drifts at her feet. Eyes forward, eyes forward. *I waited.* He wills Ann not to see him until he's well on the other side of the pane. *I waited.* Steals through the front door. Clunk-thunk on the cement step. Outside.

I waited as long as I could.

Halfway down the drive, Borys stops to net stray words with his hat. Should've worn a hood. Regardless of how it looks. Tomorrow, he thinks. I'll wear one tomorrow.

Gravel lines the roadside, tessellated chunks of concrete mixed with smaller crumbs of asphalt and mortar and punctuation. Footing is unpredictable, the loose stones sharp and unsteady. Borys relies on the cane to keep him upright. Relies too heavily on it, Jean says. As if he wouldn't smash the thing to pieces. As if it's a frivolous accessory, vain and stupid as cufflinks. Feeling Ann Miller's gaze on his back, Borys widens his stance. Tries not to lean.

Deep breath in. He looks left down the block, then right. Searches for the gleam of Artie's lid. For the Pigeon's distinct posture, hunched under a hillock of parcels, mind burdened with a slew of verbal messages, back weighed down by those written in ink. Borys imagines black-ringed letters. Artie's expression, more resigned than commiserating, as he thinks and speaks the news. Borys looks left, right, left. Doesn't see the Pigeon anywhere. Exhales.

An hour passes. Two. No one but Ann, haunting the window, pays Borys any mind. Theirs isn't an unfriendly street, but neither is it ringing with hellos, how are yous, see you laters. Backs turned, people tend allotted gardens. They board superfluous windows and doors. Pull down dangerous, shell-shattered roofs. Old ladies rake their front yards to keep young soldiers from tripping while patrolling the suburbs at night. At irregular intervals, pickups and jeeps bounce across the intersection three houses down. On silent wings, ships negotiate the airways, dodging skybunkers, clouds, each other. Jet engines are muffled but Borys senses they're up there, swimming the grey heights. In the distance, bombs drop with deep tuba *parrumps*. Rockets flare green and red over the darkening valley. Borys counts the seconds from the flash to the first pip of the missiles' piccolo trills.

He looks up the street and down.

Three hours now and no word.

I waited as long as I could . . .

A donkey ambles past, hitched to a red two-door convertible. Perched on the car's seatback, the driver *whoa*s the mule. "Need a lift somewheres?" He gestures vaguely at Borys with a horsewhip. "Discount for veterans."

Jaw clenched, Borys shakes his head once. Stiff-waves the cabbie away.

"Suit yerself." As he moves on, the driver's 'wind trails behind him. Tantalising images of bones resting, loads lifted, cradle-rocking lulls of the mule's clip-clop, laced with taunts and jibes. Purse strings cinched. Arses tight-clamped. Wizened, hobbling gimps.

Fists balled and shaking, Borys follows the cab with his eyes. Takes one unsteady step after it, then another, but stops when his gaze skips ahead. A glint of silver mesh crests the rise at the street's hilled end. The tip of a hood materialises, it seems, out of nowhere. It spills over a bulbous head, outlines unruly red bangs and sallow face, puddles on hunched shoulders. Tarnished buttons fasten the mantle to a familiar uniform, dove-hued coveralls and double-slung satchels. Borys puffs his chest, deep breath in. Hands by his sides, chin lifted, he waits as the Pigeon shares news with the driver. He steels himself for a parcel. A message. Word that Peytr's been shot. Captured. Maimed.

Anything.

He exhales.

Eighteen months since the photograph came. It had been creased, frayed around the edges. It looked old. *Antique*. All greys and whites and faded blacks. Already flaking, though it couldn't have been taken more than a week or so earlier.

"What did you do to it?" Borys had asked, running a finger over the subject's masked face. The boy, solo, was towing an armless body on a stretcher. Looked like he'd just emerged from an alleyway. Bricks and mortar and tumbledown walls flanked him. A blurred suggestion of word-smoke darkened the frame's left side. The soldier, 'windless, was running toward it. His legs fleet, frozen mid-sprint.

"Delivered in the same condition it was received," Artie had said.

"When did Peyt send it?"

"Not Peyt," the Pigeon had replied. "The combat shutterbug. Suspect he'll be sending a bill for the print one of these days."

"How much?"

Artie shrugged. "You could barter him down. Say there's no proof this here's your boy. That mask, that uniform. . . . Could be anyone's soldier."

Even without seeing his face, Borys couldn't deny that the kid pictured was Peyt. Foxing in the finish blotched his son's skin more than it already was, but he'd know those flaws anywhere. The tanned neck splashed with stark white milk. The strained forearms girded in Chantilly lace. Likewise, Jean had taken the boy's identity for granted. "They've made him a medic," was all she'd said when Borys had held the photo out for her to see. Her scarred hands not as dexterous as they once were. Her voice taking up the pinch her fingers had lost. "They've made him a *medic*."

Now the Pigeon slaps the cab-driver's mule, tips an imaginary brim at the man, and continues on down the road. Borys sucks in his stomach to keep it from churning. Deep breath in, puff the chest.

Arms rigid. Exhale in increments, one small sigh for each of the deliveryman's oncoming steps.

"Afternoon, Borys," says the Pigeon. Another tip of a make-believe brim. Pace measured, not slowing.

"Afternoon, Artie."

Deep breath in.

"Nice day today."

And exhale.

Nice day, Artie always says, when there's nothing in his satchel for Borys Gretasson and his wife. Nice day today, Borys. As if no news is good news. As if hope thrives in not knowing. Nice fuckin' day.

"Might be cloudy tomorrow. You never can tell."

"Too right," Artie says, doffing that fuckin' invisible hat. "You never can tell."

Inside, Borys stops on his way down the hall and looks into the kids' room. The girls aren't there, but their mess is. Scraps of coloured-on papers litter Euri's cot. Her collection of hair ribbons rainbow down the sheet to pool on the floor. Stuffed socks with button eyes are lined up on the little one's foam mattress, stitched mouths whispering into stitched ears. He picks up stray nighties, undershirts, spare tights, and school pinafores. Folds them. Puts them dirty into the dresser drawer, next to a pair of Peytr's old jeans. The pants are cold to the touch, damp with chill. Borys shoves them to the back of the drawer. Too small for the boy now, he thinks. Too big for the girls.

Tomorrow, he thinks, I'll do laundry.

Alone in his own bedroom, he takes off his shoes. Puts them into their box, slides it under his bed. He replaces the wedge hat on its shelf, hangs his tie. Returns the cufflinks to the breast pocket, unbuttons and hangs his shirt. Lines the pant-legs up by their pleats, drapes them over a padded rung. He leaves socks and unders on. Covers them with standard-issue overalls. Acid-washed denim with a big spoked wheel sewn in red felt on his back. Press-studs aligned in single file from gut to gullet. Long sleeves, snap-cuffed. Pants long enough to tuck into short work boots. He snaps and tucks and laces and hoods.

Deep breath in. Inhales the call of Jeanie's stew to his breakfast and her dinner. He takes up his cane. Clunk-thunk. Clunk-thunk. Clunk-thunk. And exhales.

It takes Borys over an hour to walk to the Wheels 'n' Heels, though it's less than a mile from his house. With only one bending knee, he can't ride a velo. Taking a train isn't an option. The closest station abuts a minefield; getting tickets could literally cost an arm and a leg. Their car died when Peyt was a baby and Borys still doesn't see much point resurrecting it. And he refuses to waste hard-earned coin on fuckin' mules or that piece of shit twice-a-day bus. Jean once offered to buy him a chair with that first payment she got from the gov't—said she'd even push him to work every day—but Borys won't have it. He simply will not have it.

So he walks the distance each evening, lungs bellowing, hips swivelling and jerking, blisters swelling and popping on his stump. He avoids the covered walkways linking minor and major thoroughfares, avoids the underpasses and overpasses, avoids the tunnels worming farther and deeper into the outskirts of town. Crowded and hot, stinking of piss and damp and week-old goat's cheese, these shortcuts end up adding a bad half hour to his trip. He hates the jostle of bodies cramped in underground spaces, the maelstrom of wordwinds flitting and touching, the dead insinuating air. Instead, he takes the sidewalks when he can, the open road when he can't. He likes hearing field crickets buzzing to each other in code. Likes to pretend they're actually crickets.

Slowing to ease the chafe of his brace, Borys passes the hospital, tastes iodine breezes wafting from its screened windows, antiseptics and sickness and grief. Passes the local magistrate's office, the young minister's name emblazoned in dark green up the beige side of the two-storey building. Passes housing trust blocks hunkered beside upstanding clapboard townhouses. Passes an empty park, its benches removed, its pond half-drained and reeking with fermented leaves and wormwater. A different reek follows him past the veterans' lodge—burnt weed, weak booze, and stale stories—and settles in front of the borough of refugees' tents that never seems to get any smaller.

Even here, on the outskirts, five minutes from work, he doesn't pick up the pace. He doesn't avert his eyes, doesn't block his nose against the tang of foreign-spiced air, the steam of canvas and open latrines and desperation. He meets whatever pathetic gazes seek his, sees Peytr in the youngest, the weakest, most pitiful glances. He maintains a measured *clunk-thunk, clunk-thunk, clunk-thunk*. Looking forward as well as behind.

He walks as he did when he was barely older than Peyt, a stately, disciplined, left right left. He walks 'til his hip is throbbing. Walks for the pain and to forget what caused it. And when he passes the grogger, when he's almost at the W&H, he walks and walks and walks to remember.

This, he tells himself, all of this, the nurses and pensioners and guttersnipes, the boiling stews and overflowing trash cans and empty gas tanks, the garish posters calling men to duty, the artists with enough talent—enough bright paint!—to make such posters, the flickering electricity and flickering wordwinds, the night market vendors with their cheap plastics and cheap veg and cheap grey juju, the street cleaners with their shushing brooms, the old ladies and young, the children growing and gone, this, all of this, this thriving bleeding shit-stinking life, is what he lost his leg to uphold.

He would've given the other one too, if they'd let him. But a scant month on the front was sufficient, they'd said. Go on home, they'd said. You've done all you can. A month and a leg is enough. So they said, all those years ago, so they still say. Every night, no matter how fast or how slow his pace, they dog him on his way to work.

Borys keeps walking. Always reaching the Wheels & Heels before its whistle blows the nightshift inside.

Peytr used to tell tales about the factory where Borys works.

"It's a champion horse stable," he'd say one day, and "It's a thirty-car garage" the next. Without fail, baby Zaya would clap her pudgy hands, not understanding much more than Peyt's smile. The oboe timbre of his voice. The honey coating his 'wind. The enthusiasm of his lies. Slightly more discerning, Euri chewed the ends of her frizzy brown braids as she listened. Peanut nose wrinkling. Eyelids slitting. Ideas leapfrogged her crooked part while Peytr spun his stories, mind hopping from dis- to belief. From the next room, more often than not, the Miller kid egged Peytr on. Silent, Dake's wordwind flashed secret embellishments behind the girls' backs, riddled with spelling errors and stupidity. As always, Peyt embraced the other boy's thoughts. His fine falsehoods fell to pieces under the crudeness of Daken's details.

Borys watched from the doorway, or the settee, or the kitchen table. He'd look to the children, look to Jean, and wonder how he'd ever come to live with all these happy little fools and liars.

Granted, Peytr's fabrications weren't all that far off.

The Wheels 'n' Heels factory is two main buildings: Forming and Finishing. The latter a concrete shoebox, single-storied, with twelve blue stable doors perforating its length on one side; the former, behind it, a repurposed hangar, three open storeys of corrugated iron and breeze blocks and tin. On its curved, once-retractable roof, rust weeps from blackened skylights—what Peyt used to say looked like blood dribbling from punched-out teeth. And, oh, how the boy'd cackle whenever he said it, cackle like a little speckled hen.

Borys goes to Finishing first, punches in before the nightshift whistle wails a third time. He grabs a welding mask, mesh gloves and reinforced hood from his locker. Fills his canteen at the fountain outside the change room. Stencilled signs shout on the walls, bold letters and arrows pointing to exits, sharp-angled symbols for *DANGEROUS SUBSTANCES*, colourful dots for air raid shelter locations, reminders to *WEAR PROTECTIVE GEAR AT ALL TIMES*. Borys pockets a spare pair of earplugs then makes his way through the chaos of Finishing.

Bisecting the room, two fifty-metre tables are the only straight lines in sight. On the left, semicircular workstations are scattered around vats of oil, tubs of mineral spirits, and deep, bubbling black oxide baths. Round racks of wheel-rims form ragged queues around them, waiting to be laced with spokes. Conveyor belts snake through the space, around tables and desks, carrying near-finished pieces to assembly and assembled pieces to delivery on the far right. Behind stacks of boxes, fitting tables, and shrink-wrap machines, a huge map dominates the wall, drawn on the white paint with charcoal and ink. At first, curves and squiggles and crosshatched lines were simply there as a guide, sketching out delivery zones and warehouses. Lately, pushpins and flags have been added, a few at a time, dotting the city. Plastic stars, fake carnations, little tinfoil swans. Bottle caps and faded tickets. Pictures. Thumbprints. Markers pinpointing where family members have been lost to the greys. The boss added three of his own last year.

In his locker, Borys keeps a glass bauble for Peyt.

He heads for the back door, avoiding eye contact and conversation. Perched on tall stools or sitting in wheelchairs, dozens of workers hunch over tables and cluttered desks, all within arm's reach of the slow-moving belts. With a rhythmic click of magnet against steel, practised fingers thread spokes onto rims. Wheels are trued by hand and machine before being sent to the paraplegics, who all place bets before racing new chairs down the aisles.

Fuckin' idiots, Borys thinks, deking around them as the guys hoot and holler through their safety checks. Laughing their born-crippled arses off. They have no idea what it's like. Leaving. Being away for months, a year, years. Getting back home to find your wife's a stranger, if you find her there at all.

Trolleys full of prosthetic legs and feet barricade the back door. Files rasp, metal on metal, as workers grate rough edges from the limbs Forming popped from moulds that afternoon. Chisels and spikes and small hooked gougers scrape details into ankles and toes, littering the floor with iron filings. Buckles clatter against metal shins, metal knees, metal thighs as they're fitted with braces, then clunked onto conveyors.

A moment's quiet as Borys crosses the gravel yard to Forming. Inside, furnaces and hearths suffuse the foundry with orange heat. Able-bodied men work bellows, grunting with each pull and push. The rest, like Borys, crew metal presses and benders, or crank great slag-filled ladles on winches for pouring. The air is thick with steam and sweat. The clank of boilers, kettledrums, and hydraulics. The whirr of oiled turbines. The clatter of ball bearings and rigs and pulleys. Molten metal glows into moulds. Extruded aluminium is cast into hollow, pliable bars, which Borys spends his nights coiling and cutting into rims.

He nods to Jerry, a huge troll of a man, double peg-legger, who works the bender next to his own. Jerry nods back, practised hands guiding metal bars along the rounding track.

"That there'll be my station one day," Peytr used to say, the evenings he followed Borys to the factory. Evenings when Jean was off getting brainwashed, leaving fuckin' Ann Miller to watch the kids. Peyt was so small, he wasn't much in the way. Like the rest of them, he wore helmet and mask, so was safe enough. He'd fetch water for the lads or lug iron ingots, pretending he'd the muscles for heavy lifting. But after a few minutes, chest fluttering in and out, he'd hoist himself onto a table between the benders. Scrawny legs swinging non-stop beneath him. Catching his breath while chattering away, shouting to be heard over the din. "When I'm metalled like you, Da. I'll work that bender right there."

And the stupid kid was so bloody proud at the prospect, he seemed to take Borys's shaking for laughter. Peyt would join in, giggling like a girl, before turning to talk Jer's ear off.

Take pride where you can, Borys thought then, secretly agreeing his son's future was like to be spent in a foundry. Few other options for a kid like him. The ink was weak as water when they'd written Peyt's name in the birth register, a sure sign the boy would be likewise, or so Borys once thought.

But he's proved us wrong, hasn't he? Young Peyt. Brash, speckled hen. Gone for two years now. A soldier. On the front. Two full years. Twenty-four months. At war. Fighting. Making a difference.

Having an effect.

Meanwhile, it's eight hours of coiling and cutting for Borys. Plus two overtime to help buy more seedlings for the garden. Ten hours a night, watching metal curve round and round. Off at five, five-thirty. Off to the grogger for an after-work pint with Jerry. Off home afterwards, where the older kids are off to war, the younger long off to sleep. Ann Miller off her nut. And Jean . . . off.

Lights off. Uniform off.

Round and round.

During his own tour of duty, Borys had sent his parents messages every second day. No holding back. They'd be worried, he'd thought. They'd want to know everything. That the bunkers were rotten. That the mess tent doubled as a stable, so the food smelled and tasted like shit. That the other guys in his platoon weren't soldiers, just boys. Like him. Just regular boys.

He remembers sending one letter in particular. Remembers composing it in his mind. Remembers imbuing it with colours and smells. The scent of fighting. Sulphur, sweat, and grime. The salt of hidden tears. The piss-stench of not knowing where the enemy is.

It's like they're not even there, he'd said. *But you* know *they're out there. They must be out there. They have to be. The roadsides are riddled with traps. We're bombarded from above, from below, from who-knows-where. Our guys go missing. They're returned with no eyes, no 'winds. If they're returned at all. Each time we go out on point, we all come back looking more pale and more grey, more like* them. *They're turning us into old men, Ma. Least it feels like it. They're turning us grey.*

Borys knew the message reeked of woollen blankets. The yellow urge to burrow into them each morning, to just give up and be a coward, fine, let other guys be heroes, go ahead and let them fight round and round, while he just stayed in his bunk and slept. He kept in the sour undertone of getting up anyway. The off-milk whiff of putting up a brave front. He kept it all in, every last detail, and sent the messages, humiliating or otherwise, because his parents worried. Because they'd be glad to hear his words, to smell these stinks of his being alive.

Now the Pigeon appears at the end of the street.

Borys straightens his tie, pinches his cufflinks. He imagines news of Peytr's insubordination. Inevitable, he thinks. The boy's a dreamer.

The boy can never sit still. He pictures Peyt's body, mangled and word-eaten by a grey landmine. Sentences blasting away his limbs, gnawing nerves and tendons, the way they did, once, his own. Borys scratches the inverted phrases burnt into his thigh, his forearm, his hand. Feels the shine of the scar tissue, the way it pulls his skin off-kilter, making it hard for him to straighten, permanently propping him up with a cane. As Artie approaches, Borys stands at attention. Doesn't shift, though his false leg pinches, though it chafes the raw curses on his quad. He imagines the boy in sad shape. Sad, sad shape. Too sad to send a message. Even a single line.

Still fighting would suffice.

Still here.

Would it be so hard for Peyt to send a note? If not to him, then to Jean? Or the girls? Euri and the little one? *Don't tell Da, but I think I might never be home. . . .* A line? *The food is shit but the fighting is good. . . .* A few words? *The end is in sight. . . .* Can't he just lie, the way Borys did to his own parents, every second day for a month?

Would that be so hard?

"Afternoon, Borys," says the Pigeon. Pace measured, not slowing. Imaginary hat tipping.

"Afternoon, Artie."

"Nice day today."

"If you say so," Borys replies.

At Wheels 'n' Heels, most injuries happen in the tired-out black of night. Scaldings, staplings, stabbings, severings. The foreman usually hires amputees and gimps—no chance they'll be redrafted, and they know the products firsthand—but he'd rather avoid wasting good metal shoring up limbs lost to daydreams and exhaustion. Two hours before end-of-shift, he sends a few new Finishers around with mugs of black grog, bowls of hot oats, and sticks of jerky for the foundry men. Full bellies are quiet bellies, the foreman says. At the first hint of the trolley's clattering across the gravel courtyard outside, Jerry cuts the bender's power. Signals Borys to do the same. Borys waits for the aluminium to quit coiling, takes the four-stack from the machine before switching it off. Then he rummages through the top drawer of his toolkit, sifting through all the misshapen knives, forks and spoons he fucked up trying to make Peyt a decent set to take on campaign. He digs 'til he finds the best ones he forged—the ones he'll send as replacements just as soon as the boy says he needs them.

"Got word from Chass this morning," Jerry says, thumping his lid on the table. A thick, curly beard bushes down to the third snap of his coveralls. Freed, his wordwind springs like dreadlocks from matted brown hair. Never revealing much the man wouldn't say aloud. "Spent the past fortnight shovelling dirt, he says. And he's had a gutful by the sounds of it. Says, 'I never signed up to wield a fuckin' shovel, Da. . . . Never filled so many fuckin' sandbags in my whole life!'"

"You don't say." Borys lifts his visor, but keeps his helm and hood on. Swings a leg over the low bench and sits facing Jerry. Concentrating on his hands, he unthreads the spoon from its ring. Tries to sound nonchalant. "Where's he stationed? With the local lads . . .?"

Jerry cranes his neck, squints into the orange gloom to catch sight of the newbs with their grog-trolleys. "Don't rightly know. Somewhere on the western front, I think. Near the stadium? Someplace there's a fuckload of dirt needs shovelling at any rate. Chass's got to be a bit round-about on the specifics. Y'know, in case the Pigeon gets waylaid. Suppose Peyt's just as sketchy with the details, though, isn't he."

"Yeah," Borys says. "He doesn't give much away."

Jerry nods, half-hearted. Distracted by the arrival of steaming bowls and salted meat.

Listen to me, Borys wants to say. He wants to pull Jerry's greasy beard, yank until the older man's eyes bulge to attention. "Jer," he says. Fuckin' listen to me. "Jerry."

"You want oats, B?"

"Yeah. But Jer—"

"Make that three oats," Jerry says, slapping the serving kid's 'wind when it unspools a length of *oinks*. "And an extra jar of grog."

"Rations," says the pig-kid. "You get one each."

"Jerry," says Borys. "Peyt—"

"Pah!" says Jerry. "Venderwhal is out sick. No sense wasting his share."

"Jerry, Peyt bagged three greys last week. Saw them right up close and everything. One minute the street was empty, he said, and the next he'd laid three of the fuckers low."

That catches Jerry's ear.

Borys regrets it as soon as the words are spoken.

Now they'll think Peyt's a hero.

"Well, I'll be!" Jerry claps Borys on the shoulder. "Why didn't you say something before?"

Borys tries to shrug it off, but there's no stopping Jer when he gets excited. The big oaf lets out a whoop. Cups his hands round his mouth. Bellows the news to ragged applause. "Well done," he says, rattling Borys's teeth with the force of his pride. "Bloody well done, Peytie. Two years and already the kid's right up there with the best!"

No, Borys thinks. He's no hero.

The shorter trolley-boy snorts. "All the best men lived before," he says. "Back when pavement was grass." There's no menace in the statement, no ill will. Both his tone and his wordwind are passive, deflated. Even so, it strikes a nerve.

"What fuckin' right—" Borys sputters, suddenly furious at these pasty-faced fucks, these little blond babies, who've never made sacrifices, too stupid or damaged to fight like real men, when his own son, his Peytie, not much older than them, is off becoming a hero— "What fuckin' right have you got—"

Plenty, says the pig-kid's wordwind.

The right to sling 'wind . . .

The right to catch shrapnel . . .

The right to become hamburger meat . . .

To be salted and dried and served up for lead-hounds in this fuckin' shithole . . .

"Shut up," yells Borys. 'That's my fuckin' kid you're thinking about.'

My kid, the *hero* . . .

"Whatever," says the pig. "It's just thoughts, mister. Doesn't mean anything. It's just thoughts.' As he pushes the trolley away, the kid's wordwind is guileless. Unembarrassed. Empty.

"Afternoon, Borys," says the Pigeon, slowing. Hands too busy delving into one satchel, then the other, to doff his invisible cap.

"Afternoon," Borys manages. Heart pounding, breath caught in a net of hope. Not a message, he thinks. A cemetery token. Peyt's dog-tags. His funeral mask.

Artie takes a minute to find the parcel he's after. One of many unmarked packages, uniformly wrapped in brown paper. When he does, it's no bigger than a watch box. No heavier than an army knife. The Pigeon presses it into Borys's shaking hand without looking up at his wordwind, now whizzing out of control.

At last. . . . At last. . . . At long last . . .

"Special delivery," Artie says adopting a formal, sing-song tone.

Definitely dog-tags, Borys thinks. Or the cutlery returned. All the boy's worldly possessions burnt to cinders and packed into a tiny urn.

At last. . . . At last. . . . At long last . . .

We can keep it on the mantel, he thinks. Where that kind of patriotic crap belongs. Next to Jean's old photographs and great-great-Grampa's medals. Ann Miller can dust it, if she wants, while spending her lonely fuckin' days in the living room. Out of sight, out of mind.

"Repeat after me," the Pigeon says. "From the Offices of His Honour, Prime Minister Armin Nycene. Special delivery for Jean Andrews."

Borys says nothing.

"Repeat after me," says the Pigeon. "From the Offices of—"

"I got it, Artie."

"Repeat after me—"

"I said I fuckin' got it."

"Fine," says Artie, sighing. "To confirm receipt, please leave your mark *here*." Borys takes the card offered, presses his 'wind against it until a residual signature appears. "And *here*."

Mechanical motions and a smudged imprint.

"Good enough," the deliveryman says. "See you tomorrow, Borys."

"You never can tell."

The parcel seems to pulse in Borys's grip. Taunting with its presence, with Peytr's absence. Borys feels prohibition sealing its neat folds. You can't touch me, it seems to say. You have me, but I am not yours.

"Mail," Borys calls when he steps inside the front door. "Mail, Jeanie."

And when she comes running, when she tears the box from him, saying, "Peyt? It's from Peytie?" he clunk-thunks to his room. Peels off his clothes. Places the cufflinks alone on his pillow. Bundles his pants, shirt, tie. Crams his unders into his hat. Stuffs two black socks into his shoes. Walks stark naked into the living room, carrying the lot with him. Takes Ann Miller's jar of grog and borrows her lighter. Shoves the clothes, the shoes, the yellowed underpants into the brick fireplace. Douses the pile with booze, strikes a spark. Then stands back to watch it all burn.

At *Grogs*, Borys sits in a corner booth, nursing a jar of the black stuff, leaning against the plaster wall. When he and Jerry come here in the early hours of morning, they blend in. They're just a couple of old men in a crowd full of them. Hair and 'winds sweat-slicked. Uniformed and bleary-eyed after a long night's work. Quietly throwing back a few cups of courage to face another grey day.

But at night, the red wheel on his back feels like a target. The bartender is young, her vibrant pink hair close-cropped from the tops of her ears down, spiked into a cockscomb above. Her nostrils, eyebrows, and lips bristle with metal. A single stud pierces her gullet. Borys can't, for the life of him, figure out how it stays in there. Unlike Fat Brandt, who serves the nightshifters, she watches him count out his coins. Counts them again herself, as if he's a cheat. Then looks up at him as though expecting a tip.

He slides her a penny and a scowl.

Maybe it's time we cut our losses, Borys thinks. Maybe we should just take the kids and get out of here. He props elbows on the pine table, forehead on hands. The scum of foam on his drink looks like the delivery map in Finishing. It looks like the world, the way it used to be drawn in old atlases. So many dark countries caught in the bubbles, and so many white. None of them grey.

He sticks his finger in the black liquid and churns. Above the music's thumping bass, Borys won't hear the whistle calling him to his shift. I won't hear a thing, he tells himself, looking up to catch a blue-wigged waitress's eye. Catches Artie's instead. The Pigeon clocked off for the evening, dandling a pretty little nurse on his knee. Smiling. Lacking the grace to look even slightly ashamed.

Yeah, Borys thinks, emptying his glass. I'll never hear a thing.

The grog tingles through him, warming from gut to stump and toes. Another pint and he'll go. Home to Jean. Home to talk. Let's get away, he'll say to her, to his darling wife. Let's get away from all this. He'll take her to the hospital, maybe enlist the Pigeon's young date for help. Get skin grafts for Jeanie's palms. Remove the numbers, remove all proof of her foolishness. Bundle the girls into a cab, mule or no mule, and take them somewhere brighter.

Peytr's not coming back, he'll say.

He's gone, he'll say.

Let's go.

One more pint and he'll do it.

The waitress is busy with a lunatic on the other side of the dance floor. Through sinuous, weaving bodies and a thickening fog of drunk wordwinds, Borys sees the girl flapping her hands. Up and down, slowly, as if worshipping the raving man sitting at the communal table before her.

Poor fuck's got the shock, Borys thinks, recognising the twitch in the guy's limbs. The restless rubbing, rubbing, rubbing of his palms on the wooden table top, fingers clamping onto the edge, shaking it for solidity, for reality. The flickering, rampaging nonsense of his 'wind. The lanterns clustered on the table, the windowsills, the rafters above. So bright they dispel all shadows within five feet of him. Borys has seen it before, in the ambulance that took him off the field, away from the front, not away from the war. A couple of young grunts on gurneys in the truck beside him and an old Cap sprawled on the floor, all three of them trembling with the shock of seeing too much. Of doing too much, or not enough. Soldiers who spent more time on the wards than they had on the front.

This guy's wearing his jacket inside out, but when he grabs the girls sitting beside him, begging them to stay, to keep him company, the tell-tale flash of multicams underneath give him away.

The kid's gone AWOL, Borys thinks, spitting on the sawdust-covered floor. He's a turncoat.

Borys spits again as the guy yanks the waitress's arm, pulls her down for a kiss. He gets up to intervene, but the Pigeon beats him to it. With firm hands, hands that have failed to bring Borys a single word from his son, Artie loosens the wild man's grip.

The music stops, or seems to, though Borys can still feel the bass throbbing in his chest, he can see the sawdust bouncing on speakers, see young bodies gyrating around his old one. The music stops, the whole world silent, as Artie pats the lunatic's wrists and says, "Settle down, Peyt. That's enough."

"Peyt?" Borys says, louder than the non-music, louder than the whistle not calling him in for his nightshift. "Peytr?"

And this time the Pigeon blushes. Streaks red as his hair run from bright spots in his cheeks to well in shame around his neck.

"C'mon, Ness," Artie says to the nurse, turning to go when she won't budge. Passing Borys on his way out, Artie stops.

"I can't deliver what was never sent," he says. "I've done no wrong here, Borys. There was nothing to give you. Nothing to tell."

Borys sets his jaw. Clenches and unclenches his fists until the Pigeon leaves. Stares and stares and stares at this creature whose legs are twitching so violently. Whose albino chin is scruffed with a patchy beard. Whose hands swat at any words that float near him. Whose stomach heaves and heaves, burping up letters and air. This is no soldier, he thinks. This is no hero, no man. This is his son.

The kid is haggard and dirty, like he hasn't seen a bath in years. His eyes are unfocused, but actively searching. For what? Borys wonders. For whom?

Deep breath in.

The boy knows I come here every morning after work, he thinks. Would've expected to see his Da here now, wouldn't he? Wouldn't he?

"Peyt?" he says. "Peytr, it's me."

Exhale.

Was he waiting all this time?

Grubby fingers cling to the girls in the booth. When they snuggle up to him, Peyt pushes them away. Abruptly, he stands. Jacket swinging dangerously close to the lanterns, jingling with a clatter of tin. "Who're you talking to? Not me. Not me."

Was he waiting for me?

"Peyt," Borys says, wanting to shout the boy's name over and over. Wanting to check him from tip to toe, as they did when he was newborn. Ten fingers, ten toes, a wordwind and a nose. Taking stock to be sure he's all there. "It's good to see you, boy."

Peytr shakes his head, shakes and shakes. "No, no. You haven't seen anyone, Da. I missed you. You missed me. But now, I'm not even here."

With that, he gets up. Clambers over the brunette on his left, drains his pint, and pauses no more than a foot from where Borys is standing. Peytr looks up at him. Borys looks down at his son.

He's grown, Borys thinks. But I am still taller.

"Come home," he says, arms lifting and dropping at his sides, yearning to hug the boy's skinny bones, to feel the slightness of him.

"I can't, Da," Peytr says, "I'm already gone."

"You don't have to be," Borys says, feeling the lie breeze around them before Peytr swats it out of the air. The pub door swings shut behind him, leaving no trace of his passing. Who knows how long the boy served before taking the coward's road? Could've been a year before he went AWOL. Could've been six months. A month. Maybe less.

Yeah, Borys thinks with a smile. Certainly less.

— The 'winded always rot from the head down (North/ West; oft refers to Southerners)
— Music has charms to revive the spirits (North)
— Offence is the best form of defence (Variations: all regions)
— A wise man binds thoughts fast in his breast (East)
— Balance is in the mind, not in the legs (Variations: all regions)
— Say what you think, think what you say (South)
— Beyond the clouds, there is sun (West)
— Pigeons always fly a day late (South/West)
— What can't be cured must be endured (Variations: all regions)

Aphorisms & Proverbs from Many Lands
Fragment; MS endpaper, 'wind-stained, grog-marred. Ink on A4.
Bibliotheca 11.5833° N, 165.3833° E

Running doesn't help.

There is no real logic to his movements, only the instinct to hare away, a paranoid urge to escape. His wordwind is listless when it's light out, more frantic as the days shorten. *They'll find me. . . . They'll catch me. . . . They'll force me back. . . . Find me. . . . catch me . . . force me . . . Catch force. . . . back force . . . force find . . . Force THEY. . . . THEY THEY THEY FORCE. . . . Find they. . . . FIND me. . . .* The 'wind keeping up with his feet as he runs, unsure where he's going, which *they* he's fleeing. The greys. The army. The girls at *Grogs*, the girls at home, the boys. His parents. The flavour of fear bristling from his tastebuds. The incessant echo of flesh rasping against flesh.

Hope and shame are expressed in the length of Peytr's stride, articulated in pace more than distance. He's been running for—how long? Days? At least. Weeks? Could be. Winter's long past, he knows that. Might be he's run through springtime into summer. Hard to tell when the cloud cover sits so low, more smog than rain, and the temperature is always uncomfortable. Humid and too warm. Humid and too cold. He'd have to run to the other side of the world to change that.

He tries.

He tries.

He tries.

And still the city's spires flank him, some days on the left, other days right. And the river that slops past the cheap markets on the edge of town—not one of the twelve pretty streams that once spoked through swanky districts, the high-end fashion quarter, the stockbrokers' row, the culture house mile—the deep green river that sludges along banks scummed with fluorescent algae, the river that no one in his right mind would drink from, but Peyt, so thirsty, does, the river that leaves him shitting deep green bile in the gutter beside shelters he refuses to enter, this same river never seems far from sight, no matter how far Peytr runs.

He runs like Angus used to: one eye on the ground, one on the sky. Progress is slow, and the river's still there, and the fuckin' grey-stained city. When he finally collapses in sleep, Peytr dreams of sprinting.

He runs holes in his boots.

He runs himself skinny.

He runs, long hair and wordwind whipping his back, beard scraggling over his mouth, his crack-lipped mouth, his rat-eating, roach-eating, word-eating mouth.

He runs as far as he can from the waterway. Focusing, really focusing, on keeping it at his back. Blisters searing his heels and toes. Stones invading his boots, spearing his soles. His body all sinew and leather, head bobbling, too big on this frame. He runs colour into his features. His irises a startling hazel against reddened whites, face wind-scoured a deep brown. Pale white-pink patches have climbed above the beard line and spatter his left temple and brow. Under the filth on his hands and forearms, the pigmentless skin is the bluish hue of skim milk. He runs colour into the world, runs until he sees brown and orange and ochre with hints of purple on the horizon, then keeps running until everything's bleached. The vista parched and beige as bone. Open, empty highways crackling across concrete flats. Clouds jaundiced, blue-mould clinging to their bellies in ragged strands. Buildings dotting low hills in the distance, little more than white daubs on crumpled newsprint. Peytr's wordwind pencil-sketches across the landscape as he runs, thoughts spidery, sepia, scattered.

He runs himself sweatless, breathless.

He'll run until things are clear. Until they make sense.

He keeps running.

He keeps running.

And there's the sun. The sun? A yellow-white ball in the blue. *The blue*. Nonsense. The sky is not blue, not so far away. The river, the city, never so far behind. There are no shadows, no corners, no hiding places here. Just beige and taupe and bright farness. Nonsense. Look over there. The road is shimmering, coming closer, crawling with—what? Rectangular darknesses, all in a row. Long rectangles, short rectangles, some linked together, some snuffling and scouting ahead. They grow with each step he takes. They amble closer and closer, a progression of houses. No, buses. No, cars. No, skyscrapers tipped and rolling on their sides. A caravan of nonsense snaking to a halt, trailing a curtain of dust. And there are horses, he thinks. There are dogs. Nonsense. The dogs are all gone, they've eaten their masters' words and become geniuses. Rottweilers own football teams now. Alsatians lecture at Ivy League schools. Nonsense. But there is barking. Yes, there. Hear that? And paws loping, drumming the earth. Louder the closer they come.

In his mind, Peytr runs. His wordwind runs. *Find me . . . catch me . . . force me. . . .* He races out of there—*FIND me*—muscles strong and powerful—*FORCE*—heart pumping—*catch me catch me catch me*—lungs gulping in pure, free air. In his mind. But a woman's voice, unfamiliar, accented, tells him he's not moving fast enough.

"Get up," she says.

Peytr opens his eyes. One eye. The left is pressed shut. When did that happen? He blinks at a foreign face peering down into his own, a foreign wordwind invading his space. *Dot 16. Recitative: Why sits that sorrow? (Soprano, Tenor). . . .* Scowling grinds sand deeper into the left side of his face. His legs keep running, left right left, though he's lying flat in the dirt. Palms and knees stinging. Cheek bruised and grazed. Blood iron in his mouth. Bitten tongue.

He blinks at the face's concern. At her inquisitive *Dot 34. Aria: How art thou fall'n (Bass)*. . . . At the firm black hands wedged under his armpits, lifting. Not hers—no, her hands are lighter, they are clasping her crouching-bent knees. She looks down at him for at least a year, wild black hair backlit by the sun. The sun. Decades later, he is lifted and now looking down at her. His hood flopping into place on his head, concealing, protecting. His body flopping over a broad shoulder. Arms and legs flopping. Peytr floats over the cracked ground, temples throbbing. Spots swim in front of his eyes. Each time he blinks, he summons night.

"You've come to unburden yourself," the girl says, the volume of her voice and the appearance of pointed slippers in his line of sight proof that she's following. He blinks and blinks. "Come inside. Tell us your stories."

"Nonsense," Peytr says, and darkness falls.

Euri was telling them a fable about groundhogs. The bedroom was gloomy, only a single lantern between them and the window boarded up tight, and the groundhogs were making little Zaya cry. Tears plinked one by one from her lashes. Clustered like pearls in her blue gingham skirt. She wouldn't say what was wrong, why they upset her, but Peytr thought he knew. It was the pickaxes they carried. The tiny headlamps. The way their whiskers quivered as they burrowed, tiny facial fingers groping for tremors or breezes, precursors of cave-ins. Their teensy, useless eyes. The sticks of dynamite they carried, stupid, unknowing, strapped in clumps on their backs. The hissing fuses.

Peyt knew it was all supposed to mean something—fables always had morals—but Euri showed no sign of getting to the point. She talked and talked without making a sound. Her 'wind reflected the lamplight, glinting like a crown of stars. Beautiful and illegible. Peytr and Zaya sat cross-legged beside her, atop piles of blankets and mattresses and fur. They hunched instinctively, shying from the ceiling. Reaching over, Peyt patted the toddler's inconsolable head. Straightened her bumblebee nightie so that it covered her knees. Euri made sure they were watching then stretched her arms out. *It was* this *big*.

Legs stretched into the darkness, Daken lay sprawled on his back in boxers and undershirt. One muscular arm draped over his face, the other one bent, elbow propped on Peytr's rucksack. Dake's fingers snapped quickly, a racing heartbeat, but his whistle was off-tempo. Peyt edged closer to the other boy, leaned closer, tilted to hear better. Through the quilts something jabbed him in the hip. He wriggled around to dislodge it. Each fidget released puffs of dust, the linens heavy with mildew and the scent of old soap. He laid down and was jabbed in the arm. Shifting positions, he held Daken round the waist and rested his head on his stomach. He felt the thrum of Dake's whistle, a long single note reverberating through his skull. Peytr nestled. Squeezed. Daken snorted, his 'wind feather-tickling Peyt's brow. He smiled—until the jab moved up to his ribs. Sharper now, a painful, pointed digging. Scowling, he sat up while Euri mouthed empty words and the baby howled and Daken began to deflate, groundhogs pick-picking at them all through the blankets, the furs, the skins of their dead brothers.

The whistle moaned, loud and low. Peytr placed his hand across Daken's mouth. To stop the air escaping. To silence that mournful sound. And Dake grinned, lips parting, and licked Peytr's palm.

Peyt gasped and swallowed and swallowed.

And wakes.

He's lying in a nest of oversized pillows at the far end of a long, narrow space. A light blanket strangles his waist as he shifts to lie on his back. Crates and cardboard boxes serve as a headboard; his legs extend under a sturdy pine table, feet jarring against the wall. High above him, half-length drapes cover a window as wide as the room. No boards cover the panes; the curtains' purple hems are limned with a crimped line of warm daylight. Peyt rolls onto his side, turning his back to the vulnerable glass. He rolls, and is speared in the ribs. With a grunt he fumbles under the covers, hears a dull crack, and immediately feels wetness slick his undershirt. I've been stabbed, he thinks, pulling the dagger out of his side. Staring at it in confusion. The blood glistening on his hand is not red but black; it oozes from the broken haft in his grip. The clear plastic casing is crazed from being slept on. Its ballpoint tip bent at a wrong angle. Not a knife, he realises, dropping the pen. Spattering ink on the loose-leaf notes stacked next to his pillows. A snuffed lantern is nailed to the floor beside them, right at the edge of the dais supporting his crude bed. Even in the dim light, he can read handwriting on the papers. It is neat. Precise. Well-informed.

Each page, each entry, is marked with coordinates. Longitude. Latitude. Some form of dating Peyt has never seen before. What does this mean? Where the storytellers lived? Can't be, he thinks, reading the first one, which tells of an airship sailing through the stars just to leave a boot-print on the moon. Maybe it's where their subject matter comes from? Peyt learned a bit about maps before—before. And he's pretty sure this one, about parades and street parties and wild feathered costumes, has deadzone coordinates. Yeah, that fuckin' place has been deadzoned for a hundred years. . . . So this one's either really really old, or really really wrong. His stomach clenches then rumbles noisily, but Peyt is used to ignoring it. There are more important things than hunger. Like the *Hid*— catching his eye *Hid*— wrinkling a lined yellow paper *Hid*— poking a corner out of the stack *Hid*— adding a new clamp to his guts. Shivering, he teases it out from under the others. Inches closer to the edge of the dais and the muted light filtering toward it, down the room's long aisle. Peyt swallows and swallows. Smudged with thumbprints, the scrap is torn in half but lists several coordinates under a single heading. Coordinates, he's pretty sure, that include his city. His town. His suburb.

Hidden ones.

Peytr can't breathe. He flips the sheet over, reads part of a line—"I sought them out, not the other way around,"—and wants to read more, but the page lilts to the carpet. His hands senseless. His arms shaking uncontrollably. He has to trap them under his torso, press his weight down, hard, harder, to protect himself from the greys.

She knows where they are, he guesses, watching the woman—the girl?—come in from outside. The entryway is narrow with two skinny glass doors edged in iron, propped open to let in a stream of daylight. Inside, golden beams glint on tin and steel and wood veneer. None of the girl's—the woman's—furnishings match. The dints and scratches and browned, ingrained dust, show that none of these pieces is new. Everything is either nailed to the burnished metal walls, which rise to a curved ceiling, or fixed to the floor. Strong black bolts stick out like landmine triggers through gaps in multi-coloured carpets.

Does she know?

One step, two, and she's climbed into the bus, carrying a small kettle, a thin line of steam still puffing from its short spout. Gaze turned inward, she seems to move out of habit. Wending around the driver's seat, card catalogues, pigeonholes, cabinets with wide, thin drawers. Ducking under low-hanging shelves and overhead compartments. Sitting at a little wooden desk, wedged between two leather trunks halfway down the aisle. Singing under her breath as she fills a porcelain teacup to the brim.

She *must* know, he thinks. This girl. This woman. This keeper of stories. This guardian of fantasies and truths. This Librarian.

He teeters on the edge of the dais, crushing her smudged, precise notes. Listening to her song, Peyt fails to make sense of it. Breathy words keep time with her pen's scratching, breathy wordwind captions what she writes as she sings. *Dot 2. Recitative: 'Tis nobler far (Tenor, Bass). . . . Dot 3. Aria: Pluck root and branch (Bass). . . .* The points dip and bob with her cadences, dervishes of sound and meaning that suit her somehow, that complement the turquoise skirt she's wearing over loose beige pants, that skim her white tank top and accentuate her tattoos. Arabesques ink up and down her light brown arms, sleeves of language he can't and won't ever read.

Nonsense, Peytr thinks. Nonsense.

He knows he should talk now, let her know he's awake, but he holds back. As she sings, his wordwind knits itself into a sheet. Sturdy, strong, clear thoughts settle on him like a mantle. Steady. Secure. He feels the sudden urge to curl up in this woman's gibberish, her musical knowledge, and sleep and sleep and sleep. Enveloped. Comforted. Almost at peace. But his eyes refuse to close.

Dot 4. Recitative: Our souls with ardour glow (Tenor). . . .

Panels of stained glass have been soldered over holes in the bus's side windows. They sift the morning light into a confetti of colours, speckling the woman's profile as she bends over her work. Her strong nose is softened by a smattering of crimson petals. Collarbone jewelled with eight-pointed stars in indigo, emerald, amber. Jade serpents and trees shaped like teardrops, with curved rows of fish-scales instead of leaves, ripple across her breasts.

He's never seen anyone so relaxed while working. At the factory, Borys was always wrung. Snapping when Peyt got too close to the bender, snapping when he strayed too far. Old Jer was a lot more laid back, but even he'd knock Peyt's 'wind off every now and again. Venting, he said. That's what you're here for, ain't it boy? Jean brought in her fair share of coin, but didn't exactly seem happy about it. Even though she stayed home most days and still got paid. And poor Mrs M—*Ann*—didn't work at all. Can't hack the stress, she told him once. Just can't hack it. *And Dake. . . .* And the other grunts, well. Talk about fuckin' stress. There was enough pressure in those boys to fill a bomb big enough to wreck half the country in one blow. But *this* girl. This *woman* sipped hot aniseed water and fuckin' sang. *Dot 5. Chorus: Shall we the God of Israel fear? (Persians). . . . Dot 6. Recitative: Now persecution (Tenor). . . .* Her slippers kicked off under the desk. One bare foot tucked up under her, the other threading its toes through a shaggy maroon carpet. Absentmindedly braided, her black hair hangs over one shoulder. A long tangle that coils on her thigh. Even seated, Peyt realises, she's tall. Solid, not fat. A stockman's figure. A mule-driver's muscles. Built for heavy burdens.

Dot 7. Aria: Tune your harps (Tenor). . . .

Like knowing where the greys are, he thinks. And knowing where they aren't.

"Can you tell me?" he asks, not loud, but loud enough to make her jump. Her 'wind skitters out of sequence—*Dot 21. Recitative: Who dares intrude (Tenor, Soprano)*—but she quickly catches herself. *Dot. 8. Chorus: Shall we of servitude complain?* She flutters a hand over her heart, and laughs.

"Never mind." Peyt kicks at the blanket. Shivering, sweating, he shoves it into the shadows. Papers scatter off the platform as he clambers to his knees, ink stains scattershot across his ribcage. Chest heaving, he looks for his things. His boots are heels-out beneath a low stool, just out of reach, his rucks slumped nearby on the floor. Hood and jacket are folded neatly on the seat, a plate of flatbread and soft white cheese balanced on top of them. Peyt's shoulders wilt. He wraps his arms around himself and squeezes. Mouth watering, he looks at the food. The girl. The food. The girl.

He's so hungry it hurts.

She looks back at him. Actually *looks*. One of her ears has melted into her skull; the shell of it half-dribbles down her jaw. A gold paisley medallion dangles from the other lobe, attached to an oversized sieve of an ear. It's pocked and perforated with holes; some small as his fingertip, others two knuckles wide. For a few seconds, he watches her honest words weave their odd song through the great holes in her ear. And he thinks it's just that, her ear, it's simply great, despite the ugliness, for letting the 'wind pass through unharmed. Her smile broadens as she reads his thoughts, and he feels the tension in his chest ease a bit. And he thinks, suddenly, he's become one of the boys Ma used to laugh about. The stupid, romantic ones who believe a woman's flaws make her more perfect.

"I should go," he says, barely audible.

The girl takes a sip of her drink. Squints at Peyt over the cup's rim. Watches him scramble out of her bed in his stained undershirt and pants three sizes too big. Reads all she needs to know about him in the blotches on his arms. The words caught in the scrag of his hair. The way he unlaces his boots, yanks their cracked tongues. The way he doesn't put them on.

"I'll show you out," she says, raising an eyebrow. "Whenever you wish."

"You don't have to," Peytr replies, boots swaying in his trembling hands.

She smiles and says, "I know."

She doesn't know her true name. When the Librarians found her, oh, twenty-five years ago, in the vast parking lot of an old concert hall, her parents had already gone. Dead or fled—or maybe swept by the greys. "Ironic, isn't it? Surrounded by records, but none of my own," she says with a shrug. The timing, Peyt thinks, is too perfect:

he can tell it's a well-worn joke. Mouth moving fast as her feet, she leads him across the rough circle of the library's temporary yard. Explaining that her swaddling cloth was an antique musical score. That it was labelled HWV50. That the catalogues list the title of this oratorio as *Esther*—"And so have I been called ever since."

Librarians, she explains, adopt new names whenever the mood strikes. "That's Parrot, once Javier, once Randall," Esther says, pointing out a tall black man in baggy shorts and a tropical print shirt, bald as a skeleton and almost as thin. No lashes, no brows, no 'wind. Just a series of bright pink etchings up the left side of his body. Eyes that are all iris, no whites. "Much more fitting, neh?"

Peyt agrees, but doesn't get the chance to say so.

"Picked up another stray, girl?" Parrot butts in, morning blue globes rolling in his sockets, rolling faster than Esther's own eyes.

"Keep squawking," she replies, laughing, offering a bird of her own. "With luck you'll happen upon a prettier tune."

Parrot flashes his teeth, sketches a mock bow of defeat before continuing on his way, carrying a stack of plastic chairs into a nearby pavilion. At the last minute, he lifts them high to avoid colliding with an old woman ducking beneath the tent flap.

"And this is—" Esther begins, but is silenced by the barest flick of gnarled fingers.

"Guillaume," the woman introduces herself, voice and tight silver bun severe. One of her legs is substantially shorter than the other, her gait off-kilter. She limps toward them without benefit of a cane, wearing one polished leather shoe and one black baby bootie with a twelve-inch rubber sole. She does not wave or shake hands, but keeps her arms out to the sides for balance.

"Precisely my point," Esther says, turning to Peyt. "Yesterday I was to call this one Nan."

Guillaume grunts and clicks her tongue. "Record this one's story," she says, "feed him, and bid him farewell." Rheumy-eyed stare. "In that order."

Esther dips her chin, winking at Peyt when Guillaume turns away.

"And what about you, Peytr Borysson?" Esther considers him, measures his features with her gaze. The downturned angle of his eyelids. The sad hazel of his irises. The depressions that, in plumper days, were dimples. "Fancy a change? A new name is better than a fresh change of clothes—you won't recognise yourself with it on. Perhaps Jaunty? Filippo? Louee? No, you're right. Here, take my handkerchief. No, no, don't worry. It's all right. Those names were all wrong; it's clear you are a Tristan."

Peytr sniffs and scrunches the wet from his eyes. The light lunch he ate sits like a rock in his stomach. He could hardly choke it down. His legs are weaker than water. She talks and talks, as if trying to cram her entire history into the space between the bus's black steps and the first canopy set up in the clearing. And it's weird, he thinks, that she's so open with him. So candid about the loss of her past.

"Hardly," she says, then gestures at the vehicles parked around them. "How can I have lost what has always been here? And why wouldn't I share? A story is just dead words if it isn't told."

"Knock it off," Peytr says, pulling his hood-strings tight. Buttoning his jacket up to the throat. Cinching the straps of his backpack until they bite.

Esther crosses her arms, mock serious, and playfully bumps him with her elbow. "Instructing a Librarian not to read is like commanding a soldier not to cry out in his sleep."

Peytr stops, face prickling heat. Esther pats his chest, right where his dog-tags are hidden beneath his jacket, and keeps walking, keeps talking, her wordwind teeming with numbers, categories, song lyrics, facts about the origins and significance of patronymic surnames. When Peyt doesn't follow, she doubles back. Gently gripping his elbow, she pilots him past portable kitchens, with striped awnings angled over unshuttered serving windows, and around the open-sided marquees and canopies erected in the yard. In the shade they provide from the sun—*the sun*, Peyt thinks, steeping in the stink of its heat, *what nonsense*—about twenty or thirty people sit at wooden tables laden with baskets of nuts and dried fruits, platters of cheese, and boards piled high with bread. More file in, ants to a picnic, from the deadzones, and from the city beyond. Men in coveralls, in denim jeans and blue cotton, in well-tailored but threadbare suits. Women in wool dresses and cardigans and close-fitting hats. Women in uniform, doctors, teachers. Women in red skirts. Some in no skirts at all, just short little pants and short little shirts and expressions as tough as old stone. Young people in wheelchairs. Old people carried pig-a-back. No children, only babies not yet weaned. No soldiers. No one, Peyt thinks, like him.

When the tables fill up, patrons perch on plastic crates. Lawn chairs. Wooden stools. Plates balanced on their laps, they speak between mouthfuls. Librarians ask questions, writing boards propped on knees as they listen, as they nod, as they smile and weep and frantically scribble down what's being said. Some visitors recount tear-stained biographies, recipes, family affairs. Others speak silently, shaping symbols with their hands, signs that Parrot somehow understands. And yet other stories are mythical, magical, concerning knights and dragons and, whispered darkly, tales of times when the greys were kind. These last leave a blush in the tellers' cheeks, a slump in their spines, white-knuckled kneading in laps. Whether sitting or wandering from tent to tent, the Librarians observe carefully. Hearing, certainly, but reading what can't be spoken. Experiences chiselled into human bodies. The scars and mangled limbs. The fragmented wordwinds. The absent gazes. Every detail is recorded, none too big or too small for the library's archives.

At random, it seems, people are selected from the crowd and escorted to the caravan of vehicles encircling the encampment. From the outside, the library seems utilitarian, the convoy towed mostly by oxen, stout horses and mules. Yellow school buses like Esther's and longer, articulated orange-and-whites. Armoured trucks and trailers and delivery vans. Covered stock-wagons. Refrigerated transports minus the refrigeration. "Still cooler inside than some," Esther says, directing Peytr to the library's heart. The planet to these satellite cars. The enormous, long-haul main branch.

Whatever fuel the Librarians are given is siphoned into the eighteen-wheeler, its engine rigged to drag seventy-two extra wheels behind it. All told, the branch has five great white cargo holds hitched and jiggered together, modular gangways connecting them, and a long steel ramp leading visitors into the caboose. On its other side, a safe distance away from the archives, a square bullpen has been knocked together beside a separate, smaller one, for the horses and mules. Chicken coops and goat runs are aligned atop drays, with rabbit hutches swinging between the cartwheels. A congregating stink—and noise—wafts across the camp. The bleating of many voices. The smacking of tongues and lips. The pungent oil of sun-warmed hides and decaying motors. Wet fur mixed with the salt-sweat of bodies. Stale sawdust and rotting feed. Musk and mildew. Hoofs stomping on shit. Cascades of piss and snot and tears—and over it all, a heady perfume, brewed from roses, maybe, and also their thorns, the incense burning outside in sand-filled pots exacerbating the stench instead of masking it.

It's wonderful, Peyt thinks, wrinkling his brow. A whole, mobile world.

A world built for long distances, long dreams.

"Of course," says Esther, and Peyt realises he's let his lid slip. Fuckin' sun, he thinks. Fuckin' heat. But Esther ignores his scowl. "What use is it otherwise? Stories migrate from place to place—so should libraries. It's our duty to collect, to amass—and, yes, to mobilise. Not to remain static. So many accounts, so many histories. . . . They certainly cannot be stored all together, not all in one place. Imagine the consequences! Just think of the museums . . ."

She sighs as Peytr fumbles with his hood.

"Like wordwinds," she says, taking his hand, openly reading his uncovered thoughts, "knowledge belongs in perpetual motion. It has to circulate, to spin wherever it needs, to mingle with exciting, novel ideas. To expand through contact." Esther winks and threads her fingers through his. "It's only natural."

Her touch is strong, reassuring, her skin smooth as paper. She smells bittersweet, he thinks. Like lemon curd and almonds. Like trust. Her 'wind is stark and steady and bold. Rattled, Peytr drops his gaze. A few seconds later, his hood follows. Her nails are polished, a deep sparkling burgundy. They trace secret patterns on the back of his hand.

Palms damp, he follows Esther like a sleepwalker, coasting, soles skimming dirt. She dodges guywires and ropes stretching down from the furthest canopies, steps over thick wooden pegs near the library's main ramp. He drifts by her side. He *ghosts*. Puffs of dirt and dust kick up behind her heels, greying her red slippers, leaving a dark ring on the loose cuffs of her pants. Peyt glides behind her, afloat.

I should go, he thinks, legs suddenly jerking as though pinched by grey talons. Arms shaking so hard Esther lets go his hand. "This way," she says, ambling up the ramp. Giving him time to lurch and joggle. Once he enters the archive, joining the others climbing the plank in dribs and drabs, Esther smiles and Peyt's trembling subsides.

The library's interior is as gaudy and vibrant as its exterior is drab. In the first chamber there is a riot of books—hardcover and soft, arranged by height, not colour—and a jubilee of cushions, embroidered, striped, crocheted: large on the floor, small on benches and steamer trunks and ottomans. Cats and mice are carved into lintels, reclaimed rafters, and glass-fronted cabinets—in which wooden boxes bristle with quills, pencils, erasers, plastic markers, ink bottles and blotters. Between bookshelves and cupboards, a bestiary romps across the walls: spiders and polar bears, peacocks and gazelles, lemurs with bulbous eyes. Robust succulents hang in pots, spikes scraping spots off giraffes, leopards, and stallions. Bushels of reeds shoot from urns in the corners and filigreed screens cordon off interview spaces. Skylights brighten the aisles with squares of sunshine, but glass baubles also dangle from the ceiling; lanterns to be filled with words and shaken, shaken until they effervesce and glow.

Dangerous, Peytr thinks, seeing those lamps, remembering Jean's warnings. *You must choose your words carefully. Your aim must be precise. You are your own, most precious resource—don't waste it. There is only one of you. Use yourself wisely.*

Librarians, of all people, must know how to cap such power.

They know so many things . . .

I should go, Peyt thinks again. But it is all so busy and productive and, somehow, calm. I should go with them.

Colours blur into wet and run down his cheeks.

"You are brimming, Peytr Borysson," Esther says, giving him a quick, shameless hug. "Come in, come in, and spill. We'll both be better for it."

He sits where instructed, a small table behind a decorative screen. When Esther sits across from him, familiar notepaper in hand, he yearns, he *yearns* to cooperate. But there is no beginning to the mass of words in his throat. There is no discernible end. So he sits, pulling his drawstrings out of habit, and studies the mural behind Esther's head. A tawny owl inspects him, golden gaze lazy and undemanding. Peytr blinks at the creature in silent converse. He is captivated. Mesmerised. Utterly thoughtless.

A glorious feeling.

Esther sighs and puts down her pen.

Peytr crouches in the covered wagon, clinging to the driver's seat, peering over the rough-hewn slats of its back. For two days, he's been allowed to loiter at the library, sleeping on a cot in Esther's bus, sharing her rations and, in Guillaume's words, *moping*. "Your pet needs to earn his keep," he overheard the old woman say before breakfast, when Esther went out to fill the kettle. "He can't keep borrowing without making a return."

So when Esther was assigned a morning trip to the outskirts—to chronicle news and articles from anyone too old or infirm to visit the library—Peyt volunteered to be her second.

Fuckin' idiot, he tells himself now, flinching every time the hacks balk, flinching when the wheels jam in ruts, flinching at corners and shadows. Jacket stuffed in his bag, hoodstrings set on garrotte, he shivers in his overwashed undershirt. What were they thinking, forcing him back out here? With no weapon, no backup, no fuckin' Whitey to screech when the greys fuckin' jump them. And only a few shells in his pack. Not enough for the onslaught. Not enough for the greys. Crouching, taking cover, he scans the low scrub for twickerings of movement. Stares at the tenements and portable units growing ever-taller on the horizon. Peels his eyelids wide. Refuses to blink. Glares at the concrete city wall crumbling around the buildings, *willing* himself to see through it. He hooks callused hands on the seat back, leaves damp fingerprints on the weathered wood. Legs flexing, left right left. Muscles taut, ready to spring.

Though the day is warm, goosebumps sprout all over his body. As if his own skin is recoiling, trying to distance itself from the coward who wears it. Overhead, black flecks dart between clouds, swooping, catching thermals, like words untethered, lofty and meaningless and free. Shading her eyes, Esther pulls the reins to slow the horses and watches the flyers arc and dive. The beasts' ears flick annoyance, pace unchanged. As if sensing the driver's distraction, one veers away from the beaten path, noses through patches of scrub by the roadside. Between hills and city, the land is flat, mostly gravel and shale. Cratered where grey mines once detonated—the hollows, Peyt imagines, are littered with travellers' fragmented bones. A shallow creek bed echoes the curve of the shantytown barnacling the city's tumbledown wall; it cuts across their path, dry as the bleached lichen dotting rocks along its shores. Reins laced through her fingers, Esther reaches back to touch Peyt's speckled wrist.

"Have you ever seen the skybunker girls? Up close, I mean. Have you seen their gliders? Woven from final thoughts, the last wishes and prayers of the dying. What colour, such fabric? What hue? Do the words radiate? Are they pure spirit taken flight? We have no official written records—no eyewitness accounts. Certainly no first-hand accounts." She laughs, but it isn't the hearty or impish sound Peyt's getting used to hearing. There's a new solemnity to her wondering. A wistfulness that, from anyone else, would seem bitter. "It's a soldier's privilege to see such marvels in action. And his bond, I suppose, to keep these visions under his lid. Are there rules about such things? Regulations?"

"I see what you're doing."

"Pondering?" Esther says, tattooed innocence. She yanks on the reins, chirrups the animals back on track. "Making conversation?"

"Right."

"Enlightenment isn't simply a matter of possessing knowledge," she says. "It's about insight. Asking questions. Talking. Thinking aloud. I could own all the books in the world, but without questioning what's in them—without discussion—they are only so many coffins for meaningless words."

Peytr squints at her, and they ride for a while in silence. His legs are cramping, so he crab-walks through the wagon's clutter, unearths a box sturdy enough to sit on, brings it up to the front. There's plenty of room on the seat beside Esther, but Peyt can't straighten. Can't climb over, not now, not when he's so exposed.

The city looms closer, only a mile or two away. They'll be there and back again before that ball of nonsense in the sky reaches its zenith. If not, Peyt thinks, there will be no search party. Librarians are gatherers, not hunters. They congregate where predators don't. Deadzones. Ruins. Cities where inhabitants aren't worth stealing, their eyes vacant as the buildings that house them. The library will take whatever scraps of story these shells have to offer—but at the first sign of threat, they'll scatter like minnows.

Peytr drapes an arm over the seatback and inches toward Esther. With the other hand, he unconsciously pats his waistband, searching for a pistol that isn't there. He looks up at the clouds, thinking. The skybunker girls have all gone.

"Is Guillaume really your Nan?"

"No," Esther admits. She speaks quietly, forcing him to lean in close. His cheek brushes her arm. Beard scratching flesh, he recoils. Clears his throat. Kneels on the box, raising his head to the level of her shoulder. Clinging to the wooden barrier between them.

"So why are you trying to spite her?"

"Quite the opposite. As always, I'm hoping to please her."

"Seems she'd be happier with me gone. I'm no scholar. I mean, I don't know much about debates and philosophy. I know what I know, that's all. And what I don't . . ." He shakes his head. Changes his mind, changes tack. He doesn't have the words to ask about that. Not yet. Instead, he wonders: "Why am I still here?"

"Do you like to read?"

And before Peyt can get annoyed—oh, you're so fond of questions you'll avoid mine—she runs her fingers through her curls. Caresses the heavy strands with personal, sensual gestures. As if she was alone and naked, washing her hair. Wanting him to notice, mixed in with her namesake's lyrics—*Dot 25. Aria: How can I stay (Tenor). . . . Dot 26. Recitative: With inward joy (2 Tenors) . . .*—her wordwind, raw and bare.

In her phrases, he's beautiful. Despite the beard. Maybe because of it. He's different. Intriguing. A hide-bound manuscript brimming—yes, she likes that word—*brimming . . . brimming . . . brimming . . .* with stories freshly inked. Ballads of smoke-filled battles. Odes to friends lost. Love letters to an old sweetheart. Esther imagines he is lean, not skinny. Cheekbones chiselled, not staved-in with want. Smelling of leather and oil and tobacco. She thinks he's strong. She thinks he's young. She thinks, stupid girl, he's whole.

And, openly, confidently, she lets him see it all. This invented Peyt. His attractive imperfections. She reveals the mould she's made for him, believing it isn't such a tight squeeze. It fits, she thinks. *He* fits.

Dot 4. Recitative: Our souls with ardour glow (Tenor). . . .

"Sit up here." Esther turns and pats the seat beside her. As if checking to make sure it's—he's—still there. Her breath brushes his brow, spiced liquorice and mint. Her 'wind hovers too close to read. "The view," she gestures vaguely at everything and nothing, "is much better from here."

She's nervous, Peyt realises. She's blushing.

Steeling himself, he stands on unsteady legs. Esther beams. He adjusts his grip, tenses and leans. Esther nods, encouraging with eyes and thoughts. Air whooshes from Peyt's lungs. Deep breath, he thinks, closing his eyes. Inhaling.

The hacks swerve for a patch of pale weeds, throwing Peytr off balance. He sputters and snorts, choking on an ellipsis. Gagging Esther's *ardour* down his throat. The letters wriggle and squirm, tickling his tongue, throttling, suffocating. He coughs until ribbons of saliva flutter from his lips. An 'o' clings to his beard, a stray 'r'.

Knees buckling, he half-lands, half-crashes onto the box in the back. Slumps forward, deflating. Buries his face in the crook of his arms. Hears Esther lashing the reins. Scolding the horses. Turning the wagon around for home.

Sorry, he thinks, without looking up. Without saying a word.

After dark, Esther burns candles instead of oil and doesn't snuff them until dawn.

For three days, Peyt's busied himself at the library. Reading myths from the golden age, religious treatises, political tracts. Glutting himself with story, with poetry, like he used to before. Looking at photographs, so many different peaks and points, yet all flat on matte paper: visual nonsenses of fashion, geography, porn. Blurs of grey, ghosts captured in chemical and light. He mucks out the bullpen without being asked. Cleans the rabbit hutches. Gathers eggs. When new visitors arrive, far fewer now than earlier in the week, he directs them to Parrot or Guillaume, to the archivists at the head of the convoy, to genealogists in the armoured truck. He offers no food—it's not his to give—nor does he eat. His guts heave at the smell of bread, fruit, nuts. He can barely stomach water and only in sips, not gulps. Even so, when it's daylight, when he's busy, Peyt's tremors are hardly noticeable. There's comfort in systems, he realises. Solace in order and routine, slotting things onto their appropriate shelves, disposing of crap, following logic, arranging. Avoiding unpredictable, flyaway feelings.

At night there are different distractions.

At night, the library is so dark. There are no campfires outside, no torches, no sparks unattended. Esther's candles, dim hope, are the only glimmers against stifling blackness. Against the creeping greys who, Peyt's convinced, sneak into Esther's bus and gnaw at his legs while he's asleep. So he doesn't sleep anymore. Eyes open or closed, it's all part of the same nightmare. He isn't sleeping, never sleeps, until Esther shakes him awake.

"Shhhhhhh," she says, crawling back into her den of pillows. "It's just a dream."

Of course it is. He knows it is. It's an illumination flare blazing through his skull. An interlude in the darkness. Grass, luminous green against the backs of his eyelids. Airships with banners whipping from their tailfins, dropping gifts and bubbles. A zephyr teasing the downy hair on his chest. The salt tang of ocean air. Waves buffeting a long pebbled shore in the distance. A sea of bodies, limbs, wheels, blood, grenades, letters lapping up his frozen thighs. Slurping higher and higher with each uneven breath . . .

Peyt looks at Esther. Her hair unbound, a bunched mess under her head. Cotton nightie so thin, her tatts show through the sleeves. Dingy ribbons unlaced to the breastbone, revealing a sheen of brown skin. Chest rising and falling slowly, reclaiming the rhythm of sleep.

He kicks off his sheet, pads over to her bed. His shadow falls, a veil across her face that can't dim the glint in her eyes when she opens them. She pulls back the blanket. Makes room for him to climb in.

"Tell me about meadows," he says once he's settled.

Esther's laughter tickles the nape of his neck. She doesn't ask why he hasn't said much more than "Morning" and "'Night" to her in three days. Doesn't mention the wagon. The coughing. The rejection.

"All right." That's it. No demands, no self-pity.

"All right," she says, instantly the better man.

As Esther talks, the knot in Peyt's belly tightens and loosens. She describes places where cars are flattened and stacked into towers, some more than thirty feet high. Where broken glass frosts the ground like sugar-snow. Where bald tires, reeking of rubber and tar so strong it greases the nostrils, are lobbed in great piles. Where hundreds of mirrors hang from the junkman's shack, reflecting scavengers back to themselves in hundreds of pieces, shattering them, making them tiny, insignificant enough to fit inside the crook's dark little shed, the little tin can, to pay him for the nuts and bolts he'll sell at exorbitant prices.

"No," Peyt interrupts. "Not like that. Be serious."

But Esther is nervous. She teases by default.

There are crowded bazaars, she explains. Stall after stall cramped into halls and spilling into alleyways. "Ten times the library's size," she says. Then, correcting: "Dozens of times." Beneath bright-woven awnings, merchants and collectors sell watchworks by the bucket load—cogs and gears and chains of bronze and gold and silver, laid out by size and function—and baskets of gems, rubies and sapphires and opals cheap as chalk—and reams of silk that nobody buys, "Nobody buys it! Not a stitch! While the tanner's putrid booth is daily cleaned-out of its wares"—and there are falcons and owls and songbirds in cages—"Cruel," Peytr says, but Esther ignores him. She's on a roll now; her imagination, he knows, has gotten the better of her. She conjures potatoes and carrots and rutabagas so bountiful, if any roll from the wagons, they're left on the ground, they're *trampled*, even, a feast for rats.

"And the books," Esther says, reverently. "Quartos and folios bound in lambskin, vellum scrolls, and manuscripts so old and fat they wheeze when their covers are buckled. Some handwritten, some pressed, some printed *and* handwritten—with ink sketches and marginalia . . ." She lowers her voice before continuing. "I have one such volume in my archive. I can show you, if you like."

"Tell me about the plains," Peytr says—and she describes fields full of statues. Men and women, some with wings, some cradling cherubs, some stoic, many—if not all—weeping. Wearing veils of marble, long granite robes, circlets of copper wire that radiate the strangest glow. Memorials, she calls them, each one so detailed, so realistic, you'd swear it was about to blink.

Peyt raises his eyebrows. Fuckin' waste of stone, he thinks. Much like the ancient fortresses Esther fabricates—also of stone, she says, but Peyt knows better—with labyrinthine corridors and tiered fountains and mazes in the gardens. There are galleries, she says, and other houses of stolen treasures—

"Ah," Peytr says. "You've been to our city before?" He's seen the museum. He went there, many years ago, with school. Not long before the greys destroyed it.

"No," Esther says, smiling. "Not quite. There are so many caches of knowledge, so many stories to index, and only so much time."

"Yet, somehow, you've managed to see all this?" he says, knowing it's impossible, she's too young to have gone so far, done so much, it must be a lie, but she nods and smiles so sincerely, so honestly, that he rolls over and kisses her, in the crook where neck and shoulder meet. Just like that, he kisses her, just like her smile, a spontaneous, heartfelt lie.

And when she responds, presses up against him, when she unbuckles and strokes him until he's hard, when she slides onto him and thrusts and thrusts until he's emptied and gone soft again, Peytr buries his head beneath the pillows and concentrates. He tries to relax. Does his damnedest to still the chatter in his mind. To keep his thoughts short, concise, and close.

"Good story," he says, after, and blows her wordwind tenderly away.

Dot 32. Aria: Flattering tongue, no more I hear thee. . . .

Using hands and teeth and wet lips, Esther tells the same story again.

"Good morning, Jaunty," Esther whispers, running her fingers up and down Peytr's bicep. A shuffle of skin across fabric. Pillows slipping. She snuggles against him, curls herself small, burrows her head beneath his chin. Her good ear pressed over his heart, the earring she never takes out digging in. Peytr cracks an eyelid, spies through his lashes. Her inked arm is wrapped round his waist, a dark belt against the mottled flesh of his midriff. Her hair undulates in the breeze of his breath, loosing words of contentment. *With inward joy. . . . Virtue truth and innocence. . . . Our souls glow . . .*

He exhales, hard, as if snoring. Pretends he's asleep. Flounces onto his side, tossed by a nightmare, to shake Esther off. Buries his face in the pillow. Pulls the blanket up to his neck, soft armour against her embrace.

She sits up. Not touching him now, she sits and stares and doesn't move. He can feel the stillness radiating from her, the body in stasis while the mind races. He can picture the vortex of her 'wind churning the air, churning her stomach. And he lies there, back turned, tense, his breathing unnatural, not the steady rise and fall of a sleeping man but the shallow lung-skimmings of an actor feigning death. He clutches the blanket, afraid to move. She knows he's awake. She's waiting for him to roll over and grin. To stop lying and just fuckin' roll over. In his thigh muscles, electric eels jolt and slither. He can't do anything to stop them, even though he's so obviously awake. He's awake and she knows it.

A minute passes.

Esther is a statue.

Peytr fake-snores.

A hard-knuckled rapping at the door forces Esther out of bed. She climbs over Peyt, gets dressed. Goes along with his ruse long enough to go outside to meet the caller, closing the doors behind her.

Peyt sighs, temples throbbing. Relief and guilt warring in his belly. What the fuck was he thinking? Just now. Last night. He shouldn't have. . . . No. He shouldn't. But he did. And now? He should apologise. He should stay. He should go with her, with them. He should go. She deserves better. And he just wants to be—

"Well?" Through the bus and all its shelves, Guillaume's voice is muffled. Peytr strains to hear. "Anything?"

Peyt senses Esther shaking her head, the old woman mimicking the gesture.

"There's a law of diminishing returns in research," Guillaume says after a long pause. "You know that as well as I do. This quadrant has yielded nearly all the files we're going to get, so the cost of tarrying much longer outweighs the benefit. Agreed?"

"Yes, Nan. But—"

"But what, child? Our branches are laden with ripe fruit. We have reaped what we can; now we must share this bounty lest it spoils in our trucks. Unless you'd care to stay? Winnow the bare stalks?"

"No," Esther says eventually. "I would not."

When she comes in half an hour later, Peyt's up and dressed, lacing his boots. He was hoping to be gone before she came back. His bag is packed, hood and jacket draped across his lap. A hasty apology scribbled on a scrap of foolscap, close at hand. But seeing her now, framed by the narrow doors of her bus, crazy hair backlit by the unreasonable sun, 'wind serious, subdued, he hesitates.

"We're going?" His tone light enough to lift her eyes, distracting from the paper being swept off the table and scrunched into his back pocket.

"We're going," she says, frowning. Watching him, *seeing* him. Understanding. Her 'wind, as always, is ordered, organised. *Dot 25. Aria: How can I stay (Tenor). . . . Dot 34. Aria: How art thou fall'n (Bass). . . .* But some of the phrases seem torn in odd places. Snipped and shrouded for secrecy.

She's hiding her feelings, he thinks, he knows. All the things she isn't saying. That she's sick of his fuckin' shudders, how he spills food instead of eating it, how he won't use utensils, how his thoughts veer like the horses, off track half the time and the other half stubbornly going wherever they want, how he doesn't sleep—*can't* sleep—even this morning. Even after last night.

How he sometimes calls her by the wrong name.

How he can't forget.

Her mule-driver shoulders, he thinks, aren't broad enough.

Not fuckin' broad enough for him.

"Here," Esther says, tossing a bright bundle from across the room. I've repelled her, Peyt thinks, watching the fabric unfold mid-air. I'm repellent.

"A couple days ago, I asked Parrot if he had one to spare." She watches him, so awkwardly still she might as well be fidgeting. Discomfort making her tone casual. "He washed it—well, steamed it in a cedar box. For the fragrance. . . . I just thought, you know. Parrot's such a clotheshorse and. . . . You've only got that flimsy undershirt and . . ." She shrugs. "You're always cold."

The shirt is target-red, patterned with miniature palm trees and ocean-view scenes. He slips it over his head without undoing the pearlescent buttons. Its sleeves would be short on Parrot—but on Peyt they hang midway down the forearm.

"It's really something," he says, tucking the tails into his pants before putting on his jacket, doing it all the way up. Then, somehow, he's at the bus steps. Hunching, arms outstretched. Now rigid around Esther. Hugging without using his hands. Her breasts squashed up against his ribcage. A whiff of sweet lemon off her scalp. Bitter rinds. "Really. I—"

As he pulls back, fumbling for thanks, his wordwind arcs overhead. A bridge. A rainbow. Peytr shakes his head and a word—a name—breaks loose. Snags in wisps of Esther's black hair. He hesitates, watching the letters struggle with her tousled strands. Let it go, he thinks. Just leave it.

Esther shivers when he brushes her cheek. His fingers intimate, inexperienced, groping. She leans into him, plumps her lips for a kiss.

His mouth skims hers.

"Esther," he says, wanting to say so much more. "I—"

She recoils, stiff and flat.

Gorge rising, he breaks away. Bends to grab his ruck. Licks the wriggling letters off his fingertips.

"Come on," she sighs. "Guillaume said there's time yet for one last trip into town."

"Thanks," he mumbles, shouldering his bag. "Thank you."

Before she clomps down the steps, he snatches her hand. Squeezes it. Pretends to feel her squeezing back.

"Tomorrow," she says when the team's hitched to the wagon and they're—mostly—on the road, "the library travels north."

On the bench beside her, up front, *exposed*, Peytr reaches over. Clasps Esther's knee. Massages the taut muscles around it. "Will there be meadows?" He laughs, ignoring the heat in his cheeks. He's overcompensating, pathetically, but can't stop.

He wants her to be specific, to relax, to sparkle and flirt, to get carried away as she has before. But when he asks for more details, she is withdrawn. Formal.

"Alas, my trove is depleted," she says. "What say *you* tell a story? I can record it, if you grant me permission. It is, after all, the only reason I'm here."

Peytr's throat constricts. "I don't know what I'm doing. I don't know what to say."

"Those with the most valuable insights always feel most like impostors. Only fools are bolstered by the conviction of ignorance. Brilliance is forever wed to self-doubt."

Esther flicks the reins, drives the pair on. He stares at the city, unsure if she's insulting or flattering him. They're approaching the same wall they attempted before, but from this vantage Peyt has a much better view. Vacant tenements and abandoned apartment blocks ring the inner side of the wall, but beyond them, maybe three miles further up the road, there are spires of unbroken glass. Buildings with scaffolding. Reconstruction cranes. Chimney stacks billowing smoke. There are people, he thinks. Busy people hoarding their busy stories.

"How much time have we got?"

Esther eyes him warily. "Why?"

A few hours, he says, is all they'll need to make it to the CBD and back with at least one boulevard's worth of new chronicles. A few hours to more than triple the lore they've accumulated at camp. A few more hours, he thinks, to earn forgiveness.

The prospect is enticing—a half-smile teases Esther's lips—but she isn't a fool.

"What about the greys?" she asks, and it takes every ounce of Peyt's willpower to reply, "They prefer bleak days. Just look at that big old *nonsense* 'sun. Never seen it brighter."

Esther scans the skies without even squinting. Then a brief glance at the city gates, mentally measuring the length of each shadow.

"In and out," he hears himself say, then, quavering: "They could nab us just as easily out here."

A moment passes, while Peytr watches her desire grow.

"You're the soldier," she says at last, lashing the horses.

Twenty minutes later, they're passing under the tarnished arch of the city's gates, the doors swung wide and rusted off their hinges. Their hoof-beats echo through gaps in concrete structures lining the road, hollow towers gawping blindly at them with ply-boarded windows. White-knuckles welded to the bench beneath him, Peyt's eyes are in constant motion. Sweat has soaked his new shirt. He feels it trickling down his back, under his belt, until he's sure, if he stands, he'll find a big wet arse-print on the seat. He doesn't stand.

He can't.

"We can turn around," Esther says, soft now, soft again, leaning close, clearly wanting to touch—touching. "Let's turn around."

He can't.

Ghosts caper in his peripheral vision. Grey sprinters become an old man negotiating sidewalk crevasses in his wheelchair. Dark shooters devolve into a little boy wearing a school skirt and rubber boots, following a woman—a shadow-turned-mother—through a broken store entrance. The shop owner, shielding a grey crossbowman with his fat aproned belly, sits on the curb out front. Smoking pungent herbs. Selling cans of tinned beets, five dollars a pop.

Esther halts the wagon. Introduces herself. Takes up her notebook and pen. Makes a joke about beets that isn't remotely funny. The shopkeeper chuckles. Between drags, he tells part of his story. How he'd been a doctor, once. Flown in an airship whenever he wanted, not just when the gov't allowed. How he'd treated people who weren't sick, not really.

"Their problems were all up here," the man says, blunt fingers jabbing his greasy forehead. When he invites them in—he's relaxing into his narrative, gaining momentum—Esther takes one look at Peyt and declines.

He can't.

"I'll turn around at that intersection," Esther says, taking up the reins. "Just hold your hand out like this"—the gesture doesn't register—"if you see someone coming. Make it noticeable, all right? So they'll stop."

He can't.

Someone's coming.

Someones.

"Hurry, Esther."

A herd of men—of boys—wearing windbreakers and fatigues and multicams—are marching—yes, they're marching—out of an alley on the right—now they're goosestepping—in unorthodox squadrons—must be Special Ops—and they're barking—not at each other, not at the same time—a leader, a muscle-bound Cap, is barking orders at his platoon. And the fuckin' horses are being stubborn—"Hurry, Esther, please"—not trotting, not even walking, fuckin' tiptoeing through a space in the median—and Peyt knows these boys—he thinks—he knows them—and—he thinks—they know him.

"Go." All knees and elbows and boneless between, he scrambles, kicking Esther's notepad, the shopkeeper's tale, into the dirt. "Go, go, go," he whispers, voice lodged somewhere down in his guts, as he flop-falls into the back of the wagon, under cover, out of sight, where he tries not to whimper, blood awash in his mouth, tongue throbbing, the cartwheels jostling, rattling his skull, picking up speed. "Go, go, go, go, go . . ."

He doesn't know when they stopped. His skull is still rattling, bones still shaking, teeth still thirsting for blood. The canvas cover slaps against the wagon's arched ribbing, buffeted by a strong wind. But the scene out back—the flaps are pinned up, a rush of cool air gusting in—isn't changing. The dust behind their wheels has settled.

Esther cradles Peyt's head in her lap as the fit wracks and, eventually, leaves him. She rocks him like a child. Singing under her breath, the timbre of her song less buttery, more charcoal, than it was that other day, before. Her 'wind subdued, almost transparent, dwelling on images of deserts, bombed-out meeting halls, a line of caravans, singular, thin, alone. *Dot 29. Chorus: He comes to end our woes. . . .* She notices the focus in Peyt's gaze, his senses returned, and smiles sadly.

"If love and affection could mitigate sorrow," she whispers, leaving the thought unfinished. *Dot 34. Aria: How art thou fall'n (Bass). . . .* Her words are always so fancy, he thinks. So highfaluting. But he knows exactly what she means. There are no curlicues in her wordwind, in her embrace. He sees the plain way she loves him.

She sees that it's not enough.

"I'm sorry," he says, he thinks. *Sorry . . .*

And she reads him again, reads him well, and nods *How art thou fall'n . . .* and kisses him on the eyes, soft lips smothering his lids. She lies down beside him, soothes him silently, and when they're gasping and sweating and utterly spent, when his wordwind is mingling, entangling with hers, he opens his mouth and starts talking. There are no notebooks, no scrolls, no fragile ink pens. Just his memory and hers, working in tandem. He talks about Jean and her scars and her obsession with bombs. He talks about Borys and his steel leg and the factory where it was made. He talks about the girls and the groundhogs and the trouble he has with darkness—he talks about everything he can bear to voice.

"Thank you," she says, kissing him again and again and again. And he feels hollowed, exhausted, *relieved*. At last, nuzzled against her breasts, her strong, steady heart, he sleeps.

In the cold pale before morning, he wakes alone.

Eel-jolts through his limbs, and he's upright. Scouring the wagon—the fuckin' greys have her!—feeling the pinch of their deadly fingers, scraping through their shadows. Finding nothing but his pants.

Backpack. Boots. His new shirt, neatly folded on a box—red on the coward's seat. Above the breast pocket, sloughed letters are arranged in a frown on the fabric. A precious 'wind-pressing. One-of-a-kind. The word now-forgotten in the mind of she who presented it.

Tristan.

Quiet, alone with his words, Peyt gathers his few things. The hacks are gone, burdened with the wagon's contents. He lines the bottom of his bag with the shirt, snugs his hood and jacket, and climbs onto the driver's seat. Sits there a spell. Esther's bootprints are clear in the dust, invisible on the gravel. She's made no attempt to scuff them out. Crooked as truth, they lead back to the library, dots of shade on the horizon, obscured in the twilight. In the other direction, back in the city, the nightmarkets are glowing like dawn.

Crazy, he thinks. Setting up shop like that, right in the thick of it, right in the heart.

With some effort, he gets his pack on. Follows Esther's trail for a minute or two, then stops. Retraces his steps. Shuffles toward the lights.

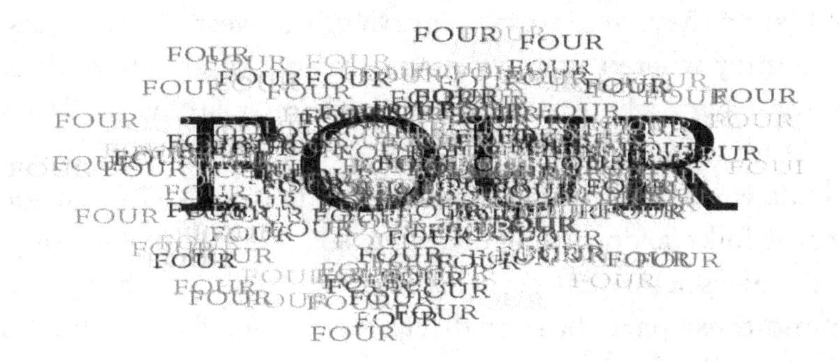

There was a show Ruby used to watch as a little girl, every night after the dinner dishes were done, and she was washed and snugged on Gramp's knee. It was so old there were holes in the picture, big yawny-melty brown mouths that gobbled up bits of the story, making Gramp swear as he got up to fix the reel. One-handed, he always managed to get the film running smooth again—but even then the sound was wonky. Voices always seemed on the verge of tears and birdsong fluted in a weird key, high-pitched and warbling straight into Ruby's tum. Sometimes she plugged her ears, quietly invented plots and effects just for herself. A show without sound was still better than anyone else had in their building, and Gramp had said Ruby was gifted in the way of imagination.

She can't say, now, what it was called; the name is buried somewhere under the many years that have layered theirselves in her memory, a great wad of time smothering details from way back when. But there were rivers in that flat colourful world, lots of them, or at least one big river, and guys on tugboats fighting over fallen trees. Ruby never understood why they all wanted the dead ones, logs shorn of their branches and bobbing to nowhere, when the shores bristled with so much live green. Maybe they didn't want to kill what had grown for so long? No, she thinks, that couldn't be it. There was one sailor, a scruffy actor with a knitted cap hiding his 'wind—actually, come to think of it, none of the characters had 'winds in that show, but not all of them wore hats. Must be they came from up north or out west, Ruby thinks. Some country where the greys' magic was off kilter, where their bombs went awry, where the fallout didn't bother survivors all that much. At least, not so obviously as it does here. It's grey magic that hauls words out of skull-darkness, she thinks. Grey magic that leaves folks so open, so vulnerable, so maimed. No way could those 'windless actors have come from round here, she thinks. No one round these parts has the discipline to keep their thoughts so tight to theirselves.

Anyway, this sailor. What was his name? Flotsam? Wrecker? No, no. She tastes it on the tip of her tongue, the copper and rust of it. . . . Relic. Yes, that's it. Relic chopped down trees with a gas-powered saw and had a stout little boat that didn't go very fast, but sure carried a lot of treasure in each episode. Leather shoes and gold trinkets and ancient caches of blown-glass; hoard after hoard of valuables Ruby would kill to sell at her night market stall. And the guys found piles of it, just by sifting through trash that'd washed up on the beach. The whole thing was that far-fetched, really, and the costumes were completely stupid, all brightly-checked shirts and alarm-yellow pants—rubber pants, no less, and rubber boots, precious rubber that could've been put to much better use. But Gramp had loved the fantasy of it all, the romance of water and pine.

And Ruby had loved Gramp, so every night she watched Relic along with him, careful not to knock his drink as she climbed onto his lap. In wheezes of laughter, the tar smell of his grog mixed with the herb of his smoke, ruffling her scribble-fine hair. Their basement apartment less dank, less cold, for that hour or two before bed. She'd cried when Gramp said she'd grown too big for snugs during show-time, when he pushed her away as she tried to get back up; when he shoved her to the floor, where she sat between his feet, shuddering against bony shins while Relic ransacked a marooned trawler on screen. Years later she'd sobbed when Gramp lost the strength to resist her, though she'd long given up trying to get that close. By then, her old Gramp was far too frail to support the weight of a fourteen-year-old girl.

Those show reels were the first things Ruby ever sold, once Gramp had gone the way of Mamie and Pap. The profit skimmed her pocket, out much faster than in, before landing in a skingirl's palm. A fair trade, Ruby still thinks. A few bucks for such well-made skirts. A few bucks and a perfectly reasonable fit. Ruby promised herself she'd stop skinning once she earned enough to buy—not rent, *buy*—a berth at the night markets. And she did stop, she did, then sublet her apartment and bartered her corset and unstitched her gear, bought a rickety hut on the market's main drag, and used all that lovely crimson to make bunting for the front of her stall.

For years she hawked dumpster gems, a clean and honest living; but it made good business sense, she thought, once her hair had turned from coal to ash, to open her legs again, earn a bit extra by helping soldiers come to terms, so to speak, with their ghosts. For the right price, with her back turned, with faded strands streaming down to her arse, she could play grey, she could act, she could sneak into the makeshift storeroom where she'd stowed a small cot, she could pinch the men invited to feign sleep upon it, she could pretend to be invisible and hide behind the stock, or, if her arthritis wasn't throbbing, she could crawl under the low bed, slit out, and let the silent men fuck theirselves empty without ever showing her face.

She could, and did. For a good while. Longer than she'd planned, yet only long enough to save up for a second kiosk and two nanny goats to raise in it. These days, Ruby's colouring is more snow than ash; far too pale to pass for grey, even if she wanted to, even if callers squinted between thrusts. Now she's best known for her edibles—tubers and cheese are always on special—but plenty of other wares crossed her polished counter while she was getting the hang of milking, churning, separating cream. Reasonable, useful goods: needles and thread, combs and lockets, shells and holsters, as-new mirrors and porcelain dolls for the little ones. Not so long ago, she'd tried her hand at apotropaics, charm-bags and rollin'-bones and the like, but was soon fed up to the teeth with complaints. These trinkets never worked the way they were supposed to, always breaking what needed fixing, rashing skin that wanted calming, spotlighting what should've been hid. If anyone accused old Ruby of being grey, she could've just pointed to the long line of dissatisfied customers outside her place to prove magic wasn't and never would be her thing.

Less than a month back, she still had luck-buyers come raging, their dirty mouths all a-yawning with ire, great noisy holes gaping in their ugly mugs as they shouted for their money back. The lot of them looked so much like Gramp's slow-burning filmstrips, Ruby got a bit misty, remembering. She turned away to wipe her eyes on the sly—only fools show emotion when coin's at stake—and there he was. Standing off to the side, away from the heated rabble, ratty and gaunt as the sailor she'd seen hundreds of times projected on Gramp's whitewashed wall: her old favourite, her own personal Relic.

Across the way, a new booth's gone up. The woman running it calls herself Belle. Folk laugh and flutter when they hear the name, as if it means something special, as if everyone knows something Ruby doesn't. Sticks in her craw, the way they all laugh and flutter, the way they visit the pretty stall-owner night after night, the way they leave her out of the joke.

"What's so funny there? She selling grog under the counter? She lacing her bannock with glass? You ever bought something like that from her, Relic?"

The boy merely shrugs, keeps scrubbing the planks that make up the floor of her shop. Most people are careless with their 'winds, letting hints drop then leaving them where they fell, littering the ground with worthless opinions, half-baked ideas, stupid nothings Ruby knows no one wants to see. If they were important, thoughts worth keeping, folk would reel them in close, make sure every last cross and dot was soaked back into the flesh, returned to the dark place where such thinkings are stored. But most people, Ruby thinks, are stupid. Even now, even after all these lean years, too many careless jerks expect to simply get back what they've frittered away. As if the world owes them. As if bleeding and breathing makes them special somehow, makes them deserve more than they're willing to earn. Skeins of mind-drivel constantly clog the drain in her goats' pen; sharp retorts burr the countertop, letters snapped off in anger and primed to hook into the softs of her unwary hand. By closing time, there'd be a fleece of forgettings on the floorboards if it wasn't for the boy.

Cleaning from true-dark 'til daybright, Relic keeps hisself to hisself, thoughts held firm as the bristle-toughs in his speckled paw. He doesn't come round every night, but when he does he works hard, he's quiet, and he's willing to slog for much less than he's worth: a jangle of copper pennies and a bag full of grub. Got enough secrets in him to burn down a house, Ruby thinks, but she doesn't pry, even when he won't take his hood off around her, even when he won't offer a name. It's not Relic, that's for certain—Ruby's older now than Gramp ever got, but she hasn't gone *that* loopy—she can still tell what is and what isn't. Got to call him something, though, and he didn't take too kindly to Spot.

"Thieving wench," Ruby says, cinching the ties on her cardigan, pulling the wool close, as though Belle's set to come steal it, too. First it was Ruby's customers—all those chuckling folk used to visit *her* stall quite regular, but not so much now Belle's come along—and now the bitch's burgling her wares.

"She is—isn't she, Relic?"

"Can't say," the boy replies, scattering sand and grit on the footpath, getting back down on his knees to scour the boards raw. Head low, he moves with slow determination, mumbling under his breath, keeping out of the shadows as he scuffles from the front of the shop toward the storeroom.

With a sigh, Ruby stares across at Belle's busy stand, at the tables piled high with veg and dairy. "Where's that barrow-load of carrots I dug," she asks, spying the dirty orange pyramid stacked atop Belle's counter. "I rolled it right there." She points at the narrow walkway connecting her shop and the goats' little barn. "Right there, Relic."

"Haven't seen them, ma'am."

"And what about those curds I bagged earlier?" Now Belle's got a string of plump cheesecloth sacks hanging across the transom, white-belly bright against the darkness, while Ruby's own stocks are suddenly low. Took all afternoon, tying those damp bundles for draining and curing, with her knuckles aching the whole time. There must've been at least a dozen, she thinks. At least ten. No less than five. There's no way she could've sold them already—Ruby's got standards, after all, and won't peddle her wares prematurely—and her purse is just as saggy as it was when she upped-awnings for business tonight.

"She's got no dirt to speak of, no nannies to give her milk—so tell me I'm wrong about this, boy. Go on." As Ruby leans over to fuss with the veg bins, her sharp hipbones jam into the counter. The vibration looses a small avalanche of onions, and though she tries, she's too stiff to catch them before they skitter onto the ground. Pain jolts through to her spine as she fumbles at turnip and potato crates, attempting to straighten. Sweat-slicked palms find little purchase on the plastic-lined bins; her back muscles are good and cricked.

"Don't just leave me kinked here," she says through gritted teeth. "Help me up."

The boy rushes to her side, but stands there gaping a while before acting. He's a bit touched, is Relic. Grey-struck by the looks of him, gets the jitters worse than Gramp ever did, though the old man had gone and done six tours before the greys nabbed his shooting arm and a fair chunk of his noggin to boot. "Caught a piece of the fucker before he scampered," Gramp used to boast whenever the rag-tags of his platoon came by to soak up the old man's pension in grog. It drove Ruby nuts, the way he'd carry on then, flopping out that dried hunk of meat he wore on a thong round his neck—cock-shaped, she always thought, but she never shared the insight with Gramp. She kept her 'wind under wraps whenever such things sprang to mind, cocks and dicks and hangdogs and the like. Let him think it was the grey's trigger finger he'd snagged for a souvenir. Let him think it was proof. Let him crow while he had the spirit for it. Let him say the greys weren't invulnerable, they weren't always so clever, not if Carson Teller had managed to bag one. Let him laugh at his own expense even while flushing with pride. Let him think the greys were losing ground, losing faith. Let him think they'd abandon their territory, the hills and stones they seemed to love so much, the plains and valleys they were endlessly trying to steal back, fighting dirty, their grey juices spilling, flowing into the red. Let him think troops of young fools were killing the fuckers piece by piece, coming home with trophies to prove it. No harm if an old man airs his delusions every now and again, Ruby thought. Let him believe whatever he wants.

"You should probably lie down," Relic says once Ruby's semi-upright and clinging to the counter for balance.

"Worst thing I could do right about now," she snipes, *Belles* in her 'wind ringing round and round her head. Across the way, the young wench is rubbing her greedy hands together, eyeing Ruby's produce through gaps in the passing crowds. Untying her apron, Belle's making a move for the door of her stall. She's bound to come stealthing over soon as Ruby's horizontal, out of sight, heedless of shadows and the greys lurking in them—for all that Gramp might've wore a cock round his wizened neck, Ruby knows they greys are out there, she knows that much. *Someone* keeps tunnelling beneath her city; someone keeps blasting mighty big holes in the ground. Shelling and crushing the pretty buildings, the clever designs—someone's making most places unfit for anyone to live in, anyone at all, on this or that side of the fight. They're determined, those murdering someones, bent on staking their claim—even if that stake destroys everything on its way to being stuck.

Lords of the boneyard, that's what the greys want to be. Masters of rubble and ruin.

Just so long as they get rid of us in the process, Ruby thinks, telling Relic to grab her that stool over there, that's it, and drag it on over here. Eliminate the competition, no matter the cost; that's the way it always has and always will be. Ruby groans as she settles her arse on the unforgiving seat. She's not a sympathiser—no, she's red through and through—but watching Bella slink back into her shiny new shop, seeing the sticky-fingered bitch setting out Ruby's own hand-rolled cheeses at discount prices, she can't help but imagine how the greys must feel.

It's only natural, she thinks. An instinct like any other. The undeniable urge to protect what's yours.

"Forget the sweeping-up for a sec," she says as Relic goes to fetch the broom. "I got a more pressing job for you. A little errand I need you to run."

Perched uncomfortably on her stool, Ruby directs Relic to the storeroom. "There's a cloth sack hanging from a hook on the back of the door," she says. "A long, skinny one—yep, that's it. Grab yourself two or three plastic bags from inside it; get ones with real sturdy handles."

Simple boy that he is, Relic does as he's told. A good start, she thinks, brushing away her 'wind before he can see its tattle-tale thoughts of dough and clay, how they're malleable until fired up. "Fill them all," she says. "Choose your favourites: beets, onions, rutabagas. Whatever you like, son. I'd do it myself but—" She gestures at the state she's in, crooked and hard-breathing, sweat damping her pits and spine as pain pulses from her lower back down. "Pack in as much as you can carry, so long as the bags don't split. Can't do nothing for it if your pay goes rolling on down the street."

Relic stops on the other side of the counter, empty bags resting on the display of fine food Ruby's grown. Looking in at her, the boy's shoulders slump. One of the straps of the pack he never takes off—not even when on hands and knees scraping shit off the floor—slips down his arm, sagging like the little frown he's now wearing.

"These are for me," he says. He's got a nice way of shaping his words, does Relic, for all that he's a bit slow. Everything that comes out his mouth is careful, well-chewed; he doesn't just spit out the first things that come to mind. Brow furrowed, he starts packing radishes and parsnips, avoiding the zucchinis Ruby sells at a premium.

"Take some, if you want them," she says, and Relic's palsied hands grope and fumble the precious green squash.

"This is too generous, ma'am." Again, he stops. Smearing a streak of dirt across his spotted cheeks, he cocks his head and says, "Too much for menial labour. I don't want to sound ungrateful, but—" He stuffs two red onions into a bag. "What's the deal?"

"When will you learn to call me Ruby?" She smiles pretty, with lips closed to cover the gaps in her teeth. Might be he's not *so* dumb, she thinks. He's got a good work ethic, this boy: he knows he won't get something for nothing.

"Take your pay," she says, when it's clear he won't keep going without her say-so. "Then I'll tell you what it's worth. If you don't think one matches the other, well." She shrugs. "It's been nice working with you these past couple weeks, all the same."

Ruby recognises the look Relic's wearing now; the calculating, figuring-out look. Balancing having a regular gig against doing something he may be less than keen on doing; weighing up the pluses and minuses. Many of the boy's nights are spent in her shop, but not all, not every last one. Young lad like him's bound to pick up work here, there and everywhere—but nothing beats a steady income. No doubt Ruby could've been living in a bungalow by now if she'd kept strutting around in red skirts, inviting hard-ons back to Gramp's tiny apartment. No doubt her Relic could likewise set himself up all right, running glass for the 'makers or bending over, as she once did, for the lonely. But such a seeking kind of life wears a person down too fast, turns the hair from coal to ash long before its time, makes a lovely girl look like a haggard old woman.

Slow and steady's the way to go, Ruby knows. Slow and steady.

While Relic takes his due, Ruby's gaze drifts past his skinny form to the street beyond. This is what she's worked for all these years, this prime location, this familiar view. Near Hack's Blade Emporium in the ground floor of a confederation hotel; the Hot Pot next door steaming up the laneway with gusts of mushroom soup air; Chachi's scrap metal spread out on tables and tartan blankets, nuts and bolts and rear-view mirrors—all a discerning cabbie might need for minor repairs; the bauble shop hung round with plastic-bead curtains, selling crystals and incense and other grey-repellents, shit that doesn't work any better than Ruby's handmade *gris-gris* did; and smelling divine, like warm bannock and pide, Antje's bakery down the road opens once a week, twice if there's a good yield, if grey shelling and burrowing doesn't destroy the season's harvest. On either side of her own modest stall, there's a couple of scavengers—Purveyors of Antiquities, they call theirselves, but everyone knows that's just a fancy way of saying they add a bit of polish and sparkle to everyday crap and pretend it's rare as diamonds. Lanterns swing from awnings and valances and rickshaw shades; on tall poles lined up and down the main drag, flambeaux add to the glow, dripping as much oil as light. Everything—from rooftops to counters to fast-moving boots—is filmed with soot and orphaned 'winds, scuffed with dirt from so many passing feet. Everything, that is, except Belle's brand-spanking new stall. Its timber struts and screen door, its yellow bunting and lace draperies, its dainty tables and steel platters covered in irresistible goods—veg and cheeses pinched from Ruby's very own stocks—well, it's all smugly a-shine, isn't it, all taunting-bright and gloating, like a perfect full-toothed smile.

"Grab me a couple of them milk bottles," Ruby says, 'wind seething and nostrils flared. "Now, Spot!"

Relic's looking skimpy, but seems he's got a temper on him. His hood's jerking against the fight in his trapped 'wind, the strings pulling under his tatty chin. Red roses bloom high in his cheeks, vivid against the white spatter creeping above the thin beard.

"That put a spark into you—didn't it, Spot? Don't take orders kindly—that right, Leopard? Don't like being barked at—do you, Dalmatian?"

Quick as, Relic spins on his heel and whips a carafe at Ruby's feet. It smashes a few inches shy of hitting her; no doubt he could've done her a sight of damage, she thinks. If he'd wanted, he could've taken her head clean off.

"Good arm," she says, pumping her fist. That's what it'll take, a bit of fire and a strong throw. . . . "Bring it on over here—with the bottles, boy. Come on, now. Two'll do just fine."

Carrying them like cudgels, Relic stomps over and thrusts the things at her.

"Hang onto them for a sec," Ruby says, wrapping her hands around his, firming and adjusting his grip. When the glass mouths are angled close enough, she tears the fury from her 'wind, stuffs the bottles with vitriol, and stoppers them with her gnarled thumbs. Then, calm, she takes them from Relic and rests the bases on her thighs. "Your turn. Top 'em up with some of that anger you got burning behind those pretty peepers of yours."

Relic hesitates. Some of the steam's gone out of him, now he's cottoned that Ruby was sniping just to get him riled. Still, she thinks. He's got more than enough pent up, more than enough that needs blowing off.

"I'll close my eyes and promise not to peek, if that'll brazen you a bit," she says. "Go on and weed out all the filthy thoughts you want, son, then add them to mine. No way I'll be able to tell which is whose."

Before she turns away, she catches the odd glance Relic gives her—same kind Gramp used to shoot when she said something funny without knowing it. All the same, the boy adds his fuel to the fire-apples; without needing to be told, he plugs the pair with shreds of greasy rag he scrounges off the storeroom shelf.

"What's the target," he says, resigned, agitating the bottles with practised flicks of the wrist. "If it's more than three bags' worth, I'll want interest."

Ruby tilts her head, acknowledgement and direction both. With her chin, she points without pointing at the frilled monstrosity across the road. At Relic's nod, she lifts a hand to stay him. "Wait 'til afternoon, right around prowling hour, when blame will follow the greys."

Violent red and orange, the *Belle*s in her 'wind spin and spin and spin . . .

"And Relic," she says after the boy tucks the loaded rabble-rousers into his pack, tightens his hood-strings, and prepares to blend into the night. Hiking the cargo onto his shoulders, he pauses on the threshold and waits for her to finish.

"Keep it contained," she says with a smile, waving him out the door. "Aim for the pantry."

After closing up at morning's first brightening, Ruby feeds the nannies, then retreats to the storeroom and its uncomfortable army cot. The walk back to Gramp's apartment gets harder every day—twenty minutes might as well be twenty hours, or so her throbbing joints say. And she thinks it might look suspicious when the Watch come, as they always do when accidents happen; it might look like guilt has chased her away, if she's off-site when Belle's supplies burn to the ground.

So she grabs what sleep she can, with her hips and spine already out of whack, and made worse by the canvas sagging between the bed's metal frame. Torture devices, these racks. Hardly fit for a child, much less a woman her age. 'Wind tossing and turning in ways her old body can't, Ruby takes in lungfuls of musty breath, listens to the street-noise hushing its way toward noon, and waits.

Relic's quiet as a grey, she thinks before drifting off. While the new girl's off burgling tonight's produce, he'll slink in and give her a little housewarming. With no pantry-shed left to hold any stores, what's now in Belle's shop'll run out soon enough. Then, Ruby thinks, *then* she won't be able to sell so much as a stick of butter without the whole market knowing it's stolen.

At dusk, groggy, tongue furred with sleep, Ruby wakes to the smell of smoke and damp cinders. Must've missed all the hoopla, she thinks, half-disappointed she'd dozed through the fuss of putting out the fire. She'd planned on making an appearance, joining the line of goodie-goods, passing a bucket of water or two to prove she had nothing against the poor girl who'd just lost her outbuildings, nothing against her at all.

Hissing through the pain as she rolls off her cot, Ruby hauls herself upright, using the shelves as brace and ladder. Panting from the exertion, she sways on the spot for a minute before mustering the strength to smooth her calico dress and shuffle into the shop to find a suitable commiseration gift. A bit of cheese seems fitting, she thinks with a snort. After some consideration, she picks a round not so big it makes her look guilty, but not so small she'll seem heartless. Beneath the counter, Relic's payment sits where the boy left it, the bags tied and waiting for him to collect them. If it'd been Ruby in his place, she'd have returned before the fire had fully blazed, demanding and taking her due for starting it. But her Relic's different—she knows that. He's mild, soft-handed. He'll come whenever he comes.

Before leaving, Ruby drapes a thick shawl over her head and shoulders; a sign of respect, of mourning, and a restraint for snitching thoughts. She doubts Chachi or Hack or any of the local hawks will squeal, even if they catch sight of the truth in her 'wind. But as

Gramp used to say, you never can be too careful; business these days is full of vindictive cunts.

Soot-prints have been tracked all over the street, from Belle's stoop all the way to Ruby's threshold. Relic's got some more overtime on the horizon, she thinks, tutting at the grime ground into her walkway. Looking up at the mess of Belle's once-pristine shop, Ruby masks her surprise. Sloppy work, she thinks, seeing how the fire's spread, crackling the shop from back to front. A real rush-job. Maybe that's why Relic's late coming back; embarrassed he let the flames best him, embarrassed he couldn't keep things under control. Under the pall of smoke, there's a whiff of roast veg, roast meat. Ruby covers her mouth and nose with a trembling hand. Whose livestock did Belle steal? Wouldn't put it past the wench to have a house full of chickens she's told no one about, a secret supply of eggs.

Pausing every few steps to catch her breath, Ruby makes her way over to the blackened husk, stopping for good at the Watch's barricade. A troop of men and women in uniform, scarves wrapped round their faces, sift through the debris; nailing in place what can't be immediately torn down, digging and shifting what might be salvaged. There's not much of either, Ruby thinks. Just a few beams that need securing, a few bits of furniture that she wouldn't recycle for pennies. A seatless chair. A pair of flower-shaped lamps. A headboard made of spindles, a matching cradle.

"Belle?" she calls over the steel and ribbon cordon, only half-feigning the shock in her voice. That must've been *some* anger Relic had bottled—no way her tired old 'wind could've conjured this kind of firepower all on its own.

Fool boy, she thinks, watching a woman traipse past carrying a singed picture frame. Must've assumed the pantry was attached to the storefront, like mine, instead of filling a swanky shed out back . . .

Taking in the sorry state of the building, Ruby shakes her head. It's good and gutted, that's for sure; little here but charred struts and blasted walls. The timber siding is crumbled in places, clinging by the nails in others. What's left of the roof is teetering dangerously above the hollowed gable, and those pressed-metal ceiling tiles that made Belle so proud are now melted blobs on the exposed rafters. All in all, the sight of it reminds Ruby of the forest fire episode Gramp had only let her watch once—it was too sad, he'd said, seeing Relic and the other sailors brought to ruin. Seeing the wreck nature had made of their lives.

No human could be blamed for such a disaster, she reckons, trying to find a way around the barrier to get a better view. Yeah, this definitely has the look of a grey storm about it.

"You in there, Belle?"

"Sorry, ma'am." A broad-beamed woman in a boxy blue jacket and pressed trousers refastens the rope Ruby's only just managed to undo. "Authorised personnel only."

"But I've got a vested interest in the owner's well-being," Ruby says in all seriousness. Patting the Watcher's thick arm, she lowers eyes and voice and tries to calm the thumping in her chest. "Put an old woman's mind to rest, dear. That's my shop across the way there. Best goats' cheese in town, if I do say so myself. I've been concerned for Belle since she moved in; keeping an eye on her, so to speak, making sure she's fitting in. . . . I won't bother you for details—you and I both know who the culprit is, don't we, dear?—but if you could just tell me one thing? How long, do you think, 'til our Belle's back in business?"

"Oh," says the Watcher. Quickly, she looks over at the hubbub behind her, then back at Ruby. Grimming her lips, the woman ducks under the cordon and gently takes Ruby by the elbow. Slowly guiding her back across the street, the Watcher tries to explain, in that way officials have, without saying anything much at all. "I'm so sorry. Circumstances have changed, ma'am."

"Is Belle—" Ruby pauses, slackening her features. "Gone?"

"It's best if you remain inside until the building is secured. Rest assured: this matter is of utmost importance to us. We will investigate fully, and deliver notices shortly. In the meantime, one of our officers will pay you a visit to install a new flambeau outside your stall; make sure it's lit at all times, ma'am. Help us help you in the fight against the greys. Can you do that for me?"

"Certainly, dear," Ruby replies, squeezing the Watcher's hand weakly, offering the round of warm cheese. "Let me know if there's anything else I can do."

With trade disrupted for the night, Ruby keeps the door of her stall closed but not locked, the awnings and shutters bound fast. Relic will knock soon enough, she thinks. And I'll holler, *Let yourself in!* Easing herself behind the small table she uses to count petty cash, she opens the safe buried in the floor beneath it. When the seven leather purses are aligned on the table top, Ruby counts out her savings—bills, coins and promissory notes—dropping not a nickel, calculating the lot down to the cent.

It won't be long until people start bidding on Belle's plot, she reckons. The shop's completely shot, that's clear as holes, but with a bit of work the turf will make a nice pasture for the goats. And with that bit of wriggle room, Ruby will revamp the beasts' pen, expand her stall into a proper shop. . . . She'll start up a payroll and her Relic will be first on it; her first official employee. Get him riled and he'd make a decent security guard, she thinks—and he's always been a deft cleaner. Brooms up every word, he does, right down to the last letter.

That's settled then, she thinks, packing away her money. The tally looks promising—she's got a good chance at the land auction—and no doubt Relic's just around the corner. What a surprise he'll have when he gets here: three bags of veg and a contract! She drops a purse, scrambles to catch the runaways, now her hands are shaking worse than the boy's. But he'll settle soon enough, won't he, he'll relax when he's safely, gainfully employed. Oh, how exciting! Ruby hobbles over to the stool, moves it so she'll be the first thing he sees when he gets in. Shifting to ease the hitch in her back, she thinks: my Relic, a full-timer! What a change. What a lot of talking it'll take to get it all sorted. And Relic's never been much of a talker. . . .

Doesn't matter, she thinks, straining for the sound of bootsteps outside. We'll sift through the nitty-gritty the very moment he comes back.

Yeah, she thinks, staring at the closed door. I'll make him a genuine offer.

Scientific Classification

Clade:	*Synapsida*
Order:	*Therapsida*
Class:	*Umbra*
Order:	*Anceps*
Family:	*Hominidae*
Tribe:	*Hominini*
Genus:	*Homo ferus*
Species:	***Hf. cineraceus***

Binominal name

Homo ferus cineraceus (cf. Linnaeus, Wadjakensis & Kleinschmidt, 51.3896° N, 30.0991° E)

I sought them out, not the other way around—there was never a finer chance. The south-central warren, collapsed in blackout shelling, would certainly hinder passage; yet the fée would have as difficult a time leaving their feral den as I would entering. Despite Bory de St. Vincent's (absurd) classifications†, these hill- and burrow-dwellers, these so-called 'hidden ones,' were not beings of smoke and air—I had seen linotypes depicting the forward-jut of their lips, the concavity of their orbital bones, the greed in their powerful fingers. These creatures could not ghost away on the breeze; they could not wheedle through crevice and shadow. After the firestorm, an entire tribe, perhaps, would be trapped underground, pinned by stone and clay and time. What a collection of specimens! What irrefutable proof! A gap in the rubble would be sufficient to confirm their corporeal presence, a spyhole through which my lens could peer. One clear snapshot of the [*Lacuna; the better half of this document is now lost. Extant displays Spencerian script. Discovered: 40.1539° N, 76.7247° W. Fragment housed at Bibliotheca 37.4000° N, 140.4667° E*]

---

†Bory de St. Vincent's controversial treatise, On the Nature and Anatomy of "Umbra Ferus," was recorded c. Evac.St.713 ±150 years, thus pre-dating Linnaeus, Wadjakensis & Kleinschmidt's humanist pamphlet, 'More Man Than Monster: Homo ferus cineraceus' (cited above by the speaker, a man commonly referred to as "Lapouge" though inked evidence of his identity is currently lacking) by at least a century. Copies of both works were pressed last month at Bibliotheca 37.4000° N, 140.4667° E, by the same hand that inscribed this note (HWV50, aka "Esther"). By today's standards, "Lapouge's" ethics were questionable; his "scholarly" pursuit of the greys' anatomy prolonged a tradition of exhumations in northern regions—and, it is rumoured, dissections performed on the infirm; those whose ashen complexions condemned them to scrutiny, those too sick or weak to defend themselves against the knife of science.

FIVE

Boys shouldn't scream like that. So shrill and unconstrained. So little-girlish. No matter how frightened they get. How happy. How angry. They shouldn't shred eardrums with their voices. They should fuckin'-well shove a gag in it. Think of the fallout of such a sound.

From afar, Peytr watches the howling pink mouth blacken, wider and wider, its head thrown back, like a baby bird. Where's your dignity, son? Even at this distance, the scream's decibel transcends all thought, all reason. It is mindless, instinctive, driven from the gut. Peytr catches a glimpse of grey, wandering through shelled tenements on the opposite verge of the shallow gully, and *wills* the kid to shut up. This fuckin' kid *is* a baby bird, he thinks. Squawking, attracting attention. Defenceless, stupid, relying on others to feed him. Gripping a bulging plastic bag in one hand, a wizened wrist in the other. Hauling on both, back bowed with the effort of pulling, of going—where? The old sewage tunnel? Peyt grunts. Stupid choice. It's too grey in there, too burrowed. The apartments above? Just as dumb. The long slope up to the parking lot? Up to Peyt? No. No. Hard enough for a grown man to skid down that scree; near impossible for a screeching kid and his silent Ma to clamber up it. But there's a footpath nearby, well-worn, crossing the gulch. It curves close to the tunnel, but then follows a bend to the right, unseen, *away*.

Maybe the kid's not so stupid after all, not so bird-brained. No, he's wily as a pup trying to get out of a cage. Yep, he's trying to get out.

Still. He's loud, way too loud.

A barking hound with tears slicking dirty channels down his black face.

Seriously. Where's your self-control, kid?

Lying on the rubble beside him, apparently. Her calico skirts splayed across the pavement, hems snagged on tumbles of cinderblock, revealing brown stick legs up to the knots of her knees. Her torso contorted, shoulder pulled from its socket from all that dragging. Peyt can't see her head, but the little pup pauses regularly, squatting to embrace *something*, cradle it to his sobbing chest. There's no blood, not anymore. Just a fog of dust and whining.

Peytr hunkers next to a sedan carcass at the far end of the gravel lot, overlooking the gully. He gets *low*, head barely cresting the trunk, compacting his body, making it small, small enough to fit in the car's rear wheel well if need be—though he doesn't test it out to be sure. Doesn't want to get trapped in there, suffocating on the ghosts of oil and tarmac and distance. What a useless way to die, stuck in one place, tormented by lack of motion. He crouches, coils, a kinetic ball, a human shell poised to spring. Shoulders bunched, arms heavy, palms callused. Hood up but compromised; words escape through a gash in the fabric. Peyt spends his coin on food, not thread. Food bought dearly from day-old tables at night markets with the few pennies he earns scrubbing stalls for this grower or that. Sweet old Ruby was the most generous, offering three full bags for other, messier, night jobs. Not sucking or fucking. Not stabbing or stealing. Just thinking incendiary thoughts, lobbing them at competitors' pantries, setting their monthly harvest alight. No one gets hurt, Peyt tells himself, no one dies. Meals get cooked a bit early, that's all.

Really.

But the greys black-and-blued him in his sleep afterwards. They tracked him off the field, followed him to the library, followed him to the markets, followed him here, beyond. They greys shoo him away from Ruby's, but show themselves only when he isn't looking. Through the night, his muscles shudder non-stop and often he froths at the mouth. Other guys in the hostel, gap-toothed and gaunt in inside-out fatigues, see Peytr roiling and moaning and biting at air, and they don't ask. They understand enough not to ask. He can't eat, though his stomach rumbles, though he can't stop buying food. Now, crab-walking slowly beside the sedan, a plastic bag with three onions, a beet, and a dry wedge of bannock bangs against his knees. He won't taste a bite of any of it.

Shut up, puppy, he thinks. Look there. Good boy. Wait— No. Over there. *Look* for fuck's sake. Shut your fuckin' trap and *look*.

Oh, boy.

Peyt's old rucksack snugs sweat to his back. His boots are knotted together by the laces, flung round his neck. Creeping forward, heel, ball, toes, each step juts sharp stones into his bare soles. The pain keeps him alert. Eyes wide, focused. Performing visual recon. About ten metres to his right: a warehouse, red brick and corrugated iron, roll-down doors padlocked and windows blacked. Quiet but not necessarily abandoned. Far to his left: a boarded-up greasy-spoon, cinder blocks, wearing a neon smile on its western side, the bulbs silent and dark. Closer: the rotting car, once blue, now faded to silver and rust. Flakes turn to powder on his jacket as he scrapes up to the doorless passenger seat, streaking his beige sleeve a darker brown. Inside the sedan: grey vinyl upholstery, cracked or knifed or both, cotton batting clouding out of gashes. The floor corroded, pedals and steering wheel and dashboard shading a bed of concrete and weeds. Bent double, Peyt climbs in, one slow leg after the other. Parcel clutched to his belly.

Springs shriek as he edges onto the seat, a grating, ancient metal yawp. He clenches—everything—and freezes. Leaning forward on the dash, butt half-descended. The windshield is gone, its glass crunching beneath Peytr's feet as he shifts, inching further into the car. Settling his weight by increments, not relaxing. Bunkering. Digging his fingernails into crusty linoleum. Gaze shooting past the kid thirty metres or so away, straight ahead, due west, wailing his fool head off in the gully. Peyt's transfixed by the herdboys emerging from the tunnel's maw. One by one, they stealth up behind the little banshee. Forming a pack of ten, eleven, twelve . . .

Peyt wants to, but can't move.

Turn around, little pup. Run, you little idiot. Run! Drop your burden and get the fuck out of here. Leave it, just leave it. You've gone and hollered yourself into prey.

Finally, Pup's seen them. The hue and pitch of his screaming changes: less mournful, more menacing. A growl twisting into a whimper snarling back into a growl. Sharp canines appear in his wordwind, curses with hooks and claws and teeth. Still holding onto the corpse's arm, he pivots around, shuffling and scuffing as if trying to shroud her under a veil of dust. His body swivels, head swaying on a scrawny neck, gaze snapping from herdboy to herdboy. Crouching, defensive stance, holding the plastic bag out before him. The herd fans out, sauntering closer. Pup's head whips back and forth, trying to keep all the strays in sight. Growl shrinks to whimper. The tallest boy, muscular, so muscular, with a wild, demented expression, purses his lips and whistles. Nonchalance in the tune; menace in his hulking slouch, in the tightening circle of his approach. Whimper snarls to growl. While the other boys pace around them, the leader stops in front of Pup. Cocks his head, cuts the warbling. Clenches and unclenches jaw and fists. Bares his teeth, imitating a smile. Peytr groans. Pup is so small. Too small.

Fault-lines of quiet radiate from the cluster of boys. A hush of tension, of waiting, of being on the cusp of violence. Quiet that shrinks the balls and twitches legs nonstop and makes Peyt giggle, giggle now until tears are streaming, and fixes him here in the deadzone, here where the herdboys roam, and rattles the gravel underfoot with earthquake tremors. Peyt squirms over to the driver's seat, lifts his feet off the ground, shifts and wriggles until he's squatting behind the steering wheel, haunches on heels, knees splayed. His guts buzz, being here, on the brink, trembling with that prescient quiet.

He flexes left right, then presses his back into the seat, feels loose springs dig into his spine. I'm alive, he thinks, settling in to watch the tallest herdboy. I'm whole. Of its own volition, his hand reaches into the plastic bag by his side. Fingers latch onto a beet and now it's in his mouth and he's chomping through delicious, filthy rough skin, tasting the earth, the burgundy flesh. He swallows, once, before his throat convulses. The greys pinch and pinch and pinch his legs, pinch his arms, pinch his cheeks, pinch his cock. Pinch his tastebuds and now the beet tastes like scalp, it tastes taboo, it tastes *stolen*. Pinch him to get moving, to get into the fray. He judders for the car door while they pinch the fuck out of him to stay put.

He spits red on the dashboard, stolen food and stolen words, and grinds his back against the springs. Stays put.

In the gully, Pup's holding his ground. Panic has tipped him from defence to offense; now he's brandishing his own little bag like a flail, swinging it round and round to gain power from momentum. "Dogs are the deadliest hunters," Peyt says to Euri, sitting close beside him, braiding a lasso for her dappled pony, while the little one, Zaya, looks on. There's no room for a fourth in the front seat; if Daken shows, he'll have to listen to the story from outside. "See how vicious he's become? And in such a short time?"

Pup's screaming again and Peyt says, "Good strategy, kid. Keep 'em laughing," while the boy's battle cry rages. A fuckin' insane bellow that cracks the herdboys right up. "But is it enough?" Peyt asks his audience, adopting a newscaster's tone. He bags the half-eaten beet, wipes the juice on his cargos, shifts position to relieve the tingling in his bruised legs. "Alpha's amused for now—see how he barks? See how his tongue lolls? He's not threatened by our Pup, not one fuckin' bit. But who knows? With the right provocation, dogs can turn. . . . Happy and healthy and sane one second, raving fuckin' beasts the next. I mean, sure, Alpha's 'wind might be all chewed to pieces." Peyt's voice catches, his mouth suddenly dry. He swallows and swallows and swallows until the words well from his throat. "But surely being chewed gives Alpha more bite."

On cue, Alpha stops laughing. With military swiftness, he punches Pup in the gut. Peyt flinches as the boy bends double, gasping, the herd bending double with glee. "Such a tough ending for one with such a tough life," he says, inventing a history for the boy who's about to become it. "His Da ghosted on the field, making Pup the man of the house when he was still swaddled. Not that he had a house to man, mind. Ma lost it along with her job. . . ." For a minute or two, Peytr's wordwind dwells on factories, production lines, conveyor belts pumping out batch after batch of prosthetic legs. A good job, he thinks. An honourable job. Anyone with a will to work would be happy to have it. . . . Ever patient, Euri waits for Peytr to continue in his own time. For years Zaya has been too young to talk, so she never interrupts. But the greys are demanding fuckers, pinch-twitching his thighs, urging him on.

"Pup's belly is filled with ash and dirt and half-gnawed clauses, all his Ma had to give. Yep, she gave it all—oh, probably no more than an hour ago. And now lookit her, lying there, skin a perfect shade of grey, already attracting flies. Herdboys bowing down before her, touching her for luck, tearing her dress, her vest, her hair—stealing relics, that's what they're doing—taking turns to rub the naked idol of her, to rub and rub and rub against it, for luck—that's right, for their own wellbeing." Peyt swallows and swallows. "See? Don't turn away, now. Remember this, Euri. Remember. That's what saints look like."

While the herd pays homage to the blessed dead, Alpha snatches the bag from Pup's limp hands. "Good," Peyt says. Too late, the kid takes a swipe, overbalances and falls again to his knees. "No, Pup. This is good. Consider it a peace offering. An apology for the ruckus. Go on, settle down. It's Alpha's—just let him have it. Keep his belly full so he's less liable to turn on you for a snack."

Peytr rustles the plastic bag on the seat beside him, adding sound effects to Alpha's actions. Arm held protectively over his plunder, the herdboy rummages for an onion. In the car, Peytr does likewise. Alpha pulls out a carrot. So does Peyt. Alpha shoves the onion into his mouth so hard, Peyt's eyes water. As the other boy feasts, Peytr firms his own lips and runs them over the papery-smooth vegetable in his hand, but does not eat. First the onion, then the carrot, disappear in Alpha's gob, disappear in Peytr's bag.

"Is it enough?" he asks, catching Euri's shrug, Zaya's gummy smile. "Are they square?" *At last . . . at long last . . . are they square?* Devouring onions, beets, carrots, bannock bread, Alpha ignores the pup and keeps the other herdboys at bay with a glare. Finished with their quiet appetiser, some boys button their flies while others kick off their pants altogether. Licking their chops, they stand at arm's length or sit, bare-arsed, and wait for their share of the scraps. Alpha leaves nothing but the greens from one carrot. These he tosses to Pup, magnanimous. The kid gulps them down, hardly chewing.

"A good sign," Peyt narrates, speaking low to avoid disturbing the wildlife while it feeds. "But Pup isn't off the hook yet. He's got Alpha onside—barely—but what about Mongrel and Rex and Rover over there? Their loyalty stretches about as long as their tails, and those tails are held firm in Alpha's paw. That's right, Pup. Lower those eyes, expose that jugular. You're fuckin' new meat, so you just keep acting the part. Do what you're told, no questions, no stalling. There's no later in war, son. There's only now. You do what you're told on the double, no matter what. No matter what."

Peytr digs his spine into the springs. Knuckles his eyes, then looks up through the car's roofless frame, arching his neck over the steel strut, no headrest.

"In groups," he says eventually, straightening up, "dogs are the deadliest hunters. They're stealthy and cunning and mean. They're not smart—they don't have to be smart. It's the pack mentality that gives them an edge." Alpha beckons the herdboys closer. They gather round, sniffing at Pup, sneering and pinching at him like the greys. "No pup wants to be abandoned, shunned, a target. Better to suffer a little hurt for the sake of company. Better to inflict a little hurt together, than be a victim alone." Their 'winds prod at Pup's, willy-nilly. Touching and poking and *mingling*. Getting in his ears, up his nose, down his shirt, in his mouth. No boundaries. No taboos. The dogs bark; Pup grunts and bucks as they continue probing. Alpha holds the puppy still, lets the pack lick him behind the ears, lick his forehead, lick his frizzy hair. They lick him until his eyes glaze. They lick him until he's amenable.

Euri's confused, Peytr thinks, practically hearing her scowl. She still doesn't get why Pup doesn't fight. Why he lets them do what they're doing.

"There's a practice among ferals," he explains, "to pin the weakest member down, gnaw his belly 'til it's sprouting entrails." Peyt falls silent for a minute, watching, thinking up a suitable term. "It's called *hanging the dog*," yeah, that'll do, "because, once he's stopped kicking, they string him up by the guts—from a lamppost or a flagpole or whatever's around—and leave him dangling there. A snack for whoever needs it. And it's usually the youngest, the weakest dog in the pack that gets wrung."

With that Peytr's voice trails off, and Euri lets it. Smart girl, he thinks. Give her the time and enough hints and she figures things out. Now she doesn't ask why Alpha allows the boys to go only so far, no farther, before belting them off. Silently, she watches Alpha pull out his cock and piss a dark yellow circle around the pack, Pup, and Pup's Ma. She doesn't need to see his wordwind to know it's jabbering about his territory, his claim, his pet, *his his his*.

Peyt lifts his jacket collar, shrinks down into it. It's the long grey of afternoon, the ridiculous sun somehow baking the earth drowsy from behind all those clouds. With appetites eased for the time being, the herdboys bunk down right there on the footpath, right out in the open, with Pup nestled in the centre. Writhing, suffocating, but protected.

I could go now, Peyt thinks. I could just do it and go. Get back to the stalls . . .

Instead he yawns. Props his ruck in the corner behind him at shoulder-level, where the door and seat intersect. Tilts his head ever-so-slightly against it. Yawns again, but keeps his lids open wide. Threads his fingers through the ration bag's plastic handles, holds tight. Stands watch as the others sleep.

Rover wakes first, maybe an hour later, to an alarm of crickets heralding the day's end. Peyt sits, drops his feet between the pedals. Tension crackles up through the gravel, jolting him back onto the seat. "D'you think he'll go for Pup while Alpha's back is turned?"

Beside him, Euri's 'wind is mute, the words too fast or too slow to be legible. After a while, he senses the shake of her head. "Nah, me neither." Both laugh at the nasal twang he managed on *nah*. "I know," he says, watching Rex and Mongrel roll over and nose Alpha awake. "Look at the greedy bastards. I know what they're saying." He *ahems*, lifts his hood so his 'wind won't ruin any punch lines, and puts on a thick accent he invents out of nowhere. It strains his throat in weird ways, talking like this; dries it out and stretches the vowels all crazy. But it makes Euri giggle, just like it used to, so he hugs the wheel, bears down, and mangles his vocabulary.

"Right now," he begins, "Rover's saying: I are fuckin' hungry! And Mongrel says, I are fuckin' hungry too!" Peyt snickers as Alpha slaps the other boys' groping hands away. "Thing is," Peyt says to his sister, "they already ate the bag of food Pup found. All that's left is whatever they can come up with themselves . . ."

Euri's raising her eyebrows, so Peyt spells it out.

"Like, right now, Rex is telling Alpha, 'Think me up some roast bird.' And since Alpha's the leader, he's got to keep proving his worth, doesn't he? No matter how fuckin' stupid it makes him, Alpha's got show he's got nouse. Right? Otherwise they'll eat him alive. . . . Okay, see what he's doing? See how his 'wind is spitting and spinning? *Hot . . . blood . . . juicy . . . meat . . . fat . . . grease . . . yummmm*. . . . That's enough for them to feed on—okay, *that's enough* . . ."

Peytr leans forward, brow furrowed, until Alpha caps his supply. It's *more* than enough for the herd—but Rex is hogging the words, sucking them fast as they come, burping and slurping and sucking some more.

"Fuckin' pig. Listen to him now, Euri. Listen to what he's saying to Alpha now:

'Gimme 'nother what you fed me afore.'

'What?'

'Gimme more.'

'More *what*, bitch?'"

Peyt snorts. "Oooh, that's bound to raise hackles—and, ha! Hear Rex growling? Selfish fuck:

'What you just fed me, only just now. I want it. Gimme more.'"

Alpha flips Pup over, uses his rump as a pillow. Rex scrabbles at Alpha's hood, fingering the stained fabric, tugging at the strings.

Alpha responds with nothing but a whistle, so Peytr sits quietly for a spell, getting a hold of himself.

"See," he says after a few minutes, feeling the pinch the pinch the pinch of grey fingers at his chest. "See how calmly Alpha deals with his pack? Never betrays what he's feeling. No fear. No regret. Just says, 'It's all aten up now, Rex. Gimme a lick of what you had, so's I can remember its flavour. Once I gots the taste for it, boy, I'll serve it up for y'all agin.'

"On second thought," Peyt says, "maybe Alpha wouldn't sound like such a fuckin' idiot. I mean, he had a good upbringing. No Da, but a half-decent replacement. An original Ma plus a stand-in. Gov't allocated sisters and a brother. He went to school, had a short stint in the army. . . . So he's got to be clever, doesn't he? Even now? I mean, he's stayed alive long enough to make Alpha. Long enough to eat more than what he's had eaten. . . . Right?"

But Euri likes the stupid voices. She thinks Alpha should sound dumb, so Peyt's got to keep making him that way.

So.

"'Get yer paws off me, bitch,' Alpha says."

But fuckin' Rex is spoiled. He yanks at Alpha's hood, yanks and yanks, shouting 'Give me 'nother somethin, Alph. I are *hungry*,' until the older dog sits up and wallops him a good one. Shuts him up—for a second. Before Alpha's snuggled back on Pup's bony arse, Rex's begging turns howl. His nose bursts bloody while the rest of the herd bursts laughter. Mongrel wrestles the crying boy down, snaps at his roasted-bird thoughts. Then Rover piles on top, blunts his teeth on Mongrel's greedy 'wind. "Rex and Rover are brothers for real," Peyt invents, and Euri agrees, seeing their matching black hair, slicked with grease, their broad features and deep-pink skin. "And brothers should protect each other . . ."

Sometimes, Peytr cries for no reason. He'll be mucking out Ruby's stall, or lying in a cot at the hostel, or sitting in a broken-down car with a full bag of food in his lap, and his face will suddenly wrinkle, and he'll feel the greys pinching, feel lava rising in his chest, swelling in his throat, and then he's heaving to get it out, cheeks stinging hot, forehead and upper lip and the crease in his chin first humid, then damp, then wet. He clutches his hands together, squeezes them bloodless, struggles to control their shaking. Through blurry eyes, he watches the herdboys grapple, gorging themselves dumber and hungrier and meaner, and tries not to wonder where their families are. Or which divisions the boys might've fought under, which regiments, before they became dogs. Or how long they'll stick with Alpha, who seems content to recline on Pup forever, plucking soporifics from his lazy wordwind, eating them lick by lick. Going nowhere but to sleep.

Peyt wonders how long it will take for the pack to turn.

When the lava subsides and he cuffs the mess from his face, Peytr starts to get antsy. The afternoon is stubbornly hauling its bulk toward dusk, dragging wan daylight with it. Peyt gauges the time by the clouds' hue. Cinder and ash: must be almost four. If he's not at the markets before the shade of charcoal, all the night-jobs will be filled. He'll wind up panhandling for hours just for a measly turnip, a parsnip if he's lucky. No bread. None of the onions that always get gobbled first.

He can't go back to Ruby's. He can't.

Springs squeal as he shimmies along the split vinyl bench, millimetre by millimetre, aiming for the passenger door. Do it quick and be out of here, he tells himself. Do it quick before anyone sees you. But now Alpha's stretching—now he's getting up! Rolling his shoulders. Twisting out the crick in his neck. Pacing around his dried-out circle, jogging around, getting the blood pumping. An easterly breeze picks up, gusting from the ridge, gullywards. Nose lifted, Alpha inhales great draughts of air, tongue working, sampling for intruders. Round and round, he sniffs and stretches and tastes. Narrow-eyed and scanning the immediate vista—tenements, warehouse, tunnel, greasy spoon, parking lot—getting primed for an evening hunt.

Peyt huddles his scent close, hopes it stays trapped in the car. Cool air rattles the diner's neon mouth, whisks burger wrappers across the gravel, skitters plastic bottles down the gulch's long slope. A rifle shot *cracks* outside the warehouse. Peyt whiplashes. Scopes for the shooter. Frantically pats himself down for bullet wounds. Checks to see which of the herdboys needs a stretcher. The pack's tumbling and fighting—the noise got them riled, too—but they all seem to be there still. Pup clinging to Alpha's belt. Mongrel straddling Rover, fists wailing. Rex nursing his hurts by sharing a visit with Pup's Ma. The rest yipping, impatient, itching for one type of thumping or the other.

So where's the fuckin' shooter? *Where?*

Peyt's gaze sweeps the warehouse's rooftop, windows, doors—and there. There it is: polished from so much use, handle straight and true . . .

Buckling, Peyt thuds his forehead against the dash, bites his lips hard. Euri and Zaya think it's hilarious. A broom. A fuckin' wooden push-broom by the building's staff entrance, smacked loud, blown over in the wind. What a fuckin' fool.

Beside him, the girls giggle themselves empty.

Now the greys poke Peytr's arse. Pinch his thighs and calves. *Get out . . . get out . . . get out. . . .* He collects the bag and his ruck. Looks up to find the herdboys have gone quiet. Even Rex has stopped his thrusting; he's tying up his shorts, standing beside the rest of the pack, standing in formation, standing eyes-forward. Staring up the ridge at Peytr.

"Boys idling dangerously through empty time," he says, but can't remember how the adage ends. What happens to them if they idle? They do what? His legs jitter—what becomes of such boys?—his stomach aches—and what? What do they do?

Go . . . go . . . go . . .

He'll never outrun them. He'll trip, he'll fall, the greys will be on him, he'll disappear, he'll vanish, like Merv said, "Just like that." The herdboys will rescue him, sure, the pack will be on him, all grabbing and snatching, saying "You're safe, you're safe," with hairy muzzles snapping, mottled tongues lapping mottled skin, chewing and fucking and pissing on him, stealing the cost of his rescue. Peyt can't run if he wanted to, his limbs aren't his, they're the greys', they're the army's, they're jittering like crazy but he's going nowhere, he's staying put, and the herdboys, the herdboys are loping.

Peyt glances to his right. "You girls should hide," he says, but Euri and Zaya are already gone. Instead, a man in overalls is there, to his right, hurrying across the lot, boot-crunching hurries, jangling keys, fumbling to get inside the warehouse's staff door.

Go . . . go . . . go . . . go . . . go . . .

The herdboys are fast, but the man is faster. The padlock clanks when it drops. He leaves it on the threshold, shoulders the door open. Takes one step and gets bowled over by a blur of red skirts and ragged blonde hair.

Wrists bound with hemp cords, pale arms muddied with blood and dirt, the skingirl's corset is shredded to the wire, flesh puckering between the gaps. She screams just like Pup did, a klaxon of fear, her wordwind scattered like broken glass. No light shines behind her, no one else comes out. Who knows how long she was in there, Peyt thinks. Alone, trapped in that dark box, all the angles the same, the featureless walls. Monsters hulking in the gloom, hemming her in, biting with sharp teeth, rasping with sandpaper tongues. She stumble-runs to escape, kicking up dust, falling, kicking and kicking, falling and kicking as the man hooks an arm around her thick waist. Starts dragging her back inside.

"Hey," Peytr whispers. "Let her go."

Go . . . go . . . go . . .

Do something, Euri pleads.

The greys pinch and pinch and pinch him in place.

The herdboys have reached the slope, but the skingirl hasn't seen them. She's intent on the few feet in front of her, the few feet after that, her focus immediate, not forward-looking. The man, though. His head's never still; up, down, up, down, he's calculating, he's weighing the odds. Skingirl takes advantage of his distraction, dead-fishes herself, drops her centre of gravity, flops to the gravel. Caught now only by her crossed wrists, she flips and wriggles, making it hard to hold onto her, making the decision for him.

Peytr's heart swells when the man takes a last look at the herdboys, and spits on her. Backhands her. Then lets her go.

Go . . . go . . . go . . .

The warehouse door slams behind him. A single bolt shunts true. Entrapping even as it releases.

"Run," Peytr says. Shouts? Thinks. *Run . . . run . . . run . . .*

Agonising seconds pass, shivering and sobbing.

Skingirl wobbles to her knees, face-plants, tries again. Bits of stone embed in her bare arm, her cheek. She gains her feet, hikes her skirts and finally, finally starts to run.

"No," Peytr says. He stretches one big toe to the gravel, instantly recoils. "No," he repeats. Aloud. But she can't hear him. She's too far, he's too quiet. What else can he do? He touches the heaving ground, pulls back. "No," he says again and again. Skingirl's disoriented. She's running the wrong way. Not past Peytr, not to the road to the highway to the markets to the corners where her kind linger in town. Not to safety in numbers. Not to people.

She runs, a blind, blooded deer, straight to the slavering herd.

"Thinking of your Ma now aren't you, Pup?"

Euri and Zaya are gone, sheltered in the safety of the past, but Peytr whispers to them still. Fervent. Furious. His 'wind lashing from the holes in his hood. The words yellow on their undersides, spotted white, and vibrating. With indignation, Peyt tells himself. Not fright. He will talk until it's all said and done. What else can he do? One man against so many. He'll just wait 'til it's over—won't be long, now—wait for the herdboys to leave. What else can he do? He'll watch, bear witness, give testimony, and remember this girl's death. His memory is long, he'll remember her for posterity. Someone has to. He can't do anything else, can he, not alone, no, not all on his own. He'll just wait. Remember. It will all be over soon.

Zigzagged scuffmarks trail across the scree, following the dogs into the gully. They've wrangled their prey back onto the footpath. Staked her out for all to see. Two pitbulls have laid claim to her ankles, pulled them as far apart as her hips will allow. Between them, Rex and Rover have mauled the skingirl free of her wire cage. Each kneeling on one of her arms, they're gnawing on her 'wind. Grunting and snuffling her terror. Pawing her breasts red. When Rover moves to do more, starts clawing at the girl's waistband, scrabbling for her cleft, Alpha boots the dog hard in the temple. Knocks his 'wind clear off its mooring, letters and punctuation bobbing loose on the breeze. Alpha kicks Rover's limp form to the side, snaps for another mutt to take his place, then leans over and tears the girl's skirts off himself. The camouflage pattern on her thighs—oval prints of yellow, blue, green—doesn't hide the pink folds and creases of her. The contrast makes them stand out even more. Soft, open targets. Weapons at the ready, the dogs clobber each other to be first to take aim.

Alpha scratches his balls. Growls everyone back—except for Pup. He fondles the kid's 'wind, whispers in his ear, then shoves him hard. The pup cries out, attempts to stand. Blood patches his little brown knees. Red grinds into the dirt as Alpha holds the kid down.

"First dibs," Peyt says. "Choicest meat. Thinking of your Ma now, Pup? What would she say? You think she's watching from over there, waiting to see how you'll treat this girl?"

Pup hesitates.

"Maybe you think it's *her*, come back to cuddle and warm you, to let you slip into her arms, those big pillows of hers plumped with life and so soft against your face. Maybe you want to nuzzle right in . . ."

And the other dogs turn to Alpha, just for a second, they turn and contemplate *really* turning, threatening, ganging up. *No fair* says the curl in their lips. *No fair* says the wrinkle in their snouts. And for a second, while the lesser, braver dogs turn, Peyt sighs, suddenly hopeful.

Do it, he thinks, and the greys pummel him, head to toe. Do it, he thinks, trying not to bite his tongue as a seizure grabs hold. Trying not to touch ground, not to be connected to the tension, the agony, the guilt coursing through the dirt. What a relief to let them do it, to be free of the responsibility of watching, to simply let Alpha go.

Alpha, so bold. With his back turned to the pack, to their fledgling, feeble betrayal. His confidence crushes theirs, postpones their mutiny. There is no later in war, Peytr thinks. Do it now. Interfere. Take him down. But doubt flickers on one mongrel mug after another. First meat is the best, their scowls agree, but sloppy seconds, thirds, fourths are better than no meat at all.

And the greys, the greys are *bruising*.

Eager for their seconds, the herdboys bark and clap and howl Pup on. They thump thump thump the kid's shoulders and butt, whooping, excited for their own turn at the hump. Pup's fumbling through it, not sure what goes where, the girl moaning and thrashing as Pup tries to fuck her, instinct-driven to pump his hips up and down, thrusting and grinding impotently through his pants. "He's too young," Peyt says, belly twisting like the skingirl, and he thinks it must hurt, pelvis smashing against pelvis, pink bits chafing against grimy denim, scalp tearing in chunks on the rough ground as she smashes and crashes and roars, and the greys jab him in place, fuckin' greys paralysing, when he should help *her, help her, fuckin' help her*, but he can't move, what can he do? He's no saint. He's no fuckin' saint.

With a resonant *crack*, a broomstick crashes over in the breeze.

Rex sags forward. Drools red on the skingirl's white breast. Mongrel laughs loud and long, calls him a slobbering hog, nudges him aside. Rex shudders, frothing at the mouth. *Crack crack!* Two more broomsticks, two more herdboys, fall. The noise ricochets around the gulch, carries with it smoke and a whiff of sulphur. Peyt's heart jackrabbits as the herdboys spin as one to face the warehouse. Peyt follows their gaze. Sees the push-broom lying, undisturbed, where it landed earlier.

Another *crack* and dust erupts near Alpha's feet. Another. Another. Shots gone wide, Peytr thinks, on purpose. Trying to distract them. To scare them. To shepherd them away from the girl. Giving her a chance. Forgotten, she gets to her knees. Worries at the knots in her bindings. Quickly gives up and begins a tripod crawl that develops into a hobbling jog away from the hounds.

"Thank you," Peyt whispers, standing. The ground is calm, steady beneath him. "Thank you." Craning through the windshield, he peers to glimpse the shooter.

Clouds steam from the Pigeon's pistol as he fires another shot. Muzzle pointed just above the herd, it shoots explosive commands. *Cease and desist! Turn around! Disperse!* The deliveryman approaches the herd cautiously, staring back at them. His uniform is garish, navy blue, pleats in the pants ironed sharp. The hood is new, denim or leather, glinting with reinforced steel. His two satchels are twice as big as Peyt's ruck, bulging with parcels. Enough for a horse to carry, but there's no horse around. Just one man and a polished word-launcher. One man against many.

"Thank you, Artie," Peytr says, digging his toes into the earth. Stability propels him from the gravel, thrums up his legs. Head clear, he swings the knapsack over his shoulder. Steady hand clutches the food bag. Get ready to go, he thinks. This will all be over soon.

The herdboys disagree.

Robbed of one snack, the dogs are keen for another. When the Pigeon breaks eye contact, looks down to reload, the pack swarms, stampedes, *pounces*. Hankering for some skin-on-skin contact. Fists on face contact. Knees in groin. Knuckles on knuckles. Feet on ribs and neck and spine and skull. . . . Now the ground quakes so violently Peyt's vision blurs. Light tunnels to a tiny circle in his sight. In it, Artie disappears, just like that, trampled under so many feet. His satchels skid to the periphery. His shining hood envelops a ball of mince. Fingers dig into the ball, dig out two white orbs, grip and pull and snap connective tendons, leave two welling black caves in the meat.

Clever hounds, says a voice, far down the dark tunnel. Wily hounds. Gouging the poor man's eyes. Using the greys as scapegoats for their crimes.

Down the tunnel, someone is screaming.

Boys shouldn't scream like that, Peytr thinks, but it's too late, the sound's out, tearing down the slope and into the gully.

Now his rucksack is open, his hands rummaging, shifting scrunched plastic bags, unworn socks, a soft red shirt, excavating an old grenade casing, one of Jean's making, and suddenly the shell's open, it's ready in his hand.

Wind whistles past Peytr's ears. Gravel becomes water and he's floating, he's sailing stormy seas, he's plunging over verges, he's cresting swells. Spewing the filthiest words into his ship's small cannon, powering full steam ahead, he launches his hatred, his remorse, his impotent rage, sees the round blackness of it soar and arc through the air, cutting through 'winds and the stolid rocks of the herd, plunging, plunging, plummeting down, making barely a splash, barely a bang, as it is swallowed by the dark waters.

The herdboys retreat as Peyt screams towards them, following his useless grenade. They take a step or two back, not far, tamping listless scattershot from their clothes. Baring yellow grins. Turning to Alpha for direction. Waiting for the order to attack.

Peytr stops, abruptly, beside the Pigeon's body. He stops no more than a metre away from the man, the dog, the leader of all these boys. Up close, his muscles are more wizened than Peyt remembers. His tanned skin gone sallow, tattooed with teeth marks and scabs. Scalp bristling with scars, a mohawk of spiked words. Lips chapped but still plump, still capable of producing the most awesome warbles. Clutching Artie's pistol, Alpha looks at Peytr, sees the bag of food shaking in his grasp, and the dog, the man, whimpers.

Around them, the herdboys fidget, hackles raised, as if sensing a shift in power. Alpha is afraid of this new dog, their posture says. Alpha is crying like an unweaned pup.

"Fuck you," Alpha says, and his voice sounds just like it always has. No trace of a stupid accent. No inbred twang. The words rasp, but the tone is perfectly familiar. "Fuck you, Peyt."

"Here," Peytr says, offering the parcel. "This is yours."

"Don't touch it," Daken barks. He turns and runs, leaving the herdboys to follow or to stay with their new Alpha. "Whatever he offers—it's poison, don't touch it!"

Tongues lolling, the herdboys look at Peytr, then look at the man he chased away. Peyt howls, throwing the food after Daken, throwing it hard as he can.

"Come back," he says, then turns on the other dogs and yells, "Get the fuck out of here." One by one they sniff the air, wrinkle their noses, turn tail. The herd scatters at his command, at the command of this strong Alpha. But Peytr doesn't feel powerful. He collapses, legs unable to hold his own weight.

Stupid, he thinks, looking at the mess he's made. What a waste.

Reaching for the Pigeon's satchels, Peytr scans the horizon for signs of the herd, for signs of leftover food, for signs of what to do next. In the rush, the dogs have left all the parcels behind, papered boxes scrawled with names and addresses, places to go wrapped up in string. He bends, rounds them up, brushes off the dirt. There's room in these packs for a week's eating, he thinks, refilling the bags. Slinging them across his shoulders. The straps pull but he doesn't slouch. There's a reassuring heft in the weight, in pockets bulging with purpose. It's too late for night work, Peyt thinks as the sky is soaked in charcoal. It's too late for gathering, but not for delivering. Adjusting his load, Peyt scopes the tenements for signs of life. Dogs bark in the hollows, unseen, unthreatening. The greys pinch Peyt's legs, urging him to *go . . . go . . . go . . .*

Gravel rumbles beneath his bare feet as he turns around, and goes.

On both sides of the driveway the front yard is already riddled with holes, so Jean decides to head out back. After kicking the dirt off her treaders, she cuts through the house, passing the den with its dusty couches and cold hearth, pausing by the formal living room. In her usual place by the picture window, the silent watcher stands, up to the ankles in a mound of grief. Woes too hard to bear remain on the floor, but so many—too many, Jean thinks—find their way back into the woman's system, soaked through skin and spirit.

"Can I get you anything, Ann?" she asks quietly. "Cup of warmth?"

Was that a nod? Jean waits, running her fingers over carved lines laddered into the door jamb, the children's names and ages scrawled beside their heights. Peyt's was always a good few inches shorter than Daken's, no matter how he stretched his little neck when she rested the ruler on his crown, no matter how liberal she was with the measurements. Just below, the girls' last gouges are primed to overtake their brother's highest mark—but really, Jean thinks, it's been such a long while since they butted heels against the baseboards, so long since they got that dandruff of paint-scratchings in their hair, that by now they've both probably outgrown him.

"All right," Jean says, pushing away from the wall. Ann glances over her shoulder, seeing but not really acknowledging. Blinking through a haze of 'wind, she blows clumps of letters away from her eyes. They drift, thick as musk, on streaks of pale blue angling through the window. Words too raw and personal for Jean to feel comfortable reading.

"I'll make us some soup in an hour or so. Holler if you need me."

That was a nod. The quick movement dislodges a tumble of unbearable, unspeakable thoughts, adding them to the jumble at Ann's feet.

In the kitchen, Jean takes one of Borys' old boilersuits off a hook by the door and jerks it on over her khakis and blouse. The briefing in town had taken longer than expected; she'd raced home from gov't house, hoping to arrive before Borys had woken for work—but his room was long cold when she got there, the bed empty, blankets taut with hospital corners. Another parcel left for her on the hallstand, special delivery. Another payment for her promise. Beneath the coveralls, Jean's best downtown outfit is sweat-stained for no good reason, clammy in the folds and creases. She tightens the belt, tucks the tail into a loop to keep it from flapping. No point changing into scruffier clothes, she thinks, when the nice ones are already so dirty. No use ruining them either, just because they're starting to stink.

Waste not, want not, as Captain Len used to say. Jean always agreed with her dad in principle, but the expression irked—still irks—whenever she heard it. We're all built to want, she thinks, unlatching the back door and propping it open, then grabbing a basket and trowel off the counter. Everyone dreams of something brighter. Something better.

Leading a good life is about more than just survival.

Bells strung on the door handle inside shout with brass tongues as Jean shuts the house up behind her. Outside, chimes jingle on the eaves and barbed wire scritches around every boarded window; but the bells are loudest, their yammering brash and insistent. The instant a grey creeper tries to sneak in—the very instant—Jean's pistol will be out of the basket and in her hand. Firing true, the way Captain Len taught.

Posture, Jeanie. Posture. Shoulders back. Chin lifted.

She can still feel the pressure of her dad's strong hands pushing, spine straightening. The knock of his boot between hers, widening her stance. Moving down the line, first to Wyatt then to Hap, correcting her brothers' positions before letting any of them shoot.

If you can't keep a book balanced on your noggin 'til the clip's empty, you're doing it wrong. Sometimes, to prove the point, he'd fetch a set of hardbacks from the living room shelves. Nudging 'winds aside, he'd slip a volume on each of their heads then tell them to take aim. *First to let it drop takes point on tonight's sweep*.

Hours passed. Blisters formed on trigger fingers. Rage and desperation were rolled into pellets, crammed into bullet casings, shoved into clips and barrels. Wooden silhouettes set up in the yard took a pounding, the grey-painted figures reduced to kindling by day's end. Stomachs rumbled, but the kids wouldn't stop shooting unless Cap's 'wind flicked them, flapping like a chequered flag. Chins up, shoulders back, they trained their thoughts, aimed, fired until they were told otherwise. Through it all books wobbled in a storm of powder and 'wind, but none fell.

Jean chuckles, thinking back on it. It's been ages since she's tasted that kind of fear, since she smelled the sulphur of it. Things are no safer these days, really. She knows that. She's seen the damage those grey bastards keep doing to her land, to her own people. Take a look at Borys, she thinks. Take a look at Peyt. But now, kneeling at the edge of the path that leads across their small, packed-dirt yard, digging into the earth, trowel rubbing the itch from her scarred palms, Jean is calm. Change is coming.

Big—monumental—change.

And she will make it happen.

For the first time, Jean feels crucial. She's in control of what's to come. When called, she'll go, join the marked forces, make use of her training, fight with body and 'wind—and she'll be one of the last to die. After she's gone, there will be no more nightly air raids, no more surprise attacks in the marketplace, no more children slaughtered in schools, no more mothers snatched from their own farmyards while hanging laundry out to dry. There will be an end. Ridiculous claims will be silenced, endless grey complaints drowned out by the singing roar of human voices.

This land is our land . . .

There will be no need for recon missions, once VERNA's screamed her piece. No need for home searches. No need for a bunch of kids to sweep the paddocks each evening before bed, checking for grey slinkers, vainly looking for signs of returned captives.

Greys are too greedy to release POWs, Jean thinks. They keep whatever they've stolen.

Gravel gouges her knees as she digs. Jabbing the point down, uprooting hunks of clay. Setting them aside until she's excavated a series of holes, each the depth and width of a balled fist. The trowel shunts in and out, ringing metallic, shifting dirt with a familiar rhythm. One-two, one-two, it beats the ground like her treaders used to when true-dark fell, Wyatt and Hap's feet clomping close behind.

Cap knew how much we dreaded going first into those fields, she thinks. Being first to maybe find Ma's body.

Despite gov't warnings, Len Andrews grew barley, crops thick and high enough to hide an invading army on the land round their farm—but the profit, he'd said, was worth the risk of attack. In one good season, they'd kitted Wyatt out for the war. A few years later, Hap had himself some brand new gear to replace the second-hand. And by her fifteenth birthday, Jean had wagonloads of iron in the smithy Cap had built out back. The shells she'd forged were strong but lightweight. Small enough to sit in a child's palm. Perfectly lethal. But even armed with pistols and grenades, traipsing through rows of shadow-thick barley had been worse than nightmares. Breath was gale-loud in the darkness, rasping from open mouths. Tears had streamed from eyes too afraid to blink. Two minutes in, the boys had needed to stop and piss out their jitters. Jean had kept watch, spying greys through rippling stalks.

Over there, she'd whispered, hammer cocked. Sifting through the rows, the greys had been impossible to get a fix on; the harder she'd stared, the more her focus had blurred. Like flare-auroras, the bastards were all a-shimmer, not a straight or clear line about them.

That's some camo they got on, Wyatt had said.

You sure it's even them?

Hap's eyes always were bad, Jean thinks, taking a loaded mine from her basket and lowering it into a fresh hole. Loosely packing gravel around it, she unfurls a length of tripwire and carefully loops it around the firing pin. With a deftness that would've made Cap proud, she smooths dry soil overtop, masking the dip in the ground. Gently, so gently, she moves to the next hollow and repeats the process, planting and stringing the first line of explosives together with a near-invisible string.

After leaning close to tie off the last mine in the row, Jean sits back on her heels, wipes her brow. Sweat trickles down her temples and in the runnels beside her nose; green glints off droplets caught in her lashes, vision sparkling as flares arc through the darkening sky. Quick-scrubbing her eyes, she wonders how Hap managed to survive so long on the front. For five years and twice as many tours, her baby brother had laid traps for the greys without once admitting he was half-blind. Refusing to wear the specs Jean bought, Hap had sent them back wrapped in blank paper, a curt message parcelled on the Pigeon's tongue.

Nothing to see out here, Jeanie.

Still, she knows he was wrong. The greys had been there all those nights in the paddocks—she's absolutely positive—they'd been there in the mornings when she pushed the plough, blades tearing into hidden bodies, mules' hoofs crushing buried skulls. Cap always said the bastards tunnelled shallow as well as deep; they'd win ground however they could, he'd said, from above and below. While gathering the harvest Jean had trod over them, just waiting for a hand to burst from the soil and snatch at her ankle, a sharp-toothed mouth to chew through the dirt and snare her with guttural spells. She'd felt their bones breaking as she fled the field, they were that close to the soles of her feet.

Of the three of them, Hap was the stubborn child. Rejecting bare truth, he went to war for his own reasons. For Ma's memory, maybe. For Len's sake. Jean was never really sure why Hap joined the fray—he'd never had Wyatt's passion for it. He'd never had Jean's conviction. Five years, ten tours, without a break in between. Without once getting a clear look at the greys before they'd swept him.

Jean had wanted to enlist. She'd been a skinny kid, but was strong from pushing the plough, stronger still from the rigours of Captain Len's training. Her aim was solid—she could shoot the pressboard cut-out through the eye from fifty paces—and her throwing arm was unmatched. Wyatt and Hap were decent shots, but they didn't have Jean's feel for glowing cherries or her skill with burrowing beetles.

Brushing dirt from her coveralls, Jean stands, twisting to ease the twinge in her back. For years, Cap had them practise with clods of earth before giving them live shells to throw. *Don't let that coin burn a hole in your pocket*, he'd say, winking as he placed 'crackers behind their ears. Sparking the long fuses, Cap judged the kids' technique in scooping 'wind, throwing fire. With the hiss of flame racing toward their faces, all three of them had learned fast.

Smooth motions, Cap'd say. *Scalp and grab, cock-and-lock, flow-and-throw.*

Bending over, Jean scrapes up a handful of clay. The damp coolness soothes her palms; the incisions itch, forever reopening, forever healing. Slow inhale, slow exhale. She rolls the muck into a compact ball, gaze soft, focusing on the black Xs spray-painted onto low concrete wall fencing the yard. Smooth motions, she thinks, breathing out, throwing.

Again, she hears Cap say.

She bends, scrapes, centres, throws—

Again.

Not moving left or right, staying on the firm path, she lobs lump after lump—

Again.

Shoulders throbbing, eyebrows and temples smooth-shining with old scars, Jean hits every target, spattering the wall until Xs become Ys or stunted Vs. She throws to keep sharp. To make her 'wind simmer. To vent suppressed frustrations.

Jean had wanted to enlist.

She'd had Len's permission—no, more: she'd had his blessing. With Wyatt, she'd volunteered at the draft; Hap wasn't yet ready, their dad had said. The bub would follow next round, maybe the round after that. Fair enough, Jean remembers thinking. Len had always been fair.

At headquarters, the Caps took in Wyatt's fine gear and muscular build and gave him diamond-marked infantry papers. Brow furrowed, her brother's smile had faded when the officers directed Jean to the airfield. "But she's an ace grenadier," he'd started, soon stifled by high-ranking glares. "She's light and wiry," came the terse reply. Ticking boxes and stamping Jean's papers with a wavy blue icon that looked, unnervingly, like a mop, the Cap had instructed: "Follow the guywires to the north end of camp. Join the other ship-monkeys."

But when she'd got there the flyers didn't need any more cleaners, slim or not, so they scribbled amendments on her ID and sent her to the corrals—where the muckers took one look at her and pointed to the mess hall. "Horses'll chomp a bit like you," the tar-spitting stableboys had teased. "Them arms of yers'd do a fair bit of damage on the pots, mind."

Thinking on it now, again, gets Jean's wordwind firing afresh. The backyard resounds with *thwaps* and *smacksmacksmacks* as she throws her anger at the wall. Decades later, it still burns that the cooks wouldn't take her—"Nothing personal, love," they'd said, sweating behind boiling saucepans, puff-headed in greasy shower-caps. "Got a new squad of stumpies in last week; they legs ain't worth shit, but they sure can stir the fuck outta Barge's gruel. Don't need any extra limbs round here at the mo." It still burns how there'd been nothing else for it, no other options. If Jean hadn't wanted to just turn-tail and go home, if she was to get any time in action, time to prove her worth, time to bag some greys—she'd have to accept the only job left open. The lowest role. The most demeaning.

Wearing mask and camo, she'd plug wounds instead of inflict them. Drive the corpse-wagon. Drag a one-man stretcher. Not fighting, but fixing up those who did. Not acting, reacting. Not leading the attack—following as a red-starred field nurse, third class, medcorps.

Len never would've forgiven her, if he'd found out. His daughter, a *medic*. In her father's mind, there was a hierarchy of achievement that peaked at killing and troughed at death. The Andrews, he'd thought, were like warriors of old: fighting in the high season, farming in the low. It wasn't for them to weave bandages or set bones; their priority was to spill enough blood to justify the soppers' existence.

"Tag-alongs, the lot of them," he'd explain, pointing to an illustration of stretcher-bearers in one of his many books. At night, after patrolling their acreage, Jean and her brothers would sit at Len's feet, soak the chill from their souls with cups of hot stock, and listen, rapt as he read aloud.

What a collection Dad had, she thinks, looking up to gauge the depth of steel in the sky, reckoning there's still time to dig another line of defence. Ann will be needing supper soon, she thinks, moving no further than the next unworked plot. In neighbouring houses, lamps begin to set windows aglow, yellow rectangles and orange squares flickering to life in the murk of twilight. Such dull hues, Jean thinks, putting her shovel to work. This weak sunset has nothing on the pictures in Len's precious books. Each cover was marked with bold symbols, icons with changeable meanings. Inside, pages were plastered with drawings, cuttings and slogans. *Stop the Spread* typed beneath a map of their country, the ragged borders blurred by grey arrows moving in from abroad. *We'll finish what they started* ran alongside an advertisement for grade-A lassos and wire snares to enhance 'windlashes. Grey creatures with hooked noses and dripping red maws crept down suburban streets, carrying a froth of eyes on their backs, a whole spectrum of irises gleaming from the page. Sketched in a bungalow with one see-through wall, a little girl just like Jeanie had binoculars raised, pointed at the creeper; in a speech bubble above her daddy's head, the slogan *See Something? Say Something* floated up to the triangle roof. But Jeanie's all-time favourite had been a two-page diagram in a thin hardcover, vibrant in shades of green, instructing soldiers on effective 'wind-loading techniques. *Because they won't shoot themselves.*

"Why do the greys hate us? What did we ever do to them?" Jeanie had asked once, tone even, refusing to sound bewildered. She'd wanted facts, plain and simple. Good intel makes the best weapon,

Captain Len had always said—but at night it wasn't Captain Len who regaled them with bedtime tales; it was plain Len, their peg-legged worry-lined old man. His advice was molasses: sweet but slow in coming.

"Depends on who's telling the story," Len had said. And though Jeanie had seen the set of his jaw, the *that's enough* twist to his mouth, the questions had kept gushing out.

"But what if they've changed their minds? What if they're attacking now only because *we're* attacking? What if they've surrendered, maybe offered a truce, and we missed it 'cause we don't speak the same language? What if they're already gone? What if we got them all without realising? What if we're just shooting other people now, thinking they're greys, and they're shooting us for the same reason? What if we're wrong, Len? What if we're wrong."

"Wash that filth out yer mouth," Len had said. Wyatt and Hap had blanched, eyes wide, breath frozen in their chests. Light-headed, Jeanie had tried to laugh it off. Thoughts tumbling fast, full-joshing, her 'wind sketched jokes about chains being yanked, legs being pulled, knees being slapped. *Wink-winks* spun round the living room, feeble and pink. *Nudge-nudges* jabbed Len in the ribs, failing to make him smile.

Stupid kid, she thinks. Pathetic. With moves like that, no wonder she'd been relegated to the red-stars. In hindsight, Jean can clearly see Jeanie's weaknesses. Naïveté. Ambition. An eagerness to please. Jeanie didn't have the control Jean now has, the power to protect her family, to give them a future.

Jeanie had deserved Len's scorn, although he'd never crowned her with that particular wreath of thorns. As far as Captain Len had known, his daughter had been a top-notch grenadier for almost a year, destroying hordes of greys, diffusing their tricks and magic. And Wyatt hadn't had a chance to disabuse him of this fancy. Oh, her big brother knew the truth all right. Jeanie'd lost count of the number of times he'd ignored her on the field, in the mess tent, at assemblies on base. Like Hap, Wyatt could see without seeing. Even when he was snagged on a grey IED, legs blown clear off and guts spilling from the canyon in his belly, even when Jeanie had loaded his half-self onto a gurney and carried him off the field—not bump-and-dragging, *carrying* with smooth motions—even when she'd laid him gently under a tenement's gutted stoop, when she'd dripped water between his frothing lips, when she'd cooed, "Shhhhhhh, shhhhhhh," and stroked his pale cheek, when she'd covered his nose and mouth with a chloroformed rag, pressing firmly down, whispering "Hush, now. You'll give away our position," as they waited for the greys to do their worst and move on—even then, *even then*, Wyatt had looked at her, eyes glazed with disappointment.

Not that she blames him.

It's almost gone true-dark. Too late now for rigging mines, but Jean's got enough pump left in her arms to turn a bit more ground. Less than a quarter of the yard is fortified; the front is good and set, but it's the back that's got her worried. Everyone knows the greys prefer stealth—why hadn't she started the dig out here?—and if she gets the PM's call before her work is finished, she'll have to leave when the house is still vulnerable. Little Zaya has a knack with knives—but with Ann being Ann and Borys being Borys, one girl with a blade probably won't be enough to keep them alive until VERNA can save them.

Just a few more holes, Jean decides. In the morning I'll fill them properly, once Borys is asleep and Ann is back at her post. As she crosses the path, a chorus of Mee-Mees screams overhead; out of habit, she crouches, grabs the pistol from her basket and jams it into her belt. Heart pounding, she counts the beats between holler and impact. *One. . . . Two. . . . Three. . . . Four. . . . Five. . . .* Once she reaches twelve without hearing thunder, she shakes the nerves from her limbs, chiding herself for acting like such a blue-head.

The bastards have set their sights East, she chortles, relief making her giddy. Shells clink together as she moves the basket, knees popping as she lowers herself down beside it. Scanning the yard, Jean squints at pooling shadows, looks for aurora shimmers out the corner of her eye.

"You fuckers keep back now," she whispers, patting the butt of her gun. "I'm quicker than I look."

Taunting, the brass bells on the back door jingle.

Posture, Jeanie—

Smooth motions—

Cock-and-lock—

Without hesitation, Jean whips to the right. She draws her gun fluidly. Aims. Pulls the trigger. Fires.

The doorframe erupts at shoulder height, bullet-hole smoking. The bare bulb over the stoop blinks on, casting stark white light down on empty steps. There's no grey corpse, no shriek of pain. Just Ann Miller in her ragged nightie, hands lifted in surrender, bleeding from the peppering of shrapnel embedded in her cheek. Crimson beads well and drip down her neck, but Ann doesn't wipe them. 'Wind startled, motionless, she stares at Jean in disbelief.

"Marten would go fuckin' nuts if he came home after all this time and found his wife dead, Jeanie. After all this time. All this time . . ."

Cold as Jean's fingers, the pistol thuds on the ground.

"Ann," she says quietly, 'wind roiling with confusion. "Oh, Ann."

I missed—

I missed—

I missed.

Ann softens, slumps into her housecoat. She filches a hankie from her drooping pocket, holds it up. Blood soaks into her collar while the tissue stalls a foot away from her face. Her hands and voice tremble. "The hour's gone charcoal, Jean. Come inside. I peeled us some carrots, but you have to do the chopping."

Jean nods—*I missed*—and nods—*I missed*—and makes no move to get up.

"Grab the med-kit from the bathroom," she finally manages. "I'll be there in a sec, promise. I'll fix you right up in a sec."

Once a medic, always a medic.

Jean winces as brass bells signal Ann's retreat.

Grabbing the gun, she packs the chamber full of her doubts. Things will change once VERNA calls. Everything will change. No longer a healer, she is a *weapon*. Taking and releasing a deep breath, she hears Len's calm instructions, steady and reassuring.

Posture, Jeanie. Posture.

Shoulders back.

Chin lifted.

Turning to face the night, Jean widens her stance. She points the gun's muzzle at moving shadows, grits her teeth, and empties her clip.

The warfare heretofore waged against the demon, has, somehow or other, progressed for centuries without betterment, without gain.

Daily, the enemy's numbers are swelled by the additions of fifties, of hundreds, and of thousands. The cause itself is reduced to cold abstract theories—the presence or absence of voices in the ether; invisible lines on territories long pounded to dust—while its effect is a living, breathing, active, and powerful foe, ever going forth conquering and to conquer. Ancient cities, valleys, glades and peaks are daily being stormed and dismantled, daily desecrated and deserted. The blare of invading armies sounds from hill to hill, from sea to sea, and from land to land, calling millions to their standard at a blast.

Here, now, are the ministers of human fate, of change, of conclusions.

Here, now, is opportunity.

Dwell no more on *right* and *wrong*, on *fair* or *unfair*, on what *has* or *has not* been done. Avoid the torment of what-might-have-beens—to have expected *them* to act otherwise than they have—to have expected them not to meet bullet with bullet, shell with shell, corpse with corpse—was to expect a reversal of their nature, which, after all that has and has not been done, can clearly never be reversed.

Burst the fetters that bind to what was, to what forever has been; turn away from *then*, away from *now*; stand tall and gaze beyond the miseries once endured; observe how easily they can all be undone, once it has finally been resolved to undo them.

Look further. Look longer. Look at what can and will come *after*.

Let every last eye be raised, far-seeing, fixed on that victory.

'The Ministers of Human Fate'; hand unknown
Bibliotheca 31.7833° N, 35.2167° E
Ballpoint on foolscap, c. Evac.St.25 ±.

Lately, Peyt finds it hard, telling the difference between ghosts and greys.

When he'd snuck home the other night, last week, last year, the house had been full of both. Small shades in his old room had pretended to be sleeping girls. Down the hall his father's bed was empty, a dark echo of his body pressed deep into the quilt. In the living room a spectre hovered by the window. Her cloudy hands were frigid, reaching, blind-searching his face. Such a searing cold, that touch, like ice-water trickling over his nose, his eyes, his naked brow. Frozen, he'd suffered it—until the greys started slapping. Full-palmed beatings around his ears and neck and head. Flinching, Peyt had dropped to his knees beside a set of blurred bare feet. Arms held up, protecting. Then the pounding stopped quick as it started, but Peyt didn't trust it was over. He stayed balled on the floor, dazed and gasping, his 'wind knocked senseless. After a minute, he'd tried to straighten. Swayed. Clutched at nightgowned legs. It's me, he'd thought. He'd mouthed. *It's me, Mrs. M. It's me.*

She'd drifted away without answering, arms listless by her sides.

I'm so sorry, Peyt had thought, teetering to stand. Afraid to touch the couch, the coffee table, the laddered shelf strewn with knick-knacks. He'd made himself small, clutching the twin satchels slung across his shoulders, hugging them close to his chest. He'd kept away from the walls. Kept his head low. As he'd made for the door, the greys mimicked his ragged breaths. He'd heard them panting in the hall.

"What are you doing here?"

Peyt had stopped. Tensed. Crushed the bags in his arms. Resisted plugging his ears. This was the greys' favourite game, Cap once told him. The fuckers loved whispering from shadows. Taunting with familiar voices. Getting into yer head.

"You look awful, Peytie." The grey peeled away from the doorjamb leading into the hall. It took a single step forward, tread silent. Wan yellow light streaked in through the living room window; the streetlamp outside was mostly obscured by a new skybunker piling planted on their front lawn. Words buzzed out of the darkness, briefly glinting like firebugs before being snuffed by the gloom. "Where've you been all this time? No, wait. Don't tell me. I don't want to know."

"I can't see you." Peyt hated the whine in his tone. "I can't hear you."

"Borys said you'd turned coward." The grey shifted to its left. A hand floated into sight, a forearm. Numbers swarmed around them, serial, encoded. Grey numbers cut into the shade's palm. Blood numbers. "I couldn't believe it. No way, I told him. Not *my* son."

Peyt closed his eyes.

"And now here you are. In the flesh." The grey's voice was even. Tired. Cruelly dispassionate. Leaning further into the light, it scratched its palm absentmindedly. "Never pegged you as a traitor," it said. "Always thought you'd be there when the war ended."

Behind Peyt's lids was an endless fog.

"I'm lost," he'd said. "Ma—"

"It's late, Peytie," she'd said. "Get going. You know you can't be found here."

Now, clad in old coveralls, camo, steel-woven leather hood, Peyt crouches in the ditch that was once Town Hall. Every few seconds he peers over the giant clock tilted against the pit's edge. Inhales dust and word-dander off the roadside: 'e's and 'o's and long streams of 'a's. A few 'r's. A throatful of fallen sighs. Pulling the neck of his t-shirt over his nose, he rubs his watering eyes. Holds his breath, looks up, and watches. There it is again, *there*: a shadow flitting near that mound of wreckage across the street. Peyt follows its movements, Jean's voice echoing in his mind. *What are you doing here? What are you doing here?* She's right, of course. It's mid-morning, downtown. Too late and too early for ghosts.

Must be a grey, then.

He lowers his head, clings to the clock's II and IV, and hopes the dead Pigeon's gear on his back will fade him from the little spirit's sight.

A minute passes. Acid burns in his muscles, but he holds the position, head down, cowering, arms locked, satchels pinned beneath him, parcels digging into his ribs. He waits until the trembling loosens his grip, until the gaze boring into his skull becomes solid steel, a rifle's cold muzzle driven into his scalp, until he hears the trigger click-clicking under a thin grey finger, and he thinks, I won't die without seeing who's killed me—

He looks up.

A gentle breeze cools the red from his face. There is no gun. No trigger. The spook is perched on a raised planter, a long fast-sprint away. It's grubbing in dark soil, piling the dirt higher and higher. Patting the conical heap with its little hands. Pouring water from a small two-handled clay jug. Tamping the muck, then digging again. Streaking its skirt with mud castle run-off.

The sky is translucent, the cloud cover streaky and thin, illuminated white from behind. Air raids have softened the cityscape below, transformed it into something almost pastoral. High-rises and spires have blunted into hills. Sidewalks have sprouted rainbow-sheened ponds. Column-fronted buildings line the central plaza, grand shells of marble and limestone and jet. Toppled lampposts fence in the three sides of the square, confining benches and huddled corpses, their backs woolly with debris. In the middle, a twenty-foot statue looms before the museum. And over it all, a haze hangs like a sheer gauze curtain, blurring details, fooling the eye. One minute, Peyt sees herdboys gathering at the jade martyr's base. Then it's a platoon of grunts. He blinks and it's neither. It's garbage tossed on the wind.

Vultures have ravaged this quadrant, beaked its bones clean. They spray-painted big pink circles around suspected landmines, barricaded the main roads, then ceded ground to the greys. There are no patrols here, which suits Peyt just fine. He has packages to deliver, socks and harmonicas and silencers, gold rings and worry-stones and a flak jacket he's tempted to keep for himself. His ruck's filled with food—some for drop-off, some for payment—and his mind's full of messages too mundane to be written, too unimportant to warrant hiring a Whitey. It's safer, taking this route. Regardless of what other Pigeons say. He'd rather run the grey gauntlet downtown every day than risk losing his load to dogs and soldiers and ghosts.

Keeping an eye on the little spirit, Peyt searches his packs for a bundle of a certain shape, a certain weight. . . . His fingers brush sharp edges and smooth, cardboard boxes and clothing, until they encounter the hard fact of paper-wrapped metal. There's always at least one, he thinks, taking it out and worrying at the parcel's string with his teeth. Laying the wrapping aside—he's only borrowing the gun, not stealing—Peyt takes a scope from his pocket. Wishes he had the Pigeon's glock to go with it. Wishes so hard that soon he plucks a rage of bullets from his 'wind. Enough to load the pistol, with ammo to spare. He braces the gun against the clock's rim. Balances the scope atop its barrel, cocks the hammer, and aims.

The child's head whips up. Through the crosshairs Peyt sees her in profile, quickly wiping hands on her skirt then lifting them, all innocence, all surrender. Her expression guilt-free. She hops down from the container, lands awkwardly. Legs buckling, she falls. Skinning knees and palms. Her face shrivels and the black hole of her mouth gapes. Five seconds later, a monotone wail ribbons across the plaza: shock, pain, defeat.

Peyt starts to climb over the ridge to help her—then freezes. Kneeling, the girl reaches with both arms for something, someone. Panning right, he follows her gaze. Across a cobbled walkway and down a paved slope, over iron railings and along a sprint of flagstones to the museum. There: crawling out of a window well. Ducking under reams of yellow tape. A young woman with the most vibrant wordwind Peyt's ever seen. She's tried taming it with a blue headscarf, but as she runs the silk slips to her shoulders, unveiling a flurry of panic. Wisps of dark blonde hair get caught in the storm, words and strands spiral into a frantic beehive. Mid-stride she beckons, urging movement—but the girl has sunk to the ground, bowing, a supplicant to misery. She weeps and whines until the woman scoops her up, hugging and scolding and dragging.

They make it halfway to the museum when the child digs in her heels, wriggles free. She dashes back to the planter—doesn't want to leave her castle half-finished, Peyt thinks—and when the woman gives chase, the girl screeches with laughter. Dodging left and right, around benches and bodies, she turns fear into a game.

Tessa! the older one shouts, cheeks flaming. Enough! Come on, Tess—

"NO!"

Both stop short at the sound of Peyt's shriek. The girl poised on the brink of a fluorescent pink circle, the woman an arm-swipe behind her.

"Get back," he shouts, firing the gun skywards. "It's a mine! Get back!"

It's . . . mine. . . . Get. . . . It's . . . mine!

Before bolting, they look around for a split-second. Spinning left and right. Trying to make sense of the echoes. Trying to guess where the next shot will come from. Ducking out of sight, Peyt fires again. Again. Again. He knows it's a risk—the greys love the reek of bullets almost as much as they do sweat and blood and fear—but he keeps shooting until the magazine is empty.

Let them come, he thinks. Only let the girls get away.

They're not your problem, he tells himself the next day.

Forget them: you're going to miss the train.

Stations, Peyt quickly realised, are the best places for scoring jobs. Ship 'ports are too busy, too dangerous for someone like him—too many recruitment officers roaming the gates, too many Watchers checking bags and features and passports. Relocating landed immigrants. Detaining nomads and evacs. Re-conscripting wayward rookies, with or without their consent. Wrangling turncoats and suspected AWOLs. Peyt had tossed his red-star papers somewhere between the barracks and the open road, but the motley of his skin is ID enough. His was a hard face to forget.

Within a few hours of enlisting, most grunts in his district had known him by reputation if not by name. They'd known him as the squadron's cum-faced corpse-runner, the youngest, the most likely to bolt. Straight off, Cap had plucked him from the ranks and called him Atlas. Said there was a whole unexplored world mapped on his body. It seemed everyone but Peyt had heard the joke that followed; but he got it, more or less, when tongues had prodded cheeks, hands dog-slapped imaginary arses, fists whacked-off empty air. The dumbest fucks in the troop had worked up a thick foam of spit, letting it dribble down their chins while Peyt stood there fuming. They'd nicknamed him Jizz and Cock-froth and Codpiece, and thought they were so fuckin' clever. And Daken had laughed with the rest of them. Later, lying on their cots after lights-out, he'd chuckled again and Peyt had felt like sinking through canvas and groundsheet, into the tunnels, into the dead earth. But then Dake had reached over and ruffled Peyt's hair. Tweaked his hot ear. Called him Dalmatian.

Now Peyt rarely works the 'ports. He does most of his pick-ups at velo stands, twice-a-day hubs and, when the shadows are quiet, train platforms. Business is better with fewer eyes watching, safer without so many soldiers around. Guys like Cap don't often ride steam. Out on the front, they'll cosy up with grunts and evacs alike—a warm body's a warm body, after all. Never hurt a soul to be fuckin' friendly. Off-field though, they'll clean the curses from their mouths, trade multicams for crisp polyester suits, and play rich until their leave passes expire. Busy spending a year's salary on cunt and glass and lexis-massages, Caps have little time for the grubs that wriggled after them out of the trenches.

At the station, the train's been and gone but Peyt earns a small crop of turnips and just enough change to buy a plate of hot pide for breakfast. A tear-stained girl hires him to deliver a flaking gold ring to an address in the valley. "If he's not there," she says, voice wavering, "smash a window or something and just chuck it inside."

"That's not how this works." If there are guidelines somewhere, headquarters with procedures and regulations, definitions of Pigeon conduct, Peyt hasn't seen them. What's left of his predecessor is rotting in a shallow grave; this past year, no one has come searching for bones. No high-ups have been there to answer Peyt's questions—or to question his taking Artie's place. Since then, he's made up the rules as he goes. He does what he can. "Whatever can't be delivered is returned. Usually within three days. My bags get too heavy otherwise."

"Don't bother," the girl says. "Keep it, for your trouble. Sell it. Makes no difference to me."

Along with the broken engagement, Peyt collects three condolences, two apologies, and a handful of *please-don't-gos*. But when a rosette vendor starts prattling a detailed order for bunting, Peyt waves him quiet. No verbal messages today.

The man takes in Peyt's appearance. The distant gaze. The overly-tight hood. A scarf pulled up to the nose. *The boy's hiding summat*, the vendor's 'wind broadcasts. He cocks his head, jowls wobbling. Winks and taps the side of his bulbous red nose. *Been on the turps, have we?*

For all the quease in his guts, the haze in his thoughts, Peyt might as well be drunk. The little ghost's—the little girl's—scream has been repeating in his mind, a circular saw whining round and round his brain all night, slicing, scraping him raw. And the older girl's face . . .

I didn't mean to scare them.

Coins suddenly leave his hand, soon replaced by a large rosette. A boutonniere, striped in alternating colours: one row flare green, the next a perfect shade of screen-blue. Stupid to buy such a pretty, feminine thing, Peyt thinks. Without someone to give it to.

They're not your problem, he tells himself, jamming the thing into his pocket as he leaves the station. They're not your problem. He takes to the oldest avenues, the widest, the most vacant. Jogs down open-air colonnades. Cobbled broadways. Tumbledown messes of ancient stone. He travels east, always east, into the mortared tomb of his city, aiming for its dead fringes, far from the living west. His legs take him far as they can get from bungalows and suburbs, from the twelve-sided front, from codenamed operations, from boys and

Caps and weapons and that hideous mistake of a stadium. Guilty, he runs. Away—and to.

No, they're not your problem.

But the voice in his head is riddled with bullet holes, and the woman's face—her lovely round face—flashes with each remembered shot. It didn't show fear, Peyt realises. It was sharp with curiosity, hurt, anger.

Not your problem, he thinks again and again, now standing in front of the museum, reaching for a clay jug half-buried in a mud castle. *This* is what the child was running back for yesterday, this chipped hunk of terracotta, its athletic black gods mucked-over with tiny fingerprints.

Peyt turns the amphora in his hands, brushes it off. She'll miss it again soon enough, he thinks, propping it on the planter's rim. A minute's fossicking in his satchel produces two beets, three onions and a bouquet of carrots—a pathetic offering, but he hates to leave more in case the local herd sniffs it out first. The vegetables fill the vase nicely. Before retreating, Peyt packs its base in the dirt to keep it from tipping.

Then he settles in behind the martyr's plinth, scopes the museum's foundations. Waits for someone hungry enough to come out.

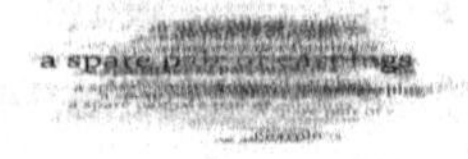

Maybe they're dead in there.

The clouds are gleaming pewter on top, grey fluff below, wisped with dreams of blue. A watery sun swims through the sky, its fat silver belly sinking as it runs out of puff. Wan light softens the museum's stone façade; the proud towers capped with saw-toothed pinnacles, the tall mullioned windows, the imposing double doors surrounded by row after row of carved arches—they're all vague impressions of grandeur glimpsed across the plaza, recalled more than seen. Peyt's gaze slides across finer details, falling instead on featureless patches of black near the ground. That gap is where the woman came from yesterday. At least, he thinks it might've been that one. Scope raised, he flicks from rupture to gash but can't penetrate the darkness. His calves are cramped from crouching and there's a kink in his neck that aches down to the collarbone. The statue's plinth has leached all warmth from his side, but he continues to lean against it, elbows on knees, shoulders bunched. A huge knot ties his stomach to his spine; it tightens with each passing minute.

Maybe they're hurt, he thinks, not for the first time. Maybe I hit one of them—or both. *Not both, please.* . . . They'd ghosted before he'd finally come to his senses, the gun hot in his shaking hands. *Please.* . . . Again, he scans flagstones and slope for signs of blood. Again he finds nothing but rocks and dust.

Maybe they need a stretcher. He clenches instinctively, gripping invisible steel handles. Maybe it's not too late . . .

Joints creaking, he shifts his weight, stamps life back into his feet. The dull thudding carries across the square, comes back redoubled. It's well past noon: surely they'd be hungry by now. Two girls alone, living in a squat—an impressive squat, he'll admit, but still a squat—is about survival, dirty and basic. No way they've got a cold-box in there, and food goes off so fast in the dank. . . . Surely they'd have come out for a morning scrounge, or at least a trip to the pumps.

That's it, he thinks, half-standing, slinging his packs. Either they're dead, or there's another way out.

Why hadn't he thought of that before? He starts punching the pins and needles from his calves, harder than necessary. Experienced squatters hole-up in rundowns with debris piled high around them, counting on bricks and trash to play guard while they sleep, blocking all entrances but one. But these girls must be new to the circuit; evacs who've only just lost their homes, who think stone walls mean protection, who don't realise many easy exits are far more dangerous than none.

Look at all those windows. . . . Hundreds of open invitations to the greys.

Peyt shakes his head. Legs still tingling, he stops. Listens. Anywhere else, the spill of pebbles would've been inaudible, the careful footsteps lost in everyday hustle. But this square was designed with performances in mind, the buildings positioned for amplification, to maximise reverberation. Peyt remembers coming here, ages ago, for school. Learning about the architect, who'd died penniless in a Lunar Street Asylum, and about the jade martyr, first in a long line of ossified men. Ma had chaperoned—for once—with Euri in tow, the toddler harnessed and kept on a leash. Even the smallest sound echoes for all time, Jean had said. Then, squeezing Peyt's fingers white, she'd opened her mouth and sung a high note for eternity.

Peyt blinks back to now. He stoops, pressing against the plinth. Focuses too late to pinpoint which part of the museum the ghost has come from. In ballet slippers and an old-fashioned tweed coat, she emerges from behind a pillar in the fossil garden near the right wing. Without hesitation, she dashes across the plaza to the planter, snatches the clay pot and sprints back to the building.

Must've seen me plant it, Peyt realises, tracking her retreat. When she disappears around the corner, he sighs, sore and disappointed. Not because she's eluded him—because she's a different, less beautiful woman than the one he'd met yesterday.

Peytr doesn't slink very well anymore. Overbalanced with his head down, he lurches from cover to cover, reaching the museum with his heart in his throat. He wasn't trained for this kind of recon. No, he wasn't trained. Edging along the building's foundations, he finds a blast-hole in the wall, crumbling and jagged. His satchels are bulky and the ruck's weighing him down; top-heavy, he stumbles, rips his pants on the way in.

As his eyes adjust to the darkness, he drops his bags behind a heap of gyprock and sandstone, buries them under grit and bricks. Unburdened, he'll move easier, quicker—but three steps inside, Peyt's staggered.

That one time he visited the museum, Peyt had marvelled at the entrance hall's splendour. Granite balustrades and brass railings had swept down staircases on each end of the vast space, guiding feet and eyes toward a prized piece of history: a gigantic beast's skeleton, seventy-five feet of majesty defleshed. On both sides, arched galleries had run the room's length. Their sandstone columns had been heavily carved with whimsical creatures—dogs riding ponies, monkeys wearing top hats, mermaids and griffins and owl-headed men. Each pillar stretched from the sunken parquet floor to vaulted, impossible heights. Decorative fretwork ribbed the ceiling, which had dazzled with stained-glass skylights. Concealed bulbs had illuminated mosaicked walls and cast golden beams upwards. When children and chaperones had shuffled past, the animals all seemed to dance.

This museum is not that one.

That museum is gone.

In its place, an arid cavern that stinks of shit. Sulphur. Sour goat's milk. The skylights are grimed over or broken, the magic bulbs crushed to powder and blown out through gaps in the walls. Shafts of bluish light sift down through decades of flies and dust; the buzzing is so loud, Peyt plugs his ears as he takes another step in. Gradually, silhouettes emerge as he crosses the landing, black on grey, resolving into lumps of destruction. Fallen capitals. Crumbled stairs. Missing columns. Gaping balconies. Peyt narrows his eyes, looking into the amphitheatre where he and Euri once watched a puppet show while Jean sat on a bench and rubbed her aching feet. From this vantage, he shouldn't be able to see the rows of burnt seats, the stage, the ripped velvet curtain. There used to be a wall there, banked with glass display cases showing ivory sewing kits, heavy wax seals, some dead emperor's tea set—over a hundred cups and saucers made of solid gold. Any cases still standing are now laden with rifles, bows, slingshots. Artefacts have been pilfered from elsewhere in the museum and jumbled together—black oak thrones, painted sarcophagi, seal-hunters' canoes, totem poles, curio cabinets—a nonsense of eras smashed and stacked for firewood.

He steps closer, boots skidding on scree. For a second, he contemplates taking them off, approaching with sock-footed stealth. Stupid, he decides, seeing so many sharp glints on the floor. Glass underfoot scritches and squeals. Not far from the balustrade Peyt stops, breathless. Cold sweating. Tasting bile and regurgitated words.

Where the monster's head used to sway on its long, strange neck, a murmuration of flies now spins a hypnotic dance. The air is thick with them, swarming and dispersing without pattern, but with a certain instinctive logic. Up and back and left right left. At the last second, they part around splintered beams. Avoiding pillars and flames and random bones. Vanishing in the darkness, reappearing a beat later in the light. Their buzz-buzz-buzzing ebbs and flows, now a steady hum, now a shout. Entranced, Peyt steps forward as if summoned. He listens close, hears what the flies are saying. He understands.

Far below, small orange tongues flick sparks up from the parquet. Some flies dip too low, singeing their bellies. Others immolate in a puff of smoke. Peyt doesn't really see the ash of their bodies lilting down like snow: he's stopped, paralysed. Eyes fixed on the crowd of greys below.

Eighty, ninety, a couple hundred of them, communing around campfires and burning oil drums. The big ones cleaning, honing, polishing weapons. Sewing patches on clothes. Stirring pots. Boiling water. Taking stock of supplies. Sitting in circles, picking nits from each other's scalps. Snapping table legs, smashing chairs. Stoking fires with scorched candelabrum. Sleeping on tapestries, lace gowns, ermine cloaks. Curling around a plump litter of their young. Chastising the toddling ones who screech while they play. Slapping their tiny loud faces, their arses, their grabbing hands. Applauding as they jump rope. Singing—yes, young and old, singing while little greys skip. Big ushering small away from hunched councils, the white-hairs talking on two frequencies. Strategizing with mouths and minds. Brewing up storm after storm of flies.

This is it, Peyt thinks, losing all feeling in his limbs. I've finally found their lair.

A pang knifes his chest as he thinks of the woman from yesterday, and the girl. So lovely, both of them. So vibrant. Such beauty, Peyt knows, stands no chance against the horde. Their straight, pretty hair is probably lining grey pillows now. Their eyes—teal blue, Peyt imagines—are adorning grey necklaces. Their pink skin is flayed and salted and already drying in strips—for grey jerky, maybe, or skin-ribbons to tie on grey effigies. Their bright red flesh is filleted for cooking, their guts are rendering to stew in grey pots. And now their stringy-meat skeletons are lying in the shadows somewhere, their empty sockets home to nibbling grey rats.

I should've taken care of them, he thinks, hands squeezing a cold grip that isn't there. Vision blurring, he tries to turn back but invisible greys have snared him. They lock onto his ankles, straddle his shoulders, hang like spoiled children from his waist. He is too heavy to move. His muscles convulse, straining to keep him upright and breathing. Ribs creaking as his lungs suck in, push weakly out. Overhead, flies become feathers become winged serifs become whirling letters become a gabble of words. So many noisy, renegade curses. So much poetry. Peyt grits his teeth, firms his mouth. Flares his nostrils, sieving as much air as he can from the buzz.

It's not enough. Spots shimmer across his eyes, spots float over the railing, spots freckle the pale creatures below. In flashes of green and blue, the spotted greys round out with radiation, they expand with it, they're all aglow. Peyt's jaw spasms, he clenches so hard. The edges of his sight vignette to black.

While he stands there blinking, the solid stone balustrade separating him from *them* shifts into a barricade of wooden idols. Then it's a collection of fat fire hydrants. It's a row of pot-bellied urns. And right in the middle—how could he have missed her?—between two piles of sandbags is a child, huddled in a red polka-dot sundress.

The girl. Peyt swears it's the same girl. Tess. Tessa. Alone on the doorstep, a rifle across her skinny thighs. She can't be a sentry, not at that age, not with her back turned. Surely not. Coatless and without a hood, she's shivering, her head lowered—no, Peyt corrects, reading her furious 'wind. He takes in the shackle around her ankle, the chain anchoring her to the staircase. She's crying.

Tessa, he wants to say. Don't be scared. I'll let you go.

But he can't breathe, can't move.

Before them, the greys become ghosts.

A blink later, the ghosts become women.

Eavesdropping, Peyt hears: "The best men are gone."

The speaker, the lady, is skinny but solid, real flesh and blood. Squatting by a brazier at the foot of the stairs, no more than ten feet away. Flushed from the flames, wrapping duct tape around a musket butt. Tearing strips from the roll with her teeth. "The best fathers."

"But we make do," says another, 'windless and slurring. A toothpick waggles from her lips as she talks. She leans over to pick up a bottle, swigs, and nearly topples into the embers. Her belly is eight months huge. "We'll survive."

"All the best ones," the first woman continues as if uninterrupted. Raising the gun, she checks the feel of it against her shoulder. She grunts, reaches for a bayonet. "All of them."

They aren't really talking to each other at all, Peyt thinks. They're just talking. Voicing stale thoughts.

"Dead," says a third. Hair shining with scum. Words shooting red sparks on her crown. Peyt holds his breath, wondering if the grease will ignite. "An entire generation—"

"Genera*tions*—"

"Gone to dirt."

"We're making do," says the pregnant one. "We're surviving."

Not greys, then, Peytr thinks. But mimicking them.

Disappearing in order to live.

Hiding to thrive.

No, he decides. Not just hiding. Another quick glance around the hall, a quick count, and Peyt realises there are at least five children to each woman. Newborns, toddlers, pre-teens. Girls, mostly. A town's worth of girls. No boys over the age of, say, ten—but even so, a good number of these. Enough to man four or five squads. A large platoon. And another few teams being carried in their mothers' bellies.

They're protesting, Peyt thinks. Quietly. Passively. Keeping the next generation of soldiers out of the firing line.

"All that life," adds a sad voice from somewhere under the landing.

"That potential life," corrects the rifleman, taping the blade to her weapon. Testing its balance. "Wasted. Trapped underground."

"For now," says the soon-to-be mother. "Where I come from it's different—"

"All that death," one of them says. "And for what."

"And for what."

"And for what."

The conversation is definitely an old one, Peyt thinks. It has the rhythm of rote to it. The mindlessness of a hymn. Of humming.

Humming a hymn. With little food, little water, the women are just talking to give their mouths something to do.

Hymning a hum, he thinks, snorting.

The girl whips around.

"Tessa," Peyt says, raising his empty hands. Harmless, see? I won't hurt you. "Tessa, wait—"

But he's too close to her now—how did he get so close?—and she's opening her gap-toothed mouth and screaming. Shackle clanking, she jumps up but doesn't run—can't run—but kicks, hard and true, sharp bursts of purple pain in Peyt's shins. She screams and claws and pulls on Peytr's hood strings, grabs his coat, his collar, and yanks. Boots thunder up the stairs beside them. Below, pistol hammers cock. Repeaters lock and load. Tessa twists, red-faced, and Peyt's got a ribful of balustrade, the broken railing, jagged marble, gouging into his side as he flails, the ceiling turned floor turned ceiling turned floor as he falls, embracing air. He lands, winded, on his back, on a cabinet, on his front, on the parquet. Cap's voice in his ear hollering *Take cover! Take cover!* and he's scrambling to knees and feet, crashing through legs—tables, children, chairs, women—shots firing from above, zinging from all sides, bullets wailing, 'winds biting, stinging, clipping his arms, his throbbing back, word-shrapnel bloodying his mouth, glancing off his hood. Spitting oaths and hate and fear, he scuttles between campfires, crouching, slipping, bodies colliding, bodies crowding, bodies cutting off his escape. Daylit breaches in the walls taunt from the sidelines, *too far, too far*, but closer holes gape in the floor, *yes, do-able*, holes in the floor, *over there, over* there.

And for a second, *stupid, fuckin' stupid*, skidding over the edge, tumbling into the black, into nothingness, maybe, into the greys' headquarters, into a dark horde of mothers, Peyt wonders if the beautiful worrier he saw yesterday is here. If she's near. If she'll be the one to kill him.

A metallic echo, like a mess-tray being punched by a bully, as a shelf buckles beneath Peytr's weight. Plaster tile-dust snows down on him and bullets ricochet off the shelf's rusted steel supports—*too close, too close*—and he quickly rolls, clutches the edge, hangs from his fingers, toes swinging. He drops and the floor rushes up, bone-jarring. Heels and shins throbbing, Peyt collapses, then rats into the gloom on hands and knees. The basement is full-shadow, pierced by a few shafts of warm light shining down from the hall above. Aisles lead in all directions, anywhere, nowhere. Far away, too far, rubble slopes all the way up to a dim gash in the ceiling, a dead end or a way out. Peytr aims for it, groping along the floor, feeling his way around locker bays and vertical cabinets. Blocks of drawers. Row after row of archival stacks, racks on wheels that scare the shit out of him, rolling into him as he passes.

The mothers follow on silent feet, lanterns blinding, bayonets glinting sharp.

Peyt hears them barking orders. Short signals in the darkness, tracking with vocal location, talking ghost. No point wasting ammo down here; they'll hunt him with numbers, with logic and blades. His palms slap the floor, faster and faster, knees clunking and banging and raw. He squeaks into a crouch, wishing he'd kicked off his boots when he'd had the chance. Glass or no glass. He'd bleed for a bit of stealth.

Huffing, thighs burning, he scrambles through the archive, heading for a ramp he can no longer see. The women circle, call out, close in.

"En't in maps 'o' the world," he hears, *close, too close*. "Got a blink on him, Cora?" *too close* "Lamps low," someone else says, *further back, thank fuck*, off to the right; maybe four, maybe five o'clock. "—run to ground."

Have to get higher, Peyt thinks, just as his boots clang *too loud, too loud* onto a tinny surface. Around him, the women instantly hush.

"Got a blink on him, Dee Dee?" asks the far voice, after a second or two.

Totally blind, Peyt reaches out with fingers stretched, willing them to come in contact with a shelf to climb. He lifts and sets his feet down in slow-motion. Slow and quiet. Reach and stretch.

"Got a blink on him, Yvie?"

Reach and step and inch and splay and—

"Over here."

—Peyt brushes against a barrier, cold and smooth as veneer.

"I thought I heard something."

Lantern light approaches as Peyt frantically soft-pats the wall—it has to be a wall—trying to find a corner, a way around. *Too fast, too fast*, blackness retreats from his hands. Searching a couple feet to the left, he butts into another wall. He turns around and paces into a third. I'm in a cupboard, he thinks, turning again. Gloom sharpens into lines. A brass railing emerges at waist height. Angles cast inwards through two sliding doors, both stuck half-open. Outside, the shadows dance.

Wedging himself into a corner, Peytr presses against a panel of rounded buttons that click and creak when he moves. Choking back a whimper, he balls up on the floor.

"Got a blink on him, Mireille?"

Peyt's teeth chatter, though he shoves his knuckles between them and bites hard. Mouth open, he drools so they won't hear him swallow. Hollows his throat and breathes in slow, hot waves, wishing he could stop breathing altogether. When the gap between doors glows an old summer yellow, Peyt crams himself hard into the shadows. Closes his eyes to hide their shine, scrubbing the wet from his sockets.

"Mireille?"

The woman's soles are supple leather, softly padding across the tiles. An intense patch of white-red swings *close, too close*, in and out and back in again, shifting the darkness behind Peyt's lids. The lantern gutters; its oil smells like burnt plastic and pine. The light dims, retreating, but Peyt is sure she's still there. He can hear leaves of air blooming on each branch of her lungs. The sneer on her face as she smells ammonia. The stew decomposing in her belly. Eggs jostling their way into her womb. Her heart squeezing life out of liquid. Rich rivers coursing through her veins. He can hear her confidence, her cunning. The bullets forming on her tongue.

I'm sorry, he thinks, biting, tasting blood.

Make it quick.

"Renaissance to Reformation: all clear," she says, loud and near.

Peyt's head jerks up.

That voice.

Peering through his lashes, he sees her silhouette, outlined through the gap in the doors. Slender hips, broad shoulders. A scarf slumped round her neck. Hair wisping in a vibrant hurricane 'wind. It's her, he thinks. *Mireille*. Chest throbbing, he misses what she says next but recognises the timbre, the cadence of her instructions.

"Head for the Mount," she calls, her light hazing, then winking out of sight.

Peyt listens, poised to flee. The Mount, he thinks. The ramp of debris. Who was she talking to? Them? Or me? Sweat trickles down his spine, sogging his shirt. His pants are clinging, reeking. His palms are too slippery for climbing. Carefully, he peels off his jacket, wipes his face and hands, then goes to scrunch it into his—

Fuck.

The satchels, his ruck—Peyt's fuckin' left them upstairs. At the entrance. All his deliveries. The food. The shirt Esther gave him. His grenades. He's fuckin' lost them. Lamps flicker past, twice, three more times, as Peyt's guts burn. Words roil against his scalp, scratching and gouging, stinging horse-flies of regret. In the dark, he lowers his hood, gives his thoughts free rein. They clatter overhead like pebbles tossed at a window, seeking attention, ready to break. By the time his legs are too numb to support him, the women's voices have dwindled, the search party called off. Still he waits. Flopped on his side, he pummels feeling back into his muscles. Points and flexes his feet. Gets on all fours. When his ears ring with silence, he takes a deep breath. Crawls out into the dark.

Gripping his jacket in one hand, Peytr stands, bracing himself against the elevator's cold metal doors as he tries to get his bearings. Three streaks of grey illuminate shelves and cabinets in the distance before him, but he can't remember which hole he fell through. Can't tell if it was any of these. Reaching back, he finds the wall. He stretches his arm out to the left. Changes his mind. Didn't he come from the right? Before he has a chance to decide, Peyt is blinded by a lantern's glare.

"Turn around."

Peyt squints, blinks water down his cheeks. Light flares in his vision, starbursts of brightness that sparkle on his lenses, on shelf fronts, on the trickle of piss on his boots. Perched on a low pedestal across from the lift, the woman is a perfect statue. An ancient idol, saint of the lost and directionless. One hand raised, holding a lamp. The other gripping a sword, the blade's tip pointing out a path through the dark.

"Go that way. The Mount's forty paces past the armoires."

Fierce. Peytr stares, his legs refusing to move. Thoughts scattered, uncontained. *Strong jaw. . . . Sharp nose. . . . A hawk. . . . A hunter. . . .* 'Wind pulsing to the beat of his heart. *I'm dead I'm dead I'm dead I'm dead. . . .* The moment stretches as he guesses her age. Eighteen? Twenty? Younger, he thinks, than she acts.

"Mireille," he says, and she scowls at her name. *Thank yyyyyyyy . . .*

Her scowl deepens.

"We're even," she says, shooing him with her weapon. "For yesterday."

"The girl," Peyt says, picturing her little foot near-stepping on the landmine. Her little foot shackled to the balustrade. He takes a step forward. "Tessa? I didn't mean to scare—"

"Don't make me scream," Mireille says. Muscles twitching in that strong jaw, clenching and unclenching. "I'm serious. Get out of here. Now."

Peyt drops his jacket. Gaze locked on Mireille's, he can't bend to pick it up again. Not without losing focus.

"Keep it," he says, though he's already shivering. "For the girl." Then he digs in his pants pocket, pulls out a sodden rosette. "And this, I think, is for you."

Mireille sniffs, her beak sharpening into a sneer. "Just go."

For three days, Peytr tries to find new satchels to match the ones he's lost. He's got no idea where the Pigeon got those shoulder bags in the first place—their straps the perfect length, the packs sectioned and lined with perfect pockets—but he guesses the place is long gone to the greys. After mucking old Jeharl's goat pens, cleaning turnips for Mischa and polishing a trove of stainless steel for the Wintersons who were richer and so stingier than most—Peyt earns just enough at the night markets to buy equipment that simply doesn't compare. The tanners' leather is cracked, thin, the wrong colour. The dressmakers' cloth is too flimsy. He doesn't have time for dump-binning in the hopes of turning up something good—every hour off the route is another meal missed, far as Peyt's concerned—and though the general outfitters clean their wares before putting them out on the rack, they still have the reek of dead evacs on them. And nowadays no one makes canvas as sturdy as the stuff Jean found, ages ago, when she stitched Peyt's rucksack together. No one makes them, like she did, to measure.

Shame to waste all that fine work.

Outside the museum, he watches the boltholes from daybreak until well past noon. None of the women emerge. No ghosts flit in the fossil garden. No greys slink around corners or hide under arches and buttresses. No little girls make mud castles in the square. Once the sky darkens from pewter to slate, Peyt sneaks up to the building. He edges along the foundations, finds the same rupture as before. Crouched next to it, he steadies himself and listens.

Wind ruffles his hair, sends his thoughts scouting ahead. A plastic bag scritches into the breach; it snags on an exposed iron strut, then crinkles and flaps an irregular rhythm. Water drips—somewhere. Nearby. From a cache, he thinks. Not a rainpipe. It hasn't rained in months.

Craning his neck, Peyt shifts closer. Peers around blasted bricks and rough stone. On the landing, his bootprints have been scuffed clean, erased by the passing of many feet. A small brass key sits on the threshold, its teeth blunt from use. Peyt picks it up. Looks, listens. He tilts his head, strains for whispers, for hammers being cocked. Last time, could he hear the hum of flies right away? The din of mothers? The children laughing, playing, crying? The rasp of blades on whetstones? He doesn't know. Can't remember.

Inside, the museum sounds cold.

The fires are banked, the embers grey. Spits and pots and jump-ropes have vanished. Weaponry cabinets are cleaned out. Barrows have been filled and rolled. Beds are nothing but rectangular gaps in the dust.

All the ghosts have now gone, except one.

Chained to the banister, she's curled on the floor. Lying on her side, knees drawn up, arms splayed. Wearing nothing but a shackle and the coat Peyt gave her. A frown. Where it's not scratched and bruised, her skin is pale clay. A pool of blood has dried beneath her temple and cheek. The proud beak of her nose is mashed, off-kilter, crusted with black-red. It whistles faintly when she inhales.

Her wordwind is faint. Drowsy. Letters float and fall on her head like ash.

Mireille. He runs to her, kneels by her side. Unsure if he's spoken aloud, he repeats her name. When he opens his mouth, her 'wind fluctuates. Her nightmares snag on his tongue. Spitting and coughing, Peyt inches back, staying close enough to touch. He jams his hands under his arms.

A sour fug wafts off her, ripe as the herdboys. Musk and crevices and stale onions and shit. She smells, Peyt thinks, like the trench.

"Mireille," he says, staring at his jacket, on her.

Slowly, her lids peel apart.

"Mireille, I'm sorry."

"Save your sorrow," she whispers, then licks her cracked lips. "Give me your water."

"Right." He jumps up and runs over to the entrance. Flexing his hands, relaxing them. The bags, thank fuck, are still there. He rummages in the ruck until he hears muffled sloshing, then dashes back to Mireille. Puts the canteen where she can reach it.

"Thirteen seconds," she says. "Plenty of time."

Peyt smiles. Can't help it. He smiles at her gumption, her practical nature. Is she ghost or grey? Or neither. Maybe this one's neither.

"What are you?" he asks, just to be sure.

Mireille swallows twice then breathes, twice more, then speaks, as if following a set pattern.

"A traitor, apparently," she says between gulps. Almost as bitter as she is exhausted. "And you—"

Peyt shakes his head. "No," he says. "No."

"—are a soldier?"

She's thumbing a white cross painted on the green bottle. While she takes another swig, Peyt thinks for a minute. Which is more reassuring—a man who carries the dead, or one who carries their parcels?

Grey or ghost?

"Field medic," he says at last. "Red star. I can set that." He gestures at the mess of her nose. "If you want. You know, so it won't heal crooked. Can't do much for your mouth, though. Sorry."

He winces when she says, "Stop apologising."

"Sorry."

Easing herself upright, Mireille grimaces but doesn't cry out. She grits her teeth and keeps pushing until she's vertical. The jacket hangs loosely from her shoulders, sagging open where buttons are missing. Revealing a scarred belly and small breasts. Spilling into her lap, hiding nothing. "The key," she says, tonguing gaps in her teeth. "You've got it, haven't you."

Reluctantly, Peyt nods.

"Well." Mireille's breath catches. Lips trembling, she swallows hard. "You know how these things work. Finders keepers."

Peytr closes his eyes and thinks, This can't be real.

Ghost or grey?

"I'm sorry."

Grey or ghost?

"This wasn't supposed to happen."

"Maybe not," Mireille says. "But it did."

And when he passes the key to her shackles, the woman's grip is solid.

"Nothing will change unless we stop fighting amongst ourselves."

The senator's voice is muffled through the thick oak door, but Euri recognises the twang Nolasco's got to her vowels. In the corridor outside the makeshift council room, Euri pauses, hand on the brass knob, not turning. *Always listen before acting*, Armin had told her once, years ago. Once was enough: Euri has always been a quick study. *Watch and wait*, he'd said, soon after he'd become Prime Minister, long before the greys prematurely ended his term. *Listen, and remember*.

Euri watches.

She waits.

She listens.

"We are our own greatest enemy," Nolasco continues. "*Mark my words*."

Grandstander, Euri thinks, picturing all the pens now forced to scratch across legal pads inside. Nolasco overuses the expression almost as badly as Yusou does—and as one of Armin's oldest advisors, she should really know better. Yusou, at least, is new to the cabinet; stole himself a seat somehow in the reshuffle, though his disbelief is as prominent as his big rubbery lips—lips that flap far too close to the new Prime Minister's ears, in Euri's opinion. For weeks Nolasco and Yusou have been getting the clerks to mark their scepticism, inscribe it in ink for posterity, while the more sensible ministers—Wroe, for instance, Carrock and Talus—keep their opinions hooded. If Armin Nycene's calculations prove accurate, if his truths, when revealed, are as effective as he'd planned all these years, it'll be political suicide to have opposed them on record.

Nycene's successor understands this well. 'Windless, Prime Minister Ashtad Cardea runs no risk of imprinting anything unintentionally—a trivial reason to earn people's trust, Euri thinks—and the woman considers her words from all sides while projecting them onto the wide glass faceplate of her helm.

"Consider them noted, senator," Cardea says. With the volume on her headset permanently turned low, it's hard to hear the new PM at the best of times. On the far side of a big room, on the wrong side of a closed door, Euri now strains to catch what's being said.

"Time is pressing on all of us, so perhaps we can move the discussion along?" There's a pause; Euri imagines the group shuffling their papers, signalling at mute clerks for water, asking typists to read out this line or that in the marked transcript. Doing anything but looking Cardea in the screen. One short month sitting at the head of a boardroom table does not a leader make, Euri thinks. Respect is the product of years, not days . . .

"Senator Rourke," Cardea says. "How go the ceasefire negotiations?"

"As instructed, twenty-five mediators were despatched last week," Rourke replies, enunciating each word carefully, slowly, to keep from stuttering. "Each carried instructions to five of our outposts before crossing into grey territory. Treating with insurgents . . ."

Behind Euri, there's a squeak of footsteps on marble tiles. She turns to see a young Pigeon squelching up the curving staircase to the second floor, water pooling around his sneakers with each step. His plaited black hair is dripping, the silver beads tipping each braid clacking together as he takes the stairs two at a time. At the landing, he stops to catch his breath. Gripping a fat brass railing that's half-worn with a patina of palm prints, he leans over and shakes the rain from his 'wind. Yet another reason Cardea chose to meet here, Euri thinks, half-turning back to the door. After trekking up all those stairs, everyone's too tired to cause trouble.

Give credit where it's due, Armin always said, and, yes, Euri will admit Cardea's temporary headquarters make sense. While gov't house is being reconstructed once again, where better to congregate than the old commonwealth bank? Even without access to the vault—no diatribe is vehement enough to blast into that steel fortress, and any keys or combinations are long lost—the building's outer walls are solid granite, four feet thick. To help prevent theft, the architects devised complicated mosaics, pillars and embossed metal ceilings to distort mentalegraph signals, so there's little chance deliberations will be overheard. The boardroom is tucked in the corner of a lofty gallery, high above the trading floor below. With no entrances but the one under guard behind Euri, no access to the second floor other than this one grand staircase, and no reason for anyone who isn't invited to come up here, the bank is an ideal substitute parliament building.

". . . to replace the ones who haven't returned. Thus far, what responses we have received from the front are as the Prime Minis—Pardon me, Your Honour—I should say, they are much as Armin Nycene predicted they would be. Our ambassadors weren't shot off the field, which is promising, but no real discussions were had. If I can be frank"—Rourke pauses, waiting for Cardea's flicker of approval—"this brand of idealism went out of fashion back when my great-grandfather was in short pants. I respect the attempt, Your Honour, I really do. But the consensus from the field is unanimous: there can be no armistice agreement with an enemy whose negotiation techniques include ambushes and scatterbombings; whose primary means of recruitment is abducting our soldiers, brainwashing them, and turning their stolen guns against us; and whose appetites are as alien as they are insatiable. Throughout this *treaty* process, the greys have been incommunicado—"

"Surprise, surprise," Yusou interjects.

"—which means we cannot simply stop proceedings now and blindly hope for the best."

"Which *means*, Senator Rourke," says Cardea. "Absolutely nothing . . ."

Euri reaches out as the Pigeon approaches, stopping him well away from the door. "I'll take that," she says, plucking a grubby envelope from grubbier fingers. Tucking it inside her jacket, she hooks two coins from the small purse in her pocket and drops them into the boy's outstretched hand. "That will be all."

"Thank you, counsellor."

Grinning, Euri shoos him away. "Please, Darrio," she calls to the oaf guarding the stairs, watching the Pigeon squeak back down them. "No interruptions while cabinet is sitting—and that includes deliveries. I trust you'll be more vigilant, when left out here on your own?"

The guard tips his hat, 'wind flushing. "Yes, ma'am."

"Good."

Euri slips inside the boardroom and eases the door shut behind her. She doesn't need to look in the envelope to know what it contains. Blessings for Prime Minister Cardea. Donations. Pledges of allegiance. 'Wind-pressed promises to the farseeing leader with her captivating blue jade eyes. Vows to do unimaginable things to help rout the greys. Bribes to help bring their boys home.

Idiots, Euri thinks, taking a seat at a curved bank of desks with the other PAs. As if this 'windless wonder is going to succeed where a *real* Prime Minister failed.

No, not *failed*, she corrects. Armin was too strong. He posed too great a threat; that's why the greys swiped him. He was simply too powerful.

Smiling apologies for her lateness, Euri picks up a pen and notepad, looks at Cardea and thinks: He was nothing like you.

Armin liked to sleep naked. Even in winter, he got so hot at night Euri often wondered if he was sick. While she was cocooned in a quilt, shivering and wriggling back into her underwear, he'd be stretched out next to her, stark as glass. He'd stay that way until morning when, stiff but not cold, he'd snake under the covers and wake her.

"How did you sleep?" he'd ask after giving Euri a good warming. Twining her fingers through the thick hair on his belly, she'd mumble something non-committal. She never slept well anymore, but it was slightly better when she wasn't alone.

"And you?" she'd ask, and the humour of his answers depended on when parliament was in session.

"I had a nightmare," he said once, "where I could feel each intestine in my gut individually. Like furrows in a field, every row was hard, rock hard, and so brown they were almost black. They pushed out of me, splitting the skin, bursting with shit and loam—but instead of shoving them back in, I strummed them. Dirt caught under my nails that I couldn't shake loose, and mushrooms bloomed at my touch. . . ." Armin laughed then, unconvincing. "What do you think it means?"

Euri listens without judgement or interpretation. She doesn't dream unless she's awake. Like when she was a kid, telling tales with Peytie or listening to Jean's bedtime stories. Or lately, before nodding off, she'd dream herself into other people's lives. It was relaxing, imagining all the things happening somewhere else in the world, right then, right that instant. *Someone's smiling. Someone's eating mash. Someone's sneezing. Someone's sending a parcel. Someone's being robbed. Someone's buying glass. Someone's being orphaned. Someone's meeting friends for a drink. Someone's dancing. Someone's falling in love. Someone's drowning in oil. Someone's burning in a foxhole. Someone's kissing for the first time. Someone's flying above the clouds. Someone's fucking. . . .* Endless possibilities ran through her 'wind like a litany, eventually lulling her into the black.

"You worry too much," she'd replied at last, but a crackle from the intercom on the wall cut her off, and Armin's hot fingers scalded her cold lips. Pressing Euri's mouth shut, he answered Verna's call instantly so she wouldn't feel the need to come to his rooms.

"Get up, love," Verna had said. More than twice Euri's age, Armin's wife had a wasp-paper voice. "No war is won in bed."

Euri smirked and bit Armin's fingers, then smothered her laugh with a pillow.

The boardroom table is long, oval; everyone easily sees everyone else without the implied equality of a circle. Ashtad Cardea sits at the head, the boxed screen on her shoulders quietly transparent. Through the helm's glass faceplate, the Prime Minister's solid blue eyes project nothing for the time being. Vents under her chin and beside her ears keep the monitor from fogging while she talks. And talks. And talks. "Transmitting," she calls it, when pictures flicker on the face-pane, accompanying her words. "Visionary" think the senators, the other ministers, the caucus that put Cardea in that high-backed chair, the morning after Nycene vacated it.

The new PM is always open to counsel. Negotiations. Discussions. More fool her, thinks Euri, taking notes while supervising the lower clerks. Armin's policy had always been *act now, apologise later*—and so things got done. Quickly. Economically. He knew how not to waste time. Under his leadership, troops were engaged. Airfields reclaimed. Skybunkers erected and manned. He'd sent tunnellers to work all over the city, in the borderlands, in territories beyond. Over the course of his long, long term, Armin had founded repat hospitals. Established sanctuaries for the malgrown, the grey-shaped, the war-formed. Created a graveyard economy that had improved these people's poor lives. Closer to home, the CBD's west end had been transformed. The stadium was recaptured, rebuilt, fortified. A warren of passageways was dug beneath its foundations, any and all burrowing greys despatched. Around the staging area, four square miles of city streets were cleared of hostiles—completely cleared!—and had been kept that way for nearly a decade. Armin persuaded with action: sound, logical action. There were discussions, of course, plans leading up to big digs. But they weren't meetings like this one: meaningless strings of opinion with no decisions made, no conclusions drawn.

Jean wouldn't have volunteered to be a screaming truth for someone like Cardea, Euri thinks. Not for an endless talker.

"And what of the 'refugees'?" Nolasco asks, leaning forward in her seat. The senator's narrow back is turned, but even from her vantage at the clerks' desk Euri can see air-quotes hovering around the word. "What of the evacs?"

"Which ones?" Cardea sighs. On her screen, black and white images flicker. Crops killed by haze plague. Villages ablaze. Streets of rubble and chalk. Houses abandoned. Houses crumbling. Rectangular afterimages scraped on the land: houses erased.

Bleeding heart, Euri thinks as Cardea reels through scene after scene of skeletal arms extended. Empty hands. Hunger-swollen bellies. Evacs rush to the cities like water into a lifeboat; no matter how quickly the gov't bails, splashing people back out into less populated territories, the tides of war bring them back in again. The boat is full, Euri thinks, but still can't bring herself to watch Cardea's visions for long. We're sinking.

Sputtering, Rourke flips through a stack of files and tallies all the reports of new arrivals his spies and Pigeons have brought. "Fourteen. . . . Fifteen. . . . Twenty-two. . . . Thirty-seven hundred relocated to stabilisation centres last week. Eight thousand more arrived yesterday, half of which were rerouted to Neuemarket. We've got the other half crammed into the stadium lots, but I must say, Your Honour, the camp is now full to bursting."

"Good," says Talus. "That's the aim."

"These are *people* we're talking about," snaps Yusou. "They didn't volunteer for this . . ."

"The tents are packed. Four—sometimes six—to a two-man bunk," Rourke continues. "And there aren't enough grunts to patrol the grounds. Eighteen parking lots and half a million evacs make for a lot of shadows. A lot of ways for greys to get in . . . and out. We could always send some of the overflow inside—"

Cardea raises a hand to stop him, but Wroe jumps in first.

"That's one option," he says from across the table, gaze shifting from PM to senator and back. Wroe's tiny eyes wouldn't feed a grey cub, Euri thinks. Leaning back in his chair, the minister lowers his hood, gives his scalp a good scratch before covering it again. Gathering his thoughts. Stalling. *Wroe's allegiances are as changeable as his 'wind, Armin had said. One minute he can't see for all the grey, and the next he swears the sun is blinding. If you can distinguish the direction Wroe thinks the light's shining on any given day, you can gauge his honesty . . .*

"Changing the scope of VERNA's content to such a degree will need further discussion. How will more screamers inside the stadium alter the ratio of numbers?"

"More importantly," adds Carrock, her round, pleasant face creased with worry, "how will it affect the impact? Will extra bodies increase the blast radius—or restrict airflow within the complex, and thus decrease the aggregate's efficiency? Will an influx of evacs in the building stifle the other screamers' breath? Or crush the tunnels we've spent so long digging under its foundations? If you'll pardon the pun," she says, "we've spent far too long accumulating numbers to blow things now."

A few of the clerks titter until Euri silences them with a glare. Outside, heavy rain thrashes against the arched windows, rattling panes. The storm has hardly let up all week. Construction on parliament house has slowed and floodwaters have turned the city's streets to rivers. Months of accumulated dust and words and dirt swill down gutters and spill over eaves, turning the world a weathered brown.

I hope they've got the stadium's dome raised, Euri thinks, mesmerized by liquid pinwheels spinning on thick window glass. No matter how dedicated, Armin's bomb won't go off if it's shivering too hard to scream.

"These are valid concerns," Cardea says, screen showing flags flown in semaphore patterns. Without turning to Euri, the PM lifts her voice and gives orders across the room. "Add another item to the agenda, counsellor. We cannot, in good conscience, proceed to a vote without analysing this matter from all possible sides."

"Yes, Your Honour." Euri finds and scans the order of today's proceedings, one eyebrow raised, lips pursed. She slots the time-waste discussion between Yusou's last-ditch attempt to defuse the screamers, and the vote that will give Cardea all the credit Armin deserves.

This is it, Euri thinks, dipping her pen in a glass inkwell. Death by committee.

Euri always suspected Armin was a believer, but never asked him outright. In bed, they'd talk dirty. They'd talk about Armin's plans to end the war. Between the two, there wasn't much space for philosophy.

"Do you really think they're so deep?" she asked one night, before he nodded off.

"Who?"

"Who else."

Armin rolls over, sleepy. "The greys are higher and lower than anyone can imagine. So, yes. We'll keep flying and keep digging. No matter where they're hiding, we'll blast them out."

"They must see us as parasites," Euri said, speaking in hypotheticals. She'd never enjoyed the comfort of certainty. If the greys were real, Peytr was a weakling. A turncoat. If they weren't real, he was lost for nothing. "We're these big, blundering, garish parasites sucking the life from their land."

Armin laughed and kissed her warm neck. "So you're a pacifist then?"

Euri shook her head.

"Only when I'm tired," she said.

"There will be collateral damage," says Yusou, veins throbbing on his neck and temples. "In addition to the sacrificial goats all numbered and accounted for—how many fit in that stadium? How many are milling in the parking lots? In addition to this immediate disaster, there will be countless, needless casualties. *Human* casualties, mark my words. Not grey."

Cardea's screen darkens. She shifts in her seat, nervous as a bride on the eve of her first ploughing. "We've been over this, senator. You've reiterated your views—time and again—and they have been heard in each instance. They have been *marked*, by ear and pen. At this hour," she looks at the bank of round clocks on the far wall, each set at different times, and all too late, "do you honestly want to go over this again?"

"If not now, when?"

"Should the results of tonight's vote not meet your standards," Cardea says wearily, "you are more than welcome to come and see me. . . . Euri?"

"You've got a *small* window open before midday, Your Honour," Euri says, her 'wind barrelling through a rolodex of public appointments, all highlighted in yellow so everyone in the room can see how busy the Prime Minister is. After years under Armin, Euri has learned to render private meetings invisible.

"There you have it," Cardea says, holding the senator's gaze. "My window is open tomorrow. Let the air of your grievances blow through it then."

Yusou's nostrils flare. "I won't be put off—"

"You will," Cardea snaps, spit flecking the inside of her helm. Around the table, wordwinds freeze. Wary eyes fix on the PM's screen, catching ten seconds of a nature documentary. Lava oozing toward the ocean, sizzling and cooling in its gentle waves. "Reschedule the repats, Euri. I will see Senator Yusou first thing. *Tomorrow*."

"Noted."

Bouncing in his seat the way Peytie used to when he thought no one was looking, Talus picks at his cuticles, collecting a little pile of hangnails on the empty notepad in front of him. "Before we make any final decisions," he says, clearing his throat, "would you mind showing us the footage of your last inspection? Is the staging area fully prepared? Are the screamers in place?"

"Certainly," Cardea says.

Immediately, Euri elbows the boy beside her, urging him to get up and help her with the lights. She cringes when he stands. Where her navy pantsuit is neatly pressed, pleats crisp and blouse starched, his looks like it's been slept in. But it's too late to choose someone else; Cardea's eyes are already glowing, projecting, her screen already buzzing with memory. Quickly, Euri and the boy shutter oil lamps on tables, walls and the great hutch dominating the room's far end, then they dim flambeaux hanging from the ceiling. The curtains are next; though the sky's already charcoal with rain, and true-dark is no more than an hour off, Euri feels grey eyes watching the bank from outside. Brass rings sing on the curtain rod as she pulls the fabric across. Behind drapes of heavy velvet, it's easier to pretend they aren't so exposed.

Euri returns to her chair, quietly moving it a few inches to the left so she can see between the senators' heads. In the room's muted light, Cardea's helm shines brightly. The picture is grainy, a bit blurred around the edges, but the details are all technicolour. A rectangular field, once turfed with vivid green grass, now concrete pocked with open craters; tunnel mouths leading down, into the warrens Armin commissioned. Over 100 metres long, the old playing surface is dwarfed by enormous tiers of blue plastic seats. The rows gradually angle up from ground level, making a shallow bowl that's fourteen storeys high at the lip. Concourses run between tiers, each one ringed with electric marquees, now dark as the concession stands beneath them. Under the retractable dome, gigantic screens hang like black flags, silent beside glassed-in penthouse suites. At both ends of the field, a giant white metal U stretches its arms to the sky. Along the boundary lines at the posts' feet, more than fifty trestle tables are perfectly aligned, covered in white sheets, manned by armed soldiers and Nycene's loyal counsellors. Sequences of numbers shine above each table, in front of which hundreds—no, thousands—of people are queued. Waiting to be processed.

Waiting to join the numbered ranks filing into the tunnels, into the seats, into the corridors and boxes and players' exclusive rooms.

Waiting to add their wordwinds to the three hundred thousand already gathering their thoughts. Honing their weapons.

The picture bobs as screen-Cardea weaves through the crowd. The din inside the stadium is near-deafening, but not loud enough to drown out the rhythmic chanting from protesters outside.

"Any trouble on the way in?" Talus asks.

Cardea pauses the replay. "Not much. A few hundred grey-lovers, cloud-worshippers, glass-eaters and the like. They're vocal, nothing more. Their 'winds are too caught up in placards and daisy chains to cause any real damage."

Back inside the stadium, the PM's security team draws close around her as she travels from queue to queue, shaking scarred hands, thanking the volunteers, promising their selflessness will not be forgotten. Skipping ahead —"It took three hours to reach the front of the line," Cardea explains—the PM takes over behind one of the registration tables. She poses for the cameras, pen poised, crossing names off the list. Flashbulbs obscure her vision, the footage starred with brilliant patches of white.

As the PM rolls through several minutes of this process—taking people's numbers, verifying their identities, giving them one last chance to withdraw—Euri jots down a note-to-self:

— *contact Librarians, re: collection of records*
— *speak to Rourke, re: photogs' pay-offs*
— *T.V.*

Anyone looking over her shoulder would think this last dot had something to do with the PM's headgear—Euri often has to get the helm repaired—and that's fine.

If you must *write*, Armin taught her, *then write credible code*.

T.V., Euri thinks. Track vote.

It's not that she wants the screamers to fail—Euri, more than anyone, wants to destroy the fuckin' greys for what they did to Armin—but neither should the plan go too smoothly. Not now that Cardea's the one enacting it. Not now that *she'll* be the hero instead of Nycene.

Track the vote, Euri thinks, not for the first time. It's D minus1, and she's been refining her strategy since D minus 30, the day after Armin was swept. She doesn't need the written reminder, there's no way she could forget, but writing calms her. The scratch of pen on paper is reassuring. The permanence of ink reinforces her ideas, makes them real. She adds another point to the list:

— *D.O.*

Day off, any snoop would think—and Euri deserves it, after this week of endless yammering. Day off, they'll think, all innocent and stupid. Training her 'wind to cycle through the To-Do list, to whirl about holidays and days spent sleeping in, Euri thinks deeply. Secretly.

She has no doubt that Carrock and Talus are believers; a month's worth of closed-door discussions won't have changed their views. Wroe and Rourke are fence-sitters, but both are driven by economic rather than ethical concerns. After so much expenditure, the cost of so many man-hours, they'll waver onto the side of supporting tomorrow's detonation. And with that, Euri thinks, we'll have the majority. It won't matter that Yusou is bound to vote against it—or that, even when Armin proposed the idea, Nolasco wasn't shy in voicing her opposition. She can add her twanging shouts to the ones outside the stadium, for all the effect they'll have now. Tonight, the ballot will come up four to two. Actually no, Euri thinks. Make that five. Cardea will add another yes to the pile, of course. Just to be on the winning side.

On screen, the Prime Minister holds a sleeping baby while its mother presses her 'wind on the registration paper, to the right of their names.

Once detonation is approved, Euri will need to watch the flesh-and-blood PM closely. After Cardea sends the order, there will be a sliver of time in which to snag the go-ahead before it reaches the staging area. Knowing what an anal-retent the PM is, she'll probably dispatch three or four copies to ensure the notice arrives on schedule.

D.O.

Delay order.

Now the PM's passing the baby back, turning to a set of triplets, making quips about their remarkable features. In unison, the three broad-bellied men let loose trumpeting baritones, the brash sound herded and amplified by their identical wordwinds.

A day's delay will be embarrassment enough, Euri thinks, wincing as the singers send their bloated 'winds up to cloud the dome. Armin's operation *will* go off—it *must*—but not when Cardea expects. If Euri intercepts the detonation order and, say, *misplaces* it until D+1. . . . The tension will be unbearable. By then, the screamers will be angrier than ever, the bomb all the more potent. . . . The blast will be incredible. It will be unforgettable—as will Cardea's incompetence.

The most important mission in living memory, Euri thinks. Botched by a boxhead.

Her smile fades as the next numbered screamer appears on Cardea's screen.

"Name?" comes the PM's canned voice. "Surname first, please."

"Andrews, Jean."

The lens focuses on the printed list in front of Cardea, but Euri only needed that short glimpse to recognise her.

"Ah, there you are," Cardea says, tapping a smudge of letters on the page. "Next of kin?"

"My husband knows I've come," Jean says. "As, I suspect, do my children."

"Even so, Madame."

The younger clerks sneak glances at Euri as her mother rattles off Peytr's details, then hers, then Zaya's. She ignores them, gaze fixed on the screen. While Cardea confirms the numbers on file match the ones on Jean's palm, tears sting Euri's eyes. Smile returning, she straightens in her seat, the warmth of pride burning her chest. She doesn't want Jean to die, of course she doesn't. But she is proud to see her go. Proud to see her join the rest of the screamers. Proud to see her fulfilling Armin's dreams. Proud to see her help end the war.

"You're too kind for your own good," Euri would say, each time she came before Armin did. In response he'd grin and keep thrusting, gaze turned inward, a dark line growing between his brows. He worried all the time, Euri knew, rotating her hips the way he liked. Even balls-deep inside her, Armin worried.

"Far too kind," she'd said as he lay panting beside her. Smoothing his sweaty black hair, she'd kissed the end of his nose. "It will get you in trouble someday."

"There was a philosopher once," Armin had replied, after his breath returned. "Not just a thinker, mind you; he was also an experienced soldier. 'In such dangerous things as war,' he said, maybe a couple hundred years ago, 'the errors which proceed from a spirit of benevolence are the worst.'" Armin sighed. The crease in his forehead deepened.

"What's your point?" Euri had asked, slipping below the sheets. Aiming to distract.

"Nothing," he'd said, running his fingers through her languid 'wind. "Just—I suppose you may be right."

The staging area is prepped, the vision on Cardea's screen promises.

The stadium is teeming, inside and under and out: everywhere, there is ammunition, shell casings of concrete and flesh and bone.

"As of midnight, everything will be in position," she says, hands folded on the boardroom table, pale white. "The screamers are prepared, mentally and physically. The tunnels are ventilated, but standing room is tight—the bowl isn't much roomier. On-site sources say there's a slow trickle of last-minute volunteers, but, as it stands, the stage is set."

"Now that we've got the numbers counted, do you foresee any change in outcomes?" Wroe asks, one last time. Cardea shakes her head. To prove it, she runs through a series of projections they've all seen before.

The stadium flattened, eight city blocks around it razed. Overhead, a ceiling of ash pressing down, impenetrable, smothering. Ghosts blurring the streets. "Dust storms," Nolasco claims, and Carrock rolls her eyes.

The stadium replaced by a bottomless cavity, a round hollow stretching for miles around. Greys roiling from the depths, snapping and eddying like wolves. "Steam," Yusou says. "A release of subterranean gases. Human life will be unsustainable."

The stadium gone, the parking lots brown with soil. The horizon free of scaffolding and cranes. In the distance, clean brick towers overlooking structures of steel and smooth concrete and glass. Crumbled buildings remain in the foreground, monuments to the past flocked with green fuzz. "It's mould," says Rourke, leaning close for a better look, face streaking with reflected light. "Maybe lichen."

"No," says Talus reverently. "It's grass."

The image flickers as Cardea blinks from channel to channel, but the essentials remain unchanged. The screamers have done their job. There are patches of blue above the skyline. Gold spills from gaps in the clouds. People rush from place to place because they want to, not out of fear.

Armin's dream, Euri thinks, wiping the mist from her eyes. His usurped dream.

"Right then," says Talus, looking from the grey world outside the bank's window to the sunny picture on Cardea's screen. "Shall we vote?"

"What do you hope to accomplish?" Euri had asked. "You know, *after*."

Armin had rolled onto his back, lit a packed-herb cigar. He puffed silently, mouthing smoke rings, breaking them with a finger. Dropping like hail on the pillow, his 'wind revealed what Armin couldn't express aloud. Snuggled up close, Euri could only read about half of the words.

Just that. . . . An after . . .

By morning, it was decided.

The small council dispersed well before dawn, taking cabs in the rain back to the suburbs, gathering their families in the dark, packing bags, quickly fleeing to the outskirts. Not abandoning the city altogether—the senators will need to be visible in the aftermath, stalwart in photographs, standing by their devastating choice—but not lingering in the CBD, either. After the meeting, Cardea's driver docks outside the bank, the car's tires sloshing through rising floodwaters, its electric engine eerily quiet. Diary in hand, Euri follows the PM onto the cold leather seat in the back. Inside, she shakes fat drops from her 'wind and prepares to press whatever briefings Cardea offers into her calendar.

The trip is a short one: the bank is two city blocks from Parliament Square, and Euri's small apartment is four blocks beyond that, past the central markets and the ugly university, squatting on a rocky outcrop down by the dwindling river.

"A team of photographers is scheduled to archive the new façade today," Cardea says, using a handkerchief to smear condensation around on her face-plate. "I'd like to go ahead with the appointment, if possible. At this stage, their images will be much clearer than my projections, and good reference detail will be invaluable once—if—we need to rebuild."

Euri nods. Gov't house is miles away from ground zero, but who's to say how far the bomb's debris will fly? If the screamers work their 'winds into the frenzy Armin had hoped for, the blast could very well reach this far. The manse's new fascia could be shredded to pieces by volatile fonts, sharp stems and counters, burning ascenders and legs and descenders. But it won't happen *today*, if things go according to Euri's plan—so when Cardea says, "They'll need supervision: will you still be around later this afternoon?" she smiles and replies, *Of course.*

There's no time for sleep, she thinks after the PM drops her off, wishing her a good night. The vote has been cast, the session closed, but the order has not yet been despatched. A staff of Pigeons and mentalegraphers is kept on site, Euri knows—Armin employed them well when he was in office—so it won't take long for Cardea to send her little birds flying. Euri's got an hour, tops, to get into position. It's enough, she tells herself, hurrying down to her building's exclusive showers. In the past, she's made it to gov't house and back in forty minutes, with a vigorous fuck in between. It's got to be enough.

After scalding the past few hours from her cold skin, warming her nervous 'wind, Euri slicks her wet hair into a tight knot at the back of her neck. Always prepared, she gets dressed for the workday in case there's no chance to duck back home after the interception. Her favourite suit is burgundy polyester, the skirt and jacket tailored to fit snugly, accentuating her curves. A gift from Armin; worthy of this special occasion. Flopping from the open collar, the long-looped bows of a navy silk blouse are tied close to the throat. She keeps her hair back, and slips her bare feet into black ballet flats, their soles stitched from the quietest leather.

Wrapped in a crinkled plastic poncho, she splurges on a taxi. Light-handed with his whip, the driver gently clicks his tongue at a mule hauling the little hatchback. The beast slops through fetlock-high water, snorting sprays of rain from his nostrils. The cab chugs along, slower than the flares popping overhead, swimming lazy green trails through the clouds. "Can't you make this thing go any faster?" Euri asks, tingling with adrenaline.

Mule and driver turn in unison, their sleepy brown eyes yawning, *What's the rush, lady?*

When they finally reach gov't house, Euri directs them to a side entrance, drops too much change in the driver's wrinkled palm and then dashes up the stone steps. In the small, plain lobby, two guards note Euri's presence with a nod. Well-used to her late-night arrivals, they return to their game of checkers while she hangs her raincoat and umbrella in the cloakroom. The pair pays little attention to the cluster of security screens on the desk behind them as Euri steps out into the corridor, disappearing behind a sliding panel in the mahogany-inlaid walls.

Armin had entrusted few people with these hidden paths, these walkways between, but he'd known Euri could keep a secret. For three years, they'd been together. Three years and none were the wiser. Three years and she'd been promoted no higher than counsellor. Three years and she'd learned every length and corner of these inner halls, every latch tucked in the moulding, every peephole, every trapdoor, every escape. Three years and she'd used none of them without Armin's knowledge. She'd never spied through the two-way mirror hung in Verna's chambers, though she *could* have, easily, she could have watched him play husband to his childhood sweetheart, his frumpy, raspy-voiced wife. She *could* have, but wouldn't and didn't.

Now she creeps through the dark on the ground floor. Spears of light shine from tiny holes all along the high wall: a constellation of intrigue and mistrust that leads Euri to the Prime Minister's office. Bolted to struts, a sturdy iron ladder leads up to a crow's nest eighteen feet up; rungs and shelf alike are worn smooth from use. Silently, Euri climbs to this lofty vantage and peers through a false speaker embedded in the wallpaper just under the ceiling cornice. The office is entirely clad in oak, from the floors to the oblong desk directly below Euri's perch, to the shuttered side-windows on her left, to the heavily-carved walls and visitors' chairs—stately furnishings that look clumsy in such a small space. To her right, a single row of stately photographs hangs at head-height, each frame centred in a square oak panel. Facing the desk, a black leather couch leaves little room for the chairs, both of which Senator Yusou has shunned.

Pacing the polished floorboards between sofa and seats, Yusou leaves a mess of puddles in his wake. Earlier, he'd withdrawn from the boardroom at Cardea's command, disgust and despair greying his features. He must've been walking since then, Euri thinks. Moping at the vote's result, tramping through the rain until the PM could be ambushed well before morning.

His voice floats through the steel mesh, clipped and desperate. Euri releases a tense breath as his words echo her thoughts. "It's not too late."

Clomping back and forth, water spilling from the wide brim of his hat, the senator wrings his hands, pleading. "Ashtad, please. Be reasonable."

From this angle, Euri can't see the PM's screen; a harsh crimson square reflects on the desk's polished surface, then fades as Cardea kneads the muscles in her neck.

"You've gone above and beyond the call of duty tonight, Orhan," she says eventually. "Now go home."

"Please," Yusou says, collapsing into a chair, words rushing from his lips in an urgent whisper. "In the past, generals sent retraction orders—encrypted, sometimes, or fragmented symbols. Indecipherable to enemy spies. Bells tolling a predetermined hymn, colour-coded vials dropped from drone ships, a single line inscribed on a Pigeon's wing: *In the interests of a future present*, it'd say, or something similar, nothing more. And those in command would know, mark my words, they'd *know* to call the operation off."

The reflection from the PM's helm is enigmatic blue. An obvious shade of indifference, Euri thinks. Cardea won't risk her career over this.

"I hear your concerns," she says. "I have certainly noted them. Understand?"

Yusou's spine straightens as he nods. Hope smooths the creases from his round face, and Euri stifles a laugh. Fool, she thinks. Idealist. This afternoon, when the bomb fails to detonate, naïve Yusou will think *he* had something to do with it, that his little outburst swayed a Prime Minister's mind. And tomorrow, when Euri releases the delayed order. . . . Oh, how she wishes she could see his expression then.

"Now if you'll excuse me," Cardea says, standing to escort her guest from the room. "I am due to receive a transmission that cannot be postponed. I will do my best, senator. Mark my words. I am doing my best."

This is it, Euri thinks, sudden worry gnawing her bowels. A call. She's going to give the order verbally.

Feet finding the ladder's top rung, Euri stands. How can she stop the PM from *speaking* the command? She sits. Maybe interrupting the message will be enough—she stands, primed to run from the hidden corridor and into the office—except now Cardea's barring the door behind Yusou. Euri sits. Peering through the speaker-holes, she exhales slowly, getting her 'wind in order. Cardea has always been a pedant when it comes to protocol, she thinks, watching as the PM returns to the desk and unlocks a bottom drawer. One by one, Cardea takes out three small flat boxes and aligns them on the slick wood. *This* is it, Euri decides, relief turning her limbs to gruel. There's no mentalegraph coming, of course there isn't; there will be no vocalising this decree. No, it's not too late—this, *now*, is the moment.

Hunched over a row of tiny scrolls, Cardea scratches a message on each strip of paper. Without even reading them, Euri can guess what they say: *Soup's on. Verna better holler for her dinner*. It took the ministers a whole mind-numbing day to come up with the right phrasing, the right punctuation; now Cardea opens the boxes and ties the carefully-worded ribbons around three identical fob watches. Then she stops. She seems to stare at the clocks for a minute, lids in hand, as if pondering the council's decision.

Don't turn coward now, Euri thinks, standing once more. Wrap those parcels in paper and twine—yes, that's it, knot them up tight—and now summon the house Pigeon, special delivery . . .

Cardea follows Euri's unspoken instructions, to a point. But when the parcels are secreted in a Pigeon's satchel, Cardea doesn't ring the deliveryman's bell. Instead, she takes off her helm and leaves it on her wingback chair. Cloaking herself in swathes of fabric taken from her personal closet, the PM covers her pocked face and stringy blonde hair, leaving the barest slit free for her eyes. She looks small, Euri thinks. Weak. Like one of the travelling women who sell gold jewellery at the central markets. She is unrecognisable, slouched like a beggar, a black rain cape drooping on her veiled shoulders.

Laden with the Pigeon's burden, Cardea walks across the room—aiming not for the door, but for Euri's wall. A few seconds later, there's a quiet hiss of air pressure being released, a door swinging on hydraulic hinges. Craning to see down into the room's corner, Euri lifts her feet and holds her breath. She can't make out more than the panel's top quarter, a shadowed edge that must open into this very rat-run. The hidden exit should be no more than two feet to Euri's right; if Cardea looks up after she passes under the lintel, there's no way she'll miss seeing her crouched above, wordwind lightning pale with fear.

Fuck fuck fuck, Euri mouths, closing her eyes like a child, praying for invisibility. The ladder's rungs grow slick under her palms. Vertigo latches onto her ears, her skull, her 'wind and swings its heavy legs, trying to dizzy her down.

I'm falling, she thinks, though she hasn't moved. Through the fast thrum of her pulse, she listens for footsteps or the gentle click of the secret panel closing—then cracks an eyelid as she realises, too late, that the corridor has remained dark. Even when the door slid open, the hallway wasn't flooded with light.

Cardea hasn't gone out, Euri thinks, clambering fast as her rubbery legs allow. She's gone *down*.

If you want an important job done properly, Armin used to say, do it yourself.

But it would be stupid for the PM to bring the order herself, Euri thinks, again and again, as if repetition will somehow generate truth. It would be reckless.

"Where do you want us?" the photographer asks, and Euri waves him in the general direction of gov't house's façade. Hours have passed since she lost Cardea in the ratways; now the rain has subsided, the new colonnades and stained glass and freshly-painted frescos are gleaming in the grey light, but Euri's mind is still caught in the darkness between walls, trying to fathom where the other woman went.

"Consider all angles," she says while the photographer's assistants set up tripods, flash reflectors, and softbox diffusers. Taking her own advice, Euri runs through all the scenarios she can imagine.

— Cardea descended into the tunnels and delivered the orders herself (ridiculous; reckless; probably impossible . . .)
— Cardea walked out right under my nose, but my eyes were closed, so I missed it (don't be stupid)
— Cardea is still inside, prolonging her moment of power (??)
— Cardea had trouble rousing the Pigeons from their drunken sleep (here's hoping)
— The Pigeons have already flown.

A thick wax of dread clogs Euri's throat at this last point. Her mind wanders, following her gaze over the outdoor amphitheatre Nycene had had constructed on the grounds in anticipation of post-grey festivities. All of Armin's hard work, she thinks, swallowing hard. Of course his plans will go off without a hitch—and for what? To keep Cardea in office, boxhead of the unbelievers, glorying in his achievements?

"Just get on with it," she snaps as the photographer waves her over. Shaking the snark from her 'wind, she straightens her jacket, dodging puddles as she crosses the yard.

"Are these to be formal or candid shots?" the man says, fussing with a flashbulb until it sparks.

"They are historical documents, Monsieur Antier," Euri replies. "Of course they should be temporally accurate and impeccably staged."

"As I thought." Antier whistles at his youngest assistant and points at the building, jibbering instructions in their northern tongue. "Please forgive Erec's stubbornness," he says, scowling at the boy. "He refuses to treat with evacs or vagrants."

"What do you mean?"

Pointing at the base of a fluted column with his half-smoked cigarette, Antier says, “I must finish with the test shots. Would you mind?”

Euri follows his gaze and sees a rambling-man slumped at the house’s entrance, ruining the artist’s shot. “Fine,” she says, turning to stride across the flags. From more than two metres away, she smells the drifter’s sour body and hears him mumbling, chewing the ragged ends of his beard. Afraid of startling him—he’s got the glazed stare and blood-stained lips of a glass-chewer, she thinks—Euri stops just out of kicking range.

“Excuse me, sir.”

“I’m *official*,” he says, slurring and coughing. Words crawl along his hairline like nits, peeking out from under his hood before scuttling back out of sight. Euri shudders and takes a step back. “I have *this* bit of business to clear up.” The man gurgles and hiccups, waving a small parcel around. “Won’t be long. Won’t be long.”

He hiccups again and holds the package out in red-crusted hands. Euri’s heart leaps. The box is the right size. . . . The newsprint torn but recognisable. . . . The twine knotted by Cardea’s manicured fingers . . .

“Here,” she says, taking in the rambler’s outfit. The satchels, the silvered hood, the sturdy boots. A Pigeon. One of Cardea’s three! If he’s still here, if he hasn’t yet managed to leave the grounds, then the other two can’t be far off either. A smile breaks out across Euri’s face and she wants to run inside, singing *It’s not too late!* louder than rockets. Reaching into her jacket, she grabs a tipping-purse and scrunches the lot into the Pigeon’s trembling hand. Excited, she pats his balled fist. “Keep it,” she says. “For your trouble.”

“All’s well,” she calls to Antier, waving at him to take a break. “I’ll be right back.”

The Pigeon mutters something about failing as she skips up the steps. She breaks stride long enough to reassure him—“You did just fine, Pigeon,” she says, hushing his complaints with other sweet nothings, “Take as long as you need”—before dashing into the lobby on silent feet. Smiling, she asks Darrio, that stupid, Pigeon-loving guard, “Any deliveries?”

"Nothing come in all day, counsellor," he says from behind the welcome desk, "but there's been a few birds hanging about."

"There have, there *have*," she says, clapping him on the arm. "It's not too late!"

Squinting up at the brass clock above the main entrance, the guard says, "Won't get late for yonks, counsellor. We got least an hour 'til true-dark . . ."

"Too right," Euri says, smiling, floating. And leaving the lout to ponder definitions of time, she skips to the Pigeons' quarters to see how much more of it she can collect.

Once upon a time, Jean used to tell them on rainy days like this, there was a city made of sand. Ancient, it was, and incredibly strong—even though its kings wore eye make-up. Thigh-length skirts. Jewelled necklaces. Even though slaves oiled the men's skin with perfumes and curled their long hair like a girl's. Hours a day, the lords would waste, with their ointments and waxes and sweet-smelling unguents. Preparing their pansy-soft bodies in life, she'd say, to be pieces of tough leather after death.

Still, Jean would say. All in all. They obviously knew a thing or two about preservation. When not chained in their boudoirs, the kings' serfs greased the city's pyramids and parapets and fortified walls. Smearing lard, maybe, some sort of god-spelled pig fat, to save antique golden sands from the monsoons.

Each year the deluge started off slow, a few fingers of rain tap-tapping on baked tiles and mudstone. But soon fingers swelled into fists and fists into feet that pounded while they ran and ran and ran. Racing down turrets and domes and awnings, the waters thumped and skidded across that magical gunk, leaving the city slimy but whole behind it. Beyond the gate, several miles to the east, the river drank and drank—just like your Nan used to, Ma always laughed. Remember?—it drank until it threw up.

Sloshing away from his apartment complex, brown water eddying up to the knee, Peytr's now pretty sure Jean made the whole thing up. A flood that licks but doesn't bite, he thinks with a snort that grows into a full-blown cough. Sandbags line the street on both sides, hessian sacks already soaked to splitting, drooling their guts into the stream. Row houses tilt forward inch by inch as the current nibbles at rotting foundations. Scaffold planks girding nearby spires and 'scrapers bloat like Ma's cardboard biscuits, thwapping as they fall into the soup below.

Even the greys are running for cover, Peyt thinks. Their boots clomping across rooftops. Their slippery fingerprints condensing on shop windows. Their breath steaming up bogged twice-a-days. Their laughter howling over flues and through doorless tenements and along alleys only skingirls and soldiers dare travel.

Real soldiers, that is.

He should've taken an umbrella like Mireille offered, but *Young soldiers have more to worry about in the field than getting a bit damp, Mimi*, he'd said. Now the words cascade overhead, lies diluted by the rain. *soldiers . . . worry . . . get*. . . . Now Peyt's muddled, sogged. *fiel . . . Mi*. . . . Now the downpour's set into his chest and sinuses. *A flood that gives more than it takes?* The storm wreaking havoc on his 'wind.

Shaking his head, Peyt lifts his collar, squinting against cold needles of rain. In Jean's tale, the river spewed for weeks but somehow always transformed into a wonderland for water buffalo and flamingos. Feathery reeds swayed in the shallows, tossed by carp and 8crocodile breezes. Dragonflies skimmed the glistening surface—and, depending on Jean's mood, sometimes there were dragons. When the deluge finally retreated, she'd say, crops blanketed the fields almost instantly. A bristling gold delta of wheat.

What a fuckin' crock.

Trash drifts past as Peyt trudges down the road. Shreds of plastic and foil wrappers. Grog bottles. Limbless floaters. No amount of pig-goop will save *them*, he thinks, smearing snot on his drenched sleeve. Coughing up clots of phlegm. He horks a gob into the slow-moving current, wipes the backsplash off his left satchel. The canvas squelches under his shrivelled fingers—and for a second, Peyt's back at base camp after lights-out. Showers pattering on the tarp overhead, on the dirt outside, stirring up shit that puts a wheeze in Cap's lungs, a thin whistle in Jepp Rhysson's nose. Cloudfever, the guys call it. Bomb-lung. And while Dake's snoring on the cot beside him, a deep-barrelled thundering, Peyt reaches out and presses his palm against the tent wall. The canvas squelches, billows, vibrates against the wind and Peytr pretends it's a strong chest rumbling.

Fuckin' rain, he thinks, splashing back to the present. So hard to think, so hard to function, with a double-squalled head. After a few deliveries, I'm going to find a flophouse somewhere. Wring out. Finally get some sleep.

It's not really lying, Peyt reminds himself, crossing an intersection against the lights. On the best of days, traffic is sparse in this neighbourhood; today it's mostly sidewalk-sloshers like him. Three or four velos wheel on the median, failing to keep chain and pedals above water. Cabbies whip their mules along the sidewalks. A raft bobs in the Good As New's parking lot, knocked together out of barrel drums and a thick sheet of ply. Peyt stops in to see if Nashani's got any inventory needs to-or-froing, and when the old lady sends him back into the storm with only a knitted blanket for his new baby, Peyt still doesn't feel like a liar.

It's a matter of duty, he thinks. Pure and simple. The way Mireille admires the shell of him—wearing his faded multicams, hauling rucks everywhere, refilling his grenades every night before he lies down beside her. The way she looks at him without looking too close. . . . The way she's always just assumed . . . *soldier* . . . and she's trusted . . . *young* . . . and she's never felt safer . . . *worry*. . . . Because he saved her *ruined her* life.

He owes it to Mimi to get deployed every once in a while, even if it's only to the outskirts of town. Soldiers, unlike Pigeons, are expected to be away. For days. Weeks, even. Regardless of new live-ins. New couplings. Newborns.

And he's so tired.

And the baby hasn't stopped screeching in days.

No matter how many times Mimi plugs its hole with nipples or rubber. No matter how strong the grog she uses to baste its raw gums.

No matter how Tantie May coos or lullabies. No matter how soothing the rain sounds on their shared apartment's tin roof. No matter how many flamingos or water buffalo Peyt adds to Jean's story. The sweaty little thing grizzles and cries and Tantie May warbles and Mireille weeps and clings and kisses and Peyt drowns in tears and smothers under sodden lips and he picks up his bags and says the platoon's been restationed and he invents a location and it's never close and he goes out into the rain and onto his same old route and stops at the Good As New and passes the consulate and passes gov't buildings and passes parliament and passes the gallows and passes the daymarkets and passes the warehouses and passes the repat hospital and passes the dead factories and passes the Wheels 'n' Heels and ducks into the grogger just to escape all the wet.

It's warm inside the pub, but far from dry. Peyt sucks in a fug of moist heat that stinks of scalp and 'pits and fermented breath. Beneath pine trestle tables, the concrete's puddled and spattered with muck. In an alcove of mirrors and boarded-up windows, a woeful little tiled floor is bogged; a thin yellow streamer cordons it off, in case anyone gets jolly enough to try dancing.

Eight days into a rainstorm, no one so much as taps their feet to the golden oldies crackling from ceiling amps. Around the bar, drips in business suits slouch over brews, a steam of letters rising from their uncovered heads. A pair of scar-faced stumpeys swig from tall pints tucked in the crook of their elbows; at the next booth over, another slurps a chunky white soup by holding the bowl with his dirty bare feet. Peyt quick-scans the cluster of coveralls slumped in steel chairs beside the woodstove—and heaves a sad sigh when Borys isn't among them. It's too late in the morning for most factory workers; nightshift ended a few hours ago, dayshift is well under way. Euri beckons Peytr over to his regular booth, on the far right beneath a double-arched window. She's wearing a flannel nightie with frilled hems, a clear plastic rain-hat and rubber boots that reach up to her knees. Letting the door swing shut behind him, he quick-waves at his little sister then descends the short stair, wending around puddles and chipped melamine tables on the way to meet her.

Hoad's playing solitaire on an inverted cask nearby, so Peyt tilts his head at him before sliding onto the wall-side pew. The other Pigeon lifts an eyebrow. Deals another card.

So much for professional courtesy, Peyt thinks, inwardly flipping Hoad the bird.

"Got fifteen minutes 'til next shift. Mind if I join ye?"

Peyt looks up. The voice's owner is backlit, her wild dreads jewelled with sarcastic quips, all limned pink in the lantern light. Not so pink as before, he realises; age and rain are getting the best of Gerte's dye. "Plenty of room," he says, nodding at the stool beside Euri. Changing his mind, he slides further down the bench and pats the spot he's just emptied. "Especially if you're buying."

"Always the charmer," Gerte says.

He shimmies a few more inches down, but stops well short of backing into the shrouded woman sitting at the seat's far end. Wrapped in scarves and long black veils, she's talking to a Pigeon Peytr's never seen before—a muscular kid who looks like he's got more beef than brains. Two cups of weak tea are going cold on the table in front of them.

"Here for a bit of the ol' truth serum?" Gerte says, taking one look at Peyt's girdle of luggage and hooking herself a stool. She tosses her balled-up apron onto the table in front of Euri, then signals at the barkeep for two pints.

Peyt almost smiles. "Something like that. What's on tap?"

"Same shite as always." When Gerte talks, a pea-sized hole yawns in the hollow at the base of her throat, where a spiked stud once bristled. As always, Peyt resists the urge to shove a finger in it. Euri has no such self-control; she kneels on her chair, bends close for a good look, prods with the end of her pinkie. Metal rings have dragged dark lines down Gerte's nostrils, the powdered skin too loose now to hold them firm. While Peyt chain-sneezes, the waitress sifts through change in her hip-pack, extra tips she's made helping Brandt behind the bar. Her forehead wrinkles as she counts coins onto the table. Empty piercings line her brows and lips, seams of black dots that stand out against her pale complexion. She looks, Peytr thinks, like a doll with its stitches plucked.

Snickering, Euri agrees.

"Got a nickel?" Gerte says.

"Probably." He digs one out of his ruck, manoeuvring around the other bags' straps without slipping them off his shoulders. Gerte makes a joke about Peyt's being into bondage—all those leashes and buckles, all that leather—but he doesn't let her tease the packs off him.

"All right, Borysson," she says after Brandt's clunked a couple of jars on the table, and told Gerte her break's up in five. "Get one of these into ye." Peyt reaches for the nearest pint, but she slaps his hand away. With a coy expression, she dips into her vest's inside pocket and pulls out a pair of glass marbles. They're not perfect spheres, more oval than round, but the lamplight catches nicely on their milk-and-nacre swirls as she rolls them around on her palm.

"What do you think?" Peyt asks and Euri shrugs. *Why not?*

"Loosen ye up," Gerte says. "Knock the cold out ye."

Outside, rain sloshes down the gutters, hisses against storm boards, smacks the flooded street. Shit weather for travelling now, but if it lets up any time soon, Peyt could still make a few pick-ups before true-dark. He could earn enough to stay in a flop . . .

"I shouldn't," he says.

"Suit yerself." Bracing the translucent balls between fingertips and table, Gerte crushes them with a delicate pop. Glass glints on the worn pine. Lacerates, then frosts Gerte's fingerprints. Sucking and licking, she laps up the mess, nibbling under nails until they bleed. Digit by digit, she dunks into the jagged piles. Cuts and collects. Swirls the sticky red remnants into her drink and chugs the whole thing down. Immediately, her smile widens. Her eyes fix on wonders Peyt can't hope to see.

After Gerte goes back to work, Peytr turns to Euri and says, "What now?"

Look, she replies. Stifling a giggle, she points at a small shard Gerte overlooked. *A perfect little petal. Smaller than my front tooth . . .*

Peyt hesitates until Brandt starts heading over with a cloth to wipe the table clean.

Quick! Quick!

The glass hooks into Peytr's fingertip before Brandt gets past two tables. It slices Peyt's lip, gouges the soft flesh inside his cheek. A long, glorious cut. Tonguing it deeper, he exhales ten years of pent breath. Euri claps, louder and louder, and Peyt—

Blinks.

Gerte's tending the bar and Blink: wiping tables and Blink: tending bar, arms a-blur, multiplying, pouring and reaching and clearing bottles and Blink: four arms, eight, whirling and Blink Blink: fog shimmers, a blind pulled down from the ceiling—*No*, Peyt says, *it's not coming down. . . . I'm rising. I'm through the roof. Hear the engines?*— fog roils from puddles and cat-slinks around ankles and Blink: fog obscures barstools and lanterns and benches and the toilet door's coin slot and Blink: fog covers stumpies and suits and coveralls and Hoad, even Hoad, is glistening with dew.

Blink.

Blink.

Peytr drops down to the rafters, perches, kicks his heels and Blink: his body sways on the bench below. *Yes, this*, he says and his limbs are syrup, so sweet, so calm, and he's laughing and Blink: relaxed, his many gazes swimming *left right left* and Blink: the young Pigeon is laughing, mouth wide and red and wet and Blink: mouth velvet, vulvar, a codpiece lined with ivory daggers and Blink: the kid's blubbering, tea shining down his face and Blink: crying like the baby and Blink: he's laughing and Blink: he's hanging with Peyt in the skybunker and Blink: he's biting gold sovereigns and Blink: he's at the bar and Blink: he's tossing the parcel to Brandt? Trading the box for a pint? and Blink: *What happened to professionalism?* and Blink: kid's chugging down the foamy black and Blink: he's shirking his delivery? and Blink: he's launching rockets from his razored teeth.

And Blink: he's gone.

And Blink: Euri's gone.

And Blink: the baby's gone.

Blink.

The noise is so loud, it's quiet.

Blink.

Beside him, the shroud's head turns and Blink: she's a silhouetted pyramid and Blink: she's a flickering boxed-screen and Blink: a cloth-wrapped secret, watching Peyt watching her. He grinds the glass hard and Blink: iron floods his tongue and he sucks pain from cheeks and Blink: salt burns from his eyes and Blink Blink: nostrils flow and he tastes slime and sharp consonants and Blink: the black veils are in motion, the shroud's silks rustling closer and Blink: she's old Ruby with her shawl slung over head and shoulders, framing a wicked glare and Blink: she's a photograph from Esther's archives, a phantom caught in flight. Peytr looks down and up and away and Blink: his head meets the wall and the boarded window rattles and Blink: a canvas tarp vibrates him to sleep.

See you in the morning, Peytie, Jean says, screwing the grenade's lid on tight, giving it a couple good hard jolts before placing it on his dresser.

He closes his eyes and breathes slow and deep until the tightness in his chest eases.

A rough cloth scrubs his nose and—*No*—a rough scalp grates his lips and—*No*—stubble scrapes and a frenzied 'wind prickles his skin as he licks and gulps and swallows and—*No*—spits and spits and spits and Blink: melted glass and blood fume through his cavities and he balloons upward, body lifting, drifting, tethered only by the cord of his skinny right arm, a flesh-ribbon clutched in the shrouded woman's cold grasp.

"Focus," she says, making another pass with the handkerchief. Peytr squirms like a pup as the woman reels him back down from the sky, grounding him with a voice firm as her hands. He feels her fingers prodding, pinching, tweaking, slapping—he thinks he feels—but she is sitting a foot away now. Stuffing the grimy cloth up her sleeve. Plying him with tea. Holding the cup to his mouth until he swallows.

"Drink," she says. "Deep swigs. That's it, Two—don't be afraid to gargle."

The brew is bitter, a pungent rosehip and lemon that stings the gashes inside Peytr's mouth. It swishes and cleans on the way down, expanding as it goes, filling his belly with lead. Euri climbs on Peyt's back, bear-hugs until his spine wilts. His lungs deflate against the table's edge. Head cradled in his hands, he can no longer hear the stars.

"What do you want?" The question is barbed, but doesn't shred his mouth so sweetly as glass. He peers at the woman sideways through the V of his arm. Slits his eyes. Focuses. "I know you."

"Says the junkie to a stranger."

"All right, *stranger*." Peytr sits up, trying not to sway as he leans in close. "Maybe you've heard of Jean—"

The woman hushes him with a smooth white hand. "No names, soldier. We do not, nor will we ever, know each other personally. Should we ever meet again, it will be for the first time. Understand?"

Blink: a box wrapped in newsprint and string appears on Peyt's lap, small as a deck of Hoad's cards.

"For now," she continues, "I'll call you Two." Pointing at the same figure scrawled in ink on the paper, she speaks slowly, as if Peyt is simple. "Consider it a tracking number."

"And should I also carve it into my palm, Your Honour?"

Cardea winces.

Blink: her eyes have no pupils. They're polished blue stone. Solid. Grey-touched.

Just like the rest of us, Peytr thinks—then snatches his sympathy before she can see it. Buries it deep in his ruck with the shells Jean gave him, long ago, before she offered to cut herself into history.

"What's the point?" he says, grabbing Cardea's hands. She stiffens but doesn't pull away. Peytr bends her fingers back, harder and harder, exposing pristine flesh. The table legs screech on the concrete as he jostles, moving so close his 'wind oozes bile onto the PM's veils. At the noise, Gerte looks up from behind the bar.

Blink: the waitress's 'wind twists into a lasso. A noose from which Peyt can hang.

Blink: she grimaces, elbowing Brandt.

"Play nice," the bartender says. "We'll bounce you quick as, Peytie boy."

"Don't call me that," Peyt snaps. Then lowering voice and hands, he turns back to Cardea. "Your cutpaws bleed so you don't have to—am I right?"

"You've no idea what you're saying, Two."

"Maybe not," Peyt says and Blink: she's wiping his tears. Blink: she's cowering under blankets of guilt. "So educate me."

"A parcel left my offices yesterday." Discreetly, she takes a pouch of coin from her purse and another filled with enough seeds to feed Peyt and Mireille's whole tenement for years. "This one needs to arrive first. That's all you need know."

"An address wouldn't hurt," Peytr says.

Cardea tilts her head, ceding the point, and passes him a tiny slip of crisp white parchment.

"Why don't you get one of your people to carry this? Send in a chopper or something. Special delivery, VIP. Bound to get there quicker by air . . ."

Blink: there's a pinch—a tug at Peyt's 'wind and

Blink: Cardea's mouth is opening, closing, her jaw is crunching and

Blink: why was he thinking of choppers?

"Proof of delivery costs extra," he says, getting back to business. Turning the paper over and over, he admires its clean grain.

"Failure to deliver will cost more."

"Whatever you say, Your Honour—" and Peyt glances at the details she's inked—inked!—in miniature cursive. An address. In theory, a simple mission. And Blink: he's back at basecamp. Blink: he's following the other vultures and Blink: he's back in the alley. Blink.

Blink.

Blink

"I can't do it," he says, paper dropping from numb fingers. "I won't."

"You can, soldier." Blink: the Prime Minister rips glowing red resistance from Peytr's wordwind, crumbles it into her cup and Blink: she's dabbing her lips. "And you will."

Peytr's legs resist carrying him across town to the stadium. He's determined to make it there—Cardea drained his reluctance along with her cup—he's determined to deliver this parcel immediately. His mind has been made up.

His body has different ideas.

Instinct kicks in: a physical fight to his flight. Stay put, his muscles shout with cramps and crippling tremors. Sweat chills every part the rain hasn't reached. His cock turtles inward, balls hiking up into his bowels. He spends over an hour in a public outhouse, squeezing panic out through his arsehole. Just get on the road, he tells himself, clutching his packs to his belly while he shits. Get it over with. Get moving. Walking usually calms him, the *left right left* flexing anxiety out with each step. Long strides and a steady pace soothe better than talk or pills or the quack meditations Tantie May says he should do; as if all his worries, his nightmares, his memories can be pounded to dust underfoot.

It galls spending coin before it's counted, but if Peyt's going to make it to the drop-off he'll have to hire four legs to replace his rebellious two.

Five taxis clatter past before Euri grabs Peyt's arm and forces him to hail one. A blue-and-white sedan with tailfins and chrome hubcaps, the hood torn off and transmission gutted, two mules hitched in the engine's place. Fat as his animals, the driver grunts while twisting to unlock a back door for them. The vinyl seat squeaks as they clamber in, adding to puddles collected in the grooved cushion. Mould blooms across the moth-eaten roof and big-bellied drops plink onto their shoulders and heads. The cab smells of damp canvas and musk and stewed onions. Peyt's stomach rumbles with hunger.

He gives the driver directions that will take them to the south end of the CBD, a few streets away from the blockade. Close enough that his traitor legs should be able to cope; far enough not to get tangled up with protesters, or to raise any suspicions. Taking roads he hasn't travelled since Daken—since *before*— he'll veer west, offloading the package at the first sentry post he sees. Let them carry it across the perimeter. Past convenience stores and schoolyards. Down alleyways choked with dead words. Over vast evac-filled parking lots to the stadium.

Let someone else do it.

Anyone.

No way he's crossing into that territory himself, Pigeon or otherwise. No fuckin' way.

Glancing in the rear-view mirror, the mule-driver sneers and says, *Thought you birds was supposed to be all high and mighty, flying come rain or sleet and all that shit.* Then he names a price that blinks Peyt into a fury—until Euri rests a small hand on his thigh. Presses a finger to her lips. Gives him the settle-down stare.

"You're right," he mutters, and the driver nods while Peyt doles out coin after coin. With his pockets sufficiently weighted, the fat man lashes the mules, who point their dripping beige muzzles toward the city's arse-end. On the way, their hooves clank across railway lines, clop under overpasses, thud along wooden bridges barely wide enough to fit the car. The driver whips the fear out of them, so the pair travels even the narrowest lanes at full speed. At the parkway, he gives them their head; their jerky canter sets Peytr's teeth rattling. Still, he admits, sleeving the steamed-up window. It's nice to be out of *that*. Faded pennants on lampposts thrash in the gale. Flags twist, throttling rooftop poles. Curtains of rain sheer down before glass-fronted buildings, obscuring the people inside. They might be greys, for all Peyt can tell. They might be friends.

Beside him, Euri's 'wind cycles through travelling songs as she traces stick figures into the condensation. Next she makes little footprints, pressing the side of her fist into the glass, using thumb and fingerprints for the toes. When she makes a mistake, Euri simply leans close, exhales an erasing fog, and starts again. Peyt wishes it was always so easy.

Heavy, he slouches. Leans against the headrest. Wishing he had another shard, he watches neighbourhoods evolve according to street signs. Blink: Brinnenberg and Blink: Kesoi—bombed-out shitholes, both, and crawling with greys. Blink: Slakt halvmåne, the first of a few blocks further north that are crammed full of tunnellers' brick cottages. Mimi once applied for housing there, years ago. Before the baby came. Thought she'd make a good digger, thought she'd fit right in. After all, she was used to being underground and wasn't afraid of the dark. Her stamina was good, she'd said with a wink. She liked the idea of proving there were no greys in the black, of unearthing, undermining. And the danger pay was good.

She had no fuckin' idea. Mireille thought packing their apartment full of garbage pilfered from the museum—cuckoo clocks, imperial doo-dads, moth-eaten tapestries, fossils of things that could never have been—made her an expert at recon. She thought stacking more and more shit along the walls and hallways, making little warrens out of each room, had trained her to cope with tight spaces. She thought using a shovel instead of a gun meant she wasn't contributing to the war effort. She thought she was being a rebel.

But accidentally plant a kid in her belly, Peyt thinks, and then see how fast she softens. Blink: she's an instant believer and Blink: she sees greys behind each city corner and Blink: gets a low-rent share apartment in the suburbs and Blink: starts paying attention to politics and Blink: wishes she'd voted in the last election.

On the sly, Peyt had gone to the polling stations. Told Mimi he was heading out of town for weapons training, then went to the bank and stood in line for hours just to press his 'wind on the Prime Minister's empty helm. One politician is as bad as the other, far as Peyt's concerned. Believers. Non-believers. Doesn't matter. As long as there are ghosts the war will go on. No screen-head's policies will change that. The whole thing's gone way too far now to change course, way too far to go back. Simply stopping is not a conclusion. There have been too many Dakens lost. Too many volunteers like Jean.

And the shells just keep on coming.

Peytr voted anyway. Out of principle, out of right. He won't pretend it made a difference.

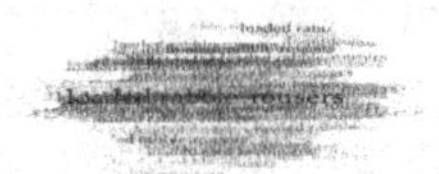

The mules slow at the parklands, wary of mines. Banners woven from childish wordwinds drape from wire fences, the writing beautiful but illegible. To the gate's left, one says גבעה מגפת, the once-red letters now faded to pink. Another reads พื้นศูนย์ and Euri laughs, saying the word looks like a little face with funny pierced ears, a little pierced nose, and irises shifty-looking over to the right. Peyt tells her to hush as the cab crunches over a dirt meadow scrapped with tall weeds, ringed by brown grass tussocks and low mounds. Under a foot of rain-churned water, any pink-painted warnings are invisible. At any second, they could roll over a grey's hideout, trigger an IED, fall into an explosive trap. Peytr rolls down his window, straining to hear the hum of bottled words. The twang of a released snare. The click that could end their lives.

Nearly there, says the driver softly, to the animals or passengers or himself.

Not so brash now, Peyt's tempted to say, but keeps his mouth shut, his 'wind hooded. He reaches over to take Euri's hand, but she shakes him off. Cross-legged on the seat beside him, one of his satchels pulled onto her lap, she's looking down at it in concentration. Digging under the canvas flap. Tugging at what's inside. Pulling it out.

Think we should open it? That other Pidge didn't give his a second look before tossing it. . . . And how much you want to bet Hoad's got the other one, propping up his deck? Why should we be the only ones to risk our necks? Without even seeing what we're in for?

"Put that away," Peyt whispers, willing the mules to move faster. Another fifty metres or so and they'll be out of the park, back on asphalt. Heading for military traffic and the camouflage of crowds.

Climbing up and down her pigtails, Euri's 'wind spells out *False hope. . . . False hope . . .* and Blink: the rough cord around the package is untied, snaked on the cab floor. Blink: the newsprint falls open around a stiff cardboard box, another string holding its lid in place.

"Don't," Peytr starts to say but then thinks, Why the fuck not? Maybe Euri's got the right idea. Whatever's inside, Cardea didn't want her own people anywhere near it. Instead she hired a trio of nobody Pigeons—loners, he realises, who can't be traced back to her. But why? What's she playing at? Something that's obviously worth paying way too much for, Peyt thinks. Something she can't—or won't—do herself.

It's a set-up, he decides, as Euri works at a tight little knot in the string. The thing's full of grey-bait; it's a box loaded with delicious eyes. That's it: I'm not supposed to make the drop. Before I even get there, the reek of trapped sight will lure the fuckers out, giving the vultures a clear shot, a perfect shot to attack out in the open. . . . Guaranteed there'll be no report filed after the grunts pump me full of verbs. I'll be ghosted while the squad celebrates, my core shunted into the black, into nothing. And then the fucking PM will pin medals on the shooters' chests while brooms brush my remains into the gutter. And when the dust settles, the roaches will feast.

As Euri pops the lid, there's a metallic clinking inside. A rattling of something like beads. Fuck, Peyt thinks, forgetting about vultures and roaches and eyes. It's a compact shell. Flat instead of round, ideal for sliding through gaps in old stadium walls or under loading bay doors or into an unsuspecting Pigeon's bag . . .

"Do you hear gears? Do you hear ticking?" he asks, heart jumping when Euri fumbles the box. The driver replies, *There's a construction site a block thataway*, but he hasn't got a fuckin' clue what he's talking about. He let a fuckin' suicide bomber into his backseat for a few fuckin' coins—what the fuck does he know? Peyt tries to calculate how long it's been since he picked up the bomb, how long before that Cardea might've ignited the thing, how long she would've given him to reach the stadium. Did she read the future in that screen-helm of hers? Did she know he'd catch a cab, this fucking slow cab with its fuckin' skittish donkeys? Or did she think he'd walk? Did she guess his route? Maybe the destination was a ruse—maybe she planned for the bombs to detonate before the Pigeons got anywhere close to the CBD.

He can't really remember what buildings are between here and there. Probably an op-shop and army surplus. A couple of groggers. The local shelter. There's a travel and passport agent somewhere, close to a ransacked Pick 'n' Mix. A hostel or two. An evac processing centre. "Stop," Peyt says, banging on the back of the driver's seat. "It's too dangerous. Let us out."

Everything's fine, the man replies, laughing as his mules jog the last few metres out of the park, pulling the cab onto firmer ground. *Road ain't even flooded up here!* He flogs them into a trot. Their shoes clatter on the pavement, ringing doom.

"Stop!" Peytr shouts.

We're going to explode, he says. He thinks.

Shortcut, says the cabbie, swerving into a narrow lane between a bottle factory and an evac centre. Sirens wail in the distance and suddenly the grey sky blooms green. Around them, the brick canyon is plunged in suffocating darkness, rusted water hissing down the walls, men hissing from behind, Cap and his lackeys hissing *pussy pussy pussy*, blocking the way out, blocking them in and

Blink: Peyt's gripping something cold, something metal and Blink: his face is burning, rubbed raw on stubble and Blink: Daken's moaning and Blink: he's moaning and Blink: he's gagging on 'e's and 'r's and 'y's and

He's gripping something cold, something metal, flat and smoothly round in his palm. It's not long, it's not a spoon, there's no handle-gouging. Through his tears he sees yellow, not silver; Borys didn't make this at the Wheels 'n' Heels, could never make something so fine. Breath shudders in and out of Peyt's mouth as he gapes, blinking, not at scraping-steel bones, not at a stealth bomb, but a man's unadorned pocket watch. Burnished gold with an ivory face, its archaic numerals of inlaid ebony. Time stopped with its hands up, frozen behind the cracked glass. Looped around the winding mechanism, a ribbon of paper, inked in a feminine script.

Typical bureaucrat, Peyt thinks, grinding the outburst from his eyes, focusing on Cardea's markings. She sure knows how to waste good words.

In the interests of a future present.

Peyt reads it over and over, but repetition does not spark understanding.

"That's it," he tells Euri. "The whole inscription."

Who cares, she says with a shrug. Eyeing the watch like a jeweller, head cocked, squinting, she continues, *It looks expensive.*

Quickly, he shoves it back in the box before the driver sees it. Anyone else gets curious the way his sister did, Peyt figures, and none of these parcels will be delivered today. Euri's not wrong: the watch will fetch a good price at the nightmarkets, even with the damage. Enough to rent them a bigger apartment. A unit maybe. A place to sleep four without anyone having to share a room. Tantie

May doesn't have kids of her own, but she's always loved the baby. And now that Mimi's almost willing to trust her—at least ready to believe she won't up stakes and run out on them in the middle of the night—May could stay on as a nanny. She could move with them, keep Mimi company while Peytr's on the road.

It's not like Cardea knows where to find him. She hired him at a *bar* for fuck's sake. No proof of delivery required, no names exchanged, no consequences. . . . And like Euri said, that fledgling Pidge ditched his load at the first opportunity—and no doubt Hoad would be Three on the PM's nameless list of Pigeons, but once his cards come out he isn't going anywhere fast. It was a risk Cardea took, a huge risk. So what does she expect?

"Pull over," he says. The cab emerges from the alleyway, rounds the corner, and the mules pull up stubborn while blue lines of Watchmen troop across the intersection, blowing whistles and flat-palm ordering the traffic to stop.

But no, Peytr thinks, clutching but not pulling the door handle. No, no, no. I'm not low as them. Guaranteed I'm the only one'll see this piece to its destination. Besides, if word got around. . . . Nobody hires a thief, Peyt knows, and he needs this job. Not just to support his family—to escape it.

Euri rolls her eyes.

A parade of recent evacs is herded down the road, whistles and batons keeping them in single file. Clothes drenched and stuck to their drooping bodies, 'winds straggling into their faces, hair soaked dark and plastered to their heads. Mothers dragging pale toddlers, fathers cradling suitcases, children wailing by the roadside as guards prod them along. White numbers sprayed across every set of slumped shoulders—across jackets and blouses, shawls and bare skin—a hurried sequence of seven figures, dripping paint.

Bet their hands are all carved up like Ma's, Euri says, and the twist in Peyt's guts tell him she's right.

Fuck her, he thinks, re-wrapping the box and loosely tying it. Fuck Cardea.

But your fare, calls the driver as Peyt opens the door. *These is nearly grey lands. . . . And we ain't that far now. . . . And d'ya even know the way?*

A bit late for honour among bastards, Peytr thinks, telling the man to keep the coin. Consider it a tip, he says. For your concern. The mules bray, long lashes slowly sweeping over milky brown eyes. Turned in his seat, the driver catfishes his mouth like an airship portal; up and down, up and down, fat lips flapping. Peyt leans in close to see if tiny passengers are lining up on his pasty tongue for the flight.

"Let's go," he says after a minute, and Euri follows.

"What you staring at, darlin'?"

Blink: an ibis.

Blink: a water buffalo.

Blink: "Flamingos," Peytr says. "But I'm looking for a hawk."

The skingirls smile and preen and ruffle their crimson skirts. Three of them, standing at the mouth of a wide alley. High and dry on a rising shore of trash. Sticking to the early afternoon shadows between a pharmacy on the ground floor of a high rise and a brownstone-turned-masonic hall. White halos flicker from fluoros mounted on the drugstore's façade: tubes curved into pill-shapes, crosses, stars. Through a haze of drizzle, the light softens the sharpest edges of the girls' faces. Hook-noses, arched brows, cheekbones, canines. It leaches life from their features, darkens the pits and hollows.

"Look at that uniform," one of the girls says. The blonde skinny one. The ibis. "Got your coat on wrong way around, though. Gutside out."

"Maybe he wants us to flip it for him," says the water buffalo, a tubby brunette wearing a bandeau so tight, her cleavage is mashed up to the rolls round her throat. She takes a step further back into the alley, leans against a dumpster and starts to unlace the ties on her skirt.

The third wrinkles her nose. If her tangled hair was pink instead of blue, Peyt thinks, this one could be Gerte's twin. "Always so desperate," she stage-whispers to the ibis, tut-tutting as she nods at the buffalo. Turning back to Peytr she says, "What kinda hawk you after, soldier? High or low-flyer? We know a lot of birds around here."

Thinking of the gold's quality, the watch's craftsmanship, Peyt shrugs, reluctant to give too much away. "Depends on who's soaring nearby."

"Ooooh, we got an eager one, Sissy," says the ibis, slinking closer. She walks her fingers up Peyt's front, toys with his hood strings. He grabs her hand to stop it from going any further; it's hard and callused and colder than Euri's.

On the street behind him, umbrellas bob in both directions, people hurrying with heads down, taking advantage of the easing rain. Velos splash after them, motors and pedals plonking, while twice-a-days trundle to and from the depot, windows streaked with passengers' breath. No one pays them any attention. Peyt had thought about catching a lift back to the suburbs, but Euri didn't want to be trapped. *We've got legs*, she'd said. Then, always the riler, *And mine are way stronger than yours.* For the past forty minutes or so they've gone east, skirting the parklands, aiming for the storm-channel that will lead them back to Peytr's neighbourhood. They've hiked almost to the other side of the city, and still Euri has had no trouble keeping up. Now she's hanging on to Peyt's belt, pulling, urging him to keep going.

"Just a minute," he says, and the skingirls chortle.

"Aw, you made him all shy, Nolene."

"Look at that blush! Never had three at once, I reckon."

"Never had even one, more like."

Peyt sputters, choking on too many words. The women cackle, their laughter forced and shrill. Euri tries to wedge herself into the huddle, but the girls are too close, too quick. Now the water buffalo adds her bulk to the group; she bumps him from behind, smothered breasts pressing against his ruck. Reaching around, she hugs him deeper into the alley while Euri shouts, *Retreat!*

"How many greys you killed, soldier," says the blue-haired Gerte, hands exploring Peyt's chest, ribs, hips, cock. He grunts as she squeezes, none too gently. Groans as she pulls him hard.

"How many greys you fucked?" he gasps.

Blink: the skingirls are eyeless

Blink: they're serpent-haired sirens

Blink: they're ghosts.

"Why," asks the flamingo, arm jerking faster. "That turn you on, Captain?"

The other girls paw Peytr's jacket, rub under his ruck and shoulder bags, pat his buzzing hood, grope his waist. They're searching, he thinks. Frisking.

"I'm not a Cap—"

Euri kicks Peyt's trembling legs, lands several punches and yells, *Retreat!*

"'Course you're not, soldier," says the ibis. "A Cap would be out on the field, wouldn't he, Sissy?"

"A Cap would wear his uniform gutside in."

"A real Cap wouldn't be hawking," says the flamingo, leading them all toward a nest of old clothes and tin cans, moulding onionskins and cellophane. "He'd be blasting the grey shit off our beat. Making it so no one's gotta sell nothing they don't want to."

"Sing it, Sissy," says the buffalo, slamming Peytr with her full weight. His face smashes into the concrete wall and

Blink: greys leer in the shadows and Blink: smoggy fists pummel Peyt's kidneys and nuts and Blink: it's three on one and Blink: the Whitey's mouth crackles *Retreat! Retreat!* and Blink: his skull crashes into a growing red patch and Blink: Euri's howling and flailing and struggling against them but her arms are pinned and Blink: "Don't hurt her!" and Blink: his arms are pinned and Blink: "Don't hurt—" and Blink: his packs are gone and Blink: his pants are down and Blink: the birds are squawking "Traitor!" and Blink: he can't escape and Blink: a gold watch isn't escape and Blink: he's balls-down on the ground and Blink: his head rammed hard into the base of the wall and Blink: rammed and Blink: rammed and Blink: he frees an arm but doesn't hit and Blink: "Coward!" and Blink: stilettos are crushing, breaking, puncturing, penetrating and Blink: he shields his wordwind, protects it, nothing else, lets them give, let them take, whatever they want, but not this. Not this. Not this.

Mimi found them a couch a few weeks ago, beige with black and brown stripes, that looks almost new by lamplight. She's sitting on the middle cushion, knitting a baby blanket out of old sweaters. To her left, Euri's perched on the sofa's fat arm, dandling the little one on her knee. The tiny girl gurgles, cheeks shining with his sister's kisses.

Peyt runs toward them. His feet wear holes in the carpet but make no progress. Wind whistles past his ears, drowning out the sound of his sobbing.

"Isn't she gorgeous?" Mireille asks, without looking up from her needles. "Couldn't you just gobble her up?"

The baby coos and

Blink: she's little Zaya and

Blink: she's little Ned.

"How can you love a kid you barely know?" Peyt cries, legs pumping, *left right left right left*, going nowhere.

Euri smirks, shifts the bundle in her arms, and says, *Retreat*.

When he comes to, it's so dark Peyt touches his sockets just to be sure his eyes aren't gone. The lids are marshmallow, gummed with blood and gunk, the lashes pulling like Velcro as he slits them open. A soft white glow beckons him from the street. A trail of light-crumbs glinting off water and buckles and scattered coins, showing him the only way out of the alley. He blinks, but there's no escape from the throbbing in his head. His back. His sides. His arse. His groin. Hands tucked under his chin, Peyt's lying in a puddle—no, *puddles*—some sticky, some piss-reeking, all numbing. Not numbing enough.

"Euri?" he croaks, then spits blood and teeth. "You there, Euri?"

The girl doesn't answer, but he thinks he hears her quiet sniffling. Muck bubbles from his nose as he releases a nervous breath. Across the alley, a balled silhouette gets on all fours and crawls over, coming close enough to touch but not touching. *Oh, Peytie. Oh, Peytie. Oh, Peytie.*

"Help me up," he says, jaw aching but intact. Euri rocks back and forth, hugging her stomach, as if she's the one with cracked ribs. Alone, Peytr gets onto his elbows, then has to wait for the spots in his vision to clear. On hands and knees, he sways with innards churning. Heaves bile until his throat burns. With one hand out, propped against the wall for support, he finally straightens. With the other, he tentatively pats himself down. Gravel and filth are ground into his pelvis, his pubic hair, the crease between his legs. Liquid weeps from a hole in his thigh—shallow, he hopes—and pebbles of glass chafe the gashes in his calves. He brushes off what he can, then explores the scrapes on his arms, the welts on his cheeks, the crooked mess of his nose. Last, he drops his hood. Runs shaking fingers through his 'wind.

Mostly whole.

Mostly.

Once Peytr's standing, Euri starts to calm down. Still folded in on herself, she manages to help haul up his pants, even rolls the waistband since the skingirls stole his belt. The cunts and their feral nest are gone—along with his provisions, Cardea's bag of seeds, and every coin he had, except the few they'd spilled and the one or two he'd stashed in his boots. Groaning with each step, he shuffles along the alleyway. Finds his ruck tossed in the mud, empty. Two of Jean's shells rolled into a sog of cardboard boxes, the shirt Esther gave him trampled in a pile of shit. Skingirls have enough red on them already, Peyt figures; their anger's strong enough without grenades. He rescues shirt and shells and, poor-pawing through the trash for a plastic bag to put them in, he finds his satchels, gutted like the Pigeon who'd made them.

"They got the watch," he says bitterly, stepping out of the dark passage and into the pharmacy's light. He leans against the wall to catch his breath, chest brewing a wracking cough that ends in splash of pink spew. A bell jingles as a customer leaves the shop, the glass door swinging shut behind her. She glances Peyt's way *just* long enough to really see him before hurrying off in the other direction. "They got the fuckin' watch."

Euri sidles up close. Carefully, she wraps her arms around Peytr's hips. Nuzzles into his belly. Squeezes until it hurts.

"Enough, kiddo," he wheezes, and Euri pulls away. She thumps his cargo pocket, a quick one-two with her palm, then skips into the drugstore without turning to see if he'll follow. Of course, Peytr thinks, tracing the flat box's outline through the cloth. Crushed, but intact. Euri must've slipped it in there before leaving the cab. She was always thinking ahead.

"Wait up," he says. "I'm coming."

The pharmacy walls are bare concrete, its floor a garish marble tile. Rows of steel shelves are cleared of anything worth stealing; what's left is a few rolls of bandages, bundles of sterilised rags, vacuum-sealed ponchos, creams and out-dated makeup, mineral spirits, neatly-stacked towers of polypropylene bottles ready to be filled. Behind the counter, a greasy-haired white coat doles out pills on a first-come, what's-in-stock basis. An old stumpey is being served while a pair of young mothers waits in line with their snotty-faced kids.

Peytr limps from aisle to aisle, wondering what kind of meds he can get for thirty cents and a couple of shells. Right about now he'd take anything to dampen the hot thumping around his cracked bones. The tear-gas-burning in his sinuses and throat. The fire of shame under his skin.

"Euri," he whispers, looking around and over shelves. "This is no time for hide 'n' seek." People sniff and scrunch up their faces as Peytr walks by—even the gibbering guy wheeling past on his way to the exit, a colostomy bag overflowing into a bucket rigged under his chair. Peyt swallows a hard lump. Even a fuckin' crip stinks less than him.

He rounds a corner into the farthest aisle, where the wall is lined with bottled jewels. Polishes of all colours, dusty but still sparkling under the ceiling fluoros. Liquid face paint and shimmering powders. Test tubes of lipstick smearing coral and ruby and antacid pink gunk onto little rectangular mirrors. Peyt catches glimpses of his reflection, but can't tell if all that red is on him, or on the glass.

Standing in front of a garish display, a straight-hipped woman with long red braids is smudging blush onto pasty cheeks. She tilts her head this way and that, trying to get a good angle in a convex mirror, under bad lighting. The colour makes her look green, Peyt thinks. And no amount of goop is going to make her any less plain.

"Euri?" he whispers again.

The red-head turns and smiles, shaking her head.

"Amelia," she says. "You Mischa?"

"What?" Peyt scowls. "No, I'm—" *No names, soldier* "—Two."

Amelia snorts and says, "Well, you're looking pretty banged up there, *Two*. Half your luck if Papa Syd has anything strong enough here for you." She clips the blush's plastic container shut, slips it into the back pocket of her jeans, and pulls the hem of her sweatshirt down to cover it. "I don't think anything in this place," she tips her head at the makeup, "is going to be much help with—" flutters her hand in the general direction of his face "—all that."

"Suppose I'll take my chances," Peyt says, stifling another wet cough. Mouth tanging with acid and blood. Thumbing crust from his nostril, he turns and looks out over the shoulder-height rows, consciously not-staring at the string of glass beads swirling around Amelia's neck.

"I don't have much," he says quietly, heart pounding. He picks up a vial of nail polish remover, puts it back down. Picks it back up again. Turns it over and over in his grimy hands while he speaks. "But I'd give it all for one of those pretty pearls you're wearing."

"Ah," she says, fingering the necklace. "These beauts are spoken for, my friend."

Peyt sighs. Puts the vial back down. "Thanks anyway."

"Tell you what," Amelia says, reaching out to stop Peyt from leaving. Startled, he looks down at her, but can only guess what she's thinking. There are no thoughts eddying above her bright copper plaits, no insights sneaking out of her pores. 'Windless, she gazes up at him without sneering or dry-retching or wincing. She doesn't brush off the crud on his sleeve, doesn't wipe her palm before ferreting in her hoodie's pouch. Brown eyes give him a quick once-over. Two seconds, tops, and Amelia seems to take everything in—from the tightly-bound hood to the sagging satchels to the walked-thin soles of his boots.

"Tell you what," she says slowly. "Clean yourself up and I'm sure we can come to some kind of arrangement."

In her hand, four silver-wrapped spheres. She tucks three deep inside his left satchel, then carefully peels the foil off the fourth. Listing three addresses—"You got to remember them all, right? Even when you got your glow on . . ."—she pops the misshapen glass marble into his mouth, and tells him to meet her at the bodega across the road when he's done.

"Right," he says, floating on sweet cuts, inhaling clouds. "Done. I just have one thing to get rid of first, and then it's done."

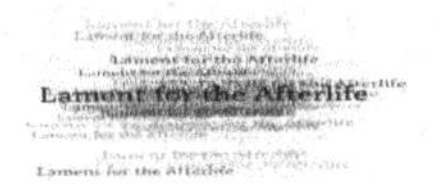

He reaches gov't house an hour or so before true-dark, whisked across town in a series of discordant blinks. They travelled in a twice-a-day, he remembers, but also in a cab pulled by two goats. Or was that before? No, he thinks. And yes. There were goats and rabbits at some point. A menagerie in paint. There were flamingos and buffalos and whores. Blink: he shuddered and Blink: he was calm. Euri held an umbrella as they trudged along streets paved with flags, as they avoided the stadium, as they swam through clouds. Peytr loop-de-looped under her little upraised arm and rain washed his face clean, rain spattered him ugly, rain soaked the blood into his soul. Soul-drenched, he thinks now, laughing through a mouthful of water. There is no umbrella at all.

A half amphitheatre of steps rises up to the columned gov't building, each curved marble slab treacherously wet. Grouped before twelve-foot double doors, construction workers and artisans and dark-suited bureaucrats pose for photos under the façade's newly rebuilt pediment. The photographer fiddles with his gear, then starts a countdown and Blink: the flash goes in a sulphurous burst and Blink: everyone's face is bleached, features obliterated and Blink: Peyt's running, taking the stairs two at a time and Blink: he's cresting the top step and Blink: gasping, slumped at the base of a classical column, ruining the politicians' shot.

There's still time, Euri says, holding a bottle of cerulean blue varnish up to the sky. The colours don't compare at all, but Peyt takes her point. An hour or so to make it to the stadium. To make the drop. To deserve the money they'd already lost.

"We'll give it back," he says, taking the box from his pocket, the timepiece from its flattened container. Though the gold is scratched and dented, it still gleams. "We'll make it up to her, somehow." Blink. "It isn't really our fault."

Euri is wan with exhaustion. She doesn't have another trip in her, Peyt thinks. Not today. Blink. "It's okay," he says. Dangling the watch from his fingertips, he pretends to hypnotise Euri and Blink: her head nods and fades and Blink: starbursts flash, silver and gold in his hands and Blink: Euri smiles and

"Excuse me, sir."

Peytr's gaze slurps through thick gelatine, bobbles around the woman towering over him. Proper, he thinks, in that snug burgundy suit, those flat shoes so quiet he didn't even hear her approach. Official, with that floppy silk bow at her throat. "I'm *official*," Peytr says, talking slow as he can, inhaling sobering breaths. In and out. In. . . . She smells so clean, like white soap and powder and Blink: he's back on his cot, a kid snuggled under flannel sheets with Jean telling them stories and Blink: his legs are twitching and Blink: the woman's 'wind mentions visiting hours, tourist seasons cancelled and Blink: *Closed for Repairs*.

"I have *this*," Peytr says, waving the watch around, "bit of business to clear up. Won't be long. Won't be long."

Blink: he's floating, seeing her eye-to-eye and

Blink: he's crashed, wheezing, blood seeping and

"Here," she says, loud and sweet and Blink: the watch is gone, her suit jacket opened and Blink: rebuttoned and Blink: a small purse is pressed between his hand and hers. She folds his fingers over the payment, communicating in reassuring smiles and squeezes and pats. "For your trouble."

Blink: her back is turned and

Blink: she's signalling, shouting something to the photographer and

"But I can't make it in time," Peytr says, feeling the coins' weight, feeling space opening inside and around him. Relief and guilt and the promise of a bigger place . . . "It's too late. I've failed."

"No no no," she says, drifting back to him like a spirit, leaning over on warm, clean gusts of nostalgia. "You did just fine, Pigeon. You couldn't possibly have done better."

"Oh," Peyt says. "Oh."

Again, he watches her walk—Blink: skip—away on silent soles. Blink: he's light and Blink: he's mostly air and Blink: he's rocking in a lullaby sky. There are no vapour trails around him. No airships cutting paths through smog. No rockets. No wordfire.

The clouds hold their breath and swallow the rain.

"I'll just rest here a minute. If that's all right," he says softly, lighter now without the watch weighing him down. Coughing, he looks around for Euri.

"Take your time," she calls over her shoulder. "Take as long as you need."

to come through
help meeee, help

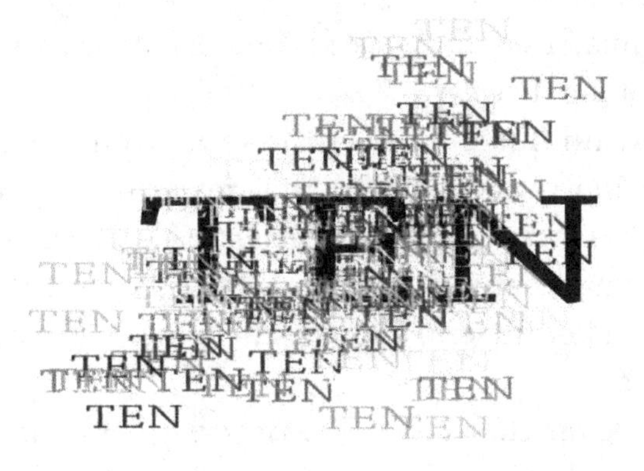

TEN

The tape measure recoils into its pocket-sized case with a satisfying snap. Ned smiles, wipes flecks of nail polish from the tape's metal tip, and slides it back into her knapsack. Today has been a long time coming. Too long.

Her toenails have lengthened more than 3mm since the last good window day. They've nearly grown bare in the dark interim, leaving the slightest crescent of colour on the tips of her toes. Cerulean blue, speckled with white polka dots. She celebrates the good days with brilliant polish—but until today, the view hasn't been worth the paint.

Not more than an hour earlier, a wedge of geese had flown past her window. What a sight! Now Ned's dying to get at her collection of varnishes. She's packed a few bottles in her knapsack—they nestle at the bottom like bubbles of promised pleasure, beside her tape measure, a fossilised rain shower (over 250 million years old!), and all the shirts Papa messy-sewed her name into last time he was home—but Tantie will kill her if she stops to repaint her nails now.

The sun breaks through the clouds, gilding Ned's face, as her matronly not-aunt accuses her of lying.

"Don't be wicked, Ned," Tantie May says. "There are no geese outside. You know that full well. Be a good girl, now; it's almost time for us to leave—"

"Call me Lavinia," Ned says. "*Please*, Tantie. It's such a lovely name. And I'm not fibbing, I swear."

Ned's wordwind flutters in V-formation around her, spilling little white lies in its wake, immediately retracing its path to cross them out. Words swirl through her hair, pale tendrils lifting as paragraphs tornado above her head. Ned pinches the slowest phrases between her fingers, popping them into her mouth before they can escape.

"We've been over this, Ned," Tantie says, her own wordwind buzzing with ferocious energy, spinning tales of naughty children, bottomless pits, and rotten cheese. "I will not call you Lavinia. Or Clarissa. Or Enchantée. Your name was set down in ink the day you were born. And that is that."

"But they made a mistake," Ned cries, wishing she knew who'd recorded her name—it was meant to be *Nell*—dooming her with their atrocious penmanship.

"Yes, Ned. They made a mistake. Just as you did when you thought you saw geese outside." Shaking her head, Tantie shoos her wordwind toward the bedroom door, swiftly following it. "Your 'wind must've obscured your vision, dear. It has been known to happen."

Turning away from her not-aunt's disappointment, Ned steps up on her school chair and peers out the window. The bedroom door clicks shut behind her. Let her leave, Ned thinks. Outside, the sun is wavering. Although it's gleamed for much of the day, its light now pulses feebly, consumed by a familiar shade of grey. The street is deserted.

Their paperwork has been stamped with official seals, and likenesses of Ned and Tantie have been inscribed—with ink—into small leather booklets. Ned thinks her picture looks funny. All the artist had wanted was to capture an impression of her face, serious and close-up, but Ned thinks she looks naked without a wordwind tap-dancing across her shoulders.

Tantie had applied for this set of transport passes more than once. More than once the applications had been rejected. But today the sun shone on them for the first time in 3mm. And then their passes arrived in the morning chute. The train departed for the 'port in less than an hour.

They've finally been given leave to go.

And there *had* been geese, even if Tantie hadn't seen them.

Ned's sure she'll never hear the end of it if she made them miss the ship, after all Tantie's done to book their passage. So she wiggles her half-polished toes into thick-soled treaders, tries not to think how much better they'd look tipped in fuchsia. A day like today definitely warrants fuchsia varnish, but that bottle has already been boxed up and sent to Mamie's.

Stepping out of her room, Ned makes sure to avoid the ladder propped up against the wall in the hallway. They aren't taking it with them—Ned had insisted. Tantie had rolled her eyes, her wordwind merging with Ned's, listing lullabies and recipes for candy as they negotiated. But Ned's mind wouldn't be changed, no matter how sweet Tantie's words were.

On the bad window days, the ladder inevitably gets positioned near the bathroom. The men ascend its length, disappearing into the ceiling, frightening Ned when she really needs to *go*. The men'll sit up there non-stop—sometimes for weeks—knocking around, repairing the machines they keep in the air shafts.

The machines that cause such a ruckus Ned can't concentrate on her schoolwork.

The ones that generate the finely sifted ash that drifts to the ground outside her window, that spoils her view with washes of red and charcoal.

The ones that make anxiety drench her pants while she avoids the bathroom.

Outside, ghostly green flashes explode on the horizon whenever the men are around, bright enough to make Ned blink. Sirens sound in the distance. Too far away to know from which direction they're coming. Ned has to draw the curtains as emergency signs switch on in the tenements a block over.

Those are the bad window days. Ned knows she and Tantie are in for it whenever the ladder comes out.

There's no way it's coming with them to Mamie's.

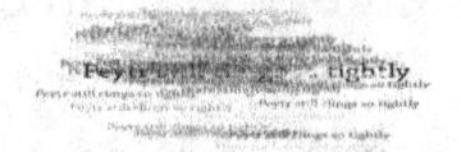

Tumbleweeds of ash and newspaper scuttle along behind Ned and Tantie as the pair hurry toward the train station. You know it's a fuchsia kind of day when people are comfortable enough to sleep outside, Ned thinks. Bodies dressed in coverall suits, faces hiding behind faded chip packets and litter, are strewn across benches or collapsed beside tree stumps. Their legs bent in foetal position, their arms draped uncomfortably across eyes. Ned adjusts her aviator goggles, pulls her hood strings until the world seems almost entirely cut off. Good thing the sleepers've got the sense to cover their eyes, she thinks, carefully tying a double-knot beneath her nose.

But where are their wordwinds? Even sleeping people are surrounded by words, whether dreams concocting incredible falsehoods over pillows, or magnetic ideas landing on slumbering figures like flies.

"Is it naptime out here, Tantie?" Ned asks, her voice muffled behind the thick canvas of her hood. "Should we wake them from their *siestas*? What if they miss the train? Then they'll never be able to leave."

Tantie doesn't reply, but her wordwind launches into a parable about dogs and wounded children. That's so like her, Ned thinks. Tantie's mouth remains firmly set. Her grip on Ned's hand is firmer still.

The train timetable skids across Ned's restricted view when the station appears on the horizon. Tantie's strides grow longer, the pressure she exerts in dragging Ned along increasing as their goal appears.

"Slow down please, Tantie," Ned says, stumbling to her knees for the third time. Her treaders are covered in soot; the palms of her hands are lacerated and embedded with chips of gravel and shrapnel.

Don't worry, Ned wants to say when Tantie pierces her with an anxious gaze. That train never runs on time—but her lungs are aching with heavy air. Loosening her hood just enough to poke her mouth out, Ned keeps silent, breathing deeply. She doesn't want to lie to Tantie. How would she know about the trains? She hasn't been outside in weeks.

The station is deserted when they arrive. Ned's overjoyed—maybe they'll get the whole train to themselves! Her wordwind paints pictures of spinning tops, magpies building nests out of rusty cogs, dented fob watches. Tantie flicks at a haywire word, sends it ricocheting off Ned's goggles.

"Take those things off, Neddie," Tantie May says. "They're ludicrous."

In response, Ned clutches the goggles' rims, presses them further into her eye sockets.

"Trust me, the greys have been gone for ages," her aunt says, taking hold of Ned's hand. "They were gone long before the screamers blew up. No one's going to steal your eyes. Promise."

Why do greys always go for the eyes, Ned wonders. Maybe it's because they want to see more clearly in our world, or maybe it gives them some advantage in theirs? Maybe they sell them on the black market, exchanging eyes for babies' livers and fresh pumpkin soup?

Tantie shakes her head as Ned's wordwind transcribes her suspicions across the air. Ned pretends she isn't looking when Tantie tucks the worst of her worries into a back pocket. Removing her gloves, Tantie works at the knot in Ned's hood strings until it releases, then pushes the cowl back from her face. Tracing a rough finger along Ned's smooth cheek, Tantie stretches the goggles upwards on their elastic strap. Ned squirms as her not-aunt unveils her grey eyes, making them a target for bloodthirsty creatures.

Brown eyes would be so much better than grey, Ned thinks. Brown is a much less troublesome colour, since the creepers seemed to like grey the best.

And everything is grey nowadays, except for Ned's toenails.

The pair of filth-encrusted lenses drop to the ground, forgotten, as an iron engine billows around the corner, chugging toward the station on elegant puffs of steam.

The 'port is a blur. A thoroughfare for travellers, all on outbound ships; but also a marketplace for storytellers, copying snippets from each other's wordwinds while they wait to depart. Ned raises her hood, tries to capture all her words beneath its insufficient shelter. She won't have anyone stealing her thoughts in this place. No way.

Preoccupied with confining her 'wind, Ned takes small notice of her surroundings as she's ushered toward the ship. Artificial breath mixes with the scent of too many bodies, uneasiness filling the unfamiliar space with its pungent aroma. A cacophony of 'winds eclipses the 'port's humming lights as the crowd ebbs and flows between the entrance and departure gates. Ned blocks her nose, wishes she hadn't lost her goggles. There are bound to be greys here, she reasons. Neither her words nor her eyes will be safe until they're both on the ship.

At the gate, guards carrying bayonets scan wordwinds for signs of trouble, looking for bold statements or those that drip red onto the passengers' luggage. Ned passes through the archway unhindered, but Tantie is asked to step aside for closer inspection.

"Tantie," Ned cries. "What's happening, Tantie? I can't go by myself! I don't know where to go." She catches a glimpse of the massive ship out the 'port window. It reminds her of a picture she once saw of a catfish. Only this one's humungous—a fish fit for a giant's breakfast—and it's made entirely of wood and steel. Its wings stretch beyond her line of sight. And, somehow, she's meant to walk straight into its mouth and sit in its belly while it flies.

Her knees buckle with relief when the guard returns Tantie's satchel, nodding her through the gates.

"Hush now, Neddie," Tantie says, clumps of black words raining into her handbag while she scoops Ned up from the floor. 'No need to make a spectacle,' she breathes. "You'll be all right." Her face is stern, but her arms quiver while she holds Ned close, carrying her onto the ship.

The window beside Ned's seat is shaped like the lozenge Tantie gives her to suck on while the ship takes off. It's smaller than the window in her room at home, but big enough to take her breath away.

An army of clouds begin waging war on the ship as soon as it soars upwards. The loss of sunlight doesn't diminish the glory of Ned's good window day in the least. It adds drama0—it adds flair!—to the pantomime being enacted beneath her. Tiny fires dot the landscape below, shining like rubies scattered across a bed of smoking grey. Ned reaches a hand out to the glass, tries to grasp one of the glowering embers between her fingertips. Her wordwind frames the window pane, asking "Who is the fairest?" as flashes of lightning shoot up from black tubes on the ground, chasing the ship across the sky.

"Have you ever seen anything so beautiful, Tantie?" Ned whispers, her face aglow with ambient light.

"No, dear," Tantie replies, her eyes fastened shut as if she's dozing. Tantie's knuckles whiten as she clutches the arms of her seat, her 'wind clunking around like the men in the ceiling, shedding stories of sorrow and loss.

"Will there be views like these where we're going, Tantie?" Ned asks, completely absorbed by the good window's spectacle. The ship shudders through a stubborn cloud, briefly surfacing into a painfully bright vista of blue and white. Ned gasps, claps her hands with delight. The sky has coloured itself to match her toes! She's so glad she hadn't repainted them after all.

Tantie swallows hard as the ship drops rapidly, enveloped once more by rampaging clouds. "If we're lucky, Neddie," she says, "you'll never see anything like this again."

Ned nods, but hasn't heard a word Tantie said. She brushes her wordwind away from the window, vies against her own imagination for a better vantage.

Have those naughty fée swapped her eyes with tricksy ones that will get her into trouble with Tantie May? She doesn't like being thought a liar. She rubs her eyelids, stretches them as wide as they'll go, and presses her face to the glass.

No, she realises. Her eyes are just fine. But Tantie will sure feel bad about not believing her, Ned thinks, as she watches a distant 'V' fly in the ship's direction.

"Look, Tantie! It's the geese," she says, jubilant with vindication. "I told you they were real."

Tantie squeezes her eyes shut as the ship reverberates with the sound of word-shot clanging off metal. Incoherent prayers spin around her head, then expand to include Ned in an embrace of benedictions and regrets. Tantie's wavering words race upwards and back around the ship's cabin, mingling with the other passengers' encyclopaedic entries on monsters, nightmares, and survival techniques. Babies cry, spilling alphabet jumbles into the mix. The air sizzles with electric uncertainties. With exclamations of horror, verbal and written.

Careering sharply to the left, their vessel's flight path turns back on itself like a broken elbow. Plumes of smoke swell from the ship's undercarriage.

"Look," Ned repeats, pointing at the battle geese descending upon them. Yellow and red starbursts bloom from metallic wings as the flock glides closer. Echoing bursts project skyward from below as earthbound creatures answer the birds' colourful calls.

"Don't be scared, Tantie. I won't let anything happen to you. Promise."

Wait 'til I tell Mamie about this, Ned thinks. How lucky we are to see all this up close! The ship plunges through a chequerboard of orange and red. Ned's 'wind flounders, turns green. The turbulence upsets her stomach. Tantie clasps Ned's hand, draws her small head to her breast.

"Don't be scared, Tantie," Ned says as her not-aunt's wordwind falls like a curtain before her eyes. Ned waves her aunt's skittish words away, gently, careful not to bruise. Turns back to the events unfolding outside her window.

Hills festooned with blackened trees seem to dart upwards, drawing the ship down, until the clouds are once more far, far above. The ship plummets with wondrous speed. Ned sits still, riveted to the view. Her 'wind latches on to Tantie's, losing some of its shine in the process.

"Don't be scared," Ned repeats while the earth rushes up to meet their ship. "Don't be scared."

ELEVEN

Standing on a footstool she found on the green road last week, Mireille presses against the cold window casement and peers through a missing slat in the blinds. Outside, rubble slopes from the roadside to her second-storey apartment, piled two-thirds of the way up the window's glass. At the top of the heap, cinderblocks and bricks. Rinds of rubber. Shredded newspapers. Plastic packaging gone brittle, disintegrating in the dry air. No trace of leaves or roots or forgotten 'winds. Not in this country, she thinks, this flamboyant city, where people talk and talk and talk without ever revealing true thoughts. Further down the panel, near the ledge, shredded rat leather is squashed between layers of fabric. Fur and tartan, both colourless with dust. And poking out of—a cardigan? a skirt?—small, fractured bones. Poor little things, she thinks. Poor little things. She can't bear to look at them. Day and night, the blinds are kept drawn. A long, thin rectangle of light sneaks into the living room, greying a streak across Mireille's eyes as she stretches up, tiptoe, on her latest treasure. Stealing glimpses out through the gap.

Across the road, a crew of sweating, ox-armed men peck at two-metre banks of wreckage with pickaxes and shovels. In the past hour, they've shifted wagonloads of concrete, slate, twisted steel bars, torn awnings, dented tin. Nothing decorative. Nothing useful.

But they've widened the thoroughfare by a good few inches. Now part of a gutter emerges, a foot of the curb.

If I don't blink before they hit sidewalk, Mireille thinks, then Peyt will be back home before May and Neddie get here.

Ten seconds pass.

Her eyes start to burn.

Sidewalks will be good, she thinks, squinting against the sting. Neddie can easily push our little barrow around while I fill it. Fifteen seconds. Or we can take turns: the girl's got a good eye for pattern and sparkle. *And*—twenty seconds—Ned's small enough to fit under that fence at the Neuemarkethub. . . . Thirty-two seconds. For weeks, Mireille's had her eye on a corner of gilded wood, poking up like an elbow from the half-caved ruins of a hotel three blocks away. She's sure it's a picture frame—and, judging from the corner, it's a big one—but the property is cordoned-off, the chain link too low for her to wriggle beneath, the top edge barbed with rusting wire and shards of glass.

Thirty-nine seconds and there's a harsh tingling in her sinuses. As the workmen cart off another load, jets arrowhead out from the clouds. Three of the guys down tools and gawk stupidly up, mouths moving silently in the glass-rattling noise. Forty-six seconds. The ships move as one toward a towering column in the distance, a sleek concrete shaft girded and buttressed with iron, its pinnacle miles above the clouds. They're going to crash, Mireille thinks. They're going to explode. Her breath rasps in and out. The blinds clatter. Tingling becomes tickling. Forty-eight. Forty-nine. Save yourselves, she thinks furiously, 'wind cursing worse than Peyt's. And as the fighters veer left at the last instant, noses angled down, spitting fire into the valley beyond, Mireille's sigh catches. Eyes watering, she tilts her head back and sneezes. Twice. Blinking both times.

Doesn't count, she thinks, sleeving tears from her cheeks and invisible grime from the venetians. Interference.

Bursts of green over the city become orange concussions on the ground, fallout drifting around high rises and cranes. Another flock of steel wings appears overhead and the workmen vanish. The grocer on the corner—who laces his grain with sawdust, and would sell flambeaux in the middle of a firestorm—has battened down his red and white awnings and sandbagged the door. Kids race out of the public toilets, a cinderblock structure near the pump and well, that stinks like shit no matter how much lime gets crushed on its thick walls. Naked, dropping towels they'll be punished for losing, they run themselves dirty; back down alleyways or through gaps in the fences around their parents' businesses and homes. Up and down the street, people go indoors then reappear, crowding apartment balconies. Families of old men and young women. Children small enough to be carried. Teenagers with thick specs stooped over railings. Talking. Smoking herbs and wrappers, filling lungs with plastic and tar. All of them watching. Waiting for action before the all-clear.

Inside her new quarters, Mireille gnaws a hangnail. Feels the sting as the thread of skin tears from her finger. Footsteps thunder past her front door, then up a set of stairs at the end of the hall. One or two floors above, a door slams. On the living room wall behind her, a cuckoo clock starts hooting the hour. Outside, clouds boom. Green and orange and billowing oceans of grey.

Mireille wonders if Peyt's in one of the ships up there, coasting the gloom, shelling targets. She wonders how much of his own sadness and anger have fuelled those bombs. No matter how much emotion he pours into the job, she thinks, it seems there's always more. Just thinking about what the greys did back home generates all the ammunition he needs to keep fighting. All those people stolen, all those poor, poor people packed into the stadium and ignited—massacred—with grey magic. Thirty thousand, Peyt kept repeating, when he came in with the news that night. A five-mile blast radius. Buildings smashed like toothpicks all around. Two-thirds of the CBD decimated in a matter of blinks. The museum, the historic gardens, the repat hospital. Everything around the stadium. Gone. And thirty thousand people inside. Outside, so many more.

"What if Neddie had been one of them," Mireille remembers saying. "What if they'd stolen our little Ned?" Peyt had stared at her. At the colicky baby grizzling on her lap. Expression blank as a stranger's. "What's the fuckin' point?" There'd been no venom in his voice then—he kept that for the next day, when PM Cardea's body was reported found in the bathtub, bled out and screenless. And the next, at her tribute, when the gov't laid blame for the city's destruction, squarely—and fairly, Mireille still thinks—at the greys' feet.

Details might've blurred with the passing years, the hows, the whos, the whys, but she will never forget the hurt in that question. "What's the fuckin' point?" The hurt, the actual physical pain—and, yes, even the pride—of seeing Peyt walk out the door a week later, hours before dawn, bearing satchels and rucksack and reinforced hood, a soldier bent on finding an answer.

"Fight hard," she'd said, whispering to keep from waking the baby. "Fight careful. Ned would like her Papa back in one piece."

Peyt's expression was inscrutable. Part frown, part disbelief.

In hindsight, Mireille realises she did this a lot. Put her words in Ned's mouth instead of voicing them herself. "She sure loves her Papa," she'd say, or "Look how she smiles to see you!" At the time, she'd given Ned all the credit for loving him. Missing him.

"Maybe you'll be assigned to your old platoon," she'd said, having no idea how these things worked, but wanting to talk to him, to stall him just that much longer before he went off to war. "Is that what happens when you go back?"

She remembers his relief that she hadn't begged him to stay. Hadn't begged him to explain why he was going. It was visible, palpable. After kissing Ned goodbye, he'd stood a bit straighter. He'd heaved a huge sigh. He'd looked at Mireille and almost smiled.

"I don't know how—"

A soldier's burden is heavy enough, she'd thought, waving the rest of Peyt's sentence away. He doesn't leave his family easily or willingly. He goes because he must. Because it is right.

"We'll be here," she's said. Then, spontaneously, "Thank you."

"For what?"

Mireille swallowed. "Protecting us."

Peyt had flinched, too humble for praise or thanks, even when it was due. Mireille had cupped his scruffy chin, kissed her mouth raw on his stubble. Despite what the mothers used to say, Mireille had thought as the door shut behind him, there is pride in action. Pride and love and fear.

Four months until he came home, missing Ned's first birthday by three days. While Tantie May fed the child mash and biscuits for breakfast, Mireille had welcomed Peyt back to her bed.

"How long's your leave?" she'd asked, fumbling with his belt. The leather was cracked and swollen, squeaking as she forced it from loops and buckle.

"I'm tired, Mimi," he'd said. He always says. Pressing her hungry hands firm against his smooth belly, he crossed his legs. Closed his eyes. "We'll talk tomorrow."

Two more bombs in quick succession and a third blaring a few miles behind.

If the last mushroom dissolves before the clock strikes nine, she thinks, I'll hear from Peyt today. Her 'wind cheers the plume on—*hurry hurry hurry*—and a skyscraper collapses in its wake. A subsonic rumbling of brick to earth. Air currents rushing to fill its negative space. Smoke quickly dispersing. The sky loses its sickening hue, fades to a dull silver-white, the mushroom gone after only eight hoots of the cuckoo.

That's it, Mireille thinks, hopping down from the stool. A good sign. Looks like I'm going out.

Her latest theory—proven, she thinks, by the certainty in her gut and the absence of ringing in her ears—is that the rubble around the apartment blocks mentalegraph signals. That's why she hasn't heard from Peyt or Tantie May for so long. She sneezes again, rubs her nose. Yes, she thinks. That's exactly it. Interference.

Before leaving the apartment, Mireille always dresses in many layers. Leggings under pants under a shin-length woollen skirt. Two tank tops under a long-sleeved thermal jersey under a loose t-shirt. A button-up cardigan tied round her waist. Ankle-socks under a lucky cotton pair that haven't yet needed darning. The calendar says it's early autumn, but the wind says it's winter. No matter the season, Mireille bundles up in case of ifs.

If she gets lost.

If she loses her house to a worthier keeper.

If the greys destroy it.

If she has to start over, again.

The bedroom is smaller than the one she and Peyt left behind—a mattress and box-spring, no frame; a three-legged table on her side, wood with steel rivets; a lowboy on his, topped with two trinket boxes, a silver-backed hairbrush, and an ugly bird-faced mask—but the wardrobe is almost walk-in and has plenty of shelves. Not empty, she thinks, looking at the chipboard surfaces, scrubbed and painted white. Waiting to be filled.

Stepping in, she reaches up to take her hat from its round box—and finds herself immersed in Peyt. Salt and skin and a spice she can't quite place, a bit like roast rabbit. Her hands drop, now arranging the hangers, sad stand-ins for Peytr's lean shoulders. She's collected a pair of pants for him and a collared shirt; a day's soaking and scrubbing got out all the stains and she stitched the little holes so tidily they're practically invisible. Peyt's camouflage jacket hangs beside the red shirt she found in his backpack a while ago. "Such a beautiful colour," she'd said, expecting a bag full of faded laundry, finding instead a shimmer of diamond dust covering this scarlet prize. "It's like all those robes we found once in the museum. Remember? Such a brilliant colour. Why don't you wear it?"

"Chafes," he replied, but the fabric was soft as Ned's fine hair. Beneath the canvas mustiness, a faint scent of lemon.

Now Mireille pushes the shirt aside, takes a scarf from the hooks at the back of the closet. Slides the hatbox off the top shelf, tucks it under her arm. With a frown, she gets her trench coat from beside Peyt's jacket.

He'd forget his own head if it wasn't screwed on, she thinks, hoping the regiment will issue him replacement multicams in the meantime.

Heading back to the lounge, she practises looking in on Ned. Leaning against the doorframe of the master bedroom, she crosses her arms, and pretends the girl is sleeping on the little cot she'd bought for her at the army surplus. Tantie May's new bunk is a slender single crammed in next to Ned's—but that's okay, Mireille thinks. May is so skinny, you could fit three of her on there and still have space for Neddie to crawl in when she's scared. Mireille flicks a switch and indulges in the sound of gas piping into frosted glass wall sconces the previous tenants had installed. Taking a box of matches from her coat pocket, she lights the closest bulb and lets it burn for a minute.

Not as bright as the old electrics back home, she thinks. But no doubt Neddie will think they're tapping dragonfire, bottling the power of fireflies or some such. Mireille can just hear her now, inventing reasons why it's so dim in here, even with the lights on. Why she has to squint to see her schoolbooks. "It's glow-in-the-dark ink, Mamie." Or "I've eaten so many carrots, I've got perfect night vision!" Or "If the greys can't see me, they won't know where to sweep . . ."

And Tantie May will roll her eyes and try to snip the girl's 'wind before it gets too rowdy.

May is so good with Neddie, Mireille thinks, snuffing the lamp. I couldn't have asked for a better caretaker. But as she closes the door behind her and crosses to the living room couch—a hideous thing, flaking brown leather-snow when she sits to lace her boots—Mireille's stomach churns. It burns that the army wouldn't fund their travel, burns that they couldn't all move together, burns that Peyt didn't take the issue up with his—who? His Commander? His General? Mireille has no idea—all she knows is he should've *tried*.

"Not even one more ticket? One set of papers? We can send for May later," her belly still squirms at the traitorous thought, "if only we can bring Neddie . . ."

"I need to go," Peyt had said. No arguing with that tone, that twitch in his jaw. "I *have* to. The way things are here, now. . . ." Mireille had seen how much the thought of leaving pained him. She'd understood. He was devoted to family; yeah, he was a family man. It hurt him, she knew, to suggest she stay behind. That she travel with Neddie and May once he'd got settled. Once he could afford the requisite bribes.

It's luxury enough for grunts to move their girls close to the base, Tantie had explained afterwards. Dragging everyone else isn't just selfish. It's obscene.

"Living with a soldier," Mireille had quipped, "you get used to obscenities."

Like when Peyt had said, "I'll send a Pigeon for the three of you. As soon as I can."

That was obscene. Mireille wouldn't wait for a *Pigeon*.

So she went with him.

They don't have a kitchen, *per se*.

A dinged-up gas hob shares a wall with the bedroom. Beside it, a deep steel basin with working drainpipe but no faucets. In front of the window, a speckled Formica table, square with chrome edgings, which they'll all use for dinner and cards. At the moment, there's only one chair—red vinyl with a fat cream stripe on the seat and back—and a single matching cup and saucer. They'll need at least three more. Four, if she can get them.

Placing the hatbox on the table, Mireille sits. Puts on the fedora inside, then tips the box, releasing a small avalanche of papers. Handwritten bills. Faded receipts. Scraps of cardboard packaging sapped of their gloss. Water-stained gift wrap. And one sheet of pristine white letterhead, embossed with a decorative *M*. Found near the train station in a manila envelope, which she's since cut open to double its surface area. The clean page, though, is kept that way. It's too perfect, too important, for regular lists, like the one she's amending now:

To Get

— *3-4 chairs*
— *3 cups, saucers (more for guests?)*
— *2 more plates*
— *3 sets of cutlery*
— *Gold frame from Neuemarkethub (Ned)*
— *Shower vouchers (extras for May)*
— *A Gran and a few more cousins*

Thinking, she lifts her hat, tangles words and knots in her hair. She chews the end of her pencil stub, then adds:

— *Mirror*

Once the first list is ready to go, she adds a couple more question marks beneath the one titled *To Sell* before picking up another, scribbled on a lined piece of paper, torn from a pocket-sized notebook. For a while, she'd kept this one memorised. Whenever a new idea struck her, she'd add it to the lot, watch the contents run through her 'wind, over and over and over. But after a few weeks, she knew she was forgetting things. One by one, older thoughts dropped off—she felt their absence in the pit of her stomach, but could do nothing to dredge them up again. So she started writing her thoughts in secret, waiting to share them with Peyt. Stockpiling a rats' nest of tidings, fears, intimacies. She scribbles *forgot your jacket*, then tucks this note into her coat with the others. Then she turns to her manila masterpiece, and plans her route for today.

The map is far from complete, but she's made a decent start. On rough pages she sketches the neighbourhood around her apartment—the toilet block, apartments around the cobbled square, the grocer's, the widening streets—then copies them, makes maps of the maps, stars her favourite rummages, exes cannons and guns, shades boroughs fallen to the greys. At night, after shopping, she corrects the drafts. Erases more than she adds.

When it's accurate, give or take, she inks, outlines, cross-hatches details on the manila.

— *Blue: to the train station (Ned and May!)*
— *Black: roadblocks / snares / regular ambushes*
— *Red: hotels / theatres / restaurants (good furniture)*
— *Green: decent rummage (also: "glass")*
— *Orange: nightmarkets*
— *White: shelters / trenches*
— *Pink: paths Peyt takes coming home*

Mireille carefully measures the distances with a wooden school ruler. Plots her weeks, her days, her hours. When she squints, the splotches and squiggles blur into masses, just like the pale continents on Peyt's hands, wrists, face. She studies the patterns, near and far, familiar and foreign. She peers through her lashes. Tries to get her bearings.

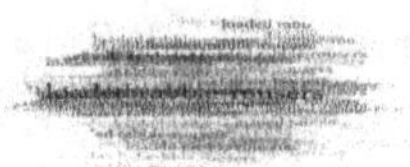

Mireille is sweating when she reaches the red road, more from anger than heat. Keeping her head down, she skirts around the overpriced bazaar, avoiding hawks and ballymen gibbering at her in their lisping, slurring tongue. They follow her, a few steps away from their stalls, eventually slowing to a stop as she hurries past without buying anything. These merchants don't smile; they bare their teeth, lips disappearing, and watch her with wide golden eyes. Now that the skies have calmed, the streets are busy once more. Mireille lifts her collar, tries to blend in with the crowd, but feels their stares penetrating the flimsy beige shield. She's sure, if she looked closely, their pupils would be pointed. Vertically slit. Like a snake's.

Just like the cobras who live upstairs, she thinks. The pythons that slither around Mireille's unit—some scaling the rubble outside her window to slide up the fire escape, others hissing past her front door—all those nasty blonde snakes with their thick eyeliner and strong perfume, their 'windless heads and sagging figures, their forked tongues forever talking about, but never to, her. Like the adder she bumped into half an hour ago, on her way out.

"Morning," Mireille had said—sweetly—lifting the corners of her mouth until her cheek muscles confirmed she was smiling. "Nice day today."

It wasn't, they both knew; it was cold and sooty and fuckin' miserable. But that's what you say to people you haven't quite met, Mireille had thought. Something neutral, friendly, insipid. You can't just launch into deep conversations—you have to give them an opening.

But the soldier's wife hadn't taken it. Her mouth had gaped soundlessly as she sketched a few symbols in the air, as if trying to ward off evil. And when Mireille clearly hadn't disappeared—she was still there with her little tin wagon, standing in the apartment's entranceway, halfway down the tunnel leading through the trash to the building's main door—the wife had gaped, exasperated, frustrated, and turned her gaze to the ragged walls, to the piss-stained threshold, to the scuffed toes of her stupid high-heeled shoes.

She's jealous, Mireille thinks. They're all jealous. Peyt's been home twice now—twice in two months! *Their* soldiers haven't shown up once. Not once. And we've got the lowest apartment, probably the biggest. Three rooms for four people, three rooms for two. . . . Yeah, they must be jealous.

But too jealous to say hello?

Just one word to make her feel welcome?

She stumbles and falls, palms and pride stinging. The wagon wheel is wedged between two crooked paving stones, stuck fast. Without slowing, the crowd parts; swirling like a muddy stream around a big, dumb rock. On hands and knees, Mireille's head starts to ache. Her inner ears thrum.

It's Peyt, she thinks, heart pounding as she gets up off the ground. Peyt's calling!

A moment passes: she clears her mind, closes her eyes, *opens* herself to the mentalegrapher's wave. Projects images of her and Peyt into the ether, an anchor for the medium to latch on to. Visions of his homecomings: how he'd tremble, seeing her, and she'd laugh to see him, laugh with joy and relief to have him, here and unharmed and whole; how he'd hug her then, fiercely; how he'd kiss her shoulders and neck, stinking of sweat and miles and vanilla. She thinks of lying in bed, his fingers tracing patterns on her naked skin; hers drumming silly rhythms on his bare arse, then making him guess the song. She imagines him getting misty when Ned learned to read, when she started to hum, to sing. In the narrow passageway, suffering bumps and glares, Mireille's mind is so open the fedora bounces on her head. Her 'wind is frenzied, drunk on memories.

Yet she hears nothing. Receives nothing but echoes from the past, snarls in her present.

It's all right, she thinks, yanking the wagon free. It's fine.

It's still early.

She trudges to the end of the red lane, turns into a green zone. A paved courtyard surrounded by ten-storey office buildings, a glass rehab centre, a soup bar, and a skinhouse. High above the rooftops, cranes swing loads of steel struts and huge spinning tubs of concrete. Patching mortar-holes, erecting watchtowers, building and rebuilding the gap-toothed skyline. Arranged in straight rows across the square below, dozens of hundred-gallon dumpsters sit with lids lifted, an aproned ladderman guarding each one. It's hard to tell which bin holds what—a long line-up doesn't necessarily point to the best goods. More often than not, the people queuing are stoolies hired by the trash collectors. For a few bucks, they'll spend their days beefing up the lines. Climbing in and out of dumpsters to pick up decoy bags made to seem full of plunder. Or, sometimes, shaking their heads, descending empty-handed—while catching or avoiding *just* enough glances to convince those waiting that pickings in that particular container aren't as dire as they appear.

One way or the other, the front row of bins usually gets picked-over first; then again, it's also first to get refilled. The far rows often get heaped with actual junk: lamps that aren't worth refitting, dishes beyond gluing, dolls with no heads or heads with melted bodies. The middle section is a hodgepodge of clutter, some trash, some treasure. Mireille once found a great photo album in the biggest junk bin—the sepia Da now hangs on their living room wall, proud in his suspenders, straddling a cross-desert motorbike—so she heads over there again, gives her twenty cents to the ladderman, and lines up. Waits for her go at the rummage.

When she's finally whistled forward, Mireille wheels her wagon up to the X marked beside the ladder. The guard, a zeppelin-bellied man dressed in chequered flannel and yellow rain pants, reaches out and blocks the rungs with the bloated stump of his arm. As always, Mireille tries not to cringe while meaningless words spit at her. She even attempts a smile. Nodding as if she understands him.

Her hat tilts and *just let me go* slips from under the brim. The ladderman recoils, swatting violently. "Sorry," she says, crimson. Before climbing up, she presses another nickel into the fat pig's hand, which he shoves into his apron with a grunt, as if it was his due.

Now up to her shoulders in the bin, she takes one look at the hoard and feels her stomach drop. Though these are supposed to be dry dumpsters, this one smells rancid, offal and curdled milk. Flies buzz out of shopping bags. Maggots congregate on soggy cardboard boxes. With the toe of her boot, she kicks back this flap and that, more and more dejected by the second. She finds:

— *plastic containers without any lids (15 ½)*
— *smashed percolators (3)*
— *a cedar tray, worm-eaten, split in two*
— *mugs with no handles, dirty brown chips in the glaze (7)*
— *chains, four different gauges and lengths*
— *empty briefcase, monogrammed "VL" (hinges shot)*
— *a metal trolley, no wheels, foxed with rust*

Nothing worth salvaging, she thinks, chucking the trolley aside. The flies dance around her, mixing with her 'wind, mocking. She squats and they follow her down. Buzzing, buzzing, buzzing tears into her eyes. What a fuckin' waste of time, she thinks. But then—*there*. She digs under a dripping green bag, stirs up another swarm. Blowing them away from her face, she uncovers a squashed carton. She smiles then, despite the wings and feelers batting her lips.

A shoebox. Universal home of valuables.

Lifting the lid, her smile widens. And fades.

Once, Mireille had a photograph of her Mamie, filched from the vanity dresser while she was sleeping. Black and white, matte finish, hand-tinted. Aurelia's cheeks and lips had been washed in coral, her irises a watery green. Her black-brown hair was bouffant, rising beyond the ebony frame. It'd been a close shot: Mamie seen from above. Crouched over a gramophone, she was looking up over her shoulder. Not smiling: coy. Flirting with the photographer, who, Mireille guessed, had been her father.

She's never had any pictures of him.

He was too temporary for that, Aurelia explained when Mireille pestered her enough. Nothing could capture him for long, she'd said. Especially not some little piece of glass.

She'd made a silent vow to return the photo before Mamie got home from the dry-docks the next morning. But when she was late for breakfast, Mireille had hung onto it. Just a bit longer, she promised. Just a while. Morning turned noon turned dusk. Still no Mamie. Still Mireille kept the frame propped against the ballerina jewellery box on her bedside table.

She'd stayed awake all night, listening. Hearing Mamie's velo in every crunch of gravel outside. Her footsteps in every creak. Her sighs in the breeze.

At dawn, Mireille realised her mistake. Bleary-eyed, she rushed into Aurelia's room and put the picture back where it belonged.

Now she'll come home, she'd thought, just as a key scratched in the front lock.

She ran to the door, ready to apologise for keeping Aurelia away so long—if only I'd done that yesterday!—but the silhouette darkening the frosted glass was too big to be her little Mamie, and much too tall. Its shoulders were way too broad, and the thing had two heads . . .

Hiding in the hall closet, she'd watched the landlords inspect the apartment, running their fingers along Mamie's prized oak table, sneering at her collection of porcelain dancing cats.

"The stiff's lease doesn't expire for three months . . ." said the man. He lifted the living room trunk, grimaced, and let the lid clunk the way Mamie always told Mireille not to. "How fast can we get the Bartletts and Singhs in here?"

"Sell what you can," said the woman, carrying a clipboard, her wordwind filled with checkmarks and dollar signs. "Junk the rest. Paul can hose the place down tonight, tomorrow at the latest."

"Good," said the man, opening and closing cupboards. When he approached the closet, Mireille read his 'wind, his intentions, his reasons for being here.

Mamie's not coming back.

Her muscles coiled, ready to spring. The man jumped after he'd slid the doors wide and saw Mireille there. He yelped like a clown when she leaped, but she didn't laugh.

Mamie's gone.

Mamie's gone.

She flew out of the closet, out the front door, out into the terrible bright.

Mamie's gone, she thought, running, running, leaving everything behind. She's gone and it's all my fault.

Now Mireille sighs, long and hard, and slumps onto an upside-down bucket. She rifles through the shoebox, knuckle-deep in its empty promise, rejecting picture after picture after picture. True, a house won't ever feel like a home without photos. Without proof that other people have smiled or held still or looked coy for someone else at least once in their lives. That—for a split-second, for now, forever—exposed and chemically-fixed, they exist. *These* people, though. Ugly as the flies invading her nostrils and ears, their static droning and insistent—and loud. Cocking her aching head, she squints to hear better.

"Is that you, Peyt?"

He's going to call soon, she thinks, pulse racing. If I find one more cousin in here, he'll call.

She flicks through the pile, faster and faster, but doesn't feel a connection with any of them. They've got to be *right*; either with Peyt's slender build or her crooked nose or dangerous grey eyes like Neddie's. Aurelia's shiny coif. A man's callused hands awkwardly cradling his baby. Something, *anything*, to make these people familiar. . . . But all she finds are freckled mutants. High-heeled snakes. Blank-eyed psychos nobody wants on her family tree.

Come on, she thinks, tearing a potential candidate in her haste. In profile, the boy's brow and chin were only *sort of* elongated, only a *bit* concave. . . . Who am I kidding, she thinks. The kid's practically a crescent moon.

There are only two snapshots left when the ladderman knocks his cane against the bin's metal side. *Time's up.*

"Just a minute," Mireille says, and the banging gets louder. The guard may not understand what she's said, but he is obviously well-versed in the tone of stallers. The dumpster gongs, rattling her skull, making it impossible to hear the mentalegrapher's signals.

"Fine," she snaps, picking the technicolour print of an almost-pretty girl. If only her fingers weren't quite so long. Her skin a bit less like weathered bark. "You'll have to do, cousin."

But as she climbs down the ladder and puts the picture in her wagon, Mireille recognises it for the cheat it is. This—creature—won't ever go up on their living room wall. She's an act of desperation, a mistake in judgement. In taking this *thing* and pretending she's a fitting addition to their gallery, Mireille has undone all the good luck she stockpiled this morning. And now Peyt probably won't be calling.

No, she thinks, scrunching the not-cousin. He definitely won't call today.

Things to tell Peyt:

— *found two new polishes for Ned (indigo, emerald)*
— *forgot your jacket*
— *one sidewalk is clear*
— *cockroaches in the cupboards*
— *grocer's awning blew away*
— *my freckles have disappeared*
— *forgot your jacket*
— *apartment echoes (a lot)*
— *job (?)*

Five more days, and no word.

She's run up the stairs to the second floor and back without making a single step squeak. She's worn the same three shirts in exactly the same way, avoiding the necklace that attracts bad news. She's kept the hat in its box, the papers arranged by size and colour on the kitchen table. She's managed to write five new lists before the kettle boiled. She's held her breath twice as long as she needs to guarantee he'd call. . . . And still, nothing.

Mireille knows Peyt won't talk about the war. She can respect this silence even without appreciating it. She gets it. She *understands*.

So she's never asked him about it.

And still.

To kill time, she'll go down to the toilet block. Brush her teeth—*no blood and he'll call*—wash her hair—*ten strands rinse down the drain at once and he'll call*—pluck her eyebrows—*don't flinch and he'll call*. Sometimes she just sits there, pants round her ankles, skirt hiked round her waist, staring at the graffiti. All the left-right, triangular, illegible words. The cocks and slits drawn in thick black marker. The question marks asking—something. Reaching out, anonymously, to a girl who gets it. Who understands.

Today, towel over one arm and hair dripping rat-tails, Mireille shivers on her way back up the slope. The apartment building looms before her, a giant marble headstone jammed into a grave of filth. Skeletons jangle in clusters at the water pump and by the taxi stand and near the tunnel to her home. Nests of snakes, she thinks. Packs of wives.

She shivers so fiercely she can't fake-smile. Instead she matches her expression to theirs, scowling. Hisses and whispers follow her up the sidewalk. They're talking, talking, talking about her. She doesn't understand the words, but still she knows what they're saying. They're staring at her wordwind, staring at her. They think she's stolen their crude little thoughts; they think she's flaunting the theft about her, wearing it like a mantle. They think she's keeping herself warm on their mean ideas.

One snake sashays across Mireille's path, intentionally bumping her towel into the dirt. Another, whose blued knees jut out beneath a red silk slip, snorts a laugh. "Look," Mireille growls, grabbing the smirker's skinny forearm, a bare stick of meat. She tightens her grip, forcing the woman to feel the chill in her fingers.

"See," she says, tugging desperately as the skingirl struggles. "See?"

Red stripes brand the other woman's arm when she wriggles free.

"Cold," Mireille calls after her. "Just like you. But you'll soon have someone to keep you warm, won't you? At least for a spell. Won't you!"

Refusing to run, to be chased from her own threshold, Mireille plods underhill to the door. Rubbing her freezing hands together until they're as pink as her cheeks.

Go on, she tells herself later, hesitating on the mentalegraphers' doorstep. It'll be fine.

Mireille looks up at the cream-coloured townhouse on the red road. The mediums couldn't have chosen a more calming location for their business. Foot traffic bustles up and down the street, but the people are well-dressed and busy—too busy to deepen their scowls, wondering what a girl like her is doing in such a nice neighbourhood. The building's smooth rendering is hardly shelled, and there isn't a sharp edge in sight. Architraves curve gently around oval windows. The house's corners look like they've been baked in a rounded cake mould. A decorative lintel projects vertically over the front door, adorned with long tubes of soft white light. Beneath her dull boots, a pale pink mat—scalloped and stitched to look like a brain—bids her *Welcome*.

Go inside. One way or another, it's someone to talk to. Sort of.

Before going in, Mireille steps aside to let a young couple past. Their faces burnished with the joy of speaking long-distance. Receiving messages from Pigeons can't compare to this kind of contact, this actual getting in touch; even if they've got a great ear for languages, Pigeons can only *report*. They'll parrot each word the senders have shaped—they'll get the order of phrases exactly right—but there's no *tone*. No certainty that what's been said will be heard the way it was intended. No feeling or emotion that Mireille doesn't read into it herself.

The mentalegraphers, on the other hand, are expressive, animated, lively. Walking into their office, she's overwhelmed by a maelstrom of voices. Waves of laughter. Cadences rising and falling.

Deep-pitched susurruses of public arguments. Wet swellings of unrestrained tears.

How spirited they are when channelling! How very life-like.

Not that they're exactly *dead*, Mireille decides, following a receptionist past several plexiglass cubicles, each furnished with a simple hardwood desk, white fibreglass tulip chairs, and a chrome pendant lamp shining blurred cones of yellow onto the figures sitting below, clasping hands across the tables. The mediums aren't *corpses*; it's just, some say they were born without souls. Mireille doesn't quite believe that, though. How can they function without at least *some* spark of their own? True, they are channels, conveying other people's thoughts—not just mimicking, *transmitting* other people's voices. But surely that doesn't mean they're empty the rest of the time.

I mean, Mireille thinks, look at this one.

The woman sitting behind the desk has more spirit than most. Her eyes, though opaque with cataracts, are alert; protruding irises fix on Mireille the instant her shadow falls across the shag carpet. Dimples pucker the medium's broad brown cheeks when she stands, open-lipped and open handed, welcoming. Her long black hair is tied back with a white velvet band, and the white fleece shawl draped across her broad shoulders is embroidered with whimsical balloons. She is matronly, almost plump. Mireille can't help feeling she'd give strong, all-encompassing hugs.

Her nametag is buffed steel, labelled *INEZ*.

Her breath—her lip gloss?—smells like vanilla.

Her smile widens, without hint of a scowl, and Mireille's pulse regulates. Inez makes her feel like a long-lost friend. Like someone she's known for years. She helps Mireille with her coat, then stalls her mid-sit. "Cash or trade?"

In her thick accent, it sounds like *kiss or tread*. It takes Mireille a moment to translate what the woman has said.

"Of course." She blushes. Fumbles through all her layers for the money belt tucked into her pants. Peyt sends funds whenever he can—coins individually wrapped in cotton batting, unclinking, so Pigeons won't know the parcel's worth stealing—but lately the grocer's prices are nearly as bad as the bazaar's. The purse is lighter than she remembered. And some things can't be rummaged: soap, milk, pencils . . .

"Trade."

Inez tilts her head, assessing. Mireille shrinks under the woman's blind scrutiny; her body stripped and inventoried in seconds.

"Destination?" she asks, and Mireille is flummoxed. How am I supposed to know where he is? Isn't that her job? To track him down? To find him?

As if attuned to her client's distress, Inez expands the field of inquiry. "Domestic or international?"

"Domestic," Mireille stammers. "I think."

"Very well." Inez nods. Gestures at the cardigan knotted around Mireille's hips. "We'll start with that and adjust if need be. If he don't pick up, you gets a full refund."

"Of course," Mireille says, more harshly than intended. With the sweater on the desk between them, she is invited to sit and place her hands palm-up on the soft wool. The medium follows suit. She pulls her chair close, intimate. Heavy breasts millimetres above the tabletop. Shadows muting her features. She leans in and exhales. The scent of vanilla so strong, it's befuddling. Mireille wonders where in the world she got perfume.

"Clear your mind," Inez instructs. "Think only of—"

"Peyt. Peytr Borysson."

"Just so," says the medium. "Think only of Peytr Borysson. Mind-trap him fully, painted in detail. What makes him *him*? Narrow it down to the blood and bone. Then hang that picture in the right room. What's around him? Got it? Got it? Now, when you're ready, call."

"Out loud?"

Inez nods. Sage. Reassuring.

Mireille does as she's told. Holding nothing back, she squeezes Inez's fingers. "Peyt?" she whispers, annoyed at the saltwater rise in her veins. She clears her throat. Swallows thick. "Darling?"

Cataracts twitch rapidly, left right left right left, and Inez's forehead pleats. Nostrils flaring, her lips become a black line. "Again."

Twice, three times, Mireille calls. Sweat trickles down her back and in runnels beside Inez's nose. It's not working, she thinks, calling,

"Peyt? Peyt?" Temples pounding, white and blue spots dancing across the desk. "Please answer, Peyt. Please—"

Inez's grip slackens.

Mireille's heart plunges.

"This was a mistake," she says, pulling back. "This was a complete waste of time."

Fool. . . . Stupid fuckin' fool . . .

The medium catches Mireille by the wrists, holds fast. Physically, her features remain unchanged—but within seconds, her bearing is transformed. She sits tall, shoulders thrust back, chin lifted. The fine brown arcs of her eyebrows dart up in surprise; Peyt's voice, when it comes, is haughty, high-pitched, almost feminine. His words, Mireille thinks, are coloured by Inez's peculiar inflections.

—Who is this?

"Peyt. Darling. It's me."

—And you are?

"Oh, Peyt." He's having an episode, she thinks. He's confused again.

All the lists stuffed in her coat pocket are forgotten. All the things she wants to tell him will keep. Until he's himself again. "It's *me*; it's your Mimi. I'm here, love—remember? Getting everything set for you and Neddie and dear Tantie to arrive. It's just about ready, too. You can come home anytime now, anytime. Come home, Peyt. Come home. There's no shame in—"

—Enough! Why are you doing this?

"*Well,*" Inez says, blinking fiercely. Gusts of sweet-vanilla air heave across the desk. A tissue appears from her sleeve; catching her breath, she pats the sweat from her brow.

"That's it? He's gone?"

"Not quite worth the price," Inez admits, making no move to return the sweater. "Make sure you see me next time. I'll give you a discount."

There won't be a next time.

Let him seek me out for once, Mireille thinks that night, her weak tea going cold on the kitchen table. Let him miss me, see how *he* likes it. Pencil in hand, list at the ready, she jots down a title, then gets up. Circumnavigates the sitting room, cracking her knuckles from pinkies to thumbs. Vitriol in motion.

She makes three laps clockwise, three widdershins, then sits. Starts writing.

Mireille is not selfish. She does what she can, all things considered. She contributes. She would do more if she could. Honestly. She's trying, even though he's not here half the time to see it. She is trying.

Things I Would Change

— *That* tone *he used today.*
— *The way he fast-talks to avoid actually talking.*
— *The way he thinks I don't notice when he does this.*
— *That he squirrels away most of his pay—who knows where? Who knows why. Sending a few coins wrapped in cotton, every once in a while. No paper, no notes. When there's Ned to consider. And May. When he says he wants better for us all, a house like the one he grew up in, or better,* better: *one that is ours. No shared walls, no shared rooms, no shared rations. A place of our own.*
— *That he's been promoted twice, however that works—higher bounty for killing greys? More time on the field? So he's earning more and is away more, but is still as close-fisted as he is close-lipped.*
— *That he won't offer a cent more than I can match.*
— *That he says it's* even *this way. It's* fair.
— *That he's often more fair than supportive.*
— *That nothing is fair, not really.*
— *Least of all love.*

Blue road for a blue sky day. Mireille's boots scuff along the chalky gravel, stirring up heel-clouds, miniature versions of the ones woolling overhead. Every few minutes, thin golden fingers streak down from above, directing her to the train station.

A good sign, she tells herself, unconvincingly. She hasn't slept well in days; now her luck metre is off. All morning she's been foggy-headed, distracted, walking green and orange paths. The wagon trundles behind her, empty, startling her with each clatter and bump. Restless, her limbs feel hollow, her hands tingling. She should eat, but her stomach is gone, disintegrated with worry. A strange, nervous feeling has lodged behind her ribs. It's almost like someone is trying to call, she thinks. But no matter how she listens the message eludes her, just beyond hearing. The muscles in her neck are hard. Her eyes are dry. Each individual lash itches. Knuckling brings no relief. At the turnstiles leading into the train station, she is seized with panic. Convinced she's left the gas-lamps burning in Neddie's room, that she'll come home to find nothing but cinder and smoke.

The platform is nearly deserted. Anyone not on the dawn run has missed out on a day's tunnelling; likewise, any shifts at the welders' three miles down the line have been filled by now. Workers with gear and gumption have been up and at it for more hours than most can fathom; the late-sleepers have tucked tail and gone to the alms-master to beg a ration of bread. Steel benches are seats for litter and rats, and wrought-iron clocks hanging from the rafters have boasted the same time for years. Pacing along the tiles, a few painted snakes click-clack in high heels, craning to see down the open-air tracks—as if staring and huffing and flicking smoke-butts on the rails will make the train magically appear. On the station side of the corridor, bannock and honey stalls are tarped and locked, the best wares saved for the evening rush.

No use peddling to ghosts from the 'port, Mireille thinks, as a big black engine crests the final rise. Out of habit, she looks at the clock. Guesses the train is about forty minutes late. Brakes shriek it home, shrilling to the roots of the teeth. Before the steam has settled, the wheels are chugging again, the shuttered carriages speckling the landing with no more than ten passengers. None of them straight-backed women. None beautiful little girls.

Tomorrow, Mireille thinks. Wishing, not quite believing. They must be coming tomorrow.

The station's revolving door spits her back onto the sun-dappled road. There are months until lunch, years before dinner. Abandoning the blue route, she turns onto the red, tread heavy as her heart.

Cranes trail shadows across her path, a confusion of lines and angles. Jackhammers rat-tat-tat behind chain-link fences, pounding asphalt and concrete to sand. Shovels scrape and scrape and scrape until there's a tang in Mireille's mouth. Sharp and metallic, like she's just bitten tinfoil.

Something isn't right, she thinks. Something is wrong.

I've done something wrong.

Peyt won't talk. Neddie and May won't come. What have I forgotten? She passes one construction site after another, jolting with each scrape of metal on stone, each screech, each *rat-tat-tat-tat*. A convoy of jets soars overhead. Mireille's shoulders bunch up, as if trying to cover her ears. Green spots swoosh in her peripheral vision as she fishes a rough map from her breast pocket. Why aren't they here? What haven't I done? With heavy strokes, she blacks out part of the red district, then rubs out a thumbprint smudging the Neuemarkethub.

Rat-tat-tat

Rat-tat-tat-tat

Brushing away eraser dust, Mireille stares down at the yellow square outlining the hotel and its off-limit hoard. She looks up, gauges the distance on land instead of paper, taking the new construction zones into account. Two blocks? Three, tops. *Rat-tat-tat*. I've got to get that gold frame, she thinks, legs suddenly pumping, propelling her forward. The wagon jerks and bounces, snags on a coil of fuses, flips with a crash. Mireille drops the handle, leaves the thing behind. I've got to get that gold—*rat-tat-tat-tat-tat*—Ned won't come until I get it—If I don't get it—she's not coming—*rat-tat-tat-tat*—if I don't—she's—*rat-tat-tat*—dead.

A wasp whizzes past Mireille's head. Her fedora blows off and scudders away. She lets it go. Around her the workmen are scowling, running to their machines. They're shouting, shouting at her—*rat-tat-tat*—and though she's gasping, churning distance with every ounce of her strength, she can't move any faster. She's sprinting through molasses. The street lengthens the further she goes. Left and right, cranes ratchet backwards, tipping at odd angles, tips aimed at the sky. *Rat-tat-tat-tat*. Clouds shred like gauze, revealing clear patches beyond the grey and flaring green. Chest heaving, Mireille sobs as a boom blasts from nowhere. Half a block away, a taxi blazes, billowing greasy smoke, hanging on the lip of a yawning crater. Running past, she sees the mule that pulled it charred to the bone. Stinking of singed hide and raw meat.

Rockets blare from cannons on rooftops, zippo raids stream red noise. High-rises in all stages of incompletion judder and grind, unsteady as drunks. Ned's dead, she thinks as a wall of heat knocks her to the ground. Neuemarkethub erupts, bombarded with fire. Stained glass sprays across the cluttered yard, chiming on the sidewalks and roads. Tiny, glittering shards nit through Mireille's hair; her 'wind scatters, incoherent, desiccated. Scrambling to her feet, she groans along with the teetering hotel. Bricks and marble and crystal and glass tumble into the yard. Burying chandeliers and tapestries and huge gold-leaf frames. Burying her little girl.

— *Ned's dead*
— *Ned's dead*
— *Ned's dead*
— *Ned's dead*
— *Ned's dead*
— *Ned's dead*
— *Ned's dead*

"Shhhhhh. Shhhhhhhhh."

The shelter is full of scowlers and snakes. They turn their backs, huddle in corners, as far from Mireille as they can get in such a confined space. Fanning the stuffy air away from their faces. Covering mouths and noses with handkerchiefs. As if the sorrow—the death—clinging to her is contagious.

Mireille doesn't stop crying.

"Shhhhhhh," says a young girl, squatting next to her on the floor. Around Ned's age, give or take. Wrapped in a shawl, with brown skin and messy black hair, the child is a perfect copy of Inez in miniature. 'Windless and wordless, her soft arm drapes across Mireille's shuddering back. Hand fluttering a comforting rhythm. *There, there.*

A good sign, Mireille starts to think, when big dimples stave in the girl's cheeks. Just like Inez. . . . Then she shakes her head, wracked with sobs.

I didn't make it in time.

Ned's dead.

This isn't a sign—

Unless.

Inez.

"I'll call them," Mireille whispers.

"Shhhhhhh," says the girl. "Shhhhhhh."

"As soon we get the all-clear, I'll call them. All of them. Ned, Tantie May." She sniffs, swallows a wad of phlegm. "And Peyt."

"Shhhhhhh."

"I know," Mireille says, snuffling into her sleeve. The girl is smart. She knows how Peyt will react. She knows calling will cause a fight. He'll say I make him feel bad for being away. That I always want him to come right home—even though he can't, not all the time, hardly ever. Then I'll apologise, and he'll say it's all right. And we'll make a deal, unspoken, untenable, that next time—next time he goes—I can't say anything about it. Not even fake good wishes. Not even *can't wait to see you again*. Not even *see you soon* because that's too restrictive. When is soon? Today? Next month? *My soon is different than your soon, Mimi. Don't make me feel bad*. So don't call. Don't ask. Shut up.

"But Ned is his *daughter*," she tells the girl, whose little hand keeps patting and patting. "He needs to *know*—"

I didn't make it in time.

"Shhhhhhh," says the girl. *There, there*.

"Welcome back."

"Trade," Mireille says instantly, shoving her trench coat at Inez. "Call my daughter."

The mentalegrapher squints as Mireille sits down. She looks tired; less beatific than she appeared yesterday. Slowly, she goes through the coat's pockets, taking out pencils and maps and lists. Glancing at them, occasionally saying, *Hmm* or *huh* before sliding them back across the desk. Ringed with blue shadows, her eyes narrow to slits.

"Ned, right?"

"Yes," Mireille says. "Ned. But how—"

Inez taps the top list with her finger.

"Oh."

"Children are sparrows," the medium says. "So flighty. Hard to catch before they're, oh, I don't know." She grasps a seven from Mireille's 'wind. "Ten? Eleven?"

"This is important." Mireille peels off her long-sleeved jersey, scrunches it into Inez's hands. "Please."

"Is she—" Inez waggles fingers at the wan letters storming overhead. "Like you?"

"Of course," she replies, taken aback. "She's my daughter."

"Of course." Inez sighs and Mireille catches a whiff of vanilla disdain. "So she'll be projecting her little thoughts all over, won't she?"

Today, Mireille takes no comfort in the medium's grip. The skin is papery but, somehow, also clammy. Between each knuckle, the flesh is gaunt despite its plump appearance. The hand that was so reassuring, so warm, now feels like a leather bag Mireille rummaged last month, filled with dice and ivory dominoes.

Closing her eyes, she clears her mind and concentrates on Ned.

After a minute, Inez clicks her tongue.

"Nothing," she says.

She's dead, Mireille thinks, heart clogging. "Call Tantie May," she manages, unlacing her boots. "I've got spare socks. Without holes."

"Done."

But it wasn't.

"Nothing," Inez says, less than thirty seconds later.

Maybe they're in the air, Mireille thinks. Maybe there's interference—

Reading her 'wind, Inez immediately says, "Sweetheart. There's nothing. No one. No one is there."

As Mireille howls, other mentalegraphers poke their heads into Inez's cubicle. She registers the disgust, the sympathetic looks they shoot at Inez. The medium grimaces and grins. Waves them out one by one, mouthing *It's okay* . . .

When the bawling subsides to a red-faced trickle, Mireille takes off her black tank top and offers it with trembling hands.

"I need to talk to him," she says. "Please. Find him."

Already, she can picture the words leaving her mind, zipping off to mingle with Peyt's, touching him like she can't . . .

Inez shakes her head. "It's not my business to harass people, Mimi."

"Please," Mireille begs. "Take my boots. My scarf. Tell me what you want, and it's yours."

Without missing a beat, the medium shrugs and replies, "Everything."

Just as quick, Mireille kicks off her boots. Her wool skirt, favourite pants, pink tank top. Peels off her scarf, ankle socks and leggings. Unfastens her bra, tosses it onto the pile. Hooks her thumbs in the waistband of her underwear—and Inez stops her.

"That'll do," she says, and Mireille sits back down, shivering.

She squeezes the medium's hands white.

This time, Inez waits a few minutes before disappointing.

"He's there," she says, "but it's blocked."

"Blocked," Mireille echoes.

"Blanked."

"Are you doing this on purpose?" Mireille gets up, gathers her scraps and pencils. Crushes them against her breasts. "Is that it? You're having a bad day?" Retreating, her bare toes snag in the thick carpet. She pauses at the cubicle door, looks at the other booths arranged in rows across the office. "What if I use someone else?"

Inez winces, remains seated. "You can try. If you think it'll help." Her tone is raw, honest as a 'wind. *Don't bother*, it says. *He's busy. He doesn't want you.*

"You must have seen *something*," Mireille says, turning to face her square-on. "Show me."

"I don't think I should . . ."

Calmly, quietly, Mireille sits back down. Piles her papers in a neat stack, pencils aligned on top. Lays her hands on the desktop, palms up. Wordwind spinning, spinning, spinning.

"Show me."

Dressed in Peyt's jacket, one of Tantie May's dresses, and a pair of men's boots Ned was supposed to grow into, Mireille sits at the kitchen table. Where they should've had family dinners together. Where they should've played cards.

Walls of Grans and Grampses, Mamies and Das, brothers and sisters and cousins stare down or across or up at her as she writes her sweet Neddie a three-pencil letter. A wide rectangle of grey light illuminates page after page; the living room blind is raised, the curtains tied back, the front door flung wide open. A breeze ruffles her paper as outside rushes in, and inside out. Her 'wind surfs the turbulent currents, tossing to and fro.

Filling an ashtray with sharpenings, Mireille tells Ned about the night she met Peyt in the museum. How frightened he was, how responsible, how endearing. She tells her of the mothers. How they'd sing the children to sleep, the same songs she herself sang to Peyt, and not too much later, to Ned. She tells her about the rummage, the nail polish, the gold frame. How the best deals appear at night, but not necessarily the best men. She draws smiley faces. She draws little hearts. She tells her not to worry so much about the greys. How it's happier, sometimes, not to see what will hurt you. Let it come in its own time, she tells her. Or just let it be.

Now her wordwind is heavy, seeping dew, but Mireille doesn't clip it. She won't press the pain into Ned's innocent letter. She won't tell her about Inez's vision. She won't describe her father, so scrawny when naked, wrestling with that red-headed snake. She won't explain that they weren't in the middle, but on the brink of, fucking. She won't tell her that the bed was turned wood, the blankets clean and well-made. She won't tell her the room was snug and richly furnished, or that it reeked of cinnamon and vanilla. She won't tell her that, one second, she was looking up at Peyt, grunting and moaning—and the next she was looking down, within licking distance of a 'windless whore. She won't describe the glistening threads connecting them all; her and Inez, Peyt and the tramp. She won't snip these details from her own 'wind, or impose them on her daughter. She won't shift that weight off her mind. She doesn't want to forget.

Instead, she tells her she's sorry. She says *see you soon*. No implications, no restrictions. Let Ned be the judge of how long *soon* should be.

When she's written calluses into her fingers, Mireille kisses the pages then gathers them into a neat stack. Going into Ned's room, she ignites the lamps. Holds the papers up to the flames. Once they're crackling hot, she trots into the sitting room and watches them dwindle to embers in the sink. No need to burn the house down, she thinks. Wouldn't want Peyt to think I've up and croaked. Before the fire dies, she collects her lists. Her maps. Her plans. Tosses them in, one after another after another, withholding a single envelope and the pristine piece of paper she's saved for a special occasion.

Leaning over the sink, Mireille gently bends the white page and scoops up every fleck of ash. Carefully, she smears the charcoal around, blackening both sides of the white paper completely. When that's done, not wanting to waste a bit, she shakes off the excess then scoops it up again. A simple fold traps the soot inside the letter, which she slides into the envelope. Picking up the pottery jug she'd filled earlier, she rinses the sink first, then her hands, then drinks the rest of the water down.

When everything is washed and in its place, she looks out the window and sees a skyful of grey. Unblinking, she twists her hair into a bun. Ties a kerchief around her 'wind. Shoulders her bag. Places the note on the table for Peytr to find. Then goes out to find a blank route, a blank home.

TWELVE

Inez has lost count of how many she's had inside her. Men who grunt more than talk; who stare at her breasts or their sweaty paws or the black-diamond shape their knees make when touching hers; who make it hard for her to get swept up in the moment, thinking, as they so often do, of their wives or girlfriends or, more than they care to admit, other men, the whole time they're together. These callers aren't all alike, of course. She's seen too many varieties to generalise: pimpled flax-braids and pale blood-nuts, tattooed ink-noggins and soul-bald scalps; slobberers with small eyes and whisperers with large; plum-face blushers and limbless herb-bringers and pathetic, grey-haunted twitchers. . . . So many—*too many*, maybe, for the cheap price she gets for letting them in. Different as they all are—if pressed she might even admit they're unique—few of these men are special. Almost none are memorable. Lately, when pressed, she imagines them as one horny lump. They leave exhausted—sapped—though *she* is the one who spends the hour concentrating, focusing, keeping them on track so they'll arrive the same instant she does. And yet, when all is said and done, they grin and say *they're* tired

Inez is tired. Of sad, desperate women sticking their miseries in her dark, hollow spaces. Of young, happy women slipping joys into her gaps; retracting them only to shove them back in again. Of their tears and their laughter and their mind-numbing anger—hours of in and out and in and out and in. *Exhausting.* Not to mention the smooth-chinners, the bare-of-mounds, the dripping little holes. Energy-leeches, all of them. She charges double for under-eighteens, triple for under-tens. Out of principle, she refuses penetration by toddlers, babies, newborns. Anyone too immature to think or speak coherently. The older kids are almost bearable—though they like and like and like so much she often wonders what it would take to make them hate—but the youngest leave her spitting, writhing in sticky-sweetness. Their hands are all over the place, as are their minds. Stupid, base-driven creatures. Prodding at Inez's tender parts, pinching and poking and take-take-taking. The selfish buggers *want*, *everyone*, *everything*, *now*.

And for each one she's let in—each bristle-beard moaner, each lonely weeper, each wailing school-pants-smirchers—Inez has been inside ten, twenty more like them. Every receiver just as vile and effusive and suffocating as the disgusting ones who sent her.

Except for Peytr, that is. There's a morose softness to him, a tears-behind-closed-doors aspect to his personality that she understands intimately. She comforts him, better even than his not-wife does. Better even *as* his not-wife, as Amelia.

First time he came to speak through Inez, Peytr had said it was a work call.

"Overdue delivery," he'd lied, hitching one of two satchels crossed over his shoulders. Eyes marble-blind, she saw him clearly. All mentalegraphers visualise sentiments, synergies, the energy of voices—to Inez, the vagaries of silence and grunts and unconscious gestures illuminate far more than they obscure. She'd had no need of light bouncing off retinas to see Peytr shuffling from foot to foot, leaving clumps of boot-muck on her ivory carpet. He'd loosened his hood, trusting her with his thoughts, inside and out. Words had beetled across his scalp, illegible scurryings that kept his thick hair in constant motion. Exposed, his face was two-toned. Wind-burnt from the lip up, while the clean-shaven chin below was whiter than her irises. Since walking into her cubicle, Peyt's temperature had increased and dipped at least twice. He was blushing, struggling for calm. Inez had smiled, dimpling. The blaze of scarlet on his cheeks and brow had warmed her belly, the limpid wash on his jaw thrilling her down to the nethers.

He would be a gentle lover, she'd thought.

"I'm here for you," she'd said.

But when he'd looked at her, Inez knew he saw someone else. The flush, the stutter-tongue, the Adam's apple pistoning up and down his mottled throat—none of it had been for *her* sake. Never was. She was a middle-aged woman, unseeing, unsightly, unseen. Such timid love-flutterings weren't ever on account of her.

"She—" Stuffing hands into pockets emptier than the sacks he carried, Peytr had tried again. "I just need to check an address."

Fibber, Inez thought, miming an understanding *ah-ha*. Taking a handful of bent nickels and a small bunch of carrots for payment, she'd kept smiling, an invitation and a shield. Within seconds, she imagined her bottom teeth growing upwards, widening beyond gums and lips, encasing her head in a shell of pearlescent enamel. At the same time, her top teeth retracted into their roots and columned upwards, tunnelling beyond skull and shell alike, clearing a broad vacuum-channel through which a caller's soul could be drawn. Fast and sharp, the shaft fused with the surrounding shell even as it broke through, stretching into a long flexible tentacle, protected by a carapace of yearning and bone. Inez pictured it arcing through the atmosphere, a glossy cable of negative space, dipping and weaving around a hundred thousand other such cords.

While he was paying, it was agreed this private channel belonged solely to Peytr. His needs alone would direct its path while Inez's innate skill would drove them home. In the meantime, almost everything else Inez was—the echo of her thoughts, the desire for company, the endless history of her clients—was to be shunted aside, crammed into the small cavity remaining behind her dry eyes.

Fitting in there was harder, now, than it had been when she'd first started.

Cramped behind a barricade of teeth, Inez was only allowed pinhole access to the goings-on in the other side of her mind. Each caller's presence inside her was a squirming of different sensations—apprehension, eagerness, self-doubt, jealousy, lust—each shaped around vibration-images and incoherent bursts of noise. Memories, experiences, dreams. All and none of them hers.

They're irrelevant, she'd thought, spinning out her rope. Soul-flotsam on the incoming tide. She didn't need to understand what these fragmented pictures all meant. She didn't need to pay them any attention. She didn't even need to see them.

But with a stranger's voice inside her she could, and did, and wanted to.

Following protocol, Inez sent the barest guywire of her own spirit through the maelstrom of her client's thoughts, into the channel, and beyond; the call's spinal cord, it connected one end to the other, conducting messages spoken and silent, animating the whole. That, Inez was told, in no uncertain terms, was the greatest part of a mentalegrapher's duties. Convey each voice with impunity. Afterwards, sever the lines. Retract them cleanly. Bid all parties farewell, and forget every word you've helped to exchange.

Be careful, the boss told her once she started mediating regular calls. No one can be in two places at once for long. Keep it to an hour, tops. Even in an emergency. If you want to burn people's brains out, Taheer had added, join the army.

But he was wrong, Inez soon realised. Clients never noticed when she widened the hole from pin to peep to port. They never flinched when she strummed their soul-chords, holding this note or that for much longer than was required. She deciphered the patterns of their mind-pictures, learned how to track sights as well as sounds. Studying the drift of their moods, the debris of their thoughts, made no difference to these out-lookers. They were always preoccupied, in a rush, nervous. Focused on more important things than an ever-thickening spirit wire or an excited shadow flitting down its length behind them.

They were oblivious, selfish soul-travellers. And in the shade of their ignorance, she was free.

With part of her spirit skull-cap protected, firmly rooted in the body at her desk, Inez had quickly learned to fly. Her body still faked enthusiasm, still squeezed clammy fingers, still overheard circular conversations and smelled the stale depths of her clients' stomach on their hot breath—but *she* was mostly elsewhere. Splitting her tethered-self in two, Inez had followed one soldier to the house where his wife and mother-in-law lived. In Vaux's mind-trap, Bren was a girl, young and glad and stiff-nippled in a negligée. But before she and Vaux plunged into the woman, Inez saw grey hair at her temples. Lines worrying her forehead. The sag of years beneath her jaw. Their talk was small, strained. *Another family moved into the second bedroom. What about the Vaughans? The missus is dead. Shame. Yeah, but Errol's still got the attic. That's good. Yeah. Thanks for the socks. You're welcome.* After the gunner had gone, Inez had kept the slightest wisp of a connection open with his wife. While she watched, Bren had tilled the backyard, planted beans. Mashed potatoes for her mother and the new kids. Filched coins from the old lady's purse and splurged them all on a hot shower. Clean as lye, she climbed the attic ladder and found more comfort there than in any of her husband's calls.

By the time Peytr had come into her cubicle that morning, Inez could split her self in three—four, even—without anyone else the wiser. Crouched behind her cataracts, smile fixed in place, she'd welcomed the Pigeon while also tunnelling through bedrock with Weasel Dan and his crew while also scaling the struts of a skybunker tower—wishing, wishing with all of her parts, she could see one of the little girl-fliers up close without having to die immediately afterwards. But within seconds of taking Peytr's hands, Inez's control had been shaken. She'd left Dan to bucket gravel and Ison to inspect girders for weaknesses and focused entirely on the slump-shouldered man fidgeting in front of her.

"This *she* you mentioned," Inez had said, taking his clammy hands. "Your boss?"

The air shifted; displaced particles swirled then rushed to fill the backdraft of his shrug. "Not quite."

"Ah. A partner, then."

In their mind, a clash of images tumbled. An ugly, bull-shouldered boy. Gold cufflinks. No, not quite: gold earrings. A red shirt that would never fit. A young stringy-haired woman. . . . Inez searched for a name to match the wan face, found *Mimi* lodged between a caravan and a high-rise apartment.

Half a beat later, she discovered *her*.

Amelia.

Peytr hesitated. It was stupid, they both knew, for him to struggle to keep his thoughts private. They were visible gnats. They were worms burrowing through Inez's brain. His voice and gaze dropped. "We have an . . . arrangement."

"As do we," Inez had said, refreshing her smile.

In their mind, Amelia's copper braids seemed lurid until Inez got used to sight, but otherwise her appearance was unremarkable. Average height, slightly too skinny. Nothing a few bowls of mash wouldn't fix. She had no wordwind. No freckles. No visible defects. She was wonderfully, beautifully, plain.

Peytr's grip tightened. "How long will this take?"

"Hush, now. Close your eyes," Inez had said. An unnecessary step from her perspective, but it helped the clients relax. "Point us at her."

Amelia shone, a flambeau beckoning from a cabin ten miles out of town. Riding Peytr pig-a-back along the airways, Inez forced herself not to whoop. She hadn't had a good flush of new love in years! And this *was* love, fresh with only a whiff of sour. Amelia wasn't desperate; if anything, she was matter-of-fact. She was instantly, pragmatically attractive. She was an entrepreneur of sorts, a glass-maker and seller of decent repute. And she trusted Peytr with her business—said he was the best Pigeon she'd ever had. He trusted her confidence.

He admired her good sense and her practical plans.

She was self-sufficient, secure, stable.

She was virtually independent.

She *was*.

Later, as Peytr knocks at Amelia's cabin door, Inez dims the ceiling light in her cubicle and says she's going on lunch. After so many hours *inside*, the last thing mentalegraphers want during breaks is more conversation, more human contact. Pockets jingling with change, they go upstairs to the staffroom and buy themselves an hour inside a solitude booth. In four rows of five, the moulded rectangular boxes are upraised on platforms in the centre of the room. Grey steps lead up to each narrow door; above sliding handles, green or red circles respectively beckon and repel. At this time of day, there are more solos available than taken: Inez takes the furthest green-dotted chamber, locks it, and sits on the cracked bench inside. The booth's vaulted ceiling is dingy white, the walls a luminous blue. Vents stipple a broad panel above the door, a mock-window that fools no one. Solo air is always turgid. Today it stinks of onions, sweat and arse-warmed plastic. Humid remnants of soup, hidden tears and regret.

Inez's stomach somersaults. Across town, Peytr's does likewise, his hands fumbling at Amelia's breasts and the many knots in his belt. This isn't the first time he's *checked an address* with her, and judging by how quickly she lifts-apron and unsnaps her jodhpurs it won't be the last. But still, there's the churn in their bellies. One part lust, five parts fear—no matter how many times Amelia shucks off her bloomers—that she won't be there when he drops by. That the wriggle in her own guts will twist from excitement to rot.

Playing matchmaker, Inez hopscotches from Peytr's chord to Amelia's. Holding firmly to both strands, she sends more and more and more of herself down the second line, subtlety be damned. Peytr is riveted as Amelia groans, trembling with the full force of a medium-surge. Taken by surprise, the other woman is quashed, compressed to a tiny cavern behind their shared eyes. Huffing and panting in the solo and in the cabin, Inez spreads their legs and shows the Pigeon how very welcome he is and will always be.

Normally Amelia doesn't use, but this afternoon she can't resist.

While the three of them fuck, Inez puts a glass-bomb in their mouth and tells Peytr to tongue it out. The bulb is imperfectly round, the size and shape of a walnut. A rainbow sheen of oil and saliva smears its clear surface, dream-coating ready to be sucked off. Tentative at first, Peytr leans in. His hips are already pumping, rigid cock deep-buried, the moment for foreplay long past. Puckering, he gets so close Inez can taste his breath—then he swerves at the last second. Nuzzling the soft curve of their jawline instead of their lips, he fishes the bomb out with his fingers. A blink later, it disappears into his mouth. With a dull pop, it crushes between tongue and roof. Shards lacerate delicate ridges then quickly melt. Blood mixes with glass-syrup, lubricating the dreams' passage into their lover's system.

Peytr's face instantly relaxes. The frantic tempo of his thrusting evens out, less herdboy now, more lap-dancing skingirl. On Amelia's lips, the drug's residue tastes like whimsy and release and the salt of far-distant seas. There's a tang of rhubarb, a bite of fire-ants on the gums. All in all the flavour wants honey, but it isn't sour. Even before meeting Rupe, who taught her everything she knows about cooking-up, Amelia had a knack for harvesting dreams from the happiest dead. No matter how many other glass-makers worked the nearest bone-orchards, her flannelette cloths always sopped up the freshest, sweetest serenity. And back home, her nimble fingers wrung gallons of the best fantasies into dust-silted pots boiling on Rupe's camp stoves.

Since his death, Amelia's trade has thrived. Unlike her once-husband, she isn't stingy. Giving free samples, she knows, keeps the glass-blowers blowing and the dealers discreetly dealing. And if they steal an extra bulb every now and again—if they need the jump so fuckin' badly—well, it's no dream off her tongue. She can spare a few daybreak fancies for the beat-walkers, some afternoon delights for the Pigeons. She can afford much more than that. Lined in ranks on slate countertops, antique coffee tables, marble benches, the sugar-pots are ever-bubbling in her cabin's spacious main room. Overhead, a frozen glass blizzard hangs from drying racks mounted in the rafters—more than enough to supply insomniacs and lonely mothers, bunker-bunnies and trench-jumpers, full-time escapists and weekenders teetering on the brink. She finds all she wants outside, where the near-dead persist in hoping, wishing, believing, dying. All the raw material she needs to survive in this business is abundant.

And Peytr deserves a bit of elsewhere, Inez thinks, popping another bomb into his gaping mouth. Jaw working as he sucks, his wordwind sloughs off in flakes. Eyes rolling back, he lets out a long, slow sigh. Ignoring the pounding behind her eye sockets, the screams thrashing at her temples,—*Enough! that's enough!*—Inez adds their moans to his as heat builds in her borrowed nethers.

That's it, she thinks. *That's* it. . . . Inside the solo, Inez's hand burrows beneath her waistband. Her palm cups the bulge of her sagging belly then pushes down, under lace and cotton, blunted fingers ploughing scant hair, slipping in and out of damp furrows. Back in the cabin, straddling Peytr on the living room floor, Inez grinds their slim hips as his inhibitions give way to dreams. Belly-to-belly, she pulls him closer, runs a nipple across his teeth until he nibbles. When he starts to shudder, she slides off and guides his hand to her wetness, letting his digits plunge and roam.

Inside their head, Amelia cries and rails. Jealous, Inez thinks, that *her* first time alone with the Pigeon had been so mundane. A quick rut on the chesterfield, clothes mostly still on. Life spurted into a handtowel because Amelia wanted Peytr to think she could still have children. Since then, she always made him pull out right when the pleasure was fierce.

Fuck that, Inez thinks while Amelia shrieks their sight spotty. "I was Awife, once," she says aloud, the words running together, exactly the way Amelia thinks them. As if there's no space between 'a' and 'wife'. As if she'd been generic, back then. Not Amelia, just some nameless hole.

"What?" Peytr asks, thumb rubbing, rubbing.

"Awife," Inez repeats. Then, laughing, gasping, "Don't stop, don't stop. Yes, you can—yes, do *whatever*—only don't ask me to sing."

"What—"

In reply, Inez shows him what a *pleaser* Amelia can be. Turning around, she leans their arse into a position gleaned from Peytr's mind, putting him places she's never had the nerve to go in her own body. Knees splayed in the solo and knees red on the living room floor, Inez thrusts and slides until the three of them are throbbing.

"Come back tomorrow and tomorrow and tomorrow," she whispers, using Amelia's voice but keeping her spirit suppressed. Though Inez's body wipes its hand on her trousers, adjusts her clothes and tidies her hair, she only sends enough of her mind back down to the office to sustain local calls. Her heart—their heart—stays in the cabin, already anticipating Peytr's return.

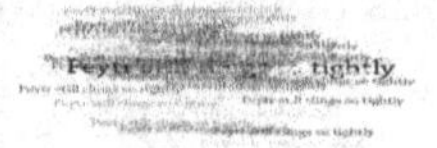

The next day he's back, but not as Inez expected. Not toting dreams to the desperate nor shuffling from foot to foot in her office, claiming he's lost an address that never existed. No, this new vision of Peytr is so much bigger than these. Suddenly, he's a born-again soldier, a volunteer-hero, a near-husband and father-of-one. He doesn't fuck strangers on chesterfields or weep in the darkness or shred his mouth raw on scraps of glass. This Peytr is stoic. This Peytr is private. He's a museum-prowler. A lover of music, a constant-dancer. A man of small appetite, culinary or otherwise. One who eats only his family's scraps. One who is often too stressed or tired—so he says—to have sex with the woman who loves him.

This Peytr lives between a caravan and a high-rise. He is blurred around the edges. An absence carried in the centre of Mimi's being, buried in cotton wool, nestled in clouds of longing.

Love is a miserable trap, Inez thinks, smiling her best protective smile, deciding then and there to wrench the poor fool free of it.

"Clear your mind," she instructs. "Think only of—"

"Peyt. Peytr Borysson."

"Just so."

As the girl's thoughts descend into the trenches, conjuring an image of Peytr masked in the grey drudges of battle, Inez finds him sprawled on Amelia's divan in boxers and socks, floating through the stratosphere in a glass balloon. His soul chord is hard to grasp; bird-pecked, worm-eaten, it soars then plummets, now a ragtime two-step, now a dirge. Inez soon gives up trying to tightrope its length, much less letting Mimi walk it with her.

"Now, when you're ready, call," she says, buying herself time. The girl does as she's told, bleats for her love, though Inez knows there can be no response. "Again," she says, watching Amelia through Peytr's slow-blinking eyes. Her hair is a waterfall of molten rubies, her skin nacre brocade. Snowflakes flurry from her lashes and moon dust from her nose while she leans over wells of past-present-future, dipping pearls. She is, plainly, the answer.

Inez sags a little as she nosedives from Peytr's heights, plunging into Amelia's depthless sorrow.

Better this betrayal than *that*, the medium thinks, mooring on the glass-seller's channel. Better to break a girl's heart kindly with part-lies than pulverise it with the whole truth. Ringing bells in Amelia's inner ear, Inez announces her presence before racing back to the office to collect Mimi.

"This was a complete waste of time."

No, Inez thinks, holding fast as Mimi pulls away. Warping the line, heavy-footing the bass to offset the treble in Amelia's voice, the medium shoves the call forward and makes the connection for her.

—Who is this?

Hold onto that joy, Inez thinks, as Mimi's features resonate silver and gold, her word-filled aura pulsating, sparkling, performing loop-de-loops. Save that glad hope for tomorrow and tomorrow and tomorrow . . .

"Peyt. Darling. It's me."

—And you are?

Quick as they flared, Mimi's fireworks are snuffed. She knows something is wrong, but refuses to admit it. Tiptoeing behind her, Inez watches excuses and justifications sprout like weeds in Mimi's mind, choking the path forward. *He's having an episode, he's confused, he isn't himself. . . .* And the faster the girl justifies, the slower she walks; soon stopping altogether, stuck in a well-worn rut of denial.

"Come home, Peyt. Come home. There's no shame in—"

A rut she needs to be forced out of. Abandoning her charge for only a second, Inez whisks into Amelia's core and *expands*. They'll have to reel Mimi in together, show her she isn't alone—

—Enough! Why are you doing this?

Amelia's screech knocks the air from Inez's swell. The force of it shunts her back to the office, shakes her from the tremulous fishing-line connection.

"*Well*," Inez says. That was close.

"That's it? He's gone?"

"Not quite worth the price," she admits, making no move to return the sweater. "Make sure you see me next time. I'll give you a discount."

In the back of Inez's mind Amelia is still shrieking, which she does too much nowadays. Peytr's away more than he's home, the demand for glass increasing with the number of sky-whales and jets bloating the air. There are too many bombs for him to deliver alone; Amelia has had to pick up the slack. The stress of farming, manufacturing, *and* supplementary shipping is too much for the poor woman to handle on her own. Lately she yells, it seems, at the slightest provocation.

"It's all right, sweetie," Inez thinks. "I'll be back to help you soon."

"What? Whatever do you mean? Virat?"

Across the desk, a man with black hair curling from beneath a snug cap blinks at her with confused brown eyes. A beard frizzes down to his collar but his upper lip and cheeks are bare; even shaped in molecule-riffs and chromatic echoes, the moustache-free look is a fashion that Inez has never liked. Let the beard take hold or shear it off completely—don't leave the pathetic strands clinging. Steel rings band his furry fingers, digging into her joints as he squeezes, pulling her hands close. "Virat? Hello? You still there?"

"Apologies, Essr. Bartos," Inez says, realising her mistake. Fixing her white stare on his dark one, she visualises the separate teeth-channels running through her head—a thin straw for Peytr, another for Amelia, a broad canal leading to her client's far-distant listener—and firms their enamel, stiffens the glossy barriers between them. No more slips, no more voicing her own thoughts. Smiling her cheeks painful, Inez finishes the call with shield intact, reassuring Bartos in Virat's rasping tones that yes, he is still here. No, of course he will *not* be back with him soon. Why would he? Yes, yes, he promises not to flee the field. What kind of question is that? He's been here this long, hasn't he? Indignant, Virat's spirit is burning, red and orange on Inez's tongue: he will stay that way, a remote blend of colours, an estranged brother, fighting a grey breach in a village Bartos hasn't seen while awake for nearly forty years.

After he leaves, Inez needs a few minutes to collect herself. She flicks off the light. Softly pings Cora and asks her to hold all callers until the afternoon rush. Closes her eyes. Then, gripping Amelia's chord, she slides along its length slowly, slowly pressing, slowly driving herself more fully in. It takes less effort today than it did yesterday, last week, last month—less force but more finesse. Amelia's gumption hasn't slackened one bit, and her instincts are raw. She's crafty, determined to outwit or outwrestle the medium at every chance; even though, with a poke, Inez can make the woman's spirit curl like a millipede.

Now they stand together in a stinking alcove on the ground floor of a high-rise, taking their finger off the buzzer to apartment 10E. The building's glass picture windows and doors have all been painted black; through watery streaks, they catch glimpses of people ghosting up and down the lobby stairs. None look their way, even though Amelia is shouting. Again.

"Orfe! ORFEO!"

"He isn't here," crackles a woman's voice through the speaker.

"Get the fuck out," Amelia says, batting an invisible fly. "Get. The. Fuck. Out."

The woman spoke over her. "He's gone, okay? Please leave."

"Listen, lady," Inez butts in, "these double-dips aren't going to fund themselves. Two days ago he promised, hand on fuckin' heart, to pay in full on delivery. Even left his spade as collateral—can't work without it, can he? And now, what. He just happens to be gone." They make air-quotes around *gone*, though the sarcasm is lost on the listener. "Fuckin' tunnellers, always reneging on expensive deals. Tell Orfe—"

"Just fuck off," the missus says, throwing Amelia's vitriol back through the speaker twofold, "before I call the Watch."

"As if those desk-jockeys can touch me," Inez brags while Amelia silently rants about discretion, secrecy, keeping her business on the down-low. "They're just clerks playing dress-up, you know. Too weak to be real soldiers . . ."

A long shadow thrums across the entrance of Inez's cubicle as, miles away, the intercom disconnects. With one hand, Inez adjusts

Amelia's satchel, heavy with unsold glass; with the other, she fumbles for the light switch. Straddling both chords—high notes in the city, low strains in the office—she gives Amelia her head, lets her rant and swear herself sweaty. While Amelia runs away, stupid-scared of police without any force, Inez straightens in her seat. A gentle rapping on the doorless wall facing her is followed by a polite throat-clearing.

"I thought I asked you to hold my calls." Cracking an eyelid, Inez sees a familiar swirl of boot-shaped atoms lingering on the threshold of the thick white shag. Well, well, well, she thinks, looking up at Mimi.

This time her smile is much more than a shield.

"Welcome back."

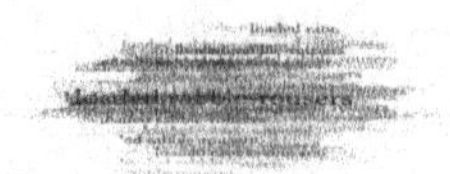

"How long was I out?" Inez always asks, innocently, when Peytr comes back to Amelia's cabin and finds her there instead.

His replies are always vague. "Not long," he'll say, or "No more than last time," or, unconvincingly, "You were gone?"

Peytr is a terrible actor.

His relief when Inez returns is palpable. Whenever she's away—sleeping, say, or dealing with a particularly demanding client—Amelia is wild. The woman sobs like a child, begs for Peytr's help, claims there's someone else in her head, someone making her *do* things . . .

Nonsense, Inez feels Peytr think, though she knows he doesn't mean it. Witnessing Amelia's deterioration, he is shaken. He sympathises as she rants and cries and fabricates lies. He is shaken, seeing her this way. He shakes.

From all sides, Inez is buffeted by whitecaps of desperation. Amelia crests at being trapped and disbelieved. Peytr peaks at just being trapped. And now this—

"I'm sorry, Mimi. There's nothing. No one. No one is there."

This is love, Inez thinks, grimacing and grinning, mouthing *It's okay* to her colleagues. But it isn't okay. Look at this girl. Just look at her. Stripped by grief, naked in love. Howling in a stranger's office, soul-bare and wrung.

There's nothing okay about her self-delusion.

"I need to talk to him," Mimi says. "Please. Find him."

Nothing okay about willingly suffering loss after loss after loss.

Nothing okay about pretending there's hope.

Make-believing she hasn't always been alone.

How can I convince her? What will it take to make her let go? Inez shrugs. "Everything."

Mimi's size-small dignity piles up on the desk, her need shed in scraps of acrylic and cotton. With each piece discarded, the girl's determination grows. Inez doesn't interrupt—words ruin the best lessons—but when Mimi reaches for her underwear, she decides, "That'll do."

Get dressed, she wants to say. Take your love letters and go home. There's nothing but hurt for you here.

Knowing Mimi won't leave without some consolation, Inez admits that Peytr is there. He's unavailable—but he's *fine*. And though not entirely true, this silence is kinder than honesty. Mimi doesn't actually want to *see* her born-again soldier with another woman. She doesn't want to see her rival smashing a harvest of living room glass, cutting Peytr off until he listens, *really listens* to what she's been saying, drying him out until he believes. She doesn't want to see him on hands and knees, bloodied from a hundred tiny scrapes and cuts, half-baked among the mess. She doesn't want to see her volunteer-hero apologising, groaning, grovel turning to snarl as he tackles Amelia and pins her dream-wrecking arms to the floor. She doesn't need to see this father-of-none brought so low.

She only thinks she does.

"You had to have seen *something*," Mimi says feebly. "Show me."

And knowing there's really no other way to convince the girl, Inez does.

"Knock knock," Taheer says, posh accent fitted as his tailored suit, neither more than a couple years old. On a small pewter tray, he's carrying two cups of tea. The pale green liquid steams up his glasses. Without invitation, he puts them down on Inez's desk, turns a handle toward her. "Quick word?"

"Sure." Immediately Inez's teeth glow full-smile, slamming through her links to Peytr and Amelia. The severed chords jangle as they retract, racing back to their owners. She gasps as the shorter ends recoil, piercing her core like ice-picks, making deep and precise holes. "Please, sit."

Disregarding the chair, her boss half-perches beside the cups. One leg propped with foot dangling, the other straight-planted on the floor. Hands clasped on his bent knee, Taheer assumes the posture and tone of a doctor primed to deliver bad news.

He watches Inez scald her tongue, then begins. "Tell me," he says, then stops to clear his throat. It's pure affectation—there's always a bottle of salt-gargle on his desk, not a skerrick of phlegm in his voice. Inez figures he does it to give people time to focus their attention on him. He thinks it makes him sound professorial. "How long has it been since you've gone on rec-leave?"

Stalling, Inez gulps down another mouthful. "Oh, I don't know."

Taheer blows on his drink, takes a delicate sip.

In the five years she's worked here, she hasn't taken a day's rec. Why would she? Where could she possibly go—alone, arthritic, low on coin and good veg—that pirated channels couldn't take her a thousand times faster? She gulps and gulps. Rec is for the unemployed.

"It's fine. Really. It hasn't been that busy," she says, keeping her voice low despite the office din. "And I get plenty of time in the solos. . . ."

Tiny bubbles of spit pop against Taheer's gums as he peels back his lips and sucks air through his straight teeth. "There have been complaints, Inez."

"Oh?"

Though he hasn't moved except to replace his cup and smooth a pleat on his pant leg, she imagines Taheer swinging his foot like a child, counting her offences off on his fingers. "Missed connections, *broken* connections, tinny reception, wire-crossings, echoes on the line. . . . And the streaker leaving your booth just now? And Essr. Bartos's botched call? Do you know how much he invests in us each month? How much cash? Medicine? Only to hear some random woman screaming in his last call? Screaming, Inez? I mean, some disruptions are to be expected—but screaming? What's going on here?"

Dread creeps up her chest, lodges in her gullet. "I could ask you the same thing. Sir." Hovering before her, the multihued quasars of Taheer's figure cease their whirling and, one by one, go black. Next the cubicle walls melt into shadow, their absence amplifying the other mentalegraphers' mindless chatter. Overhead the lamp fades, disappears. The chair is solid beneath her, the desk a cold ridge against her soft belly—but she can't see their particles or read their vibrations. If she wasn't touching them, she'd have no idea they were even there. Heart palpitating, Inez's chords and channels and enamel shield withdraw. As one, they shrink until hard and fragile as porcelain. Empty as the cup in her hands.

"What have you done to me?"

Before registering his sigh, Inez hears the slump in Taheer's shoulders. The rasp of dry fingertips across groomed chin-stubble. The bridge of his nose being pinched.

"You've earned a week off," he says at last. "Make the most of it. Come back when you're refreshed."

"But—"

"You're welcome," Taheer says. Wool scratches against the desktop as he stands. China clinks against china, clunks on pewter. His voice floats, disembodied, somewhere near the door. "Trust me, Inez. It could've been worse."

During her home-stay, Cora is Inez's only contact with the world. The receptionist visits twice daily, bringing food and a clean chamber pot. Inez doesn't dare ask about her clients—and Cora says little, using all her energy spying for their boss.

Helplessness steals Inez's appetite and makes her restless. In exile, she's dropped fifteen pounds out of sheer worry. Sleep, when it comes, is more malicious than restful, her nightmares variations on the same circular clichés. Peytr drowns while Inez stands on the shore, dropping the life-rope's frayed end into a still sea. Armed with a whip and lasso, Mimi drives Inez through snow-covered streets, lashing her clothes away layer by layer. A million Amelias float in glass bubbles, begging for rescue, but the sidewalks are impassable, the buildings impossible to scale. Countless times, Inez has sloughed the dreams off with her sweat-soaked blanket. Praying for dawn, she stares blindly at the clock only to hear it chime a quarter-hour's passing. Awake or asleep, she remains stifled in darkness.

But when Cora raises the venetians on the seventh morning, Inez is almost clear-headed. Lying on the couch, she peers through her lashes, forcing herself not to flinch. At the basin, the traitorous bint hunches with her back turned, wasting water rations on yesterday's dishes. Out the window above the sink, flares radiate over the skyline. Clouds cough purple starbursts as the little meteors lance them to the grey beyond. Beside the front door, a noisy orange miasma churns from the piss-pot. On the table, a plastic thermos reverberates a healthy beetroot red, brimming with chilled borscht. The pattern on Cora's knee-length skirt is so vibrant, Inez can hardly breathe. Awash in such a brilliant clash of colour, she closes her eyes and rolls over, hiding tears.

"Do you have coins for the shower?" Cora asks. "I'll reserve a stall for you, if you want."

"No point," Inez says into her pillow. "I'm not coming in today."

"Don't be petulant, Inez. Essr. Taheer has already been more than generous—"

"He was overly generous with the suppressant, that's for sure." Channelling a bit of Amelia's fire—oh, she can't wait to *really* tap into it—Inez flips over and sends her gaze to the ceiling, as if Cora is spidering up there. "Maybe by tomorrow this shit he's slipped me will have worn off. As for today's shift, well, I can't do a fuckin' thing about that."

Swearing, Inez has learned, is the quickest way to get rid of a reformed skingirl like Cora. Within minutes, she's packed her floppy rubber basket and flounced out the door, a perfect imitation of prissiness.

Counting to fifty and back, Inez forces herself to lie still, listening to the click-click of the receptionist's retreating heels. Racing to the window, she watches Cora hail a cab—and before the mule has dragged her to the end of the street, Inez casts three lines as far into the ether as she can. The first and nearest bounces off of Mimi; the second and third, so closely entwined they appear as one, latch onto the cabin without much resistance.

"How long was I out," Inez says, opening Amelia's eyes.

Peytr bear-hugs her so hard, Inez rattles around the vast space behind Amelia's bland brown irises. "Too long," he says, squeezing and squeezing, clinging to their hand even when Inez gently pushes him away. "I thought— I thought—"

While Peytr cries, Inez searches for—and finds—what's left of Amelia. Alert as a stuffed owl, the woman is perched on a driftwood branch under a bell jar, its walls thick with dread. Knocking on the glass doesn't rouse her. Shouting proves just as useless. There are no air-holes drilled in the flawless surface; tendrils of flesh weld the jar to the floor. There's no way for Inez to break in, no way for Amelia to break out.

"Good," Inez says, flustered from failing to tip the jar over. "Fine, then. I'll stay, thank you very much."

"Yes," Peytr says, wrapping his trembling arms around them, grinding his face into their—now *her*—shoulder. "Please stay."

And the tighter he holds her, the queasier Inez becomes. Despite the blood-shot eyes, the week-old beard gouging her skin, the musk of unwashed man oozing from his pores, Peytr reminds her too much of the sticky-sweet squirmers she's had the misfortune of channelling. Just like them, he reeks of bewilderment and dependence and misplaced affection. He holds onto her not out of love, but simply because she's there.

Crossing onto Peytr's minor chord, Inez dry-retches.

With each step, the line warbles, her tread playing his mind like a saw. All around, a kaleidoscope of memories pummels her, forcing her to crouch or fall. Digging in with fingers and toes, she plucks one murky vision after the next. Begins the long task of sifting through the past, translating random moments into a story.

Peytr sitting beside Amelia's spindle bed, watching her chest rise and fall.

Peytr wrestling her—yes, Inez recognises this part—Peytr losing his grip as she writhes. His palms are too slippery. Her thrashing too violent.

Peytr sweeping broken glass, huddling over a full dustpan, licking.

Peytr standing in an empty apartment—no, not the cabin—clutching an illegible letter, a spill of soot on his jacket and pants.

Peytr searching for a cloth to wipe blood from Amelia's mouth. The hankies are everywhere, she's got dozens of the things, flannel and terrycloth and cotton. He's afraid to use any of them lest they absorb her dreams.

Peytr's palms slipping. If he was wearing gloves he could stop her. If his hands would stop quaking, he could stop her. If he kisses her on the mouth, only this once, if he kisses her properly, he could stop her—

Peytr scooping, fingers shredded and stinging, scooping as much glass from her mouth as he can. Blood is stark against Amelia's pale skin, glistening and offensive. It looks like she's been eating entrails, ravishing a freshly-cut heart. It almost looks like she's napping, digesting, sleeping off her fragile feast.

Peytr locking the cabin door, guts churning with shame, with pity.

Peytr's palms slipping. The cryptic letter falling to the table top as a wallful of photographed strangers look on.

Peytr wiping and wiping and wiping Amelia's face plain. Wringing the scarlet dew into one of Rupe's old pots, just in case he's absorbed any secrets she wanted to keep.

Peytr assessing the damage. The ceiling's blizzard of glass is reduced to a flurry, maybe fifty crystal bombs suspended from the rafters, maybe five hundred. Tears blur his ability to count.

Peytr locking the cabin door and running, running until his legs are rubber, running until he's far-flung and sweat-clean and low.

Peytr wrestling, losing grip as Amelia writhes, not screaming anymore, whispering, whispering, *she's gone, she's gone, she's gone, she's gone . . .*

Peytr calling for Mimi, for Ned, hearing skingirls' laughter outside in the square, harsh and false and lonely.

Peytr tearing *health* and *recover* and *love* from his wordwind, burying them beneath Amelia's tongue. Apologising with hands and cloths and silence.

Peytr running alone, running until he is home again.

Peytr sitting beside Amelia's spindle bed, watching her chest rise and fall.

By the next morning, Inez knows she's done all she can and wants to do here.

She's ridden Peytr to sleep and, while he snores, she unravels the tangled skein of his thoughts. First, she rearranges them tonally and chronologically, then ranks them by degree of sadness.

Amelia. Ned. Mimi.

Mimi. Ned. Amelia.

It isn't perfect—Peytr still clings so tightly, Amelia's fingers are white from the pressure—but it's a start. Back-stepping onto Amelia's chord, Inez pulls their hand free and rolls over. They won't be his pacifier or swaddling blanket. No one woman he's met could ever be.

Luxuriating in Amelia's dark spaces, Inez has *felt*, she has *been*, she has possessed every crevice—all but one tiny bell-shaped gap.

Have it, Inez thinks, magnanimous. It's all yours.

The stuffed owl pretends not to hear.

Inez pretends being ignored doesn't bother her.

Cat-stretching, Inez tries to enjoy her new body, the vanilla scent on her skin, the twenty years shed, the tautness of breasts and belly. She tries to enjoy it in Peytr's company, tries to enjoy being on their own. But suddenly there's just too much of him, too many splotched limbs constricting, too much hot breath moistening the back of her neck, too many orphaned words spinning, spinning.

No one woman, she thinks, can care for this man.

Delving inside, Inez assembles a constellation of Amelia's happier times, strings it around the glass dome, yet fails to lure her other half out. The owl's head spins on its axis. Unblinking it stares, beyond the reflected sparkle and shine, into the dark.

"Suit yourself," Inez says, knowing her efforts have been wasted. There's nothing else she can or wants to do with these two. Virtually nothing has changed since her arrival; they're both so wrapped up in themselves, they hardly notice she's there. Though she's tried, they don't love her at all.

So when Cora comes to take her back to work, Inez wears her sharpest smile. Snapping chords with her teeth—one a saw weeping, the other a pedal-muted piano—she follows the receptionist out to the cab, polishing her shield.

Evac. #457-357-0
Age: 70 (±5)
Sight: Both eyes present; lucid with a smudge of grey.
Bibliotheca 16°37'0"N, 106°43'58"E

Great-great-great-Tantie Willa[†] was [one of?] the first skybunker flyer(s). A real fuss-pot, she was; a real neat-freak. Hated the crush of dead 'winds beneath her feet, the film of word-ash piling on flats and angles—no matter how speedy the brooms, no matter the annual rains, the world was too dirty for the likes of TW. She lived on the thirty-fifth floor of a sixty-floor building; they say TW often imagined dust building higher and higher, burying lower levels until she could step off her own balcony and stroll on the risen ground . . . [Tangent: Flrs. 25-60 destroyed in TW's youth; girl orphaned at 16; prime candidate, nowadays, for recruitment into the skycorps] . . . Even after all that, she wasn't afraid of heights. Liked to climb to empty apartments above, get the long-view to other cities, other countries where grey-changes, she thought, had no effect. TW spoke of the 'windless people who lived elsewhere; how unsettling it would be, not to know what they were thinking unless it was said aloud. [Tangent: runs through a nonsensical list of other human mutations (i.e. "grey-changes"). *Note:* 'singers' was a new one; to be added to records.] How calm it must be in the emptiness, the clean and quiet of non-'winded communities.

TW was "a real deft knitter"; scrounged for wool to clothe herself and younger sister [Tangent: teller's mother's line described at length; migrations detailed, including names of ships, 'ports, dates of landing—detailed, then repeatedly self-corrected; passion and fancy, more than fact, seemed to drive the teller's account. *Note:* no credible

---

[†]This excerpt is not included in the interview proper—see attached file—but was transcribed over tea. (Due to advanced age, the teller required frequent breaks; subject changes were frequent; stress-related stammering not uncommon. Lengthy pauses and irrelevant digressions are not recorded in full here.) The following should be filed under 'apocryphal histories,' 'speculative genealogies,' and/or 'claims to fame'; copies for the Cycle of Auto/biography have already been despatched via Pigeon.

explanation for TW's unprecedented ability to knit 'winds into gliders; nor how she "discovered" that 'winds caught and interwoven on the brink of death made for the best flights; nor why she alone took to the skybunkers while her sister, it seemed, did not. The mother's ancestors went "below"; few wanted to stay aboveground the way TW did. "Too dark and cramped in the tunnels for TW," was the teller's assessment. "Too close to grey territory down there; conditions more than bad enough to scramble anyone's 'wind." Account of sky-borne activities were equally sketchy: the bunkers are complicated, way-stations in the sky. Bird-houses? Targets for grey ships? Regularly pummelled, these platforms are common as dusk—but what a view the girls must get from up there, sunlight and stars, an invaluable aerial perspective on battle movements on the ground. Stockpiled with ammunition shorn from the freshly-dead—the amassed words were packed into bombs and dropped on grey hills? Launched upwards to perforate the cloud cover? Woven into an enormous blanket that would, one day, smother the war below? Whatever else they do, the skybunker attendants continue to look down on the war below, to see the war above at eye-level, and add to the general confusion whenever they can. Non-believers contend it isn't fée creatures who steal eyes and bodies; these girls whisk away the near-dead and the living, the naysayers claim, but of course they cannot support such assertions with proof. One way or the other, they are spies, these little flyers; they are bees gathering pollen; they are reapers.]

Skybunker architects hired TW to gather materials; they are lithe and spritely, these glider-girls, but their tasks, on the whole, are mundane. [*Note:* Romantic attempts to name these women as something grander, something more daring, more poetic than they are, went out of fashion at the beginning of the last century; since then, interpretations have been less absolute, less whimsical. People see the girls simply as they are, more or less: bombadiers, ammo-couriers, drays.] TW flew hither and yon collecting scrap metal, bolts, nails, anything worth scavenging, anything that wouldn't weigh down her sails. Got them the best building-stuffs they could want, did TW; in return, soon as the towers stretched above the smog, she was allowed to camp up there for life, away from the bustle of words. TW descended to harvest 'winds and not much else; occasionally, she sent paper-plane messages to her sister below. [Aside: teller acknowledged this last "fact" was too far-fetched to be reality; amended the story by suggesting there may have been elevators secreted in the skybunker shafts, lifting supplies and people *way way* up just as the tunnellers' rigs plunge *way way* down . . .]

Some people, they say, mistook the first flyers for greys. "What a load of rot . . ." [*Note:* Anger-inspired tangents rendered the teller mute for the duration. Understandable. By all accounts the "fée" may be hominid; however, they are too quick to *truly* be mistaken for leaden humanity, far too light and clever.]

THIRTEEN

"I haven't seen him there. Not yet." Fog wafts around O's mouth as he speaks, drawing pale curlicues on the night air. Euri leans forward to hear better, though the building is quiet around them.

"No surprise," she says, attempting levity. "Peyt— He's a good kid. He'd avoid the likes of you."

"No doubt," says O. "No doubt."

He looks like condensation, liable to slip out of sight without solidifying.

He smells like wet pavement.

"Why do you keep coming back?" she asks, 'wind whirring about penance, guilt, forgetfulness.

He looks at her, rubs a hand along his irregular jaw. Stubble creates no friction beneath his fingers; just a silent back and forth movement as he considers the question. Euri doesn't mind that he's unshaven. At least he'd set his face to rights before he came this time.

"Must be the view." The skies are thick with pamphleteers negotiating the airways around high-rises and skybunkers. They toss bundles on rooftops and lower charity packets to the sewer grates on guy wires. Balloonists touch down none too gently on army landing pads, immediately lifting off once tired soldiers have been exchanged for fresh ones. Countless lives speed past Euri's apartment, all tucked away in windowless flying boxes. She takes a sip of grog, tries hard not to think about the distance between the edge of her balcony and the ground. Once upon a time, she thinks, the gov't would've installed nets.

She drinks deep, failing to drown thoughts of what should've been saved, and what wasn't.

Selfish, taunts her 'wind. *So selfish . . .*

O smiles his lazy grin, drifts closer to Euri. Seems like he doesn't notice the deepening lines on her face, the threads of silver in her dark hair, the rattle of bomb-smog in her lungs. His ever-young hand reaches out to brush a few strands from her eyes, but doesn't complete its action. Rain slides through his retreating arms, his recoiling fingers, puddles where his body should be.

"It wasn't you, you know."

(*Blue and red lights reflected off puddles, illuminating the sidewalk ten storeys below Euri's apartment. They cast onlookers' faces in lollipop hues so at odds with the tableau. Their mouths opened; hands froze in mid-air; heads turned away from the sight at their feet. Instinctive, instantaneous, reasonable reactions. She didn't get to the scene until after, but she still sees them that way in dreams.*)

"Orfe—" Euri flushes. Feels her throat seize—she hasn't forgotten his name, just can't say it. There's a short list of them now, names she can't articulate unless fully drunk. Peyt— Armi— Carde— Orfe— She breaks eye contact with the man who, every year, gets that much younger. The latest heartbreak she won't cry for.

(*"Do you know him? Who is he? He wears a tattoo—are you his wife?" Their voices were official, prescribed, but their faces were filled with concern. And trepidation. They were afraid of how she'd react, worried she'd crumple into a wailing ball of misery there on the sidewalk. But Euri couldn't react. She couldn't even breathe.*)

Not anymore.

He sighs, turns back to the cityscape. Euri follows his gaze. Unable to count the number of times they've sat here like this, drinks in hand, impossible love in their bellies, looking out on their twilit world. Across the millions of dark rooftops and cranes before them, cluttering a panorama that might once have stretched to eternity. To the west, a black-blasted desert is ringed by skeleton buildings on the edge of the CBD. Five miles wide and fifteen years dead, it's ground that even the greys have forsaken. Another absence laid out at Euri's feet.

The wick of the lantern on O's side of the balcony is twisted short to save fuel. Down below, lamplighters are out in force, trying to create day where there can be none. The vista is illuminated with so many flambeaux, Euri thinks, you'd almost think the crowded streets have caught fire below us. Even so, the city emits nothing brighter than a soft, grey glow. Ten storeys up, shadows reign. Billows of steam cloud the horizon, pumped from 'stacks and pipes bristling out of 'scrapers linking one borough to the next. Ashen raindrops hang where once there were stars.

Euri realised long ago not everyone is built for such relentless dark.

Now O is beyond noticing such things. Rain pulls cold from the sky as it falls; Euri wraps a dusty blanket around her shoulders, holds it tight, enjoys the weight of musty wool stretching across her back. He flickers in and out of view until she almost loses sight of him.

Steam gives his limbs shape. He tries to lean against the balcony's railing; his transparent hands miss their mark and he tips forward, overbalancing. He rights himself with a chuckle. It takes him a while to readjust to Euri's surroundings each time he visits, but he can never stay long enough to really get acclimatised.

She wants to get carried away in his merriment, to giggle at the absurdity of his situation, but doesn't know if his laughter is real.

(*On good days, his smile was contagious. She could practically see through him, his joy shone so bright. Even when the fuel had dried up, and they were sunk in darkness, he seemed to reverberate with light. "How can you know the highs," he'd say, "if you won't let yourself swim the lows?" Happiness, and the lies that went with it, should've torn out his throat when he said such things. Every other day—the black days, the tunnel days, the real days—Euri knew it wasn't about* letting. *Letting implies choice. Willingness. A conscious decision to plunge into horrible spaces, places of misery and death. Places where she couldn't follow. No, there is no* letting.)

"You're the reason I stayed here so long." She feels his gaze searching her profile, her 'wind, willing her to meet it, to acknowledge what he's saying. Begging her to forgive him for leaving.

(*"Are you his wife?"*)

No. She's heard it all before. The excuses. The apologies. Everything. The glass clinks as she places it on the tiles between her rain-spattered treaders. No more business suits for Euri. No sneaking shoes. No reason to get dressed up. She's left that life behind, the luxury, the political intrigue. She changed, long before she met O. She has changed. Unlike him. He won't change now. To be fair, he probably can't.

(*"You don't need to be seeing this, ma'am. Why don't you come with us?" the Watchman said. Euri shook her head. Her feet felt stapled to the ground. Oily rainbows swirled around them. A young man at the barrier next to her turned to his girlfriend and whispered, "I wonder why . . . " He tilted his head and looked up, tried to figure out which ledge had launched such a flight; dropped his eyes back to the sidewalk behind the Watch's barricade, following an invisible trajectory from balcony to ground. The girlfriend gave him a warning look, raised her eyebrows, gestured at Euri with her head. He left his thought unfinished.*)

"Must be pretty nice there," Euri says. "I mean, you're not looking so bad anymore, you know. All things considered." Her eyes flick to the left to see if she's offended him. But he just nods. A slow, melancholic motion, as if he's been unable to shed the sadness he tried to escape, on this night—*that* night—all those years ago. Nods, and scratches at his cheek. It must be a physical memory, that scratching; a left-over instinct in his fingers, like a phantom limb. Euri can't imagine he still gets itchy.

"It's not all fluffy clouds and home-made soup, if that's what you're getting at."

"Well it's kept you this long, hasn't it? It's not like you've moved on."

(*"Morning dusk's rising, folks," the Watchman said. He had a husky voice; part of Euri thought he must've been a tunneller before he got the gig doing gov't work. "Get yourselves gone, now. Show's over." The crowd slowly dispersed. Euri stayed put. "Come back," she said. "Come back," staring at the form on the ground beyond the Watch's tape; "Come back," until her voice clogged with rain.*)

She looks at him then, straight on. His skin shimmers in the steady downpour; the haze around his face deepens as they speak. His features waver, becoming implausible.

Won't be long now, Euri thinks.

"Is that what you want? For me to move on?"

Picking up her glass, she buys time by draining it. The grog burns as it goes down; a raw, cleansing sensation. He reaches out to touch her again. This time, he doesn't hold back, doesn't stop short. She doesn't feel a thing.

"I can't ask you to be with me," he says, softly. "Not unless you're ready."

"And when might that be?" Her heart doesn't beat any faster. "We could've stayed together, avoided all this trouble. It's not such terrible living, you know. Not as bad as you used think anyway." She is calm. Still, and perfectly relaxed. "They say some airships manage to break through the stratocumulus—I heard one guy even got sunburnt a few years back. Maybe I'll get some work with them. Scope the sky-fields for greys. Stranger things have happened."

"It's too late for *maybes*, Euri. Look around you: everyone in your building's gone."

She looks at him. "Tell me about it."

He turns away.

"I'm used to it now, in a way." Clasping hands below her knees, she leans back in her seat, letting body weight pull her arms taut in front of her. "Some days, I get up and feel weightless. Buoyant, like that flier over there. Like I've become insubstantial just by waking up. Sometimes I think that's what happiness is. To let all your burdens go, all your mistakes, until you can float away."

("Darkness snuffs the brightest of us," his mates, those drunken philosophers, said when well into their cups at the wake. "Just ask his missus. Doesn't pay to dream nowadays, or am I lying?" Euri plastered a smile to her face, refilled their glasses. They turned away, contemplating their loss. "Never met a tunneller with such an urge to fly. Right then, fellas: let's pray Orfeo's found a nice shiny patch of sky somewhere. Not that prayin's a whit better than dreamin', mind.")

It was pouring in earnest now, a sure sign he's getting ready to go back. Sludgy water plinks off the railing; off the roofs of the surrounding tenements; off Euri's arms, her knees, her face. He balls his hands, still incapable of gripping anything in this world. Not long now. The rain passes through him: but his bare shoulders, his flimsy undershirt, his ragged trousers had all been soaked through ten years before. The wind doesn't tousle his uneven blond hair, though it's starting to whip hers around so much she's forced to pull it back, trap it at the nape of her neck so she can see his departure.

"Is it cold, where you are?" It isn't the first time she's asked it, but something about her tone must've tipped him off that this time is different.

"Not so's you'd notice," he says. Euri can always tell when O's smile is forced. "Like you said: it's not so bad there."

A door on one of the lower floors slams shut as the wind howls through vacant windows below. It resonates like a gunshot: Euri jumps, O fidgets with pent energy. The scent of ozone pouring off him, he adopts the stance of a man gauging how long it'll take to cross a busy intersection without getting nabbed by the greys. Euri knows what he'll say next before he even opens his mouth.

"Looks like it's about that time."

"I'm ready," she says.

I'm ready. . . . I'm ready. . . . I'm ready . . .

Eyes wide, he gazes around the balcony. At the cracked tiles; out at the distant aerial traffic; up at the cloud drifts. As if he's trying to record every detail of this world before he turns his back on it. He does this every time. Euri wonders if he's still scared, but doesn't ask.

"Did you hear me? I said *I'm ready.*"

He spins around, uncertainty transforming his features. Then his face breaks out in the first true smile she'd seen in a decade.

"I knew you'd change your mind! They said you could come with me, but I don't know— What if you don't make it? I can't see if you're behind me, I can't check until—"

His mouth grows slack before he can finish. Cataracts whiten his eyes. A few seconds later they recede and leave him looking out at a different view, one she can't see. They say separation has a way of changing a person's perspective, and Euri has learned the truth of that axiom. It's more than just time that keeps us apart.

(*The Deposer's voice thrummed in her ears at his funeral, reverberated in her hollow chest:* "Do not let your hearts be troubled. *For my yoke is easy and my burden is light. The sun shall not smite thee by day, nor the moon by night." The congregation murmured the rote response, filling the vacant columbarium with their words. She kept silent as they led him out in front of her, eyes forward as she followed.*)

"I know the rules," Euri whispers. Her 'wind scrolls through guidelines, regulations, even though she knows O can't see them anymore.

Deep breaths wrack his torso as he paces the length of the balcony, keeping his anxious steps close to the railing. He shudders, yanking his hair, fingers doing their best to puncture the top of his head. Mist seems to issue from his whole body now, great sighs of heat that Euri can't feel despite the chill. He has the look of an athlete gearing up for a big race; he's become an actor caught in a tragedy he's executed many times before. Focused. In the moment. Oblivious.

(*They said he hit the ground with the slap of a wet drumbeat. A fleshy shell, so full, made empty. An unforgettable sound, or so they told her. Before they realised who he was to her. Who he is.*)

That first time, a year to the day after he'd jumped, the shock of his return was nearly enough to send Euri to the Lunar Street Asylum. A short walk would get her there, if she avoided the greys. And if there were no vacancies at Lunar, she could've headed over to Eclipse Boulevard. There were two Stabilisation Centres on that side of the city; she knew them both well. Surely one of them would take her in again.

She hadn't even made it to the front door. He'd asked her not to go—and she'd listened. Just as she always did when he was being reasonable. She wished he'd given her the chance to convince him likewise, just one chance to say, "Don't go." Such a simple request, one that could have answered so many questions. She might've known what he'd planned, maybe why he'd done it. But at least, when she watched him re-enact his farewell all those true-darkfalls ago, just as she was watching it now, she was finally able to know *how* he'd left. And how it was she could follow.

Eyes cast down, staring over the welcoming edge, he clutches, then releases, the railing. The actions never change even though the gestures are mime-like, never connecting. He repeats the motion; the stainless steel surface would be polished to gleaming in two spots, each a hand's width across, if he'd really been touching it. Exhaling sharply, he bends his knees and sits, hovering in the air, thighs resting on the memory of a patio chair that hasn't been in that spot for nearly ten years. Takes a swig from an invisible glass of scotch; Euri can almost smell its fumes on the air. She steps back, gets out of his way. Not that her presence matters; he's on cue, and the only role she has in this play will come after.

He tosses his tumbler aside. There's still a chip in the tile where it hit the floor, sending an impressive shower of shards across the length of the balcony. The Watch reckoned that accounted for the cuts they found on the soles of his feet. He'd had a pair of genuine leather boots, only owned by a handful of people before him, that he earned on his last paying gig in the tunnels. He used to wear them everywhere, polished them every day until he could see his face reflected in their glossy black finish. Before he jumped, he polished them and put them aside. Euri has never asked why.

Unshod, he steps onto the absent chair, reaches his left hand out as if to balance against the wall. His arches settle atop the railing's curved surface, their soft flesh embracing cool steel as if he'd rehearsed the motion many times.

"I'm—"

What could he say? He'd never been one to talk about big decisions; he always let them simmer silently until, impatient at being restricted, they forced him to act. So he stood there for a moment with his lips pressed firmly together, saying nothing. For the first year after he'd gone, Euri imagined he sobbed before he leapt, that tears had come, that he'd hesitated, changed his mind. That the fall was a miscalculation, an unfortunate shift in footing at the last minute. But each time she saw him jump, only rain coated his serene face.

(The neighbours said he simply leant into the night. Nothing dramatic. Arms weren't outstretched; there was no swan-diving. Just a shift of the foot, a slump forward; leading with the shoulder, everything else following. A gentle movement and quick. They didn't even have time to respond—he was an afterimage almost before they'd seen him.)

It was cold then, as now. His breath visible, wreathing his head like a halo, then swallowed by the darkness. Euri stands, lets the blanket slip from her shoulders.

He smells like evaporation.

"Don't look back," she whispers. "I'll follow, but don't look back." She knows the rules: everyone does.

He slouches over the edge, just like the neighbours said he'd done; the way she's seen him droop off the balcony nine times before. His soiled white shirt flaps gracefully in the wind, the back fluttering behind him like wings. Footprints made of steam dissolve when his feet leave the balustrade.

(*"Are you his wife?"*)

He smells like wet pavement.

"Don't look back," she repeats, then steps up as he disappears. Her cheap treaders squeak and slide in the rain; Euri nearly loses balance before she's ready. The lantern gutters, snuffs out as she steadies herself. She takes one last look at the overcast horizon, then closes her eyes. Exhales. Leans forward until nothing but air supports her. Follows her husband's ghost over the railing, and imagines she can see day breaking.

FOURTEEN

It is twilight in the upworld: the time of seduction, of passing thresholds, of becomings. The sun, though setting and veiled with battle smoke, is much yellower than Swan expected. The rubble strewn path is a stream of chalk mortar, russet bricks, rich charcoal beneath her bare feet. Scattered shards of glass are redder than the painted spots on her skin, bluer than the shadows beneath her eyes. Grass, which is always pale turquoise or green in the pictures she lovingly studies, is now the same rich sepia as her irises. Every colour is saturated, outlandish; even commonplace grey zings beyond her optical range. Up here, grey is so vivid it hums.

Swan shivers as she moves away from the vaulted tunnels of her childhood, takes her first steps above ground. She and the rest of Thevessels, with their faux-freckled complexions and fairy-floss waists, are laced into white corsets, robed in sheer fabric and begartered with lingerie ribbons. Soft veils fall before their kohl-rimmed eyes, which are kept modestly lowered, as Themothers lead them up into an unfamiliar shade of evening.

The sky seems limitless despite its bracketing clouds. Leafless bushes click-clack in the wind, their branches twitching like mandibles as the women brush past. This year's Ladyday girls swarm out and around the downworld's largest trapdoor, a din of nervous giggles and snippets of well-rehearsed tunes. They won't venture any further without Themothers' permission. Staccato echoes of artillery in the distance ricochet around the group, bouncing along the pockmarked asphalt that had, until that moment, been the only sky Swan had ever known.

"Will you pass through the gate?" Hermother asks, offering Swan the first of two tickets. It is small and faded, paper worn thin from generations of use. Working her tongue around her mouth, Swan tries to dredge up the moisture speech requires. It is useless. Swallowing hard, she quietly takes the lucky scrap from Hermother's outstretched hand. Her stomach roils; her throat convulses and throbs. The taste of pent-up worry is thick on her tongue.

"Will you lay yourself bare, fresh skin to fresh earth? Will you dig for your unborn soul?" *Nod,* Swan mutely replies, heart palpitating. *Nod, nod*.

Themothers tut-tut her lack of response. Swan had hoped they'd mistake silence for excitement, for speechless anticipation, for awe at finally being chosen. Instead, Hermother's tone is clipped, irritated. *You know what's at stake,* her expression screams. Of course Swan knows. Of course.

"Will you pay the toll and absorb new life?"

Nod, nod.

With well-practiced movements, Themothers circle around the duo to conclude the ritual. All the women take it in turns to add ochre dots to the girl's fair cheeks, to share choruses of birthing songs, to infuse her skin with the expectation of pregnancy. Their gestures and incantations temporarily transform her: no longer Swan, today she has become Avessel.

Hermother presents the second ticket. Smiling, the matriarchs turn, and wait to hear Swan sing the accepted refrain.

They give her more than enough time, but their patience is rewarded with silence. Swan's lips quiver while she tries to convey, with devout gaze and solemnly clasped hands, that she won't disappoint them. That she will contribute, just as they have, just as all the downworlders have. That she will transcend her skills as a painter and today praise Themarys by becoming Amother. She wants to say she *will*.

She can't.

Thevessels, ushered away from the trapdoor, look eagerly ahead. But Swan lingers at Hermother's side, hoping to catch a glimpse of encouragement, a sign that she'll be welcomed home soon. Any sign. Hermother's features, once so nurturing, might be made of stone for all the hope they impart. The girl watches, unblinking, until the door clangs shuts behind Hermother's perfectly straight back.

A sulphurous breeze lifts Swan's skin into goose bumps; unbidden tears well in her eyes. May it be to me as you have said, she thinks. Still unable to give her answer voice.

Hints of sunset are too bright. Whoever is responsible for painting this sky should've invested in a stick of amber Conté. Swan shields her eyes. This palette is too gold, the application too heavy. Its weight presses on her like a stranger's unwanted embrace. She looks at her hands, inspects the rims of her nails that still bear the stains of her trade. Patches of brown, deep green, and burgundy: far more fitting colours with which to honour Themarys. She has used them all, mixed their tints out of mushroom ridges, kaolin, mould, and iron oxide; sanguine dyes for the septet of Marys adorning her chamber walls, drawn on old sheets of newspaper.

Swan yearns to imitate the illustrations she creates. To be like Themarys, plump and freckled, blue-robed on red cushions, with saturnine faces surrounded by bees, caterpillars, peonies, strawberries—evidence of fruitfulness she has only seen in two dimensions. All her knowledge of fecundity has come from Themothers' books: from abstract words, wan photographs, bleached memories. Freckled babies have been born and raised in the downworld—this all girls have seen. But how they get there remains a secret until Themothers bestow the rights of Avessel. Until then, the girls wait, and prepare.

For sixteen years Swan has pored over pages graced with Themarys' likenesses: at first admiring without understanding; then appreciating the gift of creation; then inventing artworks of her own. At night these images fill her dreams; three times a day she sings them into being while rehearsing her summoning-song. Dreams echo through her vocal chords, promising to quicken life within her.

Now she hunches, watches Elizabet's approach through the sheen of her veil. Swan hasn't slept for days—she practised so hard, sang so true, and for what? Today her voice is thinner than paper, breathier than a puff of steam on the upworld's horizon. She scowls and digs her fingernails into the soft flesh at the base of her thumbs.

Her cousin has never looked more joyful. "Don't be afraid, dear Swannie." Elizabet air-kisses each of Swan's cheeks to avoid smudging makeup, squeezes her hand, and softly chirps out a blessing: "Themarys favour you." The title breezes through her cousin's lips in a rush, too sacred to linger in profane mouths. Swan averts her gaze, unconvinced.

"Your song is amazing," Elizabet continues. "Relax, you'll be fine. Soon those freckles will be real." Then, *sotto voce*, "There's no way you won't have a girl."

Shhhhhhhhhh! Themothers' hiss shreds the still air; brows furrow, eyes blaze. The procession falters at Elizabet's jinx. Her face turns lucent with shame; her betraying mouth is pressed shut by Swan's trembling fingers.

Take it back, Swan silently implores, searching her cousin's face for hints of malice, finding none. Hurriedly, Thevessels make the sign of Themarys. Swan closes her eyes, imagines all the colours she'd use to paint over Elizabet's mistake. A prayer of hues: indigo, cerise, even brash gold. But not beige, no. And white is out of the question.

The procession passes quiet steel shells on the way to the cemetery, structures that go *up* instead of down.

It's all so ancient, Thevessels whisper. So impractical.

"Why build with such fragile material?" In her work as a scribe, Agnes makes exceptional connections, joining thin stroke to fine curves as easily as breathing. In the upworld, it seems, her mind isn't as dexterous as her hands. "Such crumbly rock," she continues, gesturing at the decrepit buildings. "Look—it's too heavy for its ribs and has fallen all to the ground!"

Concrete, Swan thinks, looking at row upon row of rectangular hulks lining the boulevard's left bank. Not rock. It must have been sturdier once.

Thevessels titter and shake their heads at Agnes. Such stupidity is bound to turn her skin tan, to see her burdened with a Lacuna child. Wouldn't that teach her? Give her a boy and confine her up here forever; *then* she'll learn how the upworld works.

"How many upbuildings have been felled by men's battles?" Thevessels demand. Humiliated, the scribe remains silent. "Hazarding a guess would be futile," they agree on her behalf. "Like trying to pinpoint the end of infinity."

A flash of green arcs high above their heads. In its unholy light all footsteps slow; some splash to a stop in late-spring puddles.

"A falling star!"

The child can't be blamed for her ignorance. Pearl is only twelve—too young to be here in Swan's opinion—and though she still has a hard time differentiating between psalms and hymns, the girl's descant won't be denied. Summoning-songs don't discriminate by age; they ring true but once, when Avessel's time is nigh. No matter if she is young or youngest.

Not a star, Swan thinks, as two sparks break away from the blaze overhead. It's a—

"Boomer!" Agnes cries, trying to redeem herself in her sisters' eyes by stating the obvious. Upbuildings loose showers of stones; Pearl squeals and breaks into a run. Themothers herd their charges: arms outstretched, they shoo the girls quickly toward the cemetery gates, casting worried glances skyward. They've travelled far from the downworld door; even if they could safely return before true-dark, none of them would. Ladyday magics are most potent at dusk and Thevessels can't afford to let the opportunity pass.

They press on.

Swan trails behind, but not far enough to go astray. Elizabet drops back to join her. Their pace is brisk and ungainly.

"I heard Lacunae hang their enemies from the street signs up here," she whispers. "You know, as a sign of conquest." Strobing boomer flares illuminate the sharp planes of Elizabet's face. For a moment she is plunged in a wash of emerald, as though submerged in Swan's paintbrush waters. A blink later, the glare dies, and the upworld is once more burnished orange with the glow of spot-fires.

Acrid smoke billows across the broad street and breaks against the buildings' vertical husks. Swan turns away from her cousin and tries to find a pocket of fresh air. She takes shallow, wheezing breaths that taste like ash and lung. Lifting a hand to her mouth, she stifles the hacking cough that claws at the base of her throat.

Where do Lacunae find shelter in this forsaken country? Nothing is whole for miles, apart from the statues flanking the cemetery's entrance; dozens of tall men, all bronzed sternness and corroded gestures. She knows they're men, or meant to be, even though they remain utterly still, not fighting. Perhaps that's how Lacunae sleep? Standing, dressed in foreign garb? Surely they must sleep between sieges. Even tanned ones must crave respite sometimes.

Even those whose songs have failed need rest.

Thinking of the Lacunae seems to conjure them into being. As Thevessels and their entourage file past the avenue of statues, they grow wary of men skulking in the shadows. Swan is the first to glimpse one, cowering in the lee of a dumpster. His uniform is unusual; dirty and inside-out, worn through at the knees, partly hidden by baggage. Hair clings to his face, bushes down to his chest. Lacunae are supposed to be shaven, Swan thinks. Aren't they? They are supposed to be fierce, not frightened. Not sad.

Stone scrapes across stone, a stream of khaki forms emerges—but from where? Swan can't tell. *These* are Lacunae, she thinks, turning to compare their garb with the other man's. Nothing but trash huddles by the dumpster. Increasingly, she can smell sour Lacunae breath, the sweat seeping through their dappled shirts, the scent of scalp and decay. They appear in broken troops, uniformed in tan and grey splotches; like magic, the fabric makes them disappear when not directly in Swan's line of sight. Looking away is a relief.

The men prowl the cemetery's perimeter, emboldened by their proximity to Thevessels. By the chance some of that fair skin will be filled with murky children, growing tan before dark falls. They scratch their brown faces, clutch dangles of metal tags, and wait for their numbers to increase. Boy children are theirs by treaty, as are their mothers. Though their contempt for the downworlders is plain, these men willingly exchange protection for the promise of replenished legions—and for spare women to raise them.

Holymarys, Swan prays. Save me from that.

Unwilling to process the desperation, the hunger, she sees in the Lacunae's appraising glances, she focuses instead on the statues' scarred faces above. The head and shoulders of the tallest are coated with splotches of—what? Paint? Fallout? Trickles and splatters of white that coat heroic features to the point of erasure.

She tries not to interpret this as an ill omen.

The cemetery's gate is always open. Its hinges support nothing but air—there's no need for a door. Lacunae enter these grounds but once in their lives and none, to Swan's knowledge, have ever returned from that journey.

Several girls run through their scales as Thevessels pass under the gate's rusted archway, *so-la-ti-dos* keeping vocal chords warm for the ceremony. Elizabet wraps her arm around Swan's waist, squeezes tightly, smiles a rainbow of happiness. Swan trembles with fever, her skin sweaty despite the afternoon chill. Red jealousy gnaws at her innards as she listens to notes projected with perfect pitch, from voices that aren't her own.

It isn't supposed to be like this.

Each time Themothers heard her summoning-song they'd exchanged significant glances. They'd asked her to demonstrate it again and again until everything in the women's bearing—from their sinfully tapping feet keeping time with her rhythm to their poorly suppressed grins, hovering between pride and relief—*everything* told Swan she would be chosen first. That she would sing to bear them a girl, and earn a promotion to prime illustrator. For that, more than anything, she promised to be a most devout Mother.

But as she steps through the gate and is confronted by its keeper, fear leaches her envy and leaves her shaken, hollow. Her throat too dry for singing.

"Absterget marianae omnen lacriman," Themother says as Swan exchanges her first ticket for entrance to the inner sanctum. *Themarys shall wipe away every tear from their eyes.* Swan doesn't want to cry, but can't seem to stop. Her tongue edges out of her mouth, catches a few moistening drops on its tip. The gatekeeper reaches beneath Swan's veil and dabs her cheeks with a woollen sleeve, then hands her a faceted lachrymal vase.

"Drink from this," the woman says, the timbre of her voice lower than Swan's spirits. "If it hurts. You know, when the time comes."

Gum trees, naked as ghosts, criss-cross the cemetery's lawns. Their slender trunks guide Thevessels through the labyrinth of plots, but otherwise there seems no method to their planting. Saplings spring up of their own volition, heedless of barrier or design. Roots infiltrate decorative plinths and hasten their decomposition; garlands of ivy choke marble cherubs; branches reach skyward from mausoleum roofs like grizzled undead hands. A symphony of crickets greets the girls as they creep through graveyard districts. Swan listens for nightingales or owls or bats, but hears nothing but the pattering of bare feet and wind sighing at their passing.

Ants crawl across paths in orderly lines, tiny foot soldiers more disciplined than the ragtag procession of girls. Swan avoids stepping on them though walking is treacherous; in places the gravel is fused together in solid, uneven slabs. There is much hobbling from stubbed toes.

Long shadows intersect with walkways, directing Thevessels to their graves, which need to be fresh to serve their purpose. A week or two old, three at most. No sign of fair young angels bidding the fallen goodnight. Unbleached titanium, a colour paler than oatmeal though not yet ivory, stripes the soft grass at the path's edge. Swan inhales sharply as she scrapes the ball of her foot on a ribcage, scatters the exposed skeleton.

With a tail of that length, the bones must be animal. The thought gives her pause. What do Lacunae carcasses look like? Surely they're bigger than this one. And dug deeper. But for all Swan knows they could very well have tails.

Themothers draw to a halt. With low voices they sing a few notes, the tune an aural blueprint of the cemetery. Taking well-rehearsed cues, Thevessels join the motet until its polyphony reveals to whom each allotment belongs. Swan's temperature rises, sweat beads her forehead. When her turn comes, she mimes a verse (a mezzosoprano's G, below middle C), and prays for her song to return. She nearly chokes on its lack.

Grave after grave is assigned to full-throated girls. But not yet for Swan. A horrifying thought nearly brings her to her knees.

What if there aren't enough?

One row over, a marble headstone, carved with bas-relief crosses. Two plots beyond that one, a limestone pillar, broken in half. A few granite tombs guard an equal number of newly-dead. Three sandstone markers, etched with intersecting swords, retreat over a low hill—none of the girls will approach those tanned monuments. Beneath the western wall, a copse of naked trees shelter seven or eight wrought-iron urns, which are perched atop decorative steles, nestled in the dank scent of turned soil.

Will there be enough?

Swan spins around. Thevessels' voices slide up a key change her ravaged larynx can't negotiate.

Will there be a grave for her?

She turns again, her breath coming hard and fast in the upworld's asthmatic air. One, two . . . five, eight. . . . Summoning-songs take flight all around her; Swan raises a hand to her parched mouth. She feels disoriented.

How many are there?

And Elizabet? Where's Elizabet?

Will there be a grave for her?

A figure clad in hoarfrost and winding sheets peels away from a nearby mausoleum. Swan stumbles to the ground; her lachrymal vase skitters out of reach. The figure's strong hand, pale as Swan's own, scoops up the small vial and holds it out. Swan takes it, and the extended hand. Standing, she nods her thanks and checks that the vial remains securely stoppered.

"Have you got your ticket?" the figure asks. Her voice is soft but strong, its cadences familiar. Swan bends to retrieve the crumpled slip, taking the opportunity to peer up into Theexhumer's shady cowl.

"This way," the woman says, lowering her hood to afford Swan a better view of her face. Swan's mouth opens in a silent gasp. Theexhumer strides toward a marble plinth that beckons from the cemetery's north-east corner. She doesn't turn back to see if Swan follows.

Ohmarys.

Under the dirt, under the winding sheets, under the layers of unkempt hair, she looks exactly as she had two years ago. Her name had been Judith before her mark was erased from the hymnal. Elizabet had partnered her in more duets than Swan can count—until Ladyday broke their harmony, leaving Elizabet to sing solo.

Swan hurries to catch up. Her guide's skin shines like white silk, utterly clear. Never Amother then, but Anexhumer.

A lost one.

Holymarys, Swan prays. Looking around, she sees Thevessels being similarly led by unhooded figures shrouded in smoky garments. Is Patrizia there too? Is Esme? Is Amelia? All Ladyday girls once, all lost. It's a jinx, thinking of them, but Swan remembers painting Amelia's shining orange hair and cannot, cannot forget.

Across the grounds, Pearl has taken her guide by the hand. Some have reached their destinations; Elizabet and Agnes are now presented with boxes. All of them, singing. Calling out for new life and a skin full of freckles.

Theexhumer stops at the foot of a grave. Up close, the plinth proves to be decorated with a flock of swallows. A good sign, Swan thinks. A symbol of motherhood. Her throat constricts.

Will it be enough?

The soil is loose; a regal brown, thank Themarys. This one hasn't been buried long. Swan fidgets with her veil. She sticks a corner of it in her mouth, hoping to generate some moisture. All around the cemetery, Thevessels raise their voices, pitching them to fill the up and down worlds; projecting their summoning-songs from this realm into the next.

"Now is the time for singing," Theexhumer says, passing Swan a wooden box.

Grasping it in both hands, she wiggles her numb feet, burrowing them into the life-giving earth. Tears fill her eyes as she releases the brass latch. Her song had been so beautiful. She'd practised so hard. Without it, what good are such tools?

The hinges creak as Swan lifts the lid; the box exhales lily-scented perfume. It is upholstered with plush crimson, possibly velvet. She has never seen anything so luxurious.

"Now is the time for singing," Theexhumer repeats, then collects a spade from behind the marble plinth.

Tears plink with metallic splashes as they land inside the box. One drops on the knife's silver blade, the other on the fork's steel tines.

Such precious bone handles will be destroyed in the dirt. Swan takes both utensils in one hand; working from tip to end, she individually polishes them with her flimsy skirts. Not clean enough, she thinks. Any paint left in the bristles will ruin a brush's point. Starting again, she methodically cleans knife and fork until the hem of her garment is snagged into webs.

And again, until cutting edges gleam.

And again, until Theexhumer tires of Swan's stalling and starts to dig.

I can't do it.

The knife rasps along the plinth's edge, growing sharper with each stroke. Swan's arm jerks back and forth, a canvas-stretching rhythm. She closes her eyes briefly, ignores the ache in her throat, pretends that's all she's doing. Beginning her next tribute to Themarys, preparing the surface upon which she will paint.

Magenta will do nicely as undertone, she thinks, but her imaginings vanish when she feels the knife warming in her grip. A foothill of dirt has accumulated beside her: Theexhumer's task is nearly complete.

Swan sneezes out a kerchief's worth of grave dust. Her eyes redden beautifully as they water. The air smells of silverware and worms; all around her, it rings with Thevessels' arias, their cantatas, their recitatives, their fugues. Summoning-songs tear through the cemetery's atmosphere, accompanied by the shrill of knives on tombstones.

This must be a nightmare. Thevessels conclude the first round of their songs and Swan has yet to sing a single note. Air wheezes in and out of her lungs. In and out, in and out—quickly, try again. No sound follows no matter how she forces her breath. She grows lightheaded.

Below, Theexhumer straightens and seeks a way out of the grave.

Ohmarys, Ohmarys, Ohmarys, Swan prays. How will the soul know where to settle, if I don't sing it home?

Theexhumer hoists herself out of the dark trough carved in the earth. Swan worries at her lips, bites at them, swallows.

Please let this be a nightmare. Oh, please.

Theexhumer brushes chunks of soil off her shroud, then gestures at the open grave. Swan leans over the verge, paralysed at the sight of her life bundle. So shrivelled. So exposed. So silent.

Sing, she tells herself. Sing now.

The cemetery is quiet. Thevessels' songs soared while knives pierced decaying flesh; they crescendoed while forks crushed rotting bones; but now they have hushed to sonorous humming. It is impolite to chew with mouths open, but humming is more than acceptable—songs mustn't be broken until final mouthfuls are swallowed.

"Eat that which is good, and let your soul delight itself in fatness," Theexhumer says, gently nudging Swan closer to her meal.

What am I supposed to do? she wants to ask. But words don't follow her mind's directions. Her mouth freezes in a pinched 'o' shape, tries to make a 'w' sound.

Air escapes out the aperture of her pursed lips—and is followed by a tiny, musical breath.

Swan's heart flutters in her chest, beating her into swift action. Thank Themarys! She takes a quick swig from her vial of tears, grabs her knife and fork, and lowers herself into the open grave.

Her whistle is sombre and wavering, its tempo leaden. It falls from her lips like a reluctant secret, a heavy oesophageal echo. Pinched, the cadences of her summoning song are unrecognisable; the tune sounds like a dirge as she slices into Lacunaic flesh. Between bites, her whistle wavers with thoughts of baby girls. Swan gulps down a crumbling tendon.

Are lyrics needed to lure spirits into our bellies?

So hard to whistle with a mouth full of corpse. Swan thanks Themarys for the gatekeeper's gift and takes another sip from her lachrymal vase. Salty tears sting the insides of her cheeks; her whistling melody falters more than it soars. So hard.

Three times she cycles through her summoning-piece—the one she once *sung* so beautifully—repeating it until all the tender bits are settled in her stomach. Silence greets her when at last she stops whistling. Silence and empty skin.

Clutching the utensils, their handles unrecognisable with mud, Swan grips the grave's ragged lip, braces her feet against its crumbling walls, and hoists herself slowly up. The effort leaves her breathless, lying on the patchy grass, half in and half out of the earth. Across the cemetery, she sees Elizabet, covered in dirt and freckles, returning her dinnerware and its gorgeous box to Theexhumer at her side. Her cousin looks stunning, bespeckled with child. She seems lighter, more confident; her spotted feet glide over the uneven ground as though

she's walked it a thousand times.

Swan resumes her whistling. Of all the girls, if Elizabet is freckled then surely it isn't too late for her. Happy Elizabet, she thinks, watching the Newmother drift away. I wish she had said goodbye.

Her whistling grows more fervent. All around, Thevessels pepper with spots, replace their cutlery, and float along the path home. Even Pearl, the youngest proving Themothers' faith warranted.

No tans so far, just freckles, thank Themarys. A mottled harvest of baby girls. Swan imagines Themothers' joyful faces as their pregnant daughters descend, leaving no fodder for the Lacunae. She stares at her skin. Is that a dot on her knee? A smattering of deep brown on her wrist, a spattering on her thigh? Swan *wills* freckles to appear.

She whistles and whistles. The only spots she sees are blue, swimming in front of her eyes from lack of oxygen. Too soon, the cemetery is vacant.

Theexhumer sidles over, places a calm hand on her shoulder. Reluctantly, Swan lets the sound die. The utensils slide from her fingers, rejoining the body that had made their fine handles.

Night has fallen. The time for quickening has passed.

Swan shrugs Theexhumer's hand off, turns her back on the woman's sorrowful expression. Three plots away from her own, a similar play is being enacted. A waifish girl—Swan can't remember her name—sobs the final notes of a lullaby while her guide prises the knife and fork from her slender fingers.

That waif is too thin to bear girls, Swan thinks. Her song always falters in the downworld; it's rumoured she hasn't a taste for it.

Up here, the girl's allotted carcass is picked clean.

And still she sings. And still she remains as pale as Swan.

Why was she chosen this year? The question is plain in the lines creasing Swan's brow as she watches the girl refuse to accept defeat.

"It is not for us to decide how, or for whom, salvation will come to pass," Theexhumer says, replying as though Swan has spoken aloud. "Our task is to ensure an opportunity is unearthed, nothing more."

"This?" Swan's voice rasps, resists each syllable. "Salvation?" She shakes her head. Emptiness consumes disappointment and leaves her feeling almost nothing. Loss is more palpable than hope, and more confusing. If she's not to be Amother, if she's not to paint, then what point is there in being "saved"?

Theexhumer reads the girl's despair; recognises it as a mantle she herself has worn many times.

"Such thoughts are best left in the downworld, Swan." No longer Avessel; this failure has stolen her past accomplishments and has left only her name. "In time, you'll see things differently. Now come."

Stepping around piles of dirt and bones, Swan lets her new sister slowly draw her toward the nearest cluster of mausoleums. The path is black, difficult to distinguish in the moments between boomer flashes, but Theexhumer's footsteps are assured. She moves swiftly, confident that the childless girl will stay close if only to avoid being alone. Eyes cast down, Swan negotiates the route, from rough patches of midnight blue scree across colourless flagstones, into the depthless ink clinging to the crypt's facade.

She slips into shadows as if into a new robe. Darkness is a comfort; it conceals her unfortunate skin more effectively than any winding sheet, any uniform. Tears warm her cheeks, erasing ceremonial spots. The tomb's chill is pervasive; Swan is soon shivering uncontrollably.

"Here," says Judith, offering a swathe of dusty grey fabric. The pads of her fingers, rough with calluses, scratch as she unlaces Swan's white corset and replaces it with Anexhumer's garb. The veil is unpinned, a hood lifted in its stead. A shovel is placed in Swan's shaking hands.

"Come. We must gather bones and fill the graves before dawn. There's bodies aplenty next field over that need preserving once the skybunker girls have their way with them. It won't take long, but watch your step—you don't want to get caught by an earthsplosion."

Swan nods. Swallows and swallows but despair is lodged firm in her throat. She clutches the spade, knuckles white, feet rooted to the floor. Looks at the flecks of paint around her nails and wonders how long they'll take to fade.

"What colour is morning here?"

Judith pauses. She looks outside, away. "Vibrant enough to shatter dreams."

Swan sniffles. *Ohmarys*—and stops. No more prayers, not to them. Seven coddled Marys: never alone, always singing. What can they do for her now? They've given nothing but the residue of hope, drier than the paintbrushes she'll never again touch, emptier than her womb.

Shuffling toward the tomb door, Swan turns away from blessed, familiar dark, and steels herself for the bleakness of a bright future.

“On yer average day,” say the Broom, “what kinds of dust will ye find in my pan?”

[*Wait for the kids’ little faces to scrunch, pondering; give their eyes time to roll left and right, up and down, seeking answers in empty air; let their ’winds (if they should have them) scroll through the wonderful nonsense of imagination—and then prompt them, again, to speak. This kind of to-and-fro story will not work without their input.*]

“On yer average day,” say the Broom, “what kinds of dust will ye find in my pan?”

— ’wind-flakes!
— shells!
— flowers! [*Make clear: the Broom cannot remove what was never there.*]
— pebbles!
— bones!
— grey fingers, toes, bums, willies . . . [*Rein them in before they get to “pooh!” else the game will be lost, the tale unsalvageable.*]

"And what do I do with all this scat?" ask the Broom. "When I sneak out my cubby and onto the street?"

— sweep!
— sweep!
— sweep!

"No," say the Broom. "I brush, scrub, scour, clean—but only them grey ones sweep."

[*"Why does the Broom waste all his time cleaning," the oldest will inevitably ask, after their younger siblings' ideas have all dribbled out, "when he could be making a difference?"*

For the record, "Everyone has a job to do" is the only response children of all ages will eventually accept. Run through the list of occupations one might have; get the kids to join in. Encourage them to make things up, new and ridiculous professions: roller-skating waitresses, nannies with magic-flying umbrellas, chefs with famous restaurants, etc. Ask them what they'd want to do, if they weren't to be soldiers. After, don't say "anything is possible." Smile and nod and tell them the plain truth: "Everyone fights in their own ways."]

'Shelter stories'; variation on 'Blackout Entertainment for Young and Old'
'The Broom's Tale', Bibliotheca 33.5130° N, 36.2920° E

Before he found clippers in the kitchen junk drawer, Peytr used to sit on the edge of Amelia's mattress once a week and bite her nails down to the quick. It often made a mess of her fingers and toes; blunted from all the glass, his teeth had clamped and torn more than nibbled. But he'd persisted, sucking rubies from her cuticles, gnawing hangnails and tips until they were raw but clean. Spat-out shards became new petals on the flowered bedspread. They became extra crunch on the floor.

Amelia never complained.

Nowadays Peytr does a tidier job. With metal and experience, he keeps her from looking so much like a corpse, yellowed claws growing long after death. Quickly, he clips and clips, while crescent buds bloom red and white. He snips, aware he'll never be quick or precise enough.

The shrillness of her nails pushing, grinding, erupting in millimetric surges keeps him awake.

Some nights, curled on a divan he's dragged near her bed, Peytr suffers the noise of Amelia's decay. The skin warm but crackling, flaking in parchment pieces. Her blood stagnating, resonant purple pools chilling the caverns of her heart. Air clotting in her lungs. The soul rattling under her ribs, scratching, clawing, trying to hitchhike its way out on her breath. He presses an ear to her slow-rising chest, the tempo of her life never changing.

Her pulse whispers. His shouts.

Most nights, Peytr reaches for the mortar and pestle. Crushes a quarter bomb, or a third, or an eighth—as small a cut as he can manage, since Amelia's stash, like its maker, is on the decline. There are about twenty full hits left, maybe three or four times that much if he's stingy. To beef up each dose he breaks filth from his 'wind, crumbles it into the mix. With unsteady hands he scoops the laced glass, grinds it into his gums. The effect is almost immediate. Sucking relief through his teeth, Peytr feels heavy. Grounded. Even with the added word-boost, he never takes quite enough to get cloudy anymore. He hasn't been above the strato for, oh, nine? Ten years? Maybe longer. Keeping track is too hard, so most of the time he doesn't bother. All he knows is he hasn't soared— He doesn't soar. Even when he bags cheap nicks from passing dealers—dealers who haven't passed his way in just about as long as he can't remember—Peytr rarely gets higher than the rafters. More and more, the shards weigh him down. He sinks onto the couch, leaden, solid. Dreaming of mountains and stone and silent blue oceans, shipwrecks pummelled to sand in the deeps.

He wakes sometime later, early.

At the first hint of daybright, snuffers clank down the Gorge Road in twos and threes, extinguishing flambeaux. They snort and hock silt onto the gravel as they pass. They laugh at mumbled jokes. Peytr always misses the punch lines.

Against pale morning, darkness coalesces into silhouettes that slink around the cabin. At the first snuffle, Peytr sits on Amelia's bed and holds her hands silent. He lifts his feet off the floor. Severs connections. As herdboys paw empty plastic bags on the stoop, muttering and pissing on the weathered planks, Peyt stares at the doorknob, expecting it to turn. It's hard to see in the dim; the windows are plastered over, caked with grime and fallout. He watches the painted posy on the porcelain handle, waiting to see the violets and bluebells move. The door's dead-bolted, he tells his racing heart. They couldn't get in if they tried.

But the greys sneak in all the time, his heart replies, without ever explaining how they get back out.

When Amelia starts to smell too ripe Peyt fills a chipped pottery bowl, washes her body with bare hands and soap. Shampoos her hair with lemon and vanilla, resisting the urge to bury his face in those sweet-scented strands, the way he used to, before, when they were more copper than white. In winter he piles on the blankets, dresses Amelia in flannel and fleece; in summer, she sweats naked under a thin cotton sheet. He constantly touches without *touching* her. Damp skin slides over bone when he kneads her limbs, when he rolls her from side to side to prevent sores. Propping her on pillows, he pries her jaw open, presses the rough slab of her tongue with a finger, strokes water and potato soup down her throat. Once, he tried starving her awake. Almost two weeks, nothing but clear liquids. Useless, of course. The only differences were in the jut of her bones and the complete absence of shit. Hungry or full, she just lies there with eyes shut, filling bedpans, soaking nightgowns.

Afterwards, he cleans her creases. Wrings the sheets. Hangs them from empty racks in the rafters. Tucks a spare blanket around her.

Years have withered Amelia's slack muscles. Time and slumber have leached the plump from her hips, the pert from her breasts, the promise of life from her belly. Not that it matters, Peytr supposes. Amelia is far too old for children. Forty-five and dormant, bleeding only from the cuts he's chewed or clipped from the tips of her. She is too flat, now, for the roundness of love and sex and babies. She is all planes and angles.

Out on the front porch, Peytr rocks on his heels. Eyes the jagged horizon. Rolls a full bomb around on his tongue. His 'wind is listless, heavy with thoughts of bedpans and food-tubes and dogs and shallow, panting breath. All morning, he'd sat and watched Amelia's veins pulse in her temples and neck. In the silence between nail clipper snips, he counted the seconds between beats in the translucent skin of her wrists. Convinced the throb was flagging, Peyt dug into his stash of painkillers and found something to thin her blood. The pills' expiry date was illegible, but the clear blisters and foil were intact. He'd popped three from the package; they'd crumbled to chalk in his palm. Mixing the powder in a small cup of water, he'd made a slurry he hoped Amelia could swallow. At worst the sugar will do her good, he'd thought, massaging the sludge down her throat. When her mouth was empty, he'd stood. Dusted off his hands. Walked into the living half of the room, plucked a dusty globe from the ceiling rack, and took a full sugar-hit of his own.

The hoarded glass gouges him skyward. He floats, empty, open, honest. Peytr doesn't justify the indulgence. He doesn't make excuses. Doesn't consider it a humungous waste, over a month's worth of flight gone in one hit. Those are tomorrow's thoughts, tomorrow's regrets. Today, he thinks, it's as simple as weakness.

He needs the escape.

He needs to soar.

He needs.

For a few minutes Peytr is a kite, a silken box of primary colours. Wind whistles through his hollows as he drifts out and up and away. He skims the clouds, tastes ozone, stiffens with pent electricity. Glass ribbons his fabric but he keeps on chewing; now he's all-over stinging, now he's cry-laughing, now he's scoured light. Before and beneath him the city glistens, frosted with crystal and tears.

What an ugly fuckin' view, he thinks, plummeting.

Closing his eyes, he tries to regain the heights. His legs are a flutter of satin, his cock a strong taut cord trailing all the way down, held by—Nobody. No one. He will be untied—yes, that's it—he'll be released. Untethered. Floating among the stars.

Squinting, he sees the promise of constellations, the glint and shimmer of *beyond*. Elsewhere. A place after this one. He glides a few metres more, then jerks to a halt. Anchored, Peytr can only float so high. Now he sinks, lower, lower, low. Hovering by the eaves, he feels Amelia's gravity weighing him down. And the city, so hideous, pulling. Distant spires and gaping holes and bunker towers. Steel scaffolding and cranes hung with dirty grey banners, company names turning this or that piece of sky into property. Air-whales with bellies full of human flotsam, tossed on the tides of war. Grey missiles darting from shadow to shadow—and far too slow behind them, impotent eruptions of light. Wheeling around flares and rockets and reinforced steeples, the skybunker girls. Sleek gliders zooming over suburbs and battlefields. Little vultures above swooping the vultures below.

The view is exactly the same and yet totally different from the one he remembers as *his* city. The one he still thinks of as home.

Here there's an annoying pretence of wealth and brightness. Sunny terracotta tiles, sandstone buildings, coral-rendering, blue corrugated iron, titanium concrete. There's a never-ending cycle of reconstruction and repair. As if destruction itself is the enemy. As if conflict can be smoothed away with high-grade plaster. As if upstanding brownstones and townhouses and rock gardens mean victory. As if the faces staring down from new balconies and through designer black-out curtains are somehow less gaunt when surrounded by colour. As if, within weeks, the fresh paint and worn panels aren't streaked with jet-drippings. Sulphur-washed. Licked with wholesale grey.

Peyt's hometown, on the other hand, is a perfect example of efficient decay. The suburbs are clad in smoke-yellow tin siding. There are fire-blackened brick units. Share-houses held together with pebble-free stucco and lengths of weathered wood. Copper roofs on government offices, purposely greened so they'll disappear in the flarelight. There's no power after dark. No flambeaux. No museums.

Back home, things are impermanent. Things are disposable. Things are easily abandoned.

Now the glass skyline flickers and sparks. Peytr can't help but think: it just isn't the same here. Take the roads, for a start.

Take the roads. . . . Take the roads. . . . Take any *road . . .*

He bats his 'wind and feels himself sink almost to ground level. So disappointing. A full bomb shouldn't wear off so quickly. It should have a few slices left in it yet.

Take the roads. . . . Take the roads. . . . Take the roads, for a start . . .

Sidewalks at home aren't smoothed featureless; they're brush-marked and so pale as to be almost white. They're swept daily, free of dead words and rubble, not buried in last week's battle-dung. Peyt *knows* those sidewalks, just like he knows the tar lines stop-gapping rifts in the streets—how they'd heat up in summer until the air smelled like oil and he and Dake and the girls would dig their toes so deep into the soft black, he sometimes still feels its warmth in his feet. How paths always seemed to lead somewhere better, more interesting. Away.

Take the roads . . .

Here, train tracks and drays and twice-a-days all come from elsewhere, but Peytr hardly ever sees them go back. Airships arrive—or they don't—but these days only evacs and soldiers leave.

Soldiers, he corrects, and Pigeons.

Invisible straps pull on Peyt's shoulders and he falls, hard. Resisting the come-down he closes his eyes, and surges forward, not up. When he opens them, the porch is thirty feet behind him; he's grounded at the end of the driveway, gravel digging into his knees. Satchels are too heavy for him to carry, they're too late, too full of important messages. So Peytr lies down on the unnatural sidewalk, beside a cracked but untarred street, and stares at unattainable clouds.

Soldiers and Pigeons and glider-girls, he adds, catching glimpses of swift triangles overhead. It's impossible to tell how many there are; they flit through the skies, now high, now low, now gone. Sprawled, he bites the insides of his cheeks. Follows them the only way he can.

Velos whizz past, powered by muscle and steam. Peyt lifts a hand to flag one down—then immediately changes his mind. The cycles are too dangerous; lately, they're the greys' favourite targets. One minute they're pedalling along, the next they're aiming their wheels for road-ruts in the busiest streets. Their little engines combust, explode, pulping bodies, blasting wordwinds and limbs, spewing metal carnage, impaling onlookers with scraps and screams. . . . No, he wants something faster, safer. Something that will take him all the way back to before. He wants to see the stadium. He wants to visit Jean's grave. He wants to get there in one piece.

Take the road. . . . Take the road. . . . Take the road . . .

He knows he can't. With his ruck, full packs, and Amelia—well. Peytr's not as young as he used to be. He can only lug so much around.

That afternoon, Peytr's drowsing in a glass mellow when the roof thunders, shouting above him. He jolts—then freezes, muscles clenched. It's a ghost, he thinks. Only his eyes rove, peeled dry-wide, following the noise's clunking roll from peak to eaves. It's the greys. *Too loud. . . . Too obvious for greys. . . .* Bedsprings squeak beside him as dust rains from the rafters. Head cocked, he listens to the screech of Amelia's ebbs and flows. As usual, the low lighting plays tricks, makes it seem like she is stirring. Peytr holds his breath and watches, but doesn't hope. Don't let it be rats, he thinks, not-seeing her arm move on the quilt. Last time she was gnawed, he'd had to trade three bombs for a small pot of salve that, when it came down to it, he was too afraid to smear into the wounds.

Overhead, something's raking over the wooden tiles. Talons, maybe. Claws. Screeches stutter into barks, short and scared. It's the herdboys, he decides, squinting at the beams. Armed with crowbars, they're going to peel open the cabin like a rotten tin can. They're going to break their way in, and eat.

But Amelia has nothing to offer. Her belly is empty. Her scalp is clean.

Licking his lips, Peyt fills his mind with filthy thoughts. As his 'wind swells, he lifts his feet onto the settee, then reaches down and quietly slides his bag and boots out from underneath. After so many years in a rough canvas sack the grenade is dented, the pin bent out of shape, the cap rusted shut. White-knuckled, he wrestles with it until his palms are raw. His grunts and curses are echoed outside.

At last the lid gives. Hands weak, trembling, he crams the cavity full of angry phrases. Vicious proverbs. A fear so old and strong it drips oil and reeks kerosene. "One whiff and they're fucked," Peyt says aloud, mustering courage with voice and lies. His aim doesn't even have to be true; close will be good enough. The backlash, he knows, will almost be worse than the blast. Fear like his can't be avoided.

Dogs pound the front of the cabin. Springs squeak—no! It's *not* springs. More like hinges. He looks at the door: it's shut, still bolted. No one's coming in. Amelia isn't stirring. Wrenching the cap back on, Peytr cups the shell carefully and clamps the pin in place with his thumb. Quickening, the grenade rattles—above the sink, the blackened window responds in kind. Hung on the wall beside it, a row of good mugs bounces on hooks. Clay figurines dance on the sill. He looks at the door. No one's coming in. The yelping and thumping are off to the right. Not quite at the house's corner . . .

Peyt's gaze alights on the stove's flue. The chimney hasn't been fastened properly—it shoots up through a round hole in the ceiling, with a rat-sized space gaping between iron and wood. Old Rupe was much better with pots and pans, Amelia liked to joke, than he ever was with hammer and nails. Her mouth alone laughed whenever she told this part of the story: "'Shut up and keep stirring,' Old Rupe said, the only time I ever nagged him about it. That was it: 'Shut up and keep stirring.' Ha! He wasn't a talker like you, Peyt." Then she'd get a really good chuckle going, and have to step away from the cooker so her tears wouldn't spoil the glass. "What a jackass," she'd say, after a while. An explanation or an apology; Peyt was never sure.

But Amelia isn't stirring, or laughing, and the metal pipe is jerking violently back and forth. The chimney's high-hat rhythm offsets the wall-bass thumping between beats.

You're going to fuckin' break it, Peytr thinks, and now he's unlocking the door, now he's turning the knob, now he's stomping on porch, winding up to throw. If he lobs the shell on the ground, not too close but not too far away from the foundations, he should scare the shit out of the fuckin' dogs without doing the house too much damage . . .

"Thank fuck," comes a sweet voice from above. "Thought I was going to have to rat my way through these straps—your eaves can't cut through leather for shit. You got a blade in there, legger? A hand wouldn't go astray neither."

Peytr blinks and blinks and blinks. The girl doesn't disappear.

He grunts in surprise; a second later he finds himself inside, the door flung wide. In the living room, everything is quiet. The squeaking has stopped. Amelia isn't stirring. Her rotting has lulled to a hum. He crosses to the divan. Buries the grenade in his pack, tucking it in a nest of shredded gauze and soft red fabric. Then he sits, elbows propped on knees, and tries to catch his breath.

It isn't her, he tells himself.

It can't be her.

"Hey, pops!" she hollers, breaking his reverie. "You gonna leave me hanging here all day?"

"No," Peyt whispers, pulling up his hood, rubbing the shine from his eyes. "I've got you, Neddie. I'm coming."

The glider's frame isn't twisted too badly. The crossbar lists to port and the keel prows upward a bit at the nose, but it's robust for something so frail. "Nothing a few good whacks with Antonine's mallet won't fix," the girl says, pacing, surveying the damage. Lying on its back, the craft is a stingray flopped out of a high blue sea: pill-white on its undercarriage, rubber-grey on the dorsum, wings rippling in the wind. Half a dozen steel hooks jewel its belly. She bends and flips the 'ray over. Winces as she straightens—then cusses a streak longer than the gash in the top-skin of her sails.

She's talking to herself, Peyt knows, but he feels like he should say something. *It's okay now. We're okay.* His mouth guppies open and closed. *I missed you.* On the porch's third step, he sits with feet planted wide, watching Ned stomp around like her leg isn't paining her, cursing like a grunt. His daughter, a lightning-dodger. Grey-struck at 12,000 feet. That's what she'd called it, grey-struck, no emphasis, as if getting shot out of the air was normal. She showed him the scars to prove that it was.

Fourth fall this month, she'd said.

"Fourth?" Peyt hopes he'd sounded more shocked than sceptical. Either way, Ned had shrugged it off.

"There's more of them up the vault nowadays," she'd said. "And their ships is fuckin' hard to see."

"So—what. They're aiming at you?"

"Nah," she'd said. "We get in their way, we go down. Simple as. They don't care enough to *aim*."

Peyt wants to hug the brave right out of her. He wants to tell her it's okay to hurt. He wants to say he's sorry. But her back is straight, her chin tilted at the level of *fine*. A stroke of luck, he thinks. Crashing into the roof's slope instead of its spiked peak. Getting rope-tangled instead of turning to jam on the concrete. The chimney cap did a number on her glider—but apart from a few scrapes, a bit of rope-burn, a thick coating of soot and ash, Neddie's intact.

Fuckin' grey-struck, Peyt thinks.

Five or ten feet away, Ned hunkers with elbows resting on bony knees. Slightly duck-footed, like her father. Boots flecked with paint, matching the grooves she'd scuffed on the cabin's siding. Goggles pushed up on her forehead. A twisted cord trapping long strands of her dust-brown hair. The knife they'd used to free her juts from the breast pocket of her jumpsuit. *Valla* is embroidered above it in charcoal cursive, a series of numbers and dashes printed beneath. Peyt chuckles, shaking his head. Ned's older now, sure, but clearly hasn't changed much. She always did hate her name, not that he blames her. So this week it's Valla, is it? Fine. It's better that way. It suits her. The double ells like the two long braids framing her round face, the V the same shape as her glider. And the whole thing has a nice dip and lift to it. vAllA. Like a rollercoaster, like a loop-de-loop in the sky.

A real highflyer's name, Peyt thinks, suddenly overwhelmed, light-headed with relief. Glad to be sitting while his body quakes him weak. Mireille must've left Ned, too. . . . And what happened to May? Peyt wipes his face when the girl glances back at him. His mouth twists, faking a smile. They must've thought poor old Ned was orphaned. The skybunker corps must've saved her from selling her skin, from being a toy for the herd.

"How're you with a needle?" Ned asks, fingering the sail's ragged edges.

Neater now than I was when you were my Neddie, he thinks. Back when he'd sewn her name into all her little clothes. Back when he'd performed surgery after surgery on the rag-and-bone dolly Mireille had found, a gangle of colour Ned toted everywhere. Back when she called him Pops, and meant it personally.

"A bit wobbly," he says. "Not terrible."

She stands, brushing dirty hands on her jumpsuit. "Got a spare? My kit's gone and done a loose-balloon. No telling where it'll land."

What happened? Peytr wants to ask as Ned reads the compass strapped to her wrist. All this *time*, he wants to yell. How did you survive? How did you know what to do? Who taught you? Who raised you? Where have you been? He clears his throat and says, "We've got a sewing box."

Ned lifts an eyebrow. "We?"

"Yeah."

For a minute, Peyt thinks he sees recognition in his daughter's expression. A squint, a glint, a too-long stare. The same look she'd given when he and Mimi had swapped her doll for one less ridden with lice. While Ned slept, he'd worked all night on the new Saralita, embroidering a tiny pinafore and bloomers to match the ones they'd burnt. Come morning, Ned eyed the doll in just this way, just like this.

"Sara's had quite the adventure," Peyt recalls saying. "She's lost her thumbs, poor girl. But we can forgive her."

"I'm going to need something stronger than thread," Ned says. "This 'we' of yours got a tackle box in there by any chance? Acrylic line? Wire? Sinew? Gutting? I'd settle for horsehair if you got it. Mind you, en't nothing tougher than musings for getting a gal off the ground . . ."

"No. She doesn't have any." Peyt's tone is too harsh, too abrupt. Clamping his hood on tight, he tries again. "I mean, you can't glean a thing from her. I mean, she keeps to herself—"

"Tack your sails, legger. I won't never ride no 'wind that weren't free-blown my way. I take my job serious, you know." Scathing, the creed *Observe*, *Gather*, *Report*, *Examine* ribbons around Ned's head.

"I en't never borne vaultwards what weren't mine to fly, got it? I know what's giving and what's taking."

They pull the glider close to the porch, then Peyt tells Ned to turn around while he yellows a rough circle around it. "Should keep the dogs off," he says, zipping his pants. Ned hardly seems to notice. Her 'wind is columned in lists and tallies, her posture saying, *Whatever gusts ya high, legger.*

"Reckon you could point me to a barterman? A hawk?" As she speaks, she unhooks severed ropes and straps from the rigging, drapes them over her shoulder. "And a Whitey? All my coin's become someone else's lucky-rain—but they still trade round here, hey?" Without waiting for Peyt's nod, she takes stock of her gear. "These boots should fetch me a roll of wire at least. And my belt oughta buy me a quick call up to Antonine." Ned grins. "The old shark worries something fierce if her 'rays are too long undercloud."

"Wait a sec," Peyt says, tripping up the stairs, trying to keep her in sight while also heading inside. "Just keep your gear on there, glider. Don't go anywhere."

"And where d'you think I'll go," she calls after him, "with my rig belly-up on the turf?"

A minute later he comes back out, a red shirt bunched in his fists. "This's got to be worth a few thread-pennies."

"Thanks all the same," she says, and Peyt hears Jean's pride in the refusal. "It's too much."

"I used to work the nightmarkets," he quickly continues, kneading the soft fabric, turning sunsets and palm trees over and over in his hands. "Learned to haggle from the best liars and cheats ever to hang tarp over table and call themselves merchants. I'll get what you need and be back before darkfall, pocketing a jangle of change."

"Oh will you, now?" The girl smirks. "And who asked you to do my dealings?"

And suddenly Peyt sees himself through Ned's eyes. Standing in the doorway, half in shade, half out. A skinny old man with glass in his gaze. Lips scabbed from a thousand little cuts. Wrists jutting from salt-stained cuffs. Pants and jacket worn inside out, worn clear through at the bends. In that smirk, he sees Ned picturing him alone for years in this cabin; she doesn't believe a woman would shack up with him, that any woman would stick around for long.

He isn't going to do this for *her*. Not exactly. Not only.

Wringing the shirt, he looks from Ned to Amelia and back. Both so much older than when they'd first loved him. One all the brighter for being out of his care, the other growing duller and duller within it.

She doesn't need me, Peytr thinks. She never has.

"Please," he says. "Take a load off. With that limp, it'll take you twice as long to find what you're after. And you know greys and crooks can smell weakness a mile off . . ."

"It's no limp," she says. "Just getting a feel for my land legs is all."

When she smiles, Ned looks nothing like Mireille. Or Jean. Or him. She's got a style of brash all her own. "I've scooped more crooks than you can imagine, pops. And en't much they can steal from me now that I won't get back in the end. One day, their 'winds'll be filling my sails with the rest of them."

Peytr's pulse races as she snatches the shirt and skips down the stairs, getting smaller and smaller as she jogs down the drive.

"Don't go," he says, too quiet for any but the greys to hear.

Pausing at the roadside, Ned turns around. Peyt takes a step forward, then another, another. Eyes stretched wide, staring at her hard as he can. Memorising.

"You wanna help?" she shouts, cupping hands around the black dot of her mouth. "Keep them so-called dogs off my rig."

He stops. Raises a hand. Keeps it up until she disappears around the corner.

After feeding Amelia, washing and changing her, Peytr places her on top of the quilt and clips her nails one last time. When he's done, he doesn't tuck her back into bed. He leaves her out in plain sight.

With the front door open, the cabin's temperature has dropped by several degrees. It's not cold enough to see frost on Amelia's breath, but the chill pinks her nose and blues her fingers and toes. Peyt sucks a shard to hush the garish noise of her suffering. Then, hoping she'll stay quiet and warm for the duration, he snugs her in gloves and socks and knee-high slippers. Jams her nightgown into wool leggings, under a long skirt that laces all the way up the front. Buttons her into the corduroy jacket Mireille neglected to take when she left them.

The chill is bracing. The glass sharpens Peyt's resolve. Ned's been gone for a couple of hours—even with a hobble, she's got to be back soon. Heat blooms in his chest and for a moment, just for a moment, he enjoys an unearned flush of pride. She's a great kid. And it's better, he thinks, that she's not too pretty. That she's toned down the surface-brightness—no girlish lustre on her fingertips, no embroidered scarves poking above her collar—saving any polish for her mind instead. Ned's a real spark, that's for sure. Shining on the inside, camouflaged in brown and grey. She's resourceful, sky-smart. But she'd have to be, wouldn't she? After all she's survived. Today and all the days that came before. Floating free. Thriving among strangers. Living off gumption and 'wind. Alone, she's more parent than Peyt's ever been. He doesn't pretend otherwise.

She's bound to take better care of Amelia than he has.

A quick rummage through the junk drawer produces two darning needles, each as long as Peyt's middle finger. They aren't as sharp as they once were. When junkies pissed her off, Amelia used them to etch sigils into the glass bombs, gouging away more than half of the dream-film. She'd tell them the symbols were potent grey magic, limited stock, and charge them double for half the hit. Now Peyt scrapes the needles clean, then hunts for suitable thread.

It doesn't have to be sinew or horsehair, the thinks, unravelling a knitted blanket and soaking the strands of wool in a metal bucket he'd found catching drips under the sink. Bringing the tools outside, he lowers his hood and listens for the lopsided drag of Ned's feet on the gravel road.

Take the road. . . . Take the road. . . . Take any road . . .

Stretched from pole to pole in all directions the power lines are mute, the hum of evening energy still a few hours off. The dogs have denned until dark, their greedy limbs curled around the growls that drive them from hiding each night. Across the way, a communal garden's gone to seed, the caretaker's hut bulldozed. Tall steel stakes jut from the flattened earth, rusted lengths spray-painted orange and green and fluorescent pink; an architect's code that builders have left half-deciphered. Two blocks over, frayed nylon cords clank against tall poles lining the highway. Tattered flags flail in the wind, guiding all eyes to an embassy too white and marble-slick for its own good. Closer to home, thermals play rooftop 'stacks like pan flutes, sending haunting notes across the construction site, parking lot and street, down the drive, up to the porch where Peytr stands listening. Hearing such longing in the music. A summons to another life. A hint of somewhere after.

Between his fingertips, he spins the wool thin. Sucks a point into its tip and threads the first needle. Starting with the left sail, Peytr sews. With uneven stitches, not too tight and not too loose, he pokes metal through fabric woven from words, quivering for flight. Gently, he pinches serifs, sentence fragments, nonsensical ramblings and holds their ragged edges together. Under his fingertips, repetitive cries for help. Confused questions. Exclamations in more languages than Peyt's ever seen. He sews them all, looping strength and flexibility into the wings. He sews until the needle breaks. Then he threads the second one, eyes on the glider, ears on the road. *Take the road. . . . Take the road. . . . Take the road. . . .* When blisters form and pop on his fingers, he rubs the liquid into each new seam, as if such a small splash of himself can seal what he's done, make it permanent. Shadows deepen as he works, forcing him further and further off the porch, into the gravel yard. Being so exposed makes him nervous, but he needs to see what he's doing even at the risk of being seen doing it.

Anxiety lends him focus. For once his limbs do what they're told. He works quickly.

The wool runs out with less than a hand's width of the right wing still to be stitched.

Close enough? He tilts the frame this way and that. Letters continue to trickle from the small tear, one or two at a time. None of the losses make sense, though. None are important commands.

None, Peytr hopes, will interfere with propulsion. Navigation. The glider's ability to soar.

Pushing harness rigging aside, he crawls underneath the reinforced tarp and takes a few deep breaths. Sucking in the smell of dirt and sweat and humid tents, he starts to shiver, then centres himself before standing, the sails a welcome weight on his back. He can hardly feel the new seams bolting in jags across the wingspan. He can hardly feel the ground.

Afternoon has slumped without his notice. The sky has adopted the 'ray's shade of rubber. Aloft, he thinks, the craft will be near-invisible, blending with cumulus and haze.

Perfect time for take-off. Peytr hefts the thing easily, getting a feel for its balance. Holding the control bar, he reaches up and strums the battens. Imagines them illuminated in flight, each strut glowing as starfire shines through bone. As he strokes the spines, countless farewells dart like minnows in the surrounding material, avoiding then pursuing his touch. Grazing the sails, his 'wind capers. Nervous words kiss nervous words. In his grip, the glider thrums.

Peyt isn't a big man, but he's heavier than the skybunker girls. Definitely heavier than Neddie—probably Ned and Amelia combined. The metal sings as he bounces the control bar on his upturned palms. How much bulk can this thing bear? Overburdened, how far can it go? How high?

How high? How high? How high?

The 'wind-fabric responds to the turbine of Peyt's thoughts, billowing with urgency. He glances at the cabin door, ears perked. Amelia isn't stirring. Turning, he scopes the road: empty from tenements to construction site to corner. Hurry, he tells himself. Hurry.

Ned is wearing the only harness, but there are straps and clasps hanging from the kingpost and crossbar. Fingers clumsy with haste, Peytr clips whatever he can to his belt. Front and back and sides, the cords tug, eager, taking control, jamming his belt up under his ribs, pulling pants up, knees up, feet up, up, up . . .

Peytr runs. Fast, faster. Legs pumping, boots crunching, soul light. Halfway down the drive, thermals pluck at the wings, tickling the skin, the whirring cloth-thoughts, catching. Faster, faster, he runs. Through the burn, the doubt—*how much can it hold?*—aching for height, aching to coast above the dead fields below. Gasping, he runs. Off the lot, across the street, to the once-garden, away. Leaving a trail of last words behind him. Approaching the stakes, their tips vibrant, runway beacons, he tilts the keel skyward. Hoping Ned isn't here to see it. Not yet. Arms strained—*will it hold?*—he jumps. Sails snap taut, 'winds gust, toes skim rocky soil, and now he is laughing, now he is weightless, now he's enveloped in air.

Until, just as quickly, he's not.

Peyt's bitten tongue throbs. His knees are scratched and bruised, not broken. There are several new dings in the 'ray's crossbar and one of the strap-hooks has yanked loose, but the wings are no worse off than before—Peyt protected them first as he fell. Shouldering the rig, he limps back to his yard. *Mamma! Mamma!* tumbles from the sails onto his head and snags in his collar. Death-blurts and final pleas glint on his wrists, apologies encrust his knuckles. When he's settled on the stoop, he presses the stray cries back into place. He is heavy enough without extra worries on his back, too heavy for one spirited glider to carry.

It needs more thrust, he thinks, watching the cloth writhe and lift with each reabsorbed word. Maybe the panic wears off after a while? The frantic energy of last thoughts, fizzling, needing bodies and blood to keep them churning. Who knows how long Ned has been weaving this material, how many layers upon layers she's salvaged from battlefields and schoolyards and shelled office blocks. . . . How much fuel she gathered from the dying before glass-makers came to wash faces and hands and chests. Who knows why girls like her carry only some wounded up to the 'bunkers, leaving so many others to rot on the ground. Are the chosen ones special? Peyt hopes not. He hopes they're all very plain.

Ned rescues more than most, he decides. She's Jean's granddaughter, after all. She's got the spine for it. She's got the fuckin' guts.

And Neddie's 'wind has always been overactive—yes, maybe that's it. Maybe the silliness Tantie scolded her for, the silliness Mimi encouraged, boosts his girl that much further than everyone else. Peytr chuckles. A stream of Ned's would-be-names pours through his mind, from Arabella to this latest, this *Valla*.

Trapping all but the last, he tears Neddie's pseudonyms into syllables—Grigognelle, Adelle, Orrelline—and crushes them into the canvas. The wings ripple, demanding more. So Peyt gives them Agnetta, Carlotta, Nanette. Serafina and Raha and Karaleen. Rowena and Tatjana and Dove—he gives them all, the inked and the spoken, the wished-for and the wished-to-be-rid-of. Finally, he gives them Ned, who was born Nell. He imagines her to life, full of colour and song, and he embroiders the glider with every detail, every flaw, every mistake that makes her his. With needle and thought, Peytr says his goodbyes.

When the girl appears at the end of the road, he sees only Valla: skybunker girl, final vision of the dying. Collector of farewells. Captain of the 'ray hovering at shoulder-height beside him.

Hurry, he thinks, wrapping his hands around the crossbar. Hurry.

It isn't working.

Peytr runs and jumps and thinks light thoughts. Steam, breezes, balloons. Airships, trapeze artists, geese flying in a vee. Even full-bombed, he's never felt so unbound, so aerodynamic. He's a jet-fighter. A missile. A human cannonball. But no matter what he thinks, Valla is getting closer—she's almost here—and he can hardly get off the ground.

A sob from nowhere, and tears, and gut-clenching frustration. Anger blooms in Peyt's chest, a heat that trembles through veins, dredging long-buried hurts, pushing sweat from pores until he's soaked, shaking, shivering, quaking with impotent motion, and he can't do a fuckin' thing about it, can he, and Amelia isn't stirring, and he's just standing here, grounded, going nowhere, and dying, dying to go.

In his grip, the glider thrums, whispering songs of the near-dead.

But that's the problem, Peyt realises, anxiety hardening to

certainty. I'm alive, he thinks, now running, now flying, away from the road, away from Valla and the driveway she's racing towards. My 'wind isn't enough. After wedging the 'ray between the porch rails, he sprints into the cabin, wordwind cursing:

I'm alive. . . . I'm alive. . . . I'm alive . . .

In the living room, he scrapes the divan over to what's left of the glass-grove, climbs on it and starts picking. With only his shirt for a basket, he harvests the whole crop—enough bombs to annihilate a full platoon. One by one he licks them, testing their strength, tossing none aside. Brewed to last, Amelia's tinctures are still potent. A final taste and halos bleed around the transparent spheres, the fingers holding them, the couch beneath Peytr's feet. Time slows as he descends. An hour passes before his soles meet the floorboards. Years stretch between each of Valla's boot steps, sprinting closer and closer outside. Cradled loosely against his body the glass chimes, a symphony of ice and mountaintops and snow.

All endings should sound like this, Peytr thinks, ignoring the sharpest notes.

The room spins until he's facing the door. Valla's slow-turning into the drive, a bag bouncing on her back. New buckles sparkle on her harness. Leather straps stretched from the fall have been clipped, repaired, reinforced. Good. He nods. That's good. No point to it if she can't support the extra weight.

Do it now, he tells himself, looking away for a second. A long, last second, looking at Amelia. Cocooned in winter layers, her cheeks have flushed. Braids have unravelled and fists have unclenched. Her lips are parted, gently curved. The extra clothes have filled her out; suddenly she looks plump and thirty again. For the first time in weeks, she looks comfortable. She looks, almost, better.

Irises bulge beneath her eyelids, roaming, following Peyt's movements across the living room. She's watching, he thinks. Not dreaming. She's picturing what this place will look like without us. Wondering how long it will take the greys to move in. For the herd to realise we're gone.

He looks at their life together, these four solid walls, the velvet warmth, the stability of treasures amassed, the wealth earned together, the wood and iron, the dreams—and nearly changes his mind.

"I'm sorry," he says, after a wordless eternity. "I hope—"

Amelia doesn't ask him to finish. Not that it matters. She isn't pink and plump and thirty again. She isn't *better*. Her eyes are sunken graves. Breath clots in her lungs. Her nails grow and grow, puncturing skin. Time is making an empty sack out of her. And Peytr doesn't know how else to stop it.

Outside, he dislodges the glider one-handed. It bobs up beside him, eager to fly. "Hold your horses," he mutters, taking the steps two at a time. At the bottom, he throws it down and pins the right wing with his feet.

"Hey, pops!"

Should've taken off my boots, he thinks, but it's too late. He steps onto the sutured panel, releases the hem of his shirt, drops the bombs. Follows them down.

"Get the fuck off her!"

On all fours, Peyt scrubs his stash into the sails. Dream-blizzards melt beneath his knees. Nightmares scrape his palms bloody. Valla's a spitfire diving, attacking, shooting at him from all sides. Hollering nonsense, she drums her small fists into his back, shoulders, ears.

"Enough," Peyt says, smearing and scouring until everything's scarlet. Crystal-coated words vibrate and buzz, the 'wind-wings crackling high. "Look."

Valla tackles him and the dream-hyped glider slips free.

"Catch it," the girl shouts and Peytr does, barely, stretched to his full height and jumping. With it firmly in hand, he locks his elbow around a porch rail to keep the thing from dragging him skyward.

"It's ready to go." He holds the 'ray up, well out of Valla's reach. She tears up the steps behind him, primed to spring. "Calm the fuck down and look at it."

Finally Valla stops. Looks. Listens to what he's saying. "So give her here, then."

"I'm trying." Peyt smiles sadly. Doesn't feel Valla's punches. Switching hands on the cross-bar, he cranes to look inside. "Please. Take her with you."

Arms crossed, Valla follows his gaze through the doorway. "She's on the brink all right. But how's she to blow my sails when she en't got no 'wind?"

"Doesn't need one," he says, smirking. "She always gets the strongest dreams."

The skybunker girl eyes her craft warily, then takes another look at Amelia and shrugs.

"Please," Peyt says again. "She's light as glass."

The next day, Peytr buries Amelia's belongings in the backyard. The camp stoves Rupe gave her, the beakers and alembics. The dancing ladies off the kitchen sill. The good mugs. The sewing kit, minus two needles. The silk handkerchiefs and embroideries. The chamber pot and sponges and threadbare towels. The fine clothes she never wore, the bed linens she always did. The clippers. He can't do much about the furniture, but he strips curtains and cushions, takes planks from the dining table, leaves cabinets without doors or drawers. It takes a day to dig a hole big enough to fit everything, and another to fill it in. His palms weep as old blisters reopen beside the new. He wraps them in Amelia's flannel cloths, keeps digging until he's exhausted. Much later, he lies curled on the bare mattress, using his full pack for a pillow. He leaves the front door open, reacquainting himself with the moon-dark cold. Listening for the herd. For the sneak and quiver of greys. He lights a candle stub, and listens to it burn.

He decides to go when the flame hushes. In the black, he'll creep from the house, hood drawn low. He'll steer clear of flambeaux. He'll focus on the near-invisible path leading away from the road, into borderlands and bonefields. He'll watch his steps. He won't look up and wonder if anyone's looking back down. He'll keep his eyes forward.

The wick sizzles and goes out. Peyt shakes the nerves from his legs as the room blends with the night. Wax hums, cooling on the headboard. Greasy smoke yawns into the air. Clutching his satchel, toes wriggling in his boots, Peytr breathes in the cabin's stink and absorbs the quiet of leaving.

SIXTEEN

"Bones or stones?"

Swathed in grey winding sheets and cloaked in grey shawls, the woman squints at Peytr and repeats her question. Louder this time, so the gale won't snatch it, tow it across the cemetery and down the headland's churned slope, drop it in the red plains below with all the other lost words. Skirmish after skirmish followed Peyt to the coast, sticking close as memory from city to town to village to battlefield graveyard. The fight moved on without him when he decided to stop, to stay. Now the ground is swarming with skybunker girls. Glass-makers. Gravediggers. In the distance, negligéed banshees kneel among statues, singing dirges, hymns, laments. Greys lurk in the shadows, thin as the little girls' keening, watching and waiting. And everywhere, everywhere Peytr looks, there is blood and skin and bones.

Bones, he thinks, dropping his pack. Cutlery hasn't been in there for years, but still he hears it clinking. Still he knows its weight. He looks away for a moment, squinting against the oncoming storm. To the east, a slate sea nudges the cliff's base. A fleet of harbour-coffins sits low in the waves, heavy with drowned reinforcements. Peytr breathes in before giving his answer. The wind off the water tastes of tears.

"Bones or stones?"

What a voice, Peyt thinks, turning back to the woman. Her smooth white hand clutches a spade's polished handle. A bare foot rests on the blade's flat jaw. Poised for digging an extra hole in the ground; equally poised to trowel the sludge she hauled up the hill in an oversized bucket. What she does with that shovel is now up to him—No, Peyt corrects, gazing at the 'windless body laid out at their feet. It's up to him.

"Stones," he says quietly, wishing Dake would sit up, knuckle-punch him, and say What you doing here, Dalmatian? Fuck off, now. Go on home.

"You sure? You'd be a lot more useful in the ground, you know."

Peytr looks down. Daken's arms are like strips of rawhide, his legs gnarled sticks strung with sinew. The muscles he was so proud of are wizened skin sacks, haze-worn and flaccid as an old man's. His fingers and toes are swollen, purpled with chilblains. Long, dexterous toes that could snatch coins off the floor or pinch hard enough to make Peytr squeal. Long, rough fingers that would tweak Peyt's ribs. Burr his 'wind. Twist his nose and ears and nipples. Long, warm fingers that often stretched out in the night, closing the distance between cots, squeezing, squeezing for comfort.

The herd has run him so fuckin' far, Peyt thinks, taking in the gashes on Dake's soles, the splints round his shins. We've run so far to get here.

Crouching, he gently strokes Daken's bruised face. Only two years older than Peyt, he seems to have aged a hundred since they last saw each other. After all he must've done for those fuckin' dogs, kept them close and safe, kept them fed and watered, they just up and left him mid-field, a grey arrow feathering his throat. Didn't take much to snap the shaft, pull it clean out. Didn't take much to lug the body—did it—to take it uphill to the graves. If Peyt hadn't been here—

If Peyt hadn't been here—

Not worth thinking about *what ifs* and *might've beens*.

Before Peytr closed them, Dake's eyes were filmed with scum; the deep creases around them made the boy, the man, near unrecognisable. If it wasn't for these. . . . Peyt traces the crooked lines and scars marring the corpse's cheeks, shaved scalp, temples. Some are short and white, traces of frantic nail-scrapings. Others are ridged, crescent-shaped: faded, decades-old bites. *These* Peyt will never forget.

"Let him rest while he can," he says to the digger. "It's my watch."

"As you wish," she replies. Her robes flap in the wind as she bends to collect Peyt's ruck and packs; the long hem lifts to knee-height, revealing gaunt calves marbled with pale blue veins. After placing the bags on a carved plywood plinth at the fresh grave's head, she takes Peytr's hand with a surprisingly firm grip, holding him steady as he climbs. Settling into the freshly-turned dirt, the box wobbles as Peyt tries to find the right stance atop it. Flexing his legs *left, right, left* he balances with feet widespread, gear slumped in between. Lowering his hood, he relaxes into the pose: arms crossed, head bowed, 'wind honest.

I'm with you. . . . I'm with you. . . . I'm with you . . .

"The burden of this one's life is not yours to carry," the woman says, slipping into a singsong tone, uttering stilted phrases as if by rote. "Will you accept its weight?" As she speaks, a girl wearing long rubber gloves and a butcher's apron over a patched denim dress crests the hill. She carries two hard plastic pails, one half-filled with oil, the other with damp flannel rags. Lifting both as if to say, *Ready?* she scuffs to a stop beside Daken's head and waits for the digger to finish her spiel.

"Will you bear the granite of this one's sorrows and forbear the feathered wing of his joys?"

Peytr doesn't hesitate. "I will."

"Will you mark all the moments of this one's life? You and no other, now and forever?"

He doesn't think of it as dying.

"I will."

"Will you stand vigil, steadfast and true, long after this one is reborn?"

It's an ending, he thinks. But also a beginning.

"I will."

"Will you take the past into your present so this one can move into the future?"

It's an overdue apology.

"I will," he says.

These past months, these weeks, and now these cemetery moments—they're all part of the same sequence, Peytr realises. A procession of final touches.

The way the glass-maker swabs Daken's scarred face, his broad chest, his limp cock. Skybunker girls have already harvested his wordwind; now the residue of Dake's hopes, his happy memories and dreams is sopped into flannel and wrung into the oil bucket. This girl doesn't have Amelia's skill, Peyt thinks, shifting to get a better look. She muddies the highs by blending them together. She drips the new in with the old. The quality of Amelia's product always reflected those of its maker: plain. More pure than sullied, more sharp than soft. Far too addictive, far too easily consumed. "Leave enough for the spirit to quicken," the digger says, but the girl doesn't have much to work with, it seems. Soon enough, she's finished.

The way Zaya had been, when Peyt went home one last time, looking for Euri, finding the little one instead. Not so little anymore, now she's done growing. Still too small, too vulnerable to live alone in that house. What's happened? he remembers asking. Her dark skin had been flawless, nothing like his, her fuzzy curls cropped close to the skull. She'd looked at him blankly, arms hanging by her slim hips, offering no welcome, no embrace.

Where is everyone? Where's your 'wind?

Ashes, he thought Zaya had said, but couldn't be sure without reading it. Behind her the front hall was empty, the living room party to ghosts. The furniture was mostly still there—the grandfather clock was missing, the curio cabinet displaying nothing but dust—but the air was cold with absence. Zaya had lifted a hand above her head, flourishing the empty space where her 'wind would be. *Look, Peytie. Just look up.*

There are no words, he'd said quietly, eyes steady, locked on hers. There's nothing to see.

It's safer, he'd thought, dropping his gaze. It's safer without 'winds.

Are you stoned? Stepping in close, she'd whipped his hood off and began to read aloud. *It's safer without . . .*

"Zaya, no—" Peytr says, and the digger frowns up at him.

"My name is Swan," she says, voice trembling, but beautiful. Singing under her breath, she turns back to her task, shovelling slop from the large bucket onto Daken's sternum.

Man, Peytr thinks as she reaches the chorus. What a warble.

The way Swan spreads muck around, uneven, concentrating on the middle and ends, avoiding the face: final touches. Covering Daken's extremities, his belly, the crown of his head. Peyt doesn't know where she got the off-white mud; the cemetery is faded grass and crushed shell, 'wind-powder and deep brown earth. Smeared on the body, the digger's paste leaches what the glass-maker left behind. Lethargy. Sadness. Regret. The bleak hue of Daken's skin.

Leaving the sludge to dry, she turns her attention to Peyt. Squatting, she brushes grime off the plinth, gouging mould from intricate images engraved in the wood. "Gourds for you," she says, interrupting her song. Leaning back on her heels to admire the patterns. "Full, not hollow. Deliverance from grief. And for this one," she tilts her chin at Daken, "a rooster. Awakening, courage, vigilance. Stone will always guard these promises—and we will help to keep them."

"Thank you."

Swan inclines her head, neither accepting nor rejecting Peyt's gratitude. Kneeling, she raises a cairn of pebbles around the plinth, slowly covering the fine decorations, the low platform and satchels, and finally Peytr's feet. Pressure builds up his arches, ankles, shins; firm and painful. Single rocks are light as onions; by the hundreds they crush fine bones in his toes, jab his tendons, pierce his trousers and bite his shins. It's almost impossible, now, to run. I could stop her, he thinks. Any time.

He waits for panic to set in with the stones.

He waits while Swan takes a blunt wooden blade from the folds of her robe and scrapes the dried mud off Daken's body, moving from the feet up. It's a tedious, methodical task. Peytr sways as she works inch by inch, tapping every last scraping back into the vessel. Chanting, she combines dry flecks in with what's left of the wet. While she stirs, the mixture darkens from cream to tar, blackened by time and hurt.

"Speak no more with words or 'wind," Swan says, dragging the pot close to the cairn. "True commemoration is a matter of expression, gesture, posture. From now on, remember this one with your body alone."

For weeks Peyt has contemplated this moment, this pose. It has to be right, it has to *mean* something. To Daken. To him. As Swan scoops the first handful of clay and grinds it against his calf, he shakes the nerves from his limbs. Releases a long, shuddering breath. Brings his hands up to his mouth. With elbows tucked close to his sides, Peytr lifts his chin and looks straight ahead. Gaze fixed on a point beyond the horizon. Fingers pressed flat, covering his lips.

Singing ice into Peytr's veins, Swan packs him in clay, weaving instructions through her verses. *Tilt back. . . . Steady now. . . . Lean forward. . . . Breathe normally. . . . Don't breathe. . . .* Without moving his head, Peyt steals glimpses at her while she smooths and scores and stipples. Her hair pale and wispy with gravedust. Her shroud flimsy but somehow obscuring. Her hands deft with trowel and brush and palette knife. Cold seeps up his legs, stiffening. Peytr stirs, loosing a shower of pebbles. Cold grips his guts. There is intimacy in being captured by an artist, he thinks. In being measured, observed, assessed. In being told what to do, how to move or not move. Cold restrains his elbows, arms, shoulders. Swan's watery eyes tangibly sketch his outlines; he feels their scrutiny like a pencil tracing his dips and ridges. In her hands, Peytr is helpless. Raw. Revealed by the millimetre.

Swan kneads and cuts and shapes until Peytr is slathered hard. Her touch is confident, practised, assertive. And that voice! What a serenade she'd sing. What a lullaby.

A dream for someone else, he thinks, knowing it's too late for the company of warm bodies. Too late for anything but final touches.

The way Swan saves his face, the tips of his fingers for last. "Shall I get rid of this?" she asks, flicking his beard with her trowel.

"Those skin-blossoms of yours will make stunning patterns in the stonework."

"Yes," he says. "All right."

Clambering down the cairn to get a blade, Swan breaks the rhythm of incantation and says, "Don't move a muscle."

Peyt's breath flutters in and out as she shaves years from his face, turns him back into a boy. When she's done, the wind off the sea stinging raw flesh, Swan trades the razor for her scraper and a tarnished silver spoon. Crouching, she swiftly gouges out Daken's eyes. Pulping them between her palms, she flicks gobs of gel onto the ground then carries the flattened shells up to Peytr. Standing on tiptoe, she peels his fingers away from his mouth. "Open wide," she says, popping the whites onto his tongue while he stammers, too encased now to cry out.

"Be brave," she says. "It's better you than them."

Swan's lullaby is sweet. Reassuring. Relaxing. It coaxes the husks down Peyt's throat, soothes him as the mud rises above his nose and cheekbones, reaching his eyes. As he swallows, he expects to have visions, to see what Daken has seen all these years, a lifetime otherwise lost in the dark. He sighs until Swan clogs his nostrils. There's nothing new here. Nothing he hasn't seen before.

Greys fog his sight but Peytr isn't afraid. Daken is lying beside him and the girls are nearby—he can hear them still, whispering. Secret fingers strum his 'wind, slowly stealing his thoughts: the filthy, the lonely, the clean. Take them, take them. There will be stories to replenish him soon. There are always stories before sleep.

Blinking takes an age. When his lids gum open, the greys are stealing closer. The girls have drifted off but Dake is here, Dake is with him. Peyt can't—doesn't need to—look down. He knows Daken will always be near.

On the horizon, a flare ignites. A strange gleam of a cold sun, dazzling bright. Peytr wants to point, to gape with all the field ants, flap with the vultures, but his arms are granite. His stone hands are fused to his mouth. He closes his eyes to shut the light out. Dark blue and green afterimages bloom before him, mushroom-clouding the crimson sky of his lids. This eruption looked much bigger than the one Jean became, much less contained. Was it some grey trick? Some sort of retaliation?

Maybe, Peyt thinks.

Maybe not.

Imagining what will happen in the next few minutes, Peytr is petrified, but not scared. He stands quietly, and listens. It isn't over, he thinks. It isn't over. But his mouth is firmly closed. His legs do not tremble. He is safe, solid stone. And he is still.

Acknowledgements

An earlier version of Chapter 10 first appeared as "The Good Window" in *Fantasy Magazine* (September 2009).

An earlier version of Chapter 13 first appeared as "Their Own Executioners" in *ChiZine* (July – September 2010).

An earlier version of Chapter 14 first appeared as "Singing Breath into the Dead" in *Music for Another World*, edited by Mark Harding (Mutation Press, 2010).

"The Ministers of Human Fate" owes much to the political stylings and righteous passion of Abraham Lincoln's "Temperance Address," given in Springfield, Illinois on February 22, 1842.

Author's thanks

Huge thanks to Brett Savory and Sandra Kasturi for giving this novel a perfect home—and for wrapping it in a gorgeous Erik Mohr cover. Still pinching myself! Many, many, many thanks to Samantha Beiko for editing the manuscript with such an astute and delicate touch (and for the tears!)—it has been such a blast working with you all. Also ranking at the top of the gratitude department: Angela Slatter, for mainlining the full manuscript in one weekend and, as always, offering unfailing support (Skype dates, surprise parcels, coffee, chocolate) while I was writing; Kirstyn McDermott, for reading early drafts and offering generous feedback; and Chad Habel, for not only supporting but feeding my addiction to war stories and films, for letting me pick his brain about politics, for beta-reading this book and totally getting it (and me).

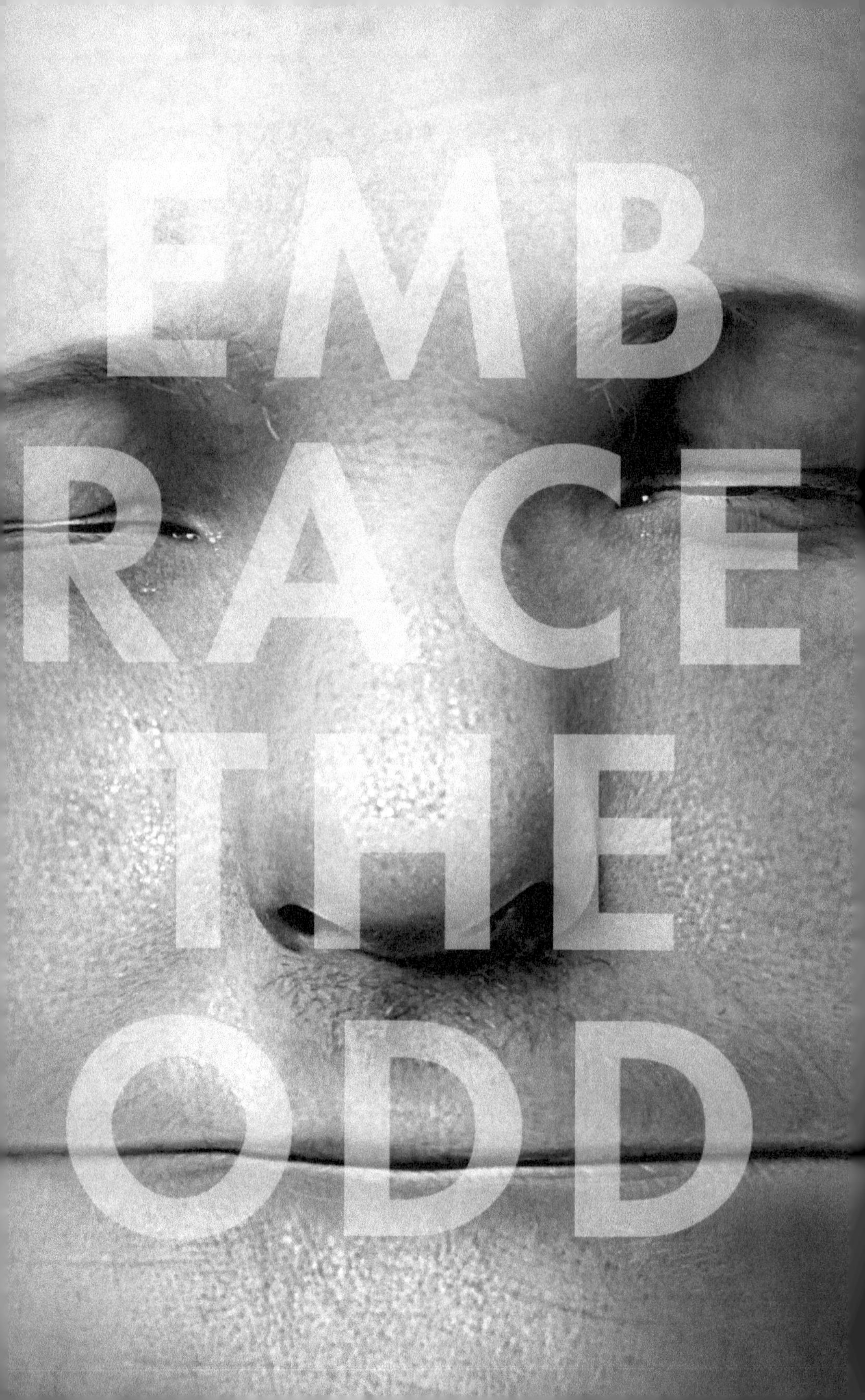

EMB
RACE
THE
ODD

WHAT WE SALVAGE

DAVID BAILLIE

Skinheads. Drug dealers. Cops. For two brothers-of-circumstance navigating the violent streets of this industrial wasteland, every urban tribe is a potential threat. Yet it is amongst the denizens of these unforgiving alleys, dangerous squat houses, and underground nightclubs that the brothers—and the small street tribe to which they belong—forge the bonds that will see them through senseless minor cruelties, the slow and constant grind of poverty, and savage boot culture violence. Friendship. Understanding. Affinity. For two brothers, these fragile ties are the only hope they have for salvation in the wake of a mutual girlfriend's suicide, an event so devastating that it drives one to seek solace far from his steel city roots, and the other to a tragic—yet miraculous—transformation, a heartbreaking metamorphosis from poet and musician to street prophet, emerging from a self-imposed cocoon an urban shaman, mad-eyed shaper of (t)ruthless reality.

AVAILABLE JULY

ISBN 978-1771483-22-3

CHIZINEPUB.COM 

THE HOUSE OF WAR AND WITNESS

MIKE, LINDA, AND LOUISE CAREY

1740. With the whole of Europe balanced on the brink of war, an Austrian regiment is sent to the furthest frontier of the empire to hold the border against the might of Prussia. Their garrison, the ancient house called Pokoj.

But Pokoj is already inhabited, by a company of ghosts from every age of the house's history. Only DROZDE, the quartermaster's mistress, can see them, and terrifyingly they welcome her as a friend. As these ageless phantoms tell their stories Drozde gets chilling glimpses not just of Pokoj's past but of a looming menace in its future.

AVAILABLE AUGUST

ISBN 978-1771483-12-4

ALSO AVAILABLE FROM CHIZINE PUBLICATIONS